# AFTER THE

Alison Layland is the author of two novels: *Someone Else's Conflict*, a compelling narrative of storytelling and the aftermath of war, was featured as a Debut of the Month on the LoveReading website, and *Riverflow*, a story of family secrets and community tensions against a background of flooding and environmental protest, was a Waterstones' Wales Book of the Month. She also writes short stories and flash fiction: she won the short story competition at the National Eisteddfod in 2002, and her story *Quirky Robbers* is featured in the Honno crime anthology, *Cast A Long Shadow*. She is the translator of a number of award-winning and best-selling novels.

When not writing, she is an environmental and social campaigner who enjoys walking, crafting, growing and foraging around her home on the beautiful coast of Anglesey.

# AFTER THE CLEARANCES

ALISON LAYLAND

*Alison Layland*

*Steddfod 2025*

HONNO MODERN FICTION

First published in Great Britain in 2025 by Honno Press
D41, Hugh Owen Building, Aberystwyth University, Ceredigion, SY23 3DY

1 2 3 4 5 6 7 8 9 10

A catalogue record for this book is available from the British Library.

Published with the financial support of the Books Council of Wales.

ISBN 978-1-916821-26-2
e-ISBN 978-1-916821-27-9
Cover Designer: Lynzie Fitzpatrick
Text design: Elaine Sharples
Printed and bound by CPI Group (UK) Ltd,
Croydon, Surrey, CRO 4YY

For my friends at OsCAH

Was the Earth made to preserve a few covetous, proud men, to live at ease, and for them to bag and barn up the treasures of the Earth from others, that these may beg or starve in a fruitful land, or was it made to preserve all her children?

Gerrard Winstanley, *The New Law of Righteousness*, 1648.

A philosophy of what I call 'enoughism'; the end of a culture of (always) 'more'. Enoughism is a concept about what and how little, economically speaking, human *needs* are.

*This Civilisation is Finished*, Rupert Read.

Ry'n ni yma o hyd
Er gwaetha pawb a phopeth
*We're still here*
*Despite everyone and everything*

Dafydd Iwan

# The journal of Glesni Jones,
## July 2056

I can't believe I ever wanted to be her friend. I've been reimagining over and over the way Sandy dealt with Madog before we left for the mainland. I've managed to keep it distanced as hideous fact, but the emotion's starting to ambush me in unexpected moments. And now I'm truly scared. Scared for my family, scared for myself and Taid, here now, and scared for everything we have back on the island.

We're not safe. Maybe we'll never be safe again. Maybe we never were; just that some of us were sheltered from knowing it. I thank them for that.

Or maybe I'm over-dramatising. Surely one woman can't undo all we've built up over the years? I hope not. But in case my fears are real, I think it's important to tell anyone who might find this notebook what we have – or perhaps, and I hate to say this, what we had.

So... Allow me to introduce myself. I'm Glesni Delyth Jones and I was the first child to be born on Ynys Hudol, the magical island, which they sometimes call Aniseed Island because most mainlanders can't speak Welsh and our pronunciation *uh-nis heed-ol* sounded like Aniseed to someone once and it stuck, so that's what it says on the few maps I've seen that bother to show it. We don't even grow aniseed. We do call our community the Seeders, or *Hadwyr*, though: partly inspired by Aniseed and partly because our aim is to grow a new way of life to cope with the changing world. *Empathy-Humility-Frugality* as it says on the mural in our roundhouse.

Others have been born, and arrived, on the island since I came into the world but still, it makes me feel a bit special. There are sixty-eight people in our community. When Sandy came, she made it sixty-nine, but Martha has died since – she was very old, so we can't blame Sandy for *that*, but now... now maybe even Madog, and who knows whether the three of us will make it back? Sandy's got plans but we're not sure what.

1

Anyway... I live with my mam Helyg, my sister Haf, my stepfather Tom, and Erik Jones, my taid (just so you know, it's pronounced 'tide' – Sandy told me early on that she imagined a name like that for an old man was to do with the unstoppable ebb and flow of life, or some indication of dependability, like the ever-present sea. She looked a bit disappointed when I told her it simply means Grandpa. I must admit her view of it makes beautiful sense). Mam arrived on the island sixteen years ago in 2040, just after Haf was born, and I came into our precarious world three years later. My dad, Gareth, drowned before I was a year old, when he was out at sea and a storm hit suddenly, despite the healthy respect we've always had for the unpredictable ways of the ocean. Taid arrived on Ynys Hudol when I was two so he's been like a father to me. My nain (pronounced 'nine') died a long time ago, which is one of the reasons Taid can be moody, but now it turns out her death might have been a lie. We daren't believe that, especially since it was Sandy who said it, although hope has a way of settling in and refusing to leave, however painful it might be when it's dashed. But that's all part of the story and I don't know the ending yet.

We were only supposed to be here for a night but it looks like the storm's going to last a good few days so we're stuck here and I'm going to try and write it all down because things are already starting to feel a bit muddled. Maybe it'll be like brainstorming and I'll think of a way to stop Sandy's scheming or Taid's self-destruction. Haf says I over-romanticise him but I know he really would give himself up for the sake of the Seeders. Me, I don't see why he should, and in any case, I wouldn't trust Sandy to keep her word.

I'm getting ahead of myself.

It's this place. I can't concentrate. The house is shaking and the winds are battering and I'm wishing I was in the solid strength of our roundhouse. I hate the mainland already – even if it is Cymru and we're all supposed to love Cymru, it's still the mainland and I can't believe how different it feels. The rocks may be the same rocks that formed Ynys Hudol millennia ago and it may all become the same seabed once again as the sea levels continue to rise, but it's the people that make the difference.

For years I've been mithering them to let me come on a mainland foraging trip, to see it all for myself, but now I'm here I have to admit I prefer security over excitement and I'm beginning to understand why a lot of people don't want to make the crossing ever again – even if that would mean doing without certain things. Of course, the circumstances don't help. And I hate to think of Mam worrying about me. She's had enough worry in her life; all the older ones have. They don't deserve to be betrayed, none of them do.

However flimsy it feels, I suppose this borrowed house has seen out a good few storms, though they're getting worse all the time. I'm sure it'll stand its ground and give me enough time to write down everything I need to. Did I say it was for people of the future to find? It's also in case I get home (which I hope isn't entirely impossible). Unlike Taid, I don't want to forget.

# PART I

# YNYS HUDOL

Our Seeder dream can only work if its people have a sense of ownership – if they feel they matter to the community and the community matters to them.

To achieve this on a small island is relatively straightforward. To take our knowledge further, back to the mainland, as a model for a fair, just, sustainable society, will be more of a challenge. We are well aware that the veneer of civilisation is thin and fragile, but we also believe passionately in the inherent human instinct for good. We have to nurture this with patience, to consolidate our knowledge and our systems with experience, before venturing forth. Despite the sweeping changes that are an inevitable consequence of climate change and the government's inadequate response to it, we anticipate hostility; to take our model out too soon may damage both ourselves and the world we seek to help.

We have been accused of selfishness, of running away. To our accusers we would say: don't all first-aid manuals tell you to ensure your own safety before attempting to help others? Neither we, nor the Seeders who have chosen to settle here with us, could achieve any real good in the failing systems handed down to us over recent decades, centuries even. Before we can help people still afflicted by those systems, we need to achieve true resilience and develop a sound plan that offers a real alternative.

Ynys Hudol is a refuge. It is also a place of learning and development. Once the latter has truly eclipsed the former, then we will be ready. Seeds can lie dormant for years, even decades, waiting to spring to life when the conditions are right. We will not scatter our seeds until they can be sure of a chance of germination and survival.

*Extract from* Seeds of Change
*by Edith Turner and Bleddyn Price, 2047.*

# WHAT A NEWCOMER MIGHT BRING

April 2056

In a twist of irony that would only later become apparent, they were learning about the Irlas Dam confrontation when Sandy first arrived. Although it could be difficult being the teacher's daughter, Glesni admired her stepfather, Tom, for telling the story in a way that held the attention of all nine in the older class. Yet however convincingly he told it, she struggled to believe that this violent incident back in 2036 – twenty years ago! – was real. The wider civil war that it heralded also felt like a distant tragedy in another world, yet she was aware that several of the adults were here on Ynys Hudol because of it.

Tom said it was common knowledge that the Irlas Dam bomb was a stitch-up, designed to brand all those occupying the doomed village as terrorists. Most of them, and the activists who came after them, were effectively silenced, many eventually dying in jail. Glesni wondered how this would be taught on the mainland. Would Tom have been imprisoned, too, for teaching the whole Irlas Dam incident, bomb and all, as a deliberate government infiltration of a peaceful protest, in order to incite an independence war that they knew Cymru could never win?

As they left the school building for lunch, she saw Gwylan making her way down the track towards the small harbour. Despite her aura of calm authority, the community's current co-leader was striding out faster than usual. The jetty was concealed from view by a rise in the land, but the sea beyond looked choppy, a dark bank of cloud gathering on the horizon. Glesni thought of Taid out there checking the tidal turbines and began to worry.

A few more people passed in the direction of the jetty, and she hurried down to the track.

9

'What's going on?' she called, her words falling over themselves like her feet on the slope as she ran towards her mam.

Helyg turned to her. 'Sounds like your Taid's rescued more than the faulty turbine,' she said with a familiar hint of disapproval. 'Someone saw him towing a boat.'

Trying not to betray her eagerness and run ahead, Glesni joined the trickle of people, fast becoming a stream, down to the water's edge.

Stopping on a rise above the stone jetty, she saw the community's boat, *Berta*, towing another that looked so run-down it was a miracle it was still afloat. She could see Taid as a shadowy presence in *Berta's* cabin and imagined him standing tall and straight as he always did, his agility belying his seventy-three years and pronounced limp. A woman in a flimsy waterproof jacket sat on the deck of the second boat, her red, curly hair blowing out in all directions, even at this distance looking sullen. Or maybe seasick.

As they neared the quieter waters of the little bay, Taid veered away, heading beyond the rocky promontory that sheltered it. The woman stood, calling something Glesni couldn't catch. He stopped the motor and let the boats drift as he went astern to try and explain. The two boats eventually moved out of view behind the promontory, heading towards the inaccessible islet that was the Quarantine Rock. Glesni moved across the hillside until the Rock came into view. She felt sorry for the poor woman, since she'd be there on her own for a couple of weeks at least.

Glesni was doubly annoyed: not only had she not been allowed to go out with Taid to bring in the faulty turbine for repair, but she'd missed the chance to be a part of this, the first arrival of a stranger since her friend Tahira and her family were washed up on their shores four years ago. No doubt she'd meet the new woman in due course, but growing up in the shadow of her pretty, confident older sister Haf meant she'd have relished the opportunity to help Taid bring her in.

It seemed to take an age for him to sort the woman out,

gesticulating while keeping a safe distance. Glesni didn't envy him that part: confining the newcomer to the desolate Quarantine Rock.

Strange to think there'd been a discussion and a vote about it only a few days ago. Protective of their community but unwilling to appear hostile, the Seeders salved their consciences with the knowledge of the rain- and windtight bothy, fully stocked with essentials and a few home comforts. From time to time between the increasingly rare arrivals, when the weather was calm and the sea as innocent as a meadow of breeze-rippled grass, they would take the boat over to the Rock and stock up, making sure the place was kept habitable for the next visitor. Or for their own people after they'd been on one of the infrequent foraging trips to the mainland. That made it seem fairer, somehow.

As if there were some collective knowledge in the air that another arrival was due, the matter had been discussed at the last weekly Gathering. A wet winter and rogue late frost had played havoc with their spring crops and there was a strong prospect of another drought this year. Had the time come to abandon the Rock and use its tinned and dried provisions? Whether it was an even more deadly strain of the flu virus or this new pandemic that was emerging in a cloud of antibiotic resistance and sweeping its way around the globe, wouldn't they be able to tell if a new arrival was a carrier? Didn't their principles compel them to extend a hand of welcome?

The vote had been only narrowly in favour of keeping the Quarantine Rock. The margins reduced every time. Those who had experienced the waves of zoonotic pandemics and their aftermath on the mainland had no doubts about upholding the system. For some of the younger ones, who knew nothing but island life, compassion was stronger than fear. Compassion or no, in favour they voted. Glesni looked back at the growing crowd watching from the jetty. Though the newcomer had her sympathy, she was sure they'd all be relieved.

Back on the Rock, the woman was standing in front of the sign, apparently resigned to her fate. Written bilingual instructions at the

11

landing point invited new arrivals to make themselves at home for the quarantine period. At one stage, someone had pointed out that the system assumed the unfortunates could read and understand Welsh or English, the island's languages; their best artist, Cerys, had added simple but expressive diagrams to the sign. There was a system of flags for signalling. If they wanted to leave, their boat would be returned to them; otherwise, it was kept on the jetty of Ynys Hudol itself, no doubt as a precaution to stop them from sneaking across and infecting the community in the middle of the night. Many of the Seeder community members, including Glesni herself, were uncomfortable with the system, hence the sporadic debates about the quarantine, but a carrier of disease would be bound to devastate their small population. Some islanders had contracted and survived one or other of the pandemics in the past, or had up-to-date vaccinations at the time they came, but no one knew how effective any of it was against what a newcomer might bring. And unless they had a miracle natural immunity, the island's children were a clean slate.

Glesni made her way down to the jetty in time to see Taid pull up with the stranger's boat in tow. The crowd were keeping a respectful distance, their wariness of someone who'd been close to a quarantined newcomer stronger than curiosity. She even heard someone mutter that he should have stayed on the Quarantine Rock himself after being in contact. Glancing at her mam, Glesni moved past them to help Taid tie the boats up. Gwylan was ahead of her and gestured her to stay clear. Her look, combined with Taid's reassuring smile, succeeded in holding her back.

Glesni was close enough to detect his irritation as he assured Gwylan, from a safe distance, that of course he hadn't been in contact with the stranger or any of her possessions – he'd thrown her the rope and he was now using a different one to secure the boat – let alone got close enough to breathe the same air as her. His protestations seemed to satisfy Gwylan, though she insisted he wore a face covering and isolated until the matter had been fully discussed at an emergency Gathering to be held that evening.

Forbidden from approaching, Glesni busied herself in the paddock close by the little harbour, coaxing one of their sturdy ponies into the harness of the cart that would be needed to bring the faulty turbine back to the workshop. She took comfort in his warm, homely smell and the feel of his tangled mane. Handling one or other of the small, semi-wild cobs was one way she could truly be useful to Taid, who was wary of the ponies. It brought solace to her now as she parked the cart at a safe distance instead of giving Taid her usual hug.

The crowd parted to let him through and he glanced at Glesni with a mischievous look in his eyes above the mask. He set off up the track, leading rein in one hand, walking stick in the other, and she followed him at a safe distance, until they met Haf and her friend Angharad coming towards them. By the time Glesni had stopped to tell them the news, pleased that for once she was a step ahead of her sister, Taid was well on the way to his workshop and cottage. She paused, and turned to look at the Quarantine Rock, feeling a brief pang of hostility and fear towards the woman, before chiding herself that it wasn't her fault her boat had broken down, and since Taid had kept his distance he'd be perfectly safe.

That evening, Haf had set off early for the Gathering, as she always did so that she and her friends could stake their corner at the back to huddle in teenage aloofness. Glesni crossed the courtyard to Taid's workshop to fetch his things to wash up. Handing the plate and cutlery across the stable door at arm's length, he brushed off her questions, saying she shouldn't be late for the Gathering and he'd have a good chat with her the following day – if necessary, while she stood outside in the fresh air. She slowed her steps as she neared the house and heard Mam arguing with Tom.

'Haf's talking about this play they'll be doing, about Irlas. What were you thinking of?'

'I only told them to write about it in their own words. It was Haf who took it into her head to start acting it out.'

'She's got a notion of performing it in the roundhouse!'

'Don't worry. She enjoyed posing around this afternoon, but that girl's never going to knuckle down to serious rehearsals unless she's pushed. And I won't be doing any pushing.'

'But even so—'

'You're overreacting, love. Understandable, after Erik's catch earlier. It's the same whenever anything happens at sea. You think of Gareth.'

Glesni rolled her eyes. Tom always seemed to bring up her father's death whenever they had an argument.

'Oh, please!' Her mam's tone echoed her feelings. 'There's no comparison. In fact, I'm glad Dad was out at sea this afternoon. Imagine if he'd...'

Glesni saw her mam move to the window and smiled, trying to adopt the expression of someone who hadn't heard a thing. They lowered their voices, but she could still catch the gist as she dragged her feet towards the door.

'The kids'll lose interest before anything comes of it,' Tom said. Out of sight, Glesni rolled her eyes – a bit of respect for the 'kids', please! 'And if they start asking too much,' he continued, 'I can just remind them of the Compassionate Silence.'

Everyone respected the unwritten agreement that, since most of them had experienced bad stuff before coming to the island, no one was expected to talk about their mainland past if they didn't want to. Glesni couldn't help wondering who, if anyone, among the Seeders had anything to do with Irlas Dam, not to mention why it was a good thing Taid had been out on the boat. She'd heard him more than once arguing passionately for non-violence, usually when the island's Defenders were under discussion; maybe Mam had been glad to avoid a rant on the subject of the first bomb attack and violent confrontation of the civil war.

They made their way to the roundhouse for the Gathering and took their usual places on one of the rings of benches. Gwylan stood, addressing the community from her seat – the central space was only used for the entertainment afterwards.

'Thank you all for coming tonight,' she said. 'I daresay you've heard that we've got a visitor on the Rock, rescued by Erik when her boat broke down. Our main purpose is to determine the extent of her quarantine – and Erik's, if any.' A few surreptitious glances were thrown at Glesni and her family. 'Today I'd like us to use our opening moments of silence to reflect on what brought us here, and our gratitude for our community, as well as our principles of equality, fairness and moderation.'

Given that Glesni had been born on the island, and therefore had no arrival story to reflect on, she wondered about Gwylan. Realising she knew only that she'd been a respected environmental activist – presumably quite prominent to judge from the way she embraced the co-leader role – Glesni spent most of the silence distracted by her awe-inspiring presence, with her colourful clothes and long, braided silvery blonde hair. Glesni fingered her own simple plaits wistfully – once, after fumbling for a while at a couple of tatty French braids, Haf had declared she couldn't be bothered playing with her little sister's hair, and Mam wasn't interested; if Glesni asked, she'd probably say she should keep it short and practical like her own. Awen, Gwylan's partner, who was presumably responsible for her awesome locks, sat next to her. She was distant, her head full of herbs and healing lore, and Glesni admired her, too, but in a different way. She caught a glimpse of Cerys, who sometimes cut people's hair when she wasn't busy with her crafts and artwork, eyes lowered in contemplation, and wondered if she could pluck up courage to ask her about hair braiding some time. Not that it worried her most of the time, just when she was supposed to be considering the values of their community. She suppressed a smile.

After a due pause, Gwylan spoke. 'Let's start this emergency Gathering by reminding ourselves what our founders had to say about new arrivals.'

She looked across at her co-leader, Cai. A copy of *Seeds of Change* in his hand, he stood, tall but not as tall as Taid, and Glesni thought he was far more approachable than Gwylan, despite being Madog's dad.

Her thoughts were cut off as he introduced a couple of paragraphs from the 'Beginnings and Recruitment' section of the book.

From the outset, we deliberately avoided drawing attention to ourselves. With the agreement of Martha, Idris and Arwel, the remaining original Trustees, we came to Ynys Hudol with a dozen or so friends who had been part of our sustainable living community, Roots and Branches, on the mainland. We knew and trusted them all, and they chose to come with us, to commit to life on the island.

To be truly sustainable, our new island community needed more people. We spread the word among communities and movements with similar values to our own proto-Seeders, and we gave every newcomer a searching interview, without at first revealing the location of Ynys Hudol, to ensure their trustworthiness, their acceptance of our money and ownership rules, and their commitment to stay.

We maintained this policy during the greater influx in the wake of the Clearances, even after we'd long since stopped our active recruitment, but as the years went by, fewer and fewer people arrived and those who did were usually so relieved and appreciative that no further questioning of their motives or commitment was needed.

Now, as our numbers have grown and the climate becomes ever fickler, with increasing incidences of failed harvests, we need to be careful about accepting newcomers, even if we're satisfied that they don't pose a threat to us. However, our primary values are based on sharing and welcome, and we need to judge each arrival on their merits and perceived need of shelter and sanctuary.

This is notwithstanding our requirement that everyone who comes to Ynys Hudol – newcomers or our own people returning from mainland trips – must spend a period, the length to be decided at a Gathering, on the Quarantine Rock, where we undertake to maintain a fully provisioned shelter for their comfort. Whatever else people – visitors or potential Seeders – may think of us, we wouldn't want to be considered inhospitable.

16

'Unfortunately, Erik, who rescued the woman, isn't here, because of course he's isolating,' Gwylan said. 'So he's asked me to pass on the little he knows.'

'How can he know anything?' Steffan, the most vocal of a few Seeders whose views earned them the epithet 'purists', spoke up to general muttering of disapproval and a dismissive wave from Gwylan.

'Let me finish. You'll have time to air your views then.' Gwylan went on to say that Erik hadn't found out much because he'd sensibly maintained a careful distance – and it had been hard to hear. 'He did think he caught her name – Sandy Welby, "or something like that" – and that she'd been looking for someone. She showed no signs of hostility so he decided to bring her here – or at least, to the Quarantine Rock – so we could find out more in due course and he could have a go at repairing her boat.'

'He should have come ashore and asked before approaching her and bringing her in.' Steffan again. 'What if she's an infiltrator? Intends to do us harm?'

'Steffan, please.' Gwylan waved at the poster on the wall showing the Gathering guidelines. 'Everyone will have a chance to speak. After we've heard the facts. And the *fact* is, she's here. The first thing is to decide on the quarantine period. Idris, what's the latest on the new pandemic?'

Idris rose to speak. He wasn't obliged to stand, but stubbornly refused to accept any concessions to his age. As if going up and down the mountain to the watchtower wasn't testimony enough to his fitness. Alongside his wildlife and weather monitoring equipment, he had a radio as cranky as he was, the island's only connection with the mainland, which he listened to sporadically to keep up with the news and report back anything of importance.

'Looks like the New Plague's still spreading,' he said without preamble. 'Incubation period seven to ten days.'

After further interventions from Steffan, the Gathering voted to allow Sandy to stay until the quarantine period was over – what else could they do, since she didn't have a functioning boat and the man best placed to fix it would also have to isolate? They decided on a two-week quarantine, both for the newcomer on the rock and for Taid in his workshop. They also agreed that he could go out for walks, strictly solitary, probably because they knew that, short of locking and barring the workshop door, they would be unable to stop him.

None of which would be a real hardship for him, a natural loner; more for Glesni, as she'd miss his company. And Madog, Taid's assistant, as it turned out. After Awen had closed the business part of the Gathering with a song, Madog approached Glesni as she was queuing for drinks, pretending as she always did that she didn't feel excluded by Haf's crowd and wishing Tahira wasn't so shy about Gatherings.

'How come you weren't out with him today?' he said.

Charming as ever. Glesni tried not to betray the way Madog unsettled her. People said he and Taid were suited as workmates, neither of them prone to small talk, but she'd never seen the slightest resemblance.

'I had school.'

'Doesn't usually stop you.'

Why did he have to be so hostile? He was the one who got to work with Taid every day. Cursing her age, Glesni had to make do with snatched opportunities to learn practical skills with him, hoping that one day she could take her own place in his workshop, even if that would mean working with Madog.

'Bit weird, isn't it? Him being out on his own the day a mainlander comes by.'

'Oh, for—'

'And bringing her back without consulting anyone. What's his game?'

'She was in trouble.'

He stared at her. She stared back. Let him give in first.

'Yeah, right,' he yielded. 'You carry on believing that, Glesni. Not everyone does.'

18

Glesni reached the drinks table. 'Like not everyone believes you're not trying to jump the queue.'

Rolling his eyes, he stepped back and wandered off. She was getting better at holding her ground, though she could have phrased it more eloquently. But he was several years older than she was and, having lived on the mainland when he was young, was far more worldly wise. Glancing out into the dark evening, the Quarantine Rock out of sight due to the lie of the land, she again felt that flash of anger at the stranger, whose presence was already sowing seeds of dissent. Why did she have to get stranded here? At the very moment Taid was out there? With that thought, she stopped her negativity, induced by Madog's suspicions, and turned her thoughts to sympathy for the poor woman stuck out there alone on the Quarantine Rock.

# WHAT ELSE WAS THERE TO DO ON A DESOLATE ROCK?

Sandy was woken from an unexpectedly good night's sleep by a ray of sun creeping through the cheerful homespun curtains and warming her face. She shifted and raised a hand to shield her eyes. Pulling on her clothes, she looked around the stone-built hut.

She hadn't been dreaming. This place – a small, cosy but smoke-smelling tiny house on an islet washed by hushing waves – was real. Just as yesterday's totally uncharacteristic recklessness had been real. Her plans to find Adam might have been crumbling, but to trust herself on impulse to a complete stranger's rickety boat...? Had she really believed that she could navigate her way across the open sea to Ireland? And manoeuvre herself safely to shore if and when she arrived there? She'd probably been lucky that it conked out no more than half an hour after leaving the run-down marina. Lucky, that is, until her rescuer, not the knight in shining armour she'd believed him to be, swerved away from the landing stage on the island. She'd yelled at the top of her voice, wondering if the old man was deaf until he finally slowed and let her boat drift closer – but not too close.

'Aren't you taking me to shore?' She waved wildly at the small crowd of onlookers.

'Can't.'

'What bloody threat do you think I could possibly be?'

He shrugged and called something back, his voice sinking into the choppy waves.

'Warranty?' she retorted. 'What?' Did he mean the boat? Or some kind of guarantee of good behaviour?

He gestured theatrically at the face mask he was wearing – which didn't help communication – and tried again, shouting across the gap he was skilfully maintaining. She managed to make out '*Quar-an-tine*. Pandemics... contagion... sorry. Not long.'

20

'How long?'

'Couple of weeks?'

'You're fucking joking! Can't you just let me go?'

He shrugged. 'I could.' He was talking more slowly now, enunciating carefully in a raised voice. 'But your boat's not working. Stay and I'll repair it.'

Knocked off balance by a swell, she thought she heard something like 'it'll be worth it' – but still her language hadn't been pretty and even now she felt her face reddening.

She could forgive herself that, she supposed, after the last few days' forlorn journey along the largely deserted lanes of rural Wales. But, having seen the desolation for herself, could she forgive herself her part in the Resettlement? From the safe distance of her civil servant's desk in Manchester, fielding phone calls and sifting forms, it had been easy enough to justify the policy that soon came to be dubbed the Clearances.

Enough of that. She really didn't want to think of her journey in search of Adam, but it insisted its way to the front of her mind. In the absence of public transport, she'd set off on her e-bike. Things got harder when she realised that the shutting down of whole regions' power supplies rendered the bike's battery useless, and she soon ditched it as no more than excess weight. Navigation hadn't been any easier since her personal device lost all trace of a signal.

Passing through deserted villages and small towns, she had no way of knowing if they were completely empty or whether eyes were watching her from dead windows. Following the sun west across a vast wilderness of moorland and unruly swathes of woodland, she eventually found what she'd hoped would be her destination – Nant-y-Wern, some kind of smallholding – but she had no directions beyond the name and the houses in the Irlas valley were derelict. Not a soul there, let alone Adam.

She spent a frustrating hour double-checking the map and negotiating lanes that were wrecked by weather and neglect, more than once shuddering as she thought she saw movement. Twice she stopped and looked around her, convinced she could feel a hostile gaze, waiting to see if the owner of the unseen eyes would reveal themselves and give her news of him. The second time, she was sure she heard a rustle. After a wait that seemed to go on forever, she called out.

'Hello?' Her voice echoed uncannily. Then nothing. Not a whisper of movement. Whoever it was, their knowledge of these woods was on a totally different level to hers, confirming her growing feeling that she should abandon her quest. As the light began to fade, she gave up and left, eager to put the valley as far behind her as possible before it became too dark to travel. She had no wish to spend a night near the fateful place that had taken Liv from her.

Her failure to account for the lack of hotels and B&Bs in the wake of the Resettlement meant she hadn't planned beyond this point. When the thickening dusk prevented her from going any further, she hunkered down in a deserted barn, glad for once of Adam's fondness for hiking and camping that had ensured she'd set out prepared with a sleeping bag and camping stove.

'You got your own way in the end, didn't you?' she muttered. She'd hated their camping trips, making every excuse not to go tramping across the moors with him, and imagined him laughing at her now. The little sleep she'd had was peppered with a succession of apparitions – Adam himself, of course, shaking his head sadly; Liv, pleading with her to forgive, forget and go home; a slim androgynous figure with a face obscured by green-man leaves, brandishing a box of matches and grabbing her, forcing her to come along and join their shady terrorist campaign.

The next day, she'd come up with a vague notion of trying to get to Ireland. Adam had always dreamed of the fabled Emerald Isle and there was a chance she might find him there – especially since she'd at least have access to reliable resources. The lack of a passport and visa, along with two more sleepless nights dampened by drizzle, were probably what led her to take a chance on that dodgy boat.

And now, after a deep night's sleep in relative security, she shook her head at the memory and instinctively thought of her bag, stashed under the bed.

As jumpy now as she'd been in the Irlas valley with its unseen leafy presence, she glanced around. She'd checked on arrival yesterday for hidden cameras but found nothing. Wrapping the brightly coloured granny-square blanket around her as the memory of cold, damp nights momentarily eclipsed the warm sunshine, she went to the door and looked out.

Despite the bilingual instruction board with its pictograms – cheerful and friendly as if to soften the intimidation of the inscrutable Welsh paragraphs – and the book she'd found, *Seeds of Change*, that looked like part memoir, part a kind of blueprint for life on the island, she had no idea who these people were, and was still unsure whether she'd be welcomed. Welcomed! She laughed out loud. Some welcome, being shoved here to fend for herself. Come on, Sandy, sleeping in a warm, comfortable bed, eating from well-stocked shelves with a working stove to cook on – call that 'fending'? There was even a vegetable patch, which the islanders must tend when the lepers weren't in residence, though the plants that she could see were too young to make a worthwhile meal. A handful of birds – she had no idea what kind – dived, presumably for fish, and she wondered if the hut's supplies included a rod and line. She reminded herself she had no idea how to use one. Her accommodation's main downside, though, apart from the obvious loneliness, was the toilet. A glorified bucket in an outhouse.

She thought of the radio programme *Desert Island Discs*, which she and her sister, Liv, had discovered back in '42 when its centenary was inescapable on every broadcast and social media channel. The quarantine hut had a violin and a guitar – another unwelcome reminder of Adam – which would do for the radio show's music choices if only she could play them. There were a few books (though no works of Shakespeare) and she assumed *Seeds of Change* might at a pinch take the place of the Bible. And her luxury? She reminded herself why she was checking for watching eyes and went back indoors to take her personal device from her bag.

Yesterday it had shown one bar of power, none of signal. She hesitated to turn the PD on, fearing that the very pressing of the button would drain the last remnants of the battery. She'd already searched the place for a socket, unsurprised to find there weren't any. The binoculars she discovered on the windowsill revealed a turbine halfway up the hill that formed the island's spine, and solar panels on the roofs of scattered houses, but the thick slates that topped the hut here supported nothing but a large cistern to collect rainwater ('Always boil and filter before drinking', the helpful instruction board had informed her). Her longed-for PD recharge would have to wait.

With a sigh, she sat in the sagging chair, her mood lifted by the balmy breeze that belied the choppy waves, and switched on her device. The battery symbol showed empty. She cradled it as if the warmth of her hands could coax the energy into lasting a little longer. She found herself looking at her screensaver, that lovely portrait of Liv as she'd been before the accident, smiling, eyes mischievous as if about to confide a wicked secret. Stop! She couldn't afford the nostalgia any more than she could afford to waste the electrons. It was easy enough to stop her fingers from automatically calling up her photo of Adam, once equally beloved, and she skipped instead to one of Liv's articles.

## A NEW UNDERSTANDING?
### Olivia Wellesby, 11 May 2036.

One of the main principles of conflict resolution is to find a starting place of common ground. However wide our differences, we all – even those we view as terrorists – have the same basic human needs: food, shelter and security. Our differences arise when we have different opinions of how to achieve them, or our needs clash.

It was with this in mind that I paid a visit to

The screen went dead. Why oh why had she not printed out a copy? But why would she? No one carried paper around anymore. But no one ventured into territory where even the quickest recharge was impossible. Oh, Liv, what drove you? If only you'd... If only she'd what? Held back from pursuing the career she loved? Sandy shook her head. Her big sister could have been a successful journalist without putting her life at risk. Without mixing with the kind of people who planted bombs to make themselves heard.

Just as Adam... just as Adam did not have to enlist for the Amazonian War. He could have had a comfortable place in the civil service, alongside her, unadventurous but allowing them to save up for something better in later life. But no, he had to prove himself. Really? Not to her, he didn't. And when they came back from the inconclusive conflict, his contracted service didn't end. He'd taken the guard's position at that dreadful prison that even she was uncomfortable with – 'the only way on offer to fulfil the contract,' as he'd claimed. She'd rather he bought himself out; they could have lived on what she earned until he found decent work. Or could they? Had she maybe, just maybe, pushed him into it? No. No! It had been *his* decision.

And where had it led them? Betrayal, that's where. Deceit. How long had he been carrying out his ridiculous scheme without telling her? He knew she'd disapprove of what he was doing even more than she hated the job itself. So he did it anyway, behind her back. Then scarpered – without her.

As if losing her job wasn't enough, he'd effectively driven her on this wild goose chase across Wales in pursuit of him. With time on her hands and a small redundancy payment, there was no way she was going to let the man she'd once loved simply vanish. To add insult to the injury of lies and betrayal, she was sure that her association with him had given the department the perfect excuse to let her go.

So he could bloody well pay for his actions. She'd make sure she found him and brought him to justice, whatever it took. In her darker moments, when it all felt too much and she was in danger of giving up her personal quest, she told herself it was also for the sake of the victims of those lower-than-low terrorists he'd helped. Regardless of what he'd done to her, that in itself was unforgivable.

She shoved the dead PD back in her bag, retrieving instead the

25

notebook she'd begun to use a few days ago when the device threatened to die on her. Come what may, she wanted a record of her journey and had taken to scribbling down daily notes. As she moved to sit at the small table by the window, she felt a slight dizziness. Some deep breaths and it was gone, but as she wrote she became aware of a nagging headache.

After taking a couple of painkillers from the well-stocked medicine cabinet, she opened a tin of peaches for breakfast – goodness knows what the use-by date was, but she'd heard tinned food could last forever, so thought it best not to look – along with a large cup of water she'd boiled the evening before. Her headache was no better afterwards, worse if anything, so after bringing her journal up-to-date – handwriting was so *slow* compared to typing! – and boiling a kettle of water to top up the water filter tank, she went to lie down. She didn't feel guilty like she normally would taking a daytime nap – what else was there to do on a desolate rock off the shore of an obscure island?

Nestled in the blankets, she looked again at the ring-bound book of handmade paper, *Seeds of Change* by Bleddyn Powell and Edith Turner, the founders of the Seeders. She wondered if the two of them had been among the crowd watching her abandonment yesterday.

After a brief introduction, the book was divided into short chapters. Intrigued by one headed 'The Clearances', as if it were personally addressed to her, she began to read.

The policy in the early '40s, disingenuously called Resettlement by the government of the day but known as the Clearances to everyone else, was implemented in the rural areas of Britain, but concentrated on Cymru in the aftermath of the War of Independence. It affected us here on Ynys Hudol, too. We may have preserved our anonymity as the Seeders, but Ynys Hudol, or Aniseed as it is shown on most of the official maps, was geographically present enough.

When the Resettlement officers – or Clearance Crew as they became known – came, with an armed escort of course, we were prepared. We simply went with them: ourselves, Martha, Arwel and the handful of Seeder pioneers who were with us at that stage. Only Idris remained, hiding from detection in a cave on the impassable eastern cliffs and then, when the coast was clear, moving to the lookout tower on the hill, a relic from the Napoleonic era, we believe.

We allowed ourselves to be 'resettled' for a few months, then gradually, in ones and twos, drifted back. Things were too chaotic for the records of the resettled to be scrutinised too closely or regularly. We were already battling with frequent and ever more destructive storms, but we considered the harvest that had been lost in our absence (despite Idris's best efforts) to be a price worth paying.

Over the next few years, we planted as randomly as we could, not in rows, to avoid detection from the air, until '47 when the policy was repealed: it had done its work by then and many abandoned rural communities have remained deserted.

We hope that, like ours, they have since been revived, and that people continue to return and reclaim.

Sandy had to smile as she read 'Clearance Crew' – she'd thought she'd heard them all – and, although she'd have to be careful to ensure that no one discovered the small part she'd played in it, she decided she was looking forward to meeting these people, especially the resourceful Idris. After her nap, she'd take another look at the hill through the binoculars to see if she could catch a glimpse of anyone watching her.

But that was for later. She picked the book up again, but her headache, with a wave of nausea, had worsened and she put it to one side.

# IF THEY HAD A CHOICE

After a couple of grey, drizzly days, the weather turned warm and sunny, so no one thought twice when no smoke rose from the chimney of the bothy on the Quarantine Rock. But as another front of wind and rain swept in and the temperature dropped, there was still no sign of life. Along with most of the islanders, Glesni began to worry.

It was one thing to subject healthy wanderers to the inevitable loneliness of the Rock. They had food, basic medicines, wonderful views, books, and even a guitar and a fiddle – both of them ancient and probably impossible to tune but the Seeders weren't there to hear. Those confined there as a couple or group had each other, and if they were alone, well, they'd made it this far without company. And there was the promise of coming to Ynys Hudol after a reasonable period of caution. But it was another thing altogether to think of Sandy, as Taid said she was called, suffering alone, too ill to look after herself, perhaps delirious, so she might even forget to drink or eat. All that confusion, fear and pain.

The arguments came and went as the days passed. Both Awen and Khaled, each with their different medicinal and healing skills, argued they should go across, to find out if she really was ill and to take fresh medical supplies. But the collective decision was that they shouldn't risk their own health, and the community couldn't risk losing their healers – for the period of their own inevitable quarantine, let alone possibly forever. In any case, the showers and strong winds eased a few consciences, since they frequently whipped up currents that would have made it nigh-on impossible to approach the Quarantine Rock safely.

Taid showed no symptoms at all, but remained stoic in his workshop, repairing the turbine he'd been inspecting when Sandy drifted in. He'd started to fret after he'd got it working, arguing that he should be allowed back out – alone, if need be – to re-site it, and to start diagnosing Sandy's boat.

Finally, on his first day out of isolation, he stopped Glesni as she was leaving for school.

'Fancy a trip out to sea, Pwt?'

The nickname made her feel like he'd never been shut away. He never called Haf that, not since she was about nine and objected, 'I'm not a scrap of a thing!' Since it was one of the few Welsh words he used regularly, Glesni felt it was something special between the two of them. He'd said he thought so, too, ever since he'd heard her nain's family calling Mam the same when she was little.

'I've cleared it with Tom, provided we wait till the afternoon.'

'But what about—'

'Madog's busy with the others, working on that leak in the roundhouse roof.' He grinned at her. 'So someone's got to eliminate the rumours that I'm going off on my own to indulge in some shady mainlander deal. You can witness that I don't get contaminated, too – I've been told to look in on our patient.'

He was waiting for her outside the school, with a packed lunch of flatbread and pickles, and the turbine ready on the cart. Although he'd obviously readied the pony and cart, or more likely got Mam to do it for him, he handed her the lead rope, as if to boost her confidence. They said little; during his isolation she'd given him the news most evenings over the stable door to the workshop, and in any case, simply being together was enough.

He loaded the turbine on board *Berta* while she turned Ffred the pony out into the small paddock by the jetty. As they readied the boat to leave, he hardly needed to instruct her, and a warm pride glowed inside her like the sun on the iridescent waves between cloud-shadows – it was one of those rare days when the sea was mercifully free from clumps of jostling plastic pollution. Her pride soon changed to sadness as they passed the sorry sight of Sandy's boat on the way out to the tidal turbine array. The Quarantine Rock came into view beyond the headland.

'Shouldn't we go to her first?'

He shrugged. 'Best get the job done. Half an hour won't make much difference.'

Glesni thought it could make all the difference in the world if Sandy had seen them setting out – waiting had a way of stretching time – but there was no sign of her and the boat's electric motor hardly made a sound, unlike the thrumming of the old boat with its smelly diesel engine that she remembered from years ago.

He read the water like she read words in a book, navigating the currents that fed the array of turbines until they came to the buoy that marked the location of the one they were to replace. They fastened up to it, and used an underwater drone to fix the repaired machinery into its cradle in the depths, before connecting it up.

'Now the wait,' he said. 'Some would say it's wasted time, but not as big a waste as having to come back out if it's not working properly.'

He got out their lunch and they sat rocking on the swell in the warm spring sun as test figures ran across a gauge.

'Have you always worked at sea?' she asked. 'Before you came to Ynys Hudol?'

He shook his head, mouth full.

'You seem so at home on the water.'

'Grew up with canals, then rivers... kind of a natural progression.'

'There was a river running through your nature reserve on the mainland, wasn't there?'

'Not big enough to sail a boat on.' He gazed out over the sun-flecked wavelets. 'But it was the lifeblood of our local ecosystem.'

'Like the one at Irlas?'

He removed his cap and rubbed his head, his remaining close-cropped hair the colour of the light clouds chasing the sun.

'What made you think of that?' he said, carefully replacing the cap.

'We were talking about it, the day you rescued Sandy.'

'Talking about it?'

'At school.'

30

He nodded as he passed her the water bottle. 'And what did Tom tell you?'

'That it was the start of the civil war. Planned deliberately in a place that was important both for nature and for Cymru, because the government wanted a civil war that we couldn't win.'

He took the bottle, tipped his head back and drank deeply.

'That sums it up nicely.'

'But our people set the bomb off,' she said. 'Played into their hands by giving up on non-violence.'

'He told you that?'

'We kind of came up with it in discussion afterwards.' Taid said nothing. 'Did you know them, the protesters at Irlas?'

He fixed his gaze on a flock of razorbills bobbing in a raft on the water. 'Most thinking people were involved in some protest or other. There was quite a network. Many of them knew each other, or of each other.'

'Was Tom one of them?'

'What makes you think that?'

'Mam was a bit weird about him covering it in class.'

'Oh?' Still without looking at her, he leaned across to examine the figures on the test screen, then straightened. 'It was a massive protest to begin with. Supporters joined it from all over. Till the police and the rest started getting heavy-handed. But I don't think Tom was there. He might even have already been here on the island by then; came straight from uni, about the time Edith and Bleddyn founded the community in '37. Who'd have left this place if they had a choice?'

'He just sounded really passionate.'

Taid shrugged, his eyes finally meeting hers. 'Whatever the rights or wrongs, it was an important incident. Changed the course of many people's lives.'

She wanted to ask more but his expression was a sobering reminder of the Compassionate Silence.

Once satisfied the turbine was functioning properly, they set off back, via the Quarantine Rock. Sandy was watching them approach, sitting by the top of the flimsy metal ladder attached to the side of the flat rock that served as a quay. She looked pale, but they were relieved to see her outside. She rose unsteadily to her feet as Taid gave Glesni a face covering and put one on himself. Sandy caught the rope they threw, fumbling to tie it to the ring. The boat nudged and clunked against the landing point.

'Thank you.' She picked up her bag and made for the edge. Taid held up a warning hand.

'You can't come aboard,' he said curtly.

She stared at him. 'You mean you haven't... you're not here to take me over?'

'Sorry.' He gazed up as the boat rocked in the swell. 'Not yet. You wouldn't be allowed ashore if I did.'

She sank back down, waving a hand at the notice. 'Two to three weeks, it says!'

'If you're not ill. We think... have you been ill?'

'Do I look a picture of health? You *think*... you knew but you didn't...?' She hugged her knees. 'You selfish bastards.'

He held out his hands, palms up. 'I need to ask you some questions. Report back. I've brought you some stuff from the doctor, in case the supplies in the bothy have run out. Painkillers. Anti-inflammatories. Decongestants...'

He threw a bag up onto the landing stage.

'Hang on – you've got a *doctor* in this godforsaken place? Why the fuck—'

'We ran out of PPE a long time ago. In fairness, he and our healer wanted to come. But it was voted down.'

'God allfuckingmighty!'

He tried to soothe her, stressing the importance of quarantine, families back on the island, the sort of thing she'd encounter anywhere, before running through the questions Khaled had given him, and asking her to take her temperature with a thermometer from the bag he'd thrown to her.

'When will you give me my boat back?' she said, jabbing the thermometer in the air like a miniature bayonet.

'When you're ready for it – and it for you. Needs a bit of work – I'm going to have a look at it. I had to isolate too, you know.'

'Oh, poor you.'

Her sarcasm rolled off him. 'I dare say you're not in a fit state to set off anywhere just yet.'

'But fit enough for you to fucking leave on my own.'

He looked at her helplessly. 'I've been here myself, you know. When I arrived. We all have. Well, not the likes of young Glesni, she was born here, but... you know...'

'I'm guessing you weren't ill.'

'Luckily not.' He looked directly into her eyes. 'But you were.'

They stared at one another for a long moment. She relented and put the thermometer in her mouth. Glesni willed the tension to break before it did.

Eventually Sandy gave them the reading. 'So what now?'

'I'll report back and tell them you're all right—'

'All right? I've been lying here for days – could be weeks, how do I know? – in agony, sweating it out with my own lungs drowning me, no one to care, not a single kind word. I come round to a freezing cold, damp room, have to crawl around—' She was momentarily halted by a hacking cough, and turned away from them. 'I'm there, crawling around making my own fire. Which won't stay lit. I've made it through all that, so yes, you can piss off back to your prehistoric clan of knuckleheads with a clear conscience.'

'Look, I'm sorry, but it's not up to me, is it?'

'Which heartless arsehole *is* it up to?'

Glesni tried to stifle a giggle as he explained that they'd hold an emergency Gathering once he'd reported back and he, or someone, would come to fetch her as soon as possible. He waved towards the bothy.

'I'd come ashore and help you if I could, you know.'

'Heaven forbid you should contaminate yourself!'

'Think of it like this,' he said. 'If we don't land here, we stand a better chance of the heartless arseholes letting us back onto the island. So we can put in a word for bringing you back as soon as we reasonably can.'

Even with the face covering, he looked friendly when he smiled. Sandy almost smiled back.

As he steered the boat back across the bay, Glesni had an absurd wish that Sandy didn't seem about half his age. However much he liked his own company, he was lonely, she was sure. But her mam told her that even though things had been difficult between him and Nain when she died, he still loved her too fiercely to find a place in his heart for anyone else. Then she'd spoil it by adding that maybe there was simply no one who would have him.

# PART II

# NANT-Y-WERN

# TO UNDERSTAND THEM AND THANK THEM

Crack snap crunch crack. A person. I always know people not animals this one a man. Man woman what do I care? They're all so careless it's their nature I know yes I do. They call this forest nature too like it's something apart like people aren't part of the whole. She told me and I listened but I know they're right to think like they do and they're not a part of it not like I'm part of these woods. She taught me that taught me how to listen how to understand the trees the fungi the weeds how to understand them and thank them I know how.

Not like the animals those people aren't, the woods belong to the animals and belong to me too and we all belong to the woods. I hear the animals the little ones mostly sometimes there's a cat one of Hers one of ours except I don't like to think I own them She didn't own them either but She thought of them as Hers. The cats are my friends there aren't many still come to the house they go their own ways but my lovely Cadi still lives in the house and Smotyn they're in the woods during daytime but come to me in the house at night. When they're away in the trees I hear the other creatures I do I hear the mice squirrels they scurry rustle pause sniff. There's lots of them here She said things were dying out but not here the woods are growing wilder every year and maybe there aren't so many big ones to eat them I haven't heard an owl since She died, sang a sad sad hoo for Her but no tu-wit and I haven't heard it since that night I think She took the owls with Her I'd like it if She had company.

I hear the scurryrustle little ones I hear their tiny sounds I do but not like when the people come, oh no it's because I choose to listen. The little ones don't crash their way into my world they rustle scurry always alert. They know I might be predator I often am and if I catch enough the cats are lucky too.

Ha ha how does this man know I don't watch him with hunger in my eyes in my bones?

Whisper rustle. I love this time of year when the trees have almost all their clothes on and I don't need so many of mine otherwise I couldn't sit here watching I'd be gone away from the road safe away from the man I'd still be listening always listening even if I couldn't be watching. Rustle whisper. The faintest movement in the leaves the creaking of a branch. If he notices he'll think it's the wind though there's only the tiniest breeze today but they don't notice things like that She told me they don't. They don't know anything they don't know the sound of me watching.

He thuds through as I sit high in my tree hating and waiting. He's hurrying keeps looking round as if he's running from something from someone. You'd think he'd be more careful but they never are. Maybe he thinks this is careful this striding looking changing his pace to walk on the grass and muffle his stomping. But there's more to staying unseen than that I know as I sit here waiting and hating. Hating and waiting wanting him gone.

He slows near the memorial and looks for somewhere to turn off the road ha even if he finds the path up the hill he won't find the way to my road and my house not since we built the wall across the gateway but I hate the road even though no one comes down our lane no one came when She was here only once and then we built the wall and when the landslide happened and the tree fell we covered it, encouraged things to grow the ivy the brambles the grass in the cracks but it's still a road and even though there's nothing here that people want She built the wall She covered the tree just in case and now he's here is he looking for us not me not Her no one knows I'm here and She's gone with the owls maybe he's looking for the *Cofeb* the old village the memorial or maybe he just came into the woods because he's running away and no one knows he's here either that's why he stopped before he came to it maybe he won't go to the *Cofeb* where people sometimes come to pay their respects it's too open maybe he's not so stupid even if he makes all that noise so every animal can hear.

But he's left the road where a tangle of bushes hides him and I hope he isn't going to pee like he's marking his territory when he's only passing through and he doesn't know I'm here to see it or sniff it anyway. But ha ha I wouldn't sniff that's animals not people and everyone needs to pee and I hear the splash yet another noise then I wait for him to come back to the road but I can sense him looking round and I'm glad the path to our higher road is narrow and steep so he doesn't come near my house I don't want visitors. She didn't want visitors either but She got me but I was only little and anyway She found me I didn't find her house my house now my garden. I think She was glad of me but we grew the thick brambles all tangled up with wild roses and sticky willie and haws and our thick nettle beds and used new paths not the old track that led from the road used ways that only we knew so we didn't get any more visitors we didn't need them didn't want them. She's gone now but I can keep people away as well as She could I don't need Her to feel safe.

He stands on the road like he can hear something I can tell he doesn't like being on the road he sees the path and even if he does climb it's still a way to my lane my house and if he goes any closer I have my bow and arrows I always carry them when I'm out in case I see something worth catching it makes a nice change from fruit and seeds and mushrooms and leaves. I have a gun too She taught me how to look after it what to do but She said I must never never use it unless I'm in terrible danger so I keep it in the house and even if using it wasn't bad I never do because it's too loud and I don't want anyone to know I'm here even if they couldn't find my house in the brambles beyond the lane with the fallen tree. I just clean it sometimes and aim at things pretend to shoot but when it's real I use the bow it's quieter. I hope he doesn't go any closer to my house because I don't want to shoot killing people is a waste I can't eat the meat She said so I'd starve first She taught me that.

He goes a few steps off the road and what does he do he sits on a log and takes the bag off his back and searches in it starts eating. I'm hungry so hungry and I wish he was somewhere else further from my tree so I could slither down without him knowing and sneak up on him and have some of whatever he's carrying in his bag but he isn't and I can't so I watch and wait and hate patiently. My hand tightens on my bow maybe it's not a waste if he's got food in his bag but however much I don't want him here he doesn't deserve killing not yet he hasn't done anything to deserve that except have food that I haven't got.

I turn my head before I've even heard it not heard it felt it. I hear a car the tyre noise I don't think the man with his food heard it his head is full of chomping then I see them pass on the road hear them stop at the *Cofeb* car doors bang I hear them stomping along the road herding though I soon know there's only two of them it sounds like more and they're certainly not trying to run away silently. I look down and now the eating man's heard it too he puts the food he hasn't eaten in his bag and ever so carefully so he doesn't make a sound he hoists it up on his shoulders. He looks up stares into the leaves as if he knows I'm there but I don't think so because he makes no sign then he starts glancing around. I hope he won't go any further up towards my house but he sets off up the path it climbs steeply I know the path but he doesn't know the woods the path I hope he'll get away I don't know why I hope this I don't know why one stupid man is better than two stupid men who I haven't seen yet but I want him to get away. I don't want it so much that I come down from my tree and show him the way to my house where to climb the wall oh no the men can have him before he has my house.

The footsteps come nearer and he's scrambling up and the path divides I will him to choose the steep part because the easier one's an animal track it soon becomes too tiny for people a trap he won't get far then the stomping men are round the corner he's still paused not chosen his path they start climbing I hope they fall but they see him and he turns he has a blade in his hand he's not so stupid after all and one of them's dead before they reach the fork in the path. Then there's a crack louder than thunder and the running-away man falls to the ground with a red hole in his leg the other one the big one has a gun he stands over him and grabs his blade off him he holds it to his throat and says something he asks where is she? I know he doesn't mean Her She's with the owls but I don't know who and the first man the running-away man says he doesn't either but I think he probably does he says he doesn't know what he's talking about and the big man says bollocks. He kicks him and I hear noises of pain then he drags him up by the hair and puts the blade against his throat again and he says tell me what you know. Nothing. He grabs a stick and shoves it in the gunshot wound in the man's leg and twists it and he yells out in agony and that makes me angry I kill if I have to but I try not to cause too much pain. And that's why even if the first man the running-away man might be as bad as the second two I don't think I just nock an arrow and shoot. The big one whirls round I almost laugh at the look on his face then he falls and as he falls he flails his arms and the blade slices through my man's shirt and I see a dark patch appear and I think who's stupid now but it can't be helped another arrow and the big one's dead too.

I didn't want this but now I've made a decision or the decision made itself I can't just leave him there wounded if there are any big animals dogs pigs I don't want them to come near my house or get him.

I climb down from my tree and he looks at me eyes screwed up like it's a real effort and says I wondered when you'd introduce yourself.

# NORMALITY HAD GONE A LONG TIME AGO

He had no idea where he was; he'd been blundering around lost, stopped to eat and then stupidly... The young woman had distracted him. No, he couldn't blame her; he'd allowed her presence to distract him. Careless. He thought he'd learned by now. At first he'd thought – when he was able to think through the fog of pain – that it was more than carelessness, that she'd somehow been watching out for him, that she'd betrayed him to them. But her actions soon redeemed her.

He recalled flashes of consciousness, agony coalescing to blackout and back, as she helped and then dragged him somewhere. Here.

Rough but well-meaning. She must be well-meaning because he was here, wounds bound, fed, raging thirst periodically quenched.

How long had he been here? It was all a blur. He sat up, pausing a moment until the whirling stopped, seeing the room clearly, possibly for the first time: he still wasn't sure what was memory, what was dream, what was now.

A movement drew his eye. No sound. He tapped the bedpost to make sure his hearing was intact; only a shadow momentarily crossing the door gave away her presence. Now he was more aware, he was amazed by her ability to move so silently.

She appeared in the doorway, a woodland sprite with spiky hair and patched clothes faded to a blend-in grey, a dead squirrel slung like a belligerent ponytail over her shoulder, and peered at him. Then vanished again. He waited, gingerly feeling the bandaged wound on his thigh and wincing at his own touch. Remembering, he raised his hand to the gash on his arm, also bandaged. A duller pain, maybe edged with the itch of healing – or maybe that was wishful thinking. Before he could decide whether to ease the dressing back for a look, his hand was batted away. She thrust a cup at him. He took it but, reluctant to succumb to a renewed loss of awareness, held it without moving to drink.

She took it from him, her eyes chiding, and held it to his mouth in a gesture that he realised had become as familiar as home. He pressed his lips together in a thin line of denial, recalling how agitated even the slightest spillage made her, how reluctant she was to waste a single drop. She put it down, her expression conveying as eloquently as words that she didn't care either way and knew that his pain would soon be enough to drive his hand to the cup. Leaving him with this thought, she was gone.

Sometime later – he thought he'd slept but couldn't be sure – he became aware of the smell of meat cooking. Swallowing saliva, he savoured the rich scent of anticipation, imagining a time in the future when he was back to normality and the smell of roasting squirrel – or some other unfortunate creature – would be a distant memory, triggering a recall of his time in this strange place.

But of course, there wouldn't be a normality to return to. Normality had gone a long time ago and even the life he'd settled into could never be got back now.

She reappeared, catlike. He nodded.

'Yes, I'll try. I'd really love to.' Then he realised she hadn't spoken. She smiled and everything about her changed – he'd been wondering if she could smile. He braced himself with his hands and sat up, surprised but relieved to find the room wasn't spinning, then gingerly lifted first one leg, then the injured one, over the side of the bed, planting his feet on the floor. He'd hardly begun to think how he intended to cross the space when she scurried in – he'd hardly noticed her leave – brandishing a large stick. He raised his hands in instinctive self-defence, but she shook her head with another smile. She planted one end on the ground, leaned on it while eyeing him quizzically, then passed it to him.

'Thanks.'

He levered himself to his feet and staggered towards the door one agonising step at a time, trying not to betray the weakness caused by days or maybe more of inactivity.

The door opened onto a hallway with stairs rising from one end; the second door on the left was where the smell and sounds of cooking were coming from. He headed towards it, pausing as a black-and-white cat emerged from the door and moved confidently towards him. Too reliant on his stick to bend, he paused to allow it to rub round his legs before entering the kitchen.

It wasn't at all what he'd imagined, though he wasn't sure what he had expected to see. Certainly not a fitted kitchen, with units painted olive green, flaking in places, and a large table in the middle of the room. He couldn't see the surface for the jumble of things – woodwork, sewing, plates, a pile of items needing mending. A stainless-steel sink and drainer with taps, though he doubted they worked, was spotless as were the counters, but a collection of potted plants on the windowsill was interlaced with cobwebs. There was an electric cooker, like the one he'd once had at home – home! – but the dust and cobwebs there, too, told him it wasn't in use.

A space had been cleared at one end of the table and in the middle was a worn china plate bearing a pile of rough cuts of meat, served with a large bowl of leaves that could have been spinach. She emerged from a side room with two age-opaque glasses and a bottle of some unidentifiable brew, sat down and poured. Tutting, she gestured impatiently for him to sit, too. Then she handed him a glass before roughly loading two plates and passing one to him along with a knife and fork. She sat opposite him, still for once. He realised how attractive she was, in a rough-hewn kind of way. Probably in her early twenties though she seemed ageless, somehow hinting at a life too full of tribulation for one who must be little more than half his age.

The squirrel was tender and he'd already decided before he knew what it was that he liked the taste. He savoured it along with the greens she'd conjured from somewhere – he didn't yet know whether she cultivated a garden or foraged the forest undergrowth.

Probably both. Despite the simplicity and lack of presentation, she was a surprisingly good cook and he wondered where she'd learned. He'd half-expected her to tear apart the carcass and gnaw at the raw flesh. He felt guilty for even thinking it. Despite his uncharitable thoughts, the silence seemed companionable.

'Thank you,' he said as he savoured the drink. Some kind of wine. 'Cheers.'

Her only reply was to catch his eye as she reached for the plate of bones and gristle. As she tipped the scraps into a bowl in a corner, two cats appeared, the black-and-white one he'd met earlier and a tabby. She took the bones outside and the cawing of crows or rooks, which he realised had been a constant backdrop to his convalescence, intensified as they squabbled over the remains.

She reappeared, poured again and sat down, looking at him inquisitively.

'I'm Winter,' he said, tapping his chest, not for the first time. 'And you are...?'

She continued her silent scrutiny. Draining the last of her wine, she held out her hand for his glass, forcing him to finish it more quickly than he thought wise as he had no idea of the strength, nor what effect it would have in combination with her painkilling concoction. She took the dishes outside and he heard her pouring water. He limped to the door to watch her wash up in a pot warmed by a wood-fired stove in an open-fronted lean-to. She dried the plates and glasses with a worn but clean-looking cloth and shooed him inside ahead of her as she returned to put them away neatly in one of the cupboards.

She then led him down the corridor into a small room with a worn sofa and two faded armchairs, one of them occupied by the tabby cat. He eased himself painfully onto the sofa and she settled in the vacant chair. She picked up a half-formed shirt and began to sew, fixing a plain blue sleeve to the green-and-brown checked body. He watched her with convalescent's eyes, conscious thought ebbing and flowing like the vagaries of a poor PD signal. He shut out the

45

memories the sensation triggered, concentrating on her needle moving in-and-out like a mantra. It seemed weirdly natural to realise the shirt was his own, or at least the body and the untouched sleeve were his.

'Why?' he asked, his hand moving involuntarily to the bandage on his arm.

She kept her head bowed over her work, her shoulders tensing visibly.

'Why did you take me in?'

*Shut up*, her shoulders said.

He continued to watch, silently willing her to reply. Surely the same compassion that had led her to bring him here should mean she would at least attempt to communicate with him? He tried again.

'I—'

A cloud of dust rose as she slammed the shirt down onto the arm of the chair, jabbing the needle into it like a weapon. Without so much as a glance at him, she stood and flitted from the room. He made no attempt to follow her. He wanted to give her time, but how much time did he have? His two pursuers had been dispatched, and he had no doubt she would have dealt with the bodies. The bodies... Two of them, dead. How was he so certain? Maybe he'd asked her from his sickbed, and she'd somehow confirmed it. He felt momentarily nauseous. Yes, he'd killed before, during military service, yet he'd never become hardened to it. And this – so close, so visceral. No doubt death would have been his own fate if he hadn't. Even now, it was likely that sooner or later, their failure to return or send word would in itself raise the alarm. They had tracked him down, and so would others.

Darkness coagulated around him like the blood of memory and still there was no sign of her return. The black-and-white cat came in and jumped up to join the tabby, who batted it away. Disdaining Winter, the cat settled in the chair the young woman had vacated, as if to confirm she wouldn't be back that evening. He felt

46

frustration and anger rising in him; tried to suppress the draining emotions when he needed all his energy to heal. Weariness descended and rather than fall asleep waiting, he manoeuvred himself painfully from the sofa and, with a last glance at the abandoned sewing, went back to the room she'd made up for him.

# AT NIGHT I STILL LOOK TO THE STARS

I think I'm safe he sleeps he wakes he eats he's going to be all right I know what to do. Her herbs are good I know it's working he looks more comfortable and he gets up but he can't go far I want him to be better but I like him not going far I'm safe I can look after him and feed him and that's good but sometimes I wish he wasn't here I don't know what will happen whether he'll be a threat when he gets better. I miss Her She'd know what to do I wish She was here She'd have told me to leave him where he was or She'd have told me it was right to bring him in I wish She was here to tell me maybe that's why I helped him maybe her house needs another person maybe I do I just wish it was Her not him.

When I'm in the woods hunting food and healing plants for his badness I hear everything I know the little ones I become them to know their ways and catch them I reach out to the trees that warned me of him and they're all quiet they don't warn me I think he's safe and I'm safe and no one comes to find him those bad ones were the only ones that wanted him or others don't know where to look. They aren't here at my house and I've been working to hide the signs that the first two were here buried them far away from where I buried Her She's precious they're not. Pushed the car down the hill covered it with branches they won't find it the trees the little ones know it's there but any new people who come won't know. I hunt with animal eyes and the slow instincts of trees but now I look at how I hid the burial place the car tracks brushed away the boot marks of the pursuers I look at them with people eyes I can see what others see and they won't see me. But at night I still look to the stars through the leaves and long for the owls and ask Her to keep the men far away from the woods from him.

# PART III

# YNYS HUDOL

*Empathy – Humility – Frugality*

We first saw this motto on banners at a number of protests in the early '20s. It fitted perfectly with the principles we envisaged for our new community, so we adopted it. Thank you to the unknown person(s) who first devised it. We hope you approve.

The society we envisage can't work if hierarchies are allowed to develop. To this end we hold weekly Cyfarfodydd/Gatherings, in a public place – at first we met outside, unless the weather drove us to the schoolroom, but in recent years, as our numbers have grown, we have the beautiful roundhouse we built together.

We proposed – and the idea was developed and accepted at an early Gathering – to have the role of Arweinydd/Leader, since someone needs to facilitate our Gatherings and undertake other coordinating tasks. The roles – because two people share the job – alternate, and the co-leaders are chosen at random to prevent power and control creeping in. We refused the proposal that the first holders of the roles should automatically be us, or indeed Martha, Idris or Arwel, the island's Trustees before we came. Instead, our first Leaders were chosen by lots, a practice that continues to this day. We realise that not everyone has obvious leadership skills, but just as the practical tasks are allocated and shared on a rolling basis, so we envisage the leadership roles. If someone is adamant that they can't undertake the role for whatever reason, people won't force them, or judge them for refusing, but everyone is strongly encouraged to take their turn – who knows what hidden benefits different personalities could bring to the position of Leader? And of course, all decisions are made at the Gatherings, where every Seeder has the opportunity to speak and to vote.

*Extract from* Seeds of Change
*by Edith Turner and Bleddyn Price, 2047.*

# A REASONABLE PERIOD OF HOSPITALITY

True to his word, the old man returned to the Rock the day after he'd come to check up on her. Confirming his name as Erik Jones – he'd probably told her before but the wind and waves, if not her fever-addled memory, had obscured it from Sandy's mind – he introduced their doctor, a friendly, Asian-looking man called Khaled, and Gwylan, a striking woman who said she was one of the Seeder community's co-leaders.

'We had a Gathering yesterday after Erik came to check on you,' Gwylan said, 'and I'm pleased to say we should be able to take you back and give you the welcome you deserve. Provided Khaled thinks it's OK.'

Keeping a safe distance but with a reassuring smile, Khaled asked her a series of questions in accented English about how she'd been feeling and how she was now. She answered with an accuracy that seemed to surprise them, even throwing in some figures from the temperature readings she'd taken last night and this morning, deliberately implying she was blessed with powers of memory she didn't possess, while keeping her notebook concealed. She was still getting used to actual writing on actual non-password-protected paper, and she hoped the secret compartment in her bag would be sufficient until she found a more secure hiding place.

'You see? I came back as soon as I could,' Erik said as he reached for her bag then offered her a supporting arm to help her down into the boat. She found his northern accent, albeit from the 'wrong' side of the Pennines, strangely comforting, an antidote to her convalescent's weakness. 'I hope you understand—'

'Of course I do,' Sandy said as she steadied herself in the rocking boat and took the seat Gwylan indicated in the little cabin. She'd managed to convince herself not to blame the islanders for their quarantine practices. After all, she'd been given food, shelter and even medication to supplement the meagre supplies she hoped they wouldn't find when they inevitably searched her bag. 'I'm sorry if I was a bit harsh yesterday.'

'Not to worry. I'd have reacted similarly, I'm sure,' Erik said. Sandy noticed Gwylan frown slightly, as if he were questioning the community's quarantine practices. 'Any road, let's get back.'

He unhitched the boat and as they crossed the narrow strait he told her he'd arranged for her to stay with his family – his daughter, Helyg, her partner and their two young daughters – at least until he got her boat repaired. Longer if she wanted to stay on. He sounded hesitant, as if merely satisfying a responsibility he'd accidentally taken upon himself by rescuing her. Wondering if the welcome would be as warm as Gwylan had implied, she held her backpack close.

A few days later, Sandy was enjoying her view of the sea from the room she'd been given in the Jones house. The girls' voices drifted in through the open window. Although she couldn't understand their words – like most people on the island, they spoke Welsh, though everyone courteously turned to English for Sandy and the few Seeders who weren't fluent in the language – she recognised with painful nostalgia the tones of sisterly bickering. She tried not to think of Liv; she'd been troubled by her sister's ghost far too often while alone and delirious on the miserable Rock. She had been on the island proper for what – two days? Three? – and was beginning to enjoy the ups and downs of family life, although she felt in the way most of the time, especially since she'd realised the girls were now having to share a room because of her. Her time in isolation seemed like a distant fever dream with a different perspective as she'd gazed across the bay to the small harbour, which seemed rarely used except for when Erik, whom she mostly heard referred to as Taid, which she'd learned meant Grandpa, had come to fetch her.

As yet they hadn't been in a hurry to search the bag – naïveté?

Fear of contamination? Or maybe it was simply to make amends for her harsh treatment with exaggerated hospitality.

She went downstairs to the sound of the girls' arguing becoming more heated. Helyg looked across from where she was peeling potatoes in the kitchen and rolled her eyes. 'They're rattier than usual.'

Sandy smiled. Aware of the probable reason for their squabbling, she thought wistfully of the room she'd shared with Liv all those years ago. Maybe time and her sister's fate had coloured her memories, but she couldn't imagine growing up without the closeness of that shared space.

Haf appeared at the door. The sulky outrage of her voice needed no translation.

'Excuse me.' Helyg vanished.

When she returned, she gave a world-weary sigh.

'It's never-ending. You've seen how Glesni's in and out of Dad's workshop; she loves learning the practical stuff, you know? But Haf's forever accusing her of shirking her chores so she can finish early to go and help her taid.'

Like several of the houses, theirs had a walled courtyard with high walls to protect the garden within from winds and storms, and a range of outbuildings. Erik had a workshop and cottage converted from one of these, to which he made himself scarce most of the time. Sandy couldn't help feeling he was avoiding her, as if embarrassed by his own compassion. He joined the family for the shared evening meal, and what he did say to her was kind, friendly even, but it wasn't much. As soon as they'd finished, he'd vanish again, walking down to the rocky shore or along the path that wound up the hill through garish yellow gorse. The chill wind and spring showers never seemed to deter him.

The girls spent their mornings in a classroom in the old school building, a routine that Sandy found surprisingly civilised. As was their teacher, Tom, Helyg's partner, a stocky, dark-haired man who'd welcomed her with a ready smile when she arrived on the island. She'd naturally assumed he was the girls' father until she discovered his surname, Pritchard, and overheard Glesni calling him Tom. Helyg told her he was their stepfather and had only been living with them for a couple of years. The girls' father, Gareth, had been drowned at sea when they were little.

There had been a succession of people to the house, asking her how she was liking it here. Most of them brought gifts: a bunch of wildflowers, food or surprisingly attractive homespun clothing. Like the sage-green shirt she was wearing now, most of the garments fit perfectly; she considered herself of average height and build, but even so they had a good eye, and it was a relief from having to share Helyg's spare clothes. Despite the weight Sandy had lost during her trek across Wales, and her illness, those were tight on her, and short. Her hostess had inherited her father's skinny build, but was as small as he was tall.

A visit was another excuse for Helyg, Tom or the girls to produce a variety of herbal infusions, the staple of which seemed to be nettle. They all insisted she drank it by the mugful because of its amazing health-giving properties, boosts to the immune system, blah blah. Even with the novel blends of fruits and flowers, she'd have traded it all for a good, strong mug of builders' tea.

The girls' voices, joined by friends and more amicable by now, were interrupted by Erik – the welcome familiarity of English like a ray of sunshine cutting through the mysterious mists of Welsh – calling Glesni over to the workshop, to muttered protestations from her sister. Sandy wondered, not for the first time, whether he was the best person to ask if there was anywhere she could charge up her PD. She'd kept its presence to herself, fairly sure they'd confiscate it if they knew of its existence. It was unlikely they'd be able to hack into it, and she had no idea how much the contents would mean to them, out-of-date as it would all be by now, but she was unwilling to risk losing it. The very thought of it revived an itchy urge to scroll, tap and feel connected.

Helyg went out so, glancing out of the window to make sure no one was around, Sandy went back upstairs and removed the loose floorboard she'd discovered under her bed. An obvious place, but what choice did she have? She kept her bag in the cupboard with the rest of her things – to have hidden it would no doubt have aroused suspicion – but one or two items from it were best kept to herself, at least for now.

She retrieved the PD, replaced the floorboard and gazed at the dormant device. Dormant – or dead? Terminal, she thought and a smile caught her unawares. Though feeble, the joke felt too unfamiliar; how long was it since she'd enjoyed simple, easy conversation? Helyg managed to keep her distance while remaining polite. Glesni was lovely but so earnest – and young. Haf remained disdainfully aloof, as if to distance herself from her little sister by emulating her mother's reserve. Sandy had been harbouring a tiny hope that a couple of weeks' rest might have revived a remnant of charge, though she had no idea about signal, but the PD glared blankly back. It was weeks since she'd connected with friends or former colleagues, weeks since she'd signed on for her housing benefit. They'd be suspecting her of absconding by now and she wondered if she'd have a home to return to. She'd make what excuses she needed when she returned, hopefully with Adam, a trophy that would exonerate her. Who knew, it might even mean she could beg her job back.

In the meantime, didn't a girl deserve a few days' convalescence? These Seeders seemed OK on the whole. She wondered what Liv would have had to say on the matter. Her sister would probably have been fascinated, telling Sandy how lucky she was, that she should stay here for as long as she could and forget all thoughts of finding Adam. She still missed Liv's calm and common sense, however much she'd disagreed with her political views when she had the luxury of doing so.

She turned the PD face down as if to shut off a flow of infiltrating confusion. Maybe the things never died, however powerless they seemed. Perhaps she was being observed even now.

She heard footsteps on the stairs and Glesni appeared in the doorway. The girl hovered nervously. 'Sorry, wrong room. I... forget I've moved sometimes. I just came in to fetch my UV protection hat. It's sweltering out there, but we've got to get back to work. I said we should go to the woods and catch up on some coppicing.' She mimed fanning herself. 'Shade, you know?'

Sandy held back the comment that even mainlanders knew the concept of trees providing shade. She checked the instinct to reach out and hide the PD, lying beside her on the quilt: to move would be to draw attention to it.

'But no, the plan was for the garden this afternoon,' Glesni continued, 'so the garden it is. Gwylan's so... inflexible, you know?'

She glanced at Sandy as if she'd been disloyal. Sandy smiled: her guilty secret was safe.

'And to add insult to injury, I was supposed to be helping Taid this afternoon, but Madog's just dragged him off...' She trailed off as her eyes fell on the PD. Damn, talk about guilty secrets. 'Wow. Is that a mobile?'

Sandy found the old-fashioned term endearing from one so young. 'It's a PD,' she said.

Glesni looked from her to the device.

'Personal device. A phone's one of its functions, but—'

'I know,' the girl said as if she used one every day.

Sandy hadn't seen one all the time she'd been here, but then, she hadn't yet left the house.

Glesni sank down on the bedside chair. 'No one's going to miss me for a few moments. Can I have a look?'

Sandy's hand moved protectively to cover it, relieved that her bag wasn't also on display. 'No point. It's not charged up.'

"Course not.'

'In any case, there hasn't been a signal since halfway across Wales and I doubt it's any different here.'

'It isn't. Idris has a radio up in the watchtower if you—'

'It's OK; there's no one I need to get in touch with.'

'Good. The radio's only there for essential news. Not that there's much would affect *us*, but it pays to know what's happening out there.' She gazed out of the window as if keeping a lookout for a fleet of violent hordes heading across the sea towards them. She returned her attention to the device, still under Sandy's hand on the quilt. 'Can I have a look anyway?'

Why hadn't she put it away in time? Sandy hesitated, but there was no denying it was dead, so it was probably best to let the girl satisfy her curiosity.

Glesni turned it over in her hands, taking in the retro floral cover, before staring at the screen as if she could penetrate the depths of data behind it.

'How d'you switch it on?'

'It's dead.'

'I know. Just asking.'

Sandy frowned at the implied invasion of privacy. 'Only I could do it anyway,' she said. 'It's the *personal* in PD – it's got a full array of biometrics.'

Glesni ran her finger over it, staring as if she expected it to burst into life.

'I don't know what you think you're going to see,' Sandy said irritably. 'It won't be that different from a smartphone. You... you have seen one?'

Glesni smiled. 'Sort of. Like yours, there's none of them working any more. The last ones came when the Husseins arrived. I wasn't involved but I heard them having a bit of a row when Khaled tried to use his.'

'A row? With the people your mam calls the purists?'

'Nah. It was more a case of the signal getting intercepted, you know? People on the mainland must know we exist, and we do have the Defenders, whatever good that might do, but the less attention we draw to ourselves the better.'

Interesting. True, Sandy hadn't heard of Aniseed before ending up here, but she didn't know every inch of the coast, all the ins and outs of every illicit off-grid community of Resettlement refuseniks. It had never occurred to her that her ignorance might be the result of a deliberate policy.

'Of course, there was an element of "the Devil's instrument".' Glesni pulled a face. 'Though I can't see what difference a couple of phones with no charge and no signal would make to the innocence of my generation... Besides, Tom's been through it all with us.'

She paused, apparently enjoying Sandy's questioning look. 'You know, part of our modern history lessons.'

She stood and began to walk around the room, staring at the PD screen, running her finger over it. She paused, glanced at Sandy. 'Sorry. I probably look ridiculous.' She looked like an average teenager. 'Doing it all wrong.'

Apart from the fact that she probably had no idea what the screen would show if it could, or what the gestures meant, to a casual observer she could have grown up with one.

'Tom said that people living their lives through these caused all kinds of mental health issues. Loss of real community and support systems, you know? So people didn't pull together when they needed to. Didn't believe the climate and nature crisis was real. Supported conflicts that were wrong to any objective observer. Preferred to believe the fake news they got on antisocial media. Or sat there immersed in Screwflix while the real world and its problems passed them by. Distanced from nature, real life, like... like... You'll probably think I'm utterly stupid here, taken in by some purist nonsense, but they say there were some people who didn't even know where their food came from, beyond the "supermarket" shelves.'

'I'm sorry to say you're right about that one. Though most people have had a rude awakening one way or another.' The implied question in the way Glesni said *supermarket* made Sandy think of the Seeders' store – a combination of shop and warehouse – and their complex system of tokens and bartering for goods and work.

It seemed to function, though so far she found it unfathomable. Another thing to get her head round if she was going to stay beyond a reasonable period of hospitality and convalescence. Where had that notion popped up from? The daunting immensity of the search for Adam meant she wasn't about to dismiss it out of hand.

Glesni put the PD back down on the bed with exaggerated caution – maybe as if to prove that she didn't think it was the Devil's Instrument to be cast violently from her. 'It all sounded pretty far-fetched to me,' she said. 'As if people wouldn't... But even Taid said it was a fair picture, if a bit exaggerated perhaps. And he's more inclined than most to see the benefits of technology, if it's used wisely.'

Sandy wondered if he was considered a bad influence on his granddaughter. She still hadn't worked out the undercurrents and wondered if his views were at least partly responsible for his apartness.

'So,' Glesni said, 'now I've got a real mainlander to talk to, tell me where Tom got it wrong. Tell me the good side.'

Sandy began to talk about information sharing and contact – the need for both highlighted by the waves of pandemics – all the time eyeing Glesni for her reaction.

'I'm not denying that what you've been taught has some truth in it – the downside of people's greed, and the drive for ever more development, regardless of its actual value...' The girl was definitely having some kind of effect on her; Sandy couldn't believe her own words. 'But technology such as this,' she brandished the PD before finally tucking it out of sight in a pocket, 'has helped us to live with the consequences. I certainly noticed its absence on my travels in Cymru, when I couldn't get a signal. Boy, did I feel lost!'

'Because of the *Digartrefu* – sorry, the Clearances?'

'I guess so.'

'So it's as bad as they say?'

'I didn't see many people around.' Sandy was beginning to feel uncomfortable.

61

'How could they force people to leave like that?'

'Most went of their own accord.'

'So they weren't edged out by deliberate power cuts, more or less non-existent health services and food shortages?'

Sandy wished she'd never started this by mentioning her journey. 'Well... it was the same for people in the towns and cities too, just... house prices had been spiralling out of control, and second homes in rural areas took the heart out of communities, so when tourism took a dive because of the pandemics and the cost of living, a lot of people left for the new towns. And it was easier to help hard-pressed resources and services to go round if people lived in centres of population, so those who stayed were... um... encouraged to leave. Given the offer of quality homes at discounted prices in new towns where they'd be better provided for.'

'Leaving behind all that meant anything to them.'

Glesni was relentless. It wasn't hard to imagine the way this was taught in the little school, or the conversations among the Seeders.

'Have you always lived in Manchester?'

'I grew up there. Adam and I lived in Hulme. But believe me, our poky little flat was nothing special. We often wished *we'd* be offered a cushy new apartment in a new town.'

'So you don't think that home, family, community and tradition mean anything?'

'Look, the policy wasn't ideal, and it was very unpopular. To the extent that it's no longer being actively pursued.'

Glesni looked triumphant, like a politician about to deal the deciding argument. 'So people can go back to their homes now?'

Sandy shrugged. 'I said "actively". I don't think the services are any better, to be honest. Not from what I saw on my travels. So...'

'It's awful!'

Sandy nodded. 'There were probably better ways, but... I'm sure things will get better over time.'

'Sorry. I suppose it's not your fault.'

Sandy was relieved at the sound of footsteps entering the house.

'Glesni!' They heard Haf storm in.

Glesni glanced at Sandy. 'Better go.'

She was met at the bedroom door by her sister.

'Your hat,' Sandy said, interrupting a flow of angry-sounding Welsh.

Haf glared daggers at her as if this were some insidious mainlander code. Sandy was glad her PD was out of sight this time.

'Glesni came to fetch her sun hat,' she said calmly. 'You can tell Gwylan it's my fault for keeping her talking.'

As the girls stomped down the stairs, she hoped that Glesni wouldn't tell anyone about their conversation. Maybe it wouldn't be such a bad thing if she did. She didn't feel quite right keeping secrets from her hosts, and from what she'd learned, she felt sure they wouldn't steal it if she promised not to use it. As she stowed the device back under the floorboards, she was surprised to find that she had no desire to use it.

# IF THINGS WERE USED WISELY

As Glesni followed Taid towards the shore, she revelled in one of those rare spring days that behaved as the adults were always saying a spring day should. The sun was warm but gentle and a light breeze delivered comforting scents of growth and fruitfulness. There was not a hint of excess sun, wind or rain, and the green of young crops in the fields sought to erase all memory of failure and shortage. She tried to concentrate on the uneven track beneath her feet to keep her focus away from the lower fields. She was supposed to be with the other kids and Tom, learning about plants, soil and weather, which was another way of saying helping in the fields, but with Taid's help she'd persuaded Mam and Tom that it would be a good thing if she learned more about how the boats worked.

Most islanders knew the basics about all aspects of island life, but since he came to Ynys Hudol eleven years ago, Taid had become the undisputed expert with boats, machines and electricity. He often worried that the young ones had all their learning time divided between food cultivation and history so they didn't repeat humanity's mistakes. A bit of an exaggeration, but she got his point.

Steffan, Marc and the other purists thought the mechanical things no longer mattered because they were part of the old life and once they wore out beyond repair, the community could live without them. Most of the Seeders, Glesni's family included, considered those views extremist and short-sighted and insisted that hands-on technical skills were just as important. If things were used wisely, they could be just as much a part of that not-making-mistakes learning – as well as helping to make everyone's lives worth living, in the same way that music and books and play made their lives worth living. Glesni was sure that even the purists would miss light in the evenings, and additional entertainment like amplified or recorded music and DVD showings in the roundhouse.

She'd been looking forward to helping Taid and Gwylan, hoping that a new boat would persuade some of the doubters to accept Sandy in a bit more of a welcoming spirit. The boat was propped upright and they'd established a simple scaffold around it. Gwylan had set up the ladder against this, and Glesni's first job was to pass tools and paintbrushes up to her, while Taid looked through the collection of old paint pots in the store shed to see what they had that matched the boat's original colours. As if summoned by the tapping of her feet on the ladder, Steffan, the purest of the purists, appeared.

'What are you doing here, lass? There'll be time enough to mess with boats when the fields are planted and it's certain there'll be enough to eat.' He turned his attention from Glesni to Gwylan. 'I'd have thought you'd have known better. 'Specially in your leadership years.'

He placed his hand on the ladder and Glesni smiled inwardly – even if she'd had the slightest intention of scurrying off to the fields, the stupid man himself was in her way.

'Excuse me.' Taid elbowed past him and handed two large paint pots up, one by one. Gwylan beckoned her over and started discussing the preparation work they needed to do before the painting itself. Glesni couldn't help being distracted by Steffan's protests and Taid's calm replies.

'I'm surprised at you, Erik. What sort of a message does it give the child, allowing her to shirk her duties for the frivolity of painting a stranger's boat?'

'Come on, mate. Sparing Glesni from the fields for a day or two isn't going to lead to starvation. Any road, I'd have thought you'd approve of good maintenance to prolong the life of a perfectly sound if rather neglected boat.'

'But—'

'A boat that we'll be able to use as long as Sandy stays here.'

Glesni was tempted to remind Taid that the purists refused to accept fishing, were suspicious of the kelp farming and frowned on mainland trips.

Steffan's wittering made Glesni even prouder of her desire to learn about the boats and machinery. Not least because, despite the childhood belief she sometimes still clung to, she knew in her heart that Taid wouldn't be there forever and she wanted his knowledge to live on in her. She often wished she'd been born earlier and could have taken Madog's place as his assistant.

Sandy's boat, *Otranto*, was in reasonable shape beneath the shabby exterior, with functioning solar panels and a sizeable battery bank, and after Taid's expert attention the motor was working fine; they'd confirm that with a test run later. It looked patchy because they'd begun to prepare it for painting, but Gwylan assured her it was sound. Once he'd dispatched Steffan, Taid spent some time showing Glesni how it all functioned. Then they had to finish rubbing it down ready for painting. Another anti-*Otranto* argument, that: the community's paint wouldn't last forever and should be kept for *Berta*, the existing boat. Why did they need two?

In fact, until the most recent storm they'd had three boats. The winds were stronger and the waves higher than any they'd recorded, which meant that two were torn from their moorings, one carried away and one dashed to pieces. At least they still had *Berta*, named after murdered Honduran activist, Berta Cáceres, whose name was in turn honoured in the boat that formed the centrepiece of the big climate rebellion in 2019 – though the Seeders' resources certainly didn't extend to bright pink paint like that one.

Whatever the objections, it had been agreed at the last Gathering that another boat would be useful, at least for as long as Sandy stayed, and they could get paint on the next foraging trip – which, of course, the purists didn't approve of.

However great her curiosity about the mainland, Glesni hadn't asked for a while about another foraging trip, and whether she could go. It was guaranteed to start disputes – apart from the risks, obtaining things from the mainland was considered a failure by the purists, who argued that the community should simply do without them. She'd decided not to raise it until she'd safely established she was regularly allowed to work on mechanical stuff with Taid. Choose your battles, he always told her.

The rubbing-down was getting tedious. Glesni was dying to start applying the paint, but they'd insisted that this was the most important part of the job, preparing the boat's surface so the precious paint would have maximum effect while not using up too much. The three of them were working away, each sunk in their own thoughts, when she sensed someone was watching. Now she was recovered, Sandy had a way of appearing unexpectedly.

'Wow,' she said. 'Looking good. Who'd have thought it?'

Gwylan paused and looked down. 'It's in remarkably good shape now we've got the motor fixed.'

'I never expected... I don't know what I can do to repay you.'

Glesni tried to listen without slowing her sanding.

'You'll get your chance,' Gwylan said. 'I assume you're not intending to leave immediately.'

'No, I...'

She seemed lost for words. It made Glesni realise how little Sandy had told her. She seemed to have a way of steering the conversation towards the Seeder community and island life while sharing very little about herself.

'As long as you're here, the boat will be useful to us,' Gwylan said. 'That's payment in itself. Do you want to see what we've done?'

With a hesitancy that suggested she'd rather not, Sandy climbed the ladder and half tumbled into the boat. Gwylan took her into the little cabin and showed her all the things she and Taid had just shown Glesni, then came out on deck and talked some more. She winked at Taid once, as it was obvious how little Sandy knew about practicalities, and Glesni almost felt sorry for their guest. The small guided tour over, Gwylan said she was meeting Cai at the roundhouse that afternoon for their regular co-leaders' discussion and offered to walk back with Sandy.

'You two will be all right here, won't you?' she said.

As they watched the two women leave, Taid grinned. 'I said from the start of her time that Gwylan would be good leadership material.'

Glesni nodded. 'I'm sure she'll get more out of Sandy by the time they get back to the village than the rest of us have in all the days that she's been living with us.'

Taid shook his head and brandished his sandpaper. 'I was thinking more of her delegation skills.'

He was a hard taskmaster, and they finished the preparation in time to put a grey undercoat on the hull. After they'd finished cleaning the brushes, they sat on the grass by the jetty, watching the sunset, the waves splashing on the rocks by the harbour wall below them. Glesni imagined them out at sea, just the two of them. After savouring the moment for a while, she took her opportunity. Producing her notebook, which she'd been carrying in her pocket in the hope of just such a chance, she showed him the drawing she'd made from what she could remember of the logo on Sandy's PD. It showed some kind of intricate crest.

'Do you know what this is?'

He stared at it. At first she thought he was trying to decipher the sketchiness of her drawing, but soon realised his frown wasn't one of concentration. She was about to say it didn't matter, when he turned to her.

'Where did you get that from?'

'It was on Sandy's PD.' She felt her face reddening. So much for keeping her secret. 'She... I walked in when she was looking at it the other day. It's totally dead; she can't—'

'Does anyone else know about it? Gwylan? Cai?'

She shook her head.

'Don't fret, Pwt.' He smiled suddenly, shaking off his earlier gloom. 'None of my business.'

'So?' She looked at the piece of paper.

'Looks like something official,' he said. He sounded just a bit too casual. 'Did she say anything to you?'

Glesni shook her head. 'It was hidden by a cover. Semi-transparent. I wasn't supposed to be looking that closely. What do you think?'

He shrugged, then turned sharply towards the harbour. 'What was that? Did you see something move over there?'

Glesni looked and saw a cormorant fly off. Nothing unusual about that. He was obviously avoiding her question and she knew she'd get nothing more from him.

# COMPASSIONATE SILENCE

That evening, annoyed at how exhausted she was after her exertion – exertion! Walking to the harbour and climbing a ladder to look at a bloody boat! – Sandy was grateful for a hot bath, even if it was a metal tub in a side kitchen. Helyg warned her that this was only during her convalescence; she'd already shown her the bathing pool below the spring – healthier for her, so she claimed, and less wasteful of precious water. She might have been joking, but Sandy hadn't liked to ask and was still unsure. In any case, she'd been relieved to discover that drinking water was collected upstream of the pool, though downstream it was carefully channelled for irrigation and cleaning. There was only one sizeable spring on the island, which sometimes dried up, and they had a series of cisterns to collect and store as much rainwater as possible, since droughts were unpredictable and their length ever-increasing.

The tin bath, which had seemed primitive to begin with, was already beginning to feel like a luxury. She was also grudgingly impressed by their electricity supply, better than the situation she'd seen in most places after she crossed the border into Cymru. Her hosts had been proud to tell her about the tidal turbines – without which she wouldn't have been seen and rescued – and the wind turbine she'd seen from the Rock, cleverly sited on the lower slopes where it caught the wind but the peak of the central hill prevented it from standing out against the skyline. There were numerous roof-mounted solar panels, too – everything presumably brought over from the mainland. Despite the central collection of batteries, electricity was rationed. She didn't need telling that this was to conserve these artificial resources, since they were not in a position to manufacture new equipment and there was a limit to even the best engineer's ability to patch and repair. But Glesni had also told her, with that serious air of youthful wisdom that impressed and irritated her in equal measure, that it was partly a matter of principle. They were eager to remind themselves, and teach the children, that nothing should be taken for granted; things didn't just happen at the flick of a switch.

Depending on the weather and the seasons, the girls usually spent the afternoons outdoors at various tasks, which was closer to Sandy's preconceptions of a community like the Seeders than their regular morning schooling. One evening, Glesni had assured her that this was an equally valuable part of their education. She also said that several people saw Sandy's arrival as an omen. Her expression indicated she didn't share their belief.

'In what way?' she asked.

'You know we'd just had a vote on whether or not to continue maintaining the quarantine bothy on the Rock?' Glesni shrugged expansively. 'You came; you were ill. As if our debate had summoned you.' She laughed.

'And what did it prove — that compassion or safety was more important?'

The girl smiled. 'I'm sure it's the same where you come from. Each side twists it to prove their argument. I'd still vote the same way, though — I'm sure we could have isolated you safely while giving you proper care.'

Sandy was surprised, not by the outcome of the vote, but by the fact that Glesni had been party to it. The girl had told her she was thirteen.

'What?' Glesni frowned and Sandy realised her surprise must have shown. 'You mean you agree that the way you were treated—'

'Not that. You... voted?' Sandy smiled to soften her incredulity.

'Why wouldn't I?'

'So children take part generally?'

'Define child.' She waved a hand as if to question the maturity of some of the older members of the community. 'We have our opinions like anyone else. If we're interested, and if whatever-it-is has been covered in school and Tom or the others are satisfied we understand, we can vote.' She gave one of her ready smiles. 'There are far more adults than kids so we're hardly going to take over.'

'But... don't important decisions require a bit of life experience?' She cut herself off from saying more. Adults or children, the Seeders' lives could hardly be called typical experience.

'You must remember the school climate strike movement,' Glesni said. 'We learned about it recently. Fridays for Future. Wish I'd been there.'

Sandy remembered wishing she could have gone with her big sister, though unlike Liv, her motive would have been more about bunking off school than principle.

'Weren't they proved right?' Glesni waved a hand as if to indicate the whole range of unreliable, extreme weather. '*They* were kids. They could see instinctively what the adults were blinded to. Anyway, you don't have to take my word for the rights and wrongs. You can ask Gwylan and Cai when they come to see you.'

'Your mum said the other day they'd be calling round.'

Sandy was relieved to hear that the leadership system at least was for adults.


The following morning, she was feeling better as she waited for the promised visit from the community's leaders. Ambushed by a twinge of guilt at sitting in the sunny living room, looking out at a group working in one of the patchwork fields that undulated down to the sea, she reminded herself how knackered she'd felt after her outing to look at the boat. Helyg was working at the raised beds in the sheltered courtyard garden, having told her to call if she needed anything. A copy of *Seeds of Change* lay in her lap. She'd hardly begun to look at it on the Quarantine Rock before she became too ill to read. Now, she was busy catching up.

She had learned how a succession of government policies, followed by the ultimate blow of what they insisted on calling the civil war, had forced the trust that ran the island as a nature reserve to sell up in 2036. They hoped that by doing so before it was inevitably dissolved, they could have some control over who took over, rather than leaving it to less scrupulous hands. The book was a record of the new owners' early experiences and intentions for the community and so far she was enjoying learning about the naïve but strangely appealing rationale behind it.

Glancing out at Helyg, she was keen to find out more about how they managed for food in this tough environment.

It was decided at an early Gathering that a largely plant-based diet would be the choice of the community, many of whom were already vegetarian or vegan. It also enabled us to maximise the amount of food we could obtain from our cultivated land. Those of us from the Roots and Branches community on the mainland, and several others, brought farming and gardening skills which, together with the limited foraging opportunities on Ynys Hudol, meant that from the start we made a good show of being self-sufficient in food.

We did continue the policy of limited managed grazing – a few goats we use for milk and spinning the hair, and a small herd of roaming native ponies we use for transport and which some people love to ride.

There were a few heated arguments from some, who argued that it was wrong to keep livestock at all. Although we use the animals' milk to a limited extent and keep hens for eggs, the main purpose is to encourage a variety of habitats and ecosystems. This wasn't good enough for the purists, who maintained that managed biodiversity was human arrogance worthy of mainlanders, and we should let nature take its course. They still continue to raise this at intervals, along with the issue of fishing, which we do to a limited degree, particularly when crops fail, and the beehives we nurture for honey and beeswax. But they continue to be voted down at Gatherings, in the belief that we need to be pragmatic to survive, increasingly so as the climate deteriorates.

Despite the vagaries of storms and droughts, we've established a wide range of vegetables, cereals and fruit trees and bushes. We have also successfully established a kelp farm, originally harvested to fertilise the fields, but which we are learning how to process for food.

Core elements of family meals, and the weekly communal meal, are prepared centrally to conserve resources and share the work. The weekly communal meal, held on a different day from the Gathering, is a cornerstone of our community. Seeders are encouraged to attend, though they can always opt out and have the weekly shared meal delivered to their home, if there is good reason for it.

A brewery was established at an early stage (notably not a target for the purists' disdain) and an enterprising group recently came back from a mainland trip with distillery equipment. The results are eagerly anticipated.

Sandy was smiling at this when Helyg popped her head round the door to announce Cai's arrival. He was on his own, saying Gwylan would be along later. Helyg showed him in and left to make tea. Sandy would have stood to greet him but he gestured for her to stay seated. It might not have been his intention, but it emphasised the humbling weakness of her convalescence. She recognised him from the day of her arrival on the island. He had an easy smile but with his average build and light-brown hair and beard, she probably wouldn't have remembered him except for a certain resemblance to Adam.

He sat down and indicated the book with a smile. He told her he'd been given it to read, too, when he arrived.

'Is it some kind of bible?' she asked.

He laughed – slightly unfairly, she thought. 'Nothing of the kind! Though it's useful to keep reminding ourselves of our founding principles, especially since the community's constantly evolving, both with time and with the different people who come and settle here.'

'It says here you don't get many new arrivals any more.'

'Not now. During the first few years, the Seeders grew from a handful to something over fifty, many but not all arriving during the civil war.'

She deemed it wise not to comment; of course a Welsh community would use the term 'civil war' to refer to the rioting and violent unrest following their failed bid for independence.

74

'The last major change was when Bleddyn died a couple of years ago.'

'I'm sorry to hear it. How?'

'Heart attack.'

'That must be scary in a place like this. So far away—'

'Don't you believe it. When I was last on the mainland it was a lottery if you'd get an ambulance. Though I admit that *if* you did, with intensive care, specialised doctors, all the things we don't have here, he might still be alive.'

'I'm sorry—'

'But then, he could have been killed by a speeding car, or poisoned by pollution. Also things we don't have here... Who knows, maybe he lived longer than he would have on the mainland. But we're not big on what-ifs here.'

She wondered if he was simply proving a point about their lives, or trying to justify their treatment of her, abandoning her in the hut on the Rock. 'Have you been here long?' she asked when the pause became uncomfortable.

'Madog, my son, and I arrived in 2042.'

'2042.'

They regarded one another across a wary silence.

'I don't know what you're thinking, but it wasn't a direct result of the *Digartrefu*.'

She recognised the Welsh word they used for the Clearances – even that was frowned upon by most people she knew.

'So why did you come?' she asked.

'I'd grown bone-weary of my life, my job. I heard of this place at a time when I was sick of the way the world was going and my part in it.'

'Which was?'

As if on cue, Helyg came in with two mugs, which she set down before them.

'Gwylan sent a message. She's been held up.' She glanced at Cai. 'You know, the same-old-same-old about the irrigation channel down in the lower fields. She says carry on without her; you had a good chat with her yesterday down at the boat, didn't you, Sandy?'

Cai nodded and picked up his mug as Helyg left.

'So, what brings you to these parts?'

She was sure he'd deliberately left her own question hanging. She let it go, but pared her story right down. 'I'm looking for someone.'

'On Ynys Hudol?'

It was her turn to laugh. 'Honest to God, I'd never heard of Aniseed or the Seeders before I ended up stranded here—'

She was about to launch into an account of her rescue, which he and everyone else would doubtless already have heard, when he cut her off. 'Where, then?'

'Ireland.' She hoped he wouldn't ask for more detail – she didn't have any, and didn't want to sound evasive. His next question was no easier to answer.

'Where had you launched from?'

'I don't know.' She held his gaze. 'Seriously. I'd got as far as a place that turned out to be a couple of miles inland. A village? Small town? Called Lan-something-unpronounceable.'

'That narrows it down.'

'I'm sorry. No disrespect.' His expression said otherwise. 'I just... I'd been lost for ages, my PD had given up the ghost, paper map destroyed in the rain and well out-of-date in any case, and... I'd seen the village name signs, but you know how it is...' He was shaking his head. 'It just didn't sink in. My bad. Anyway, there was a roadblock just outside the place that looked like trouble and, in a nutshell, I legged it. I made it to a run-down harbour town,' (she thought it best not to attempt a pronunciation) 'and came across a couple of people, in what was left of a marina, sorting their boat out. The only living souls I'd seen for ages and the only boat that looked remotely functional. I made them an offer and the *Otranto* was mine. They showed me the basics of how to work it and I couldn't leave the damn place fast enough. I know nothing about the price of boats

76

but thought it seemed ridiculously cheap. It gave out on me after less than an hour, so I guess I got what I deserved.'

'And how much did you give them?'

He tried to sound concerned that these people had conned her, though it was more likely he was sussing out whether she was the sort who'd steal a boat.

'Couple of grand.'

'You were carrying that kind of cash?'

'Reckless I know, but with everything I'd heard about the blackouts and all... I didn't know if my chip would get me very far once I was into Wales.'

'Sounds reasonable.' But, his tone said the opposite; he must be wondering how she came to get her hands on such a large amount of cash. Or maybe he'd guessed she wanted to travel incognito and was wondering why. Wonder on, friend, she thought.

'You're lucky you didn't get robbed.'

She nodded, though it wasn't only a matter of luck.

'Look, I didn't come to give you the third degree.'

She gave him a half smile. 'Doesn't sound like it.'

'Sorry. But who did you say you were looking for?'

'My partner. Adam.'

'What brings you – him – here from...?'

'Manchester. He... he was a security guard.' That wasn't *too* far from the truth. She continued in a similar vein. 'Paid well; we needed the money. Anyway, there was some trouble with a client, and he vanished. Left me a message. He was heading to a friend's in Wales, and from there they were going on to Ireland. The house at the address I had seems to have fallen prey to the Resettlement so I was on my way over the Irish Sea. In that wreck of a boat – I'd have no chance of getting a visa to go through the normal channels, would I?'

He nodded, then picked up his mug and stared into it as if pained at having to ask. 'What was the trouble... with his client?'

She laughed. 'Don't think I've been here long enough for that kind of trust, do you?'

He put his tea down, looked at her and smiled. It seemed genuine, or maybe it was that occasional hint of Adam in his expression. 'Fair enough. But trust works both ways. Sooner or later people might want to... But... well, in general, our policy – has anyone told you about the Compassionate Silence?' She shook her head. 'In a nutshell, people only need share as much personal information as they want to. We believe everyone should be given a chance, but we need to make sure it's not putting us at risk. So... see how you feel. We might even be able to help you. You can talk to me, or Gwylan. Or one of the Joneses if you like, if you'd feel more comfortable.' He drained his drink. 'Are they looking after you all right?'

'They're really kind,' she said with a smile.

'Glad to hear it. And if anyone makes you feel unwelcome, just ignore them. I hope you'll understand, but the spring's been relentlessly wet and we've lost some of the early crops.' He sighed. 'Then the next few weeks look set to be hot and dry so we'll no doubt have to ration the water again. That's happening all too often now. So you can see that to some less hospitable souls, you're another mouth to feed.'

'I hope I'll be another pair of hands when I get my strength back,' she said, pleased to see from his face that it was an appropriate response.

'Some of us arrived here by chance, some knew about the Seeders and made their way here to join the community,' he said. 'Whichever, we know we're lucky and are willing to share – or should be.'

After he left, she thought about what he'd said. Whatever the spin around compassion and respect, what kind of secrets did they keep from each other? She'd have thought this was the most open of communities. Or maybe this apparently unassuming man was trying to lull her into a false sense of security.

# ALONE TIME

Glesni was often an early riser, but this time there was a reason for it. She'd woken from a dream about an invasion from the mainland of strange half-human, half-machine creatures, summoned by Sandy. As the first amphibious craft approached the beach of her favourite cove – impossible for landing, but dreams didn't care about the impossible – she stood there, desperate to run to the village and raise the alarm but unable to move. As she woke, terrified, the immediacy of the nightmare receding slightly, she felt guilty for the implied slur on their guest. Her lingering unease remained as she dressed quickly and silently, careful not to wake Haf – no fear there; if the mainlanders sent a fleet of piercing foghorns her sister would sleep through it – and made her way out into the translucent dawn light. She hoped the reality of her favourite cove would dispel this persistent sense of wrongness. As she came closer to the rhythmic hushing of waves, with no sign of marauding craft, she began to feel calmer. A bobbing seal stared at her and cushions of thrift nodded pinkly in the breeze. Often, she would sit on a grassy tussock looking out over the little bay, but today she felt compelled to scramble down to the very edge of the sizzling wavelets, allowing them to wash away the last wisps of nightmare and clear her mind.

She was almost down to the pebbles that sloped away to shingle when she saw the gull. The poor bird was writhing on the shore, something unnaturally bright and spiky poking out of its gullet, goodness knows what attached to it inside. Its cry came out as a feeble squawk. The blood told Glesni that it wouldn't last long. To put it out of its misery would be merciful.

Hating what she was about to do, she picked up a large stone, aimed, closed her eyes…

As she buried it under a cairn of pebbles, a respectful ritual, but also to prevent some predator from seizing the carrion and with it the deadly wire, the sense of unease flooded back, washing all comfort out to sea. She returned to the rocks above the cove and sat, gazing past the thrift out over the waves. The seal was no longer there, its absence a statement of disapproval. A few gulls circled. The tribe of the dead one? Did they know? Did they hate her for it? She watched them soaring on thermals and air currents. It usually soothed her, but today she could imagine them gathering to swoop on her in retribution for their murdered friend. She wanted to shout into the breeze: *It wasn't my fault!*

Free as a bird, as the saying went. Living on Ynys Hudol and observing the migrating birds – fewer, different species every year, according to their observations – she was aware that they weren't free at all; they were bound by the need for food just like the islanders were. Their food was scarcer, if anything. People would envy their ability to soar on outspread wings, surveying the ground beneath, free of it all, gliding around simply to admire the beauty. But perhaps the birds were looking down on them, wishing they didn't have to make all that effort to hover, fly and dive in search of shoals that were dwindling or moving elsewhere as the changing climate ravaged the oceans faster than the birds' abilities to adapt.

And then they had to face the floating mini-islands of rubbish that often nudged up against the shore. Clearing the shallows and beaches was a regular Seeder task, shared by rota. But, as this poor gull had testified, their efforts only scraped the surface; a drop in the ocean. *Piso dryw bach yn y môr.* Glesni imagined the little wren in the Welsh version expressing its disgust at humankind by pissing on the rubbish in the sea.

Realising the sun, with its unmistakable promise of a scorching day, had neared its breakfast-time height, she stood and set off for home. She resisted the temptation to go the long way home, past Tahira's house. It wouldn't do to be late back and cause Mam to worry or Haf to start asking questions. Her sister wouldn't understand either the nightmare or the problem of brutally dispatching a seagull.

Tahira wasn't in school, which simply added to the weirdness of the day. At lunchtime, Glesni told Haf she wasn't hungry and wove her way between the houses to the far end of the village. It wouldn't be the first, or the last, time her friend stayed away from school. It was condoned because of her family's history; people were reluctant to put pressure on her. And in any case, it was no slur on Tom's teaching to say that she was probably better educated than any of them. On their refugee ship there had been little else to do than read; her uncle Khaled had seen to it that learning was something she and her brother Rashid would not be deprived of.

Their door was open; Rashid looked up from the plans he was working on. 'She's not here, sorry, Gles.'

'Any idea where she's gone?'

He shook his head. 'Went off this morning. Don't worry, she's fine. Just... alone time.'

He meant that she wasn't depressed, and Glesni understood alone time. It was one of the things she and her friend had in common. Normally she'd have asked him what he was working on – if only he could have been Taid's regular assistant instead of moody Madog – but she wanted to find Tahira. Although she was a few years older than Glesni, the two of them had become friends.

About the time the Husseins arrived, Glesni and Haf had reached the age where her sister's crowd were making her feel like an irritation. Little nuisance. Though if anyone was actually nasty to her, Haf defended her like a mother tiger. More than once she heard one of the adults saying age didn't matter, but it didn't feel that way to Glesni, caught in the no-man's-land between Haf's clique and the little ones.

Although she enjoyed her own company, it still nagged sometimes that she didn't have a special friend. There were times when she could talk to Haf, when they were doing their chores, laughing and sharing impressions of the adults – her sister was a hilarious mimic – and sometimes the other kids. But too often for comfort it would end with some hurtful remark, enough to unsettle but not quite enough for Glesni to precociously remind her of the Seeder principles of non-judgemental co-existence.

Those principles had been tested to their limits when Tahira, Rashid and Khaled washed ashore on one of the little beaches to the west of the island in a battered dinghy. Glesni was only nine when they arrived, but she remembered how the newcomers had caused some animated discussions among the Seeders: there had been a particularly prolonged drought, causing a year and a half of unpredictable harvests, and stores were low. But they knew the horror stories of the wars and famines where the Husseins came from, and Khaled was a doctor.

Once the little family was allowed across from Quarantine Rock, their story confirmed to any doubters that they were doing the right thing. Khaled and his orphaned niece and nephew had ended up on one of the infamous refugee ships moored in the English Channel at an out-of-sight-out-of-mind distance from the shore. Tahira, a toddler when they'd left their home country, hadn't known life anywhere else. As the intervals between supply drones stretched to breaking point, one by one families made lifeboats from furniture, and left like seed pods launching from a dying plant. After hesitating for too long because of the duty Khaled felt towards those unwilling or unable to try, Tahira's family had taken their chance, and when the vagaries of the sea brought them to Ynys Hudol, they must have thought it a magical island indeed.

Even the most zealous guardians of crops and community supplies were moved by their story, and a group pitched in to empty one of the stores in an outbuilding in the Tŷ Heulog courtyard and convert it to a home. The two men's contribution to community life grew with their returning health and strength. Khaled soon became friends with Jo, who'd been a midwife on the mainland, and Awen, who was a fount of knowledge on traditional healing and herbal lore. From a basis of mutual respect, they each contributed in their own ways to the community's health and wellbeing.

Tahira remained invisible for weeks, rarely leaving the house, staring glassy-eyed the few times her brother coaxed her to the roundhouse for a social Gathering or shared supper. No one saw her eat a morsel and he soon stopped trying, opting to eat at home with her instead.

After months of regarding her with awe and pity, Glesni finally spoke to her on a blustery autumn day. She'd finished her chores and was sitting above a cove on the rocky north shore. Two of the ponies had wandered down from the mountainside and were watching her curiously while grazing. Above the constant swell of the waves she heard a pebble skittering down the rocks.

And there she was: Tahira looked terrified, whether from the small but rugged climb down or from the attention, she couldn't tell.

'You don't mind?' Tahira gestured to a smooth rock next to where Glesni was perched.

Glesni felt a surge of joy and wanted to bombard her with all the questions that had been building up inside.

'Not at all,' she said, managing to dam a flood of words with a smile. 'Do you like it here?'

'Of course.'

'How—' She checked herself. Ever since they arrived, she'd been aching to know what had happened to Tahira's mother and father. But she thought of the Compassionate Silence and instead waved at the ponies. 'Have you met Ffred and Siani? Do you like horses?'

Tahira shrugged. 'They are beautiful. But I've never...'

Glesni stood and beckoned Tahira to approach. Siani shied away, making her new friend jump, but Ffred came steadily towards them. Glesni stroked his nose in the way he liked and looked across at Tahira, who kept her distance. 'He won't hurt you.'

She shook her head. Glesni understood – horses on a refugee ship? It must all be so strange for her. She found it hard to imagine that for the previous decade or so, Tahira had never felt the earth beneath her feet, never known the waves crashing on rocks – merely slapping against the unforgiving hulk of the ship. What was it like to be born to a life of imprisonment? No wonder she'd been slow to talk to anyone.

The pony stood, patiently, as if he knew to give her time. Tentatively, following Glesni's example, she stroked his rough coat, ran a hand through his mane. He responded to her touch and she murmured a few words in her own language. He turned his head and rubbed against her, an undemanding listener.

Glesni smiled. 'He knows you now. He'll come if you call.'

Tahira smiled back.

It took time, something they had plenty of, but they eventually grew close. Tahira told her that the island's wide-open spaces, the hall full of strangers, terrified her. People's well-meant concern felt stifling. Glesni had no idea what to say, but maybe her silent listening was what her new friend needed. Once she'd braved the great outdoors to follow her, Tahira was in her element, especially when it came to the animals. Delighted that she'd chosen her over the girls her own age, Glesni loved showing her all the best secret places on the rocky shore to the west and the top of the dangerous but awe-inspiring mountainside plunging into the sea to the north and east, from where they could see the mainland on a clear day. One thing Tahira couldn't grasp was Glesni's powerful desire to go on a mainland foraging trip.

'Why do you want to go from here? This island is so beautiful.'

'It might be beautiful on the mainland, too. I want to see for myself.'

'But you are safe here.'

'I'd be safe with the foraging party. Nothing's ever happened to anyone before.'

'I wish you wouldn't go.'

Tahira became visibly upset whenever Glesni mentioned the mainland, and it was one thing she never felt able to talk to her about.

Yet she treasured their moments of closeness.

Tahira seemed to know by a sixth sense when she was feeling lonely – but not today, it seemed. Glesni walked down to her favourite cove, feeling guilty as Rashid's *alone time* rang in her head but increasingly weighed down by the need to talk to someone. Even the ponies were distant specks on the other side of the island. Finding the beach deserted, Glesni's eyes were drawn to the seagull's cairn and she couldn't stay.

In the absence of her friend, only one other person could reassure her, but Taid's workshop and his house were empty. Longing to talk to him, about the gull and the dream, knowing he would understand, or simply listen, she set off in search of him. He wasn't in any of his usual haunts and the harbour was quiet. The two most likely places to find him, then, would be the cave on the far side of the mountain or Idris's watchtower. He spent time in both places as if the salt-laden sea air or the crackling radio could bring him closer to his memory of her nain, his wife. He never talked about her, neither did Mam, but her absence was as much a part of their family as herself or Haf.

The early afternoon felt too hot to strike out on the exposed path up the hill, but having made her decision she was determined to find him. Where the path dog-legged up and a tangle of brambles hid a disorderly set of steps down the sheer drop towards the sea cave, she paused, thinking guiltily that if he was there, it meant he wanted solitude. She wasn't in the mood for rejection, so she took the steeper route up to the tower. If Taid was there, he'd be with Idris and neither of them would mind her interrupting.

One of the last remaining pre-Seeder islanders and still their main observer and recorder, Idris had been employed as a warden on Ynys Hudol since before the arrival of Edith and Bleddyn, with Anti Martha and a couple of others, when it had been a nature reserve. The island's wildlife continued to dwindle despite his best efforts and the work of those like him, though maybe it was faring better here than elsewhere; Idris still kept meticulous records but had little to compare them with. He was rarely seen in the community, with the exception of the weekly Gatherings, which he never missed. Hardly anyone visited him in the watchtower, except for Taid, who actually enjoyed his company.

Glesni never knew what to make of Idris and often wondered what the two of them found to talk about. Taid told her his friend needed someone to share his observations and statistics with, clinging to the migratory birds that returned, mourning those he missed, shaking his head over weather patterns that were mere abstractions. Normally fascinated by minutiae, even Taid sometimes tired of his obsessions. Yet he still went and Glesni realised that, after a brief exchange, they didn't need to talk about anything. They'd said it all before. Maybe they found comfort in having said it all before.

The last wispy clouds had melted, leaving a hot day without a breath of wind, the kind of day where she felt as if her skin was peeling after a minute's exposure. She manoeuvred her sun hat to cover the back of her neck, smoothed the biggest plantain leaves she could find into her sandals to protect her feet and rolled her sleeves down over her hands, which she shoved into her pockets. Not an inch of skin showing.

The climb seemed endless. She stopped a few times, despite the lure of the cool haven within the squat tower's thick stone walls. The nearer she got, the more she could feel Idris watching her.

'Hello, Glesni *fach*.'

The endearment felt strange coming from him.

'Hello,' she said. 'Is Taid here?'

He shook his head. No need to say more, since he knew she'd have searched all the usual places before coming up to the tower. She felt guilty for getting straight to the point, for not being there on a social visit, so when he stepped back to usher her in from the harsh sunlight, she followed him in.

'You look troubled. Shall I put the kettle on?'

What she really wanted was to continue her search for Taid, but after her hot climb she accepted a drink of water. They sat in the two chairs that seemed to fill the ground-floor room of the tower, their worn arms poking out from beneath equally threadbare throws. Idris's silences were uniquely eloquent and she found herself telling him about the gull. The dream was far too personal to talk about, but the gull was a different matter; he could share her anger at the mainlanders' wanton filling of the sea with plastic waste. Depending on the tides, sometimes it felt like most of it jostled up around their island. Leaving her to look after the birds it killed.

'You mustn't upset yourself. That gull would've died anyway.'

She didn't need his consolation; it was enough to know that he sympathised.

'Don't we all die eventually?' he continued. 'But too many of them perish earlier than they should. Which is our fault collectively – humans' – but not yours. You're innocent of plastic, at least.'

His eyes were piercing, as if challenging her to confess all the ways in which she wasn't innocent. As if they each had a duty to be guilty of something. Not what she needed; she should have thanked him for the water and continued on her way.

'Not nice, killing, is it?' He widened his eyes in a way that made her wonder what – or who, even – he'd killed in his time. He relaxed and smiled. 'But you did the right thing. Sometimes we have to make difficult choices.'

She sipped her water, nodding.

'You see, I like that in someone.' He shifted in his seat and she was both flattered and unsettled by his words. 'That you care.'

She could feel herself frowning. Didn't they all care?

'It's so important, caring,' he said as if he'd heard her thoughts. 'When so many people live as closely together as we do.'

Sometimes it felt like there were a lot of them – depending on her mood, on any running disputes – but most of the older ones who'd lived on the mainland spoke of anything from a 'small community' to 'isolation'. It was all a matter of perspective. Glesni sometimes tried to imagine communities much bigger than theirs, where you constantly mixed with people you didn't know. Remembering that his early life as a warden on the island was spent with just a couple of others and the birds for company, she thought the Seeders, all sixty-eight of them, must seem like an overwhelming crowd to him, even though he hardly lived 'closely together' with them.

'You think they care,' he said, 'then you just have to see the way they bicker.' She wondered how much he truly saw from his hermitage in the watchtower. 'It's all words, their kind of caring. It's deeds that count. They talk about respect but I know what they think of me. "Crazy old fool up there on his hill." I'm surprised they trust me to keep watch, and you know what, *fach*? Sometimes I think that if I saw trouble approaching,' he waved his arm, 'from land or sea, you know what, I might just let them come. I might even light a bonfire to show them the way.'

His eyes challenged hers. He unnerved her when he talked like this, though she knew there was some truth in his complaints of mockery. But she also knew that most of the islanders respected him deep down. And that there was no way he'd betray them. However much he remained aloof, he knew – they all knew – that the alternative was worse.

'Loneliness,' he continued. 'You wouldn't think it. They'd have you believe we all look out for one another. Empathy, humility, frugality. But there's no escaping loneliness.'

His words made her think of the gulf between alone time, which she understood, and loneliness, of which she had little experience.

'Nothing's changed. The world as we know it is dying – we didn't manage to mend that – and we have to cope with it, accept it and move on. Wouldn't you think that would unite us, make sure those of us who are left can learn from our mistakes and flourish? But even within this little sheltered world we have our outsiders.'

Her mind conjured images of herself and the others as little kids, sneaking up to the tower, daring each other to knock and run away, tipping water they could ill afford to waste into his precious rain gauge. As if he hadn't known.

He looked at her, right through the guilt of a dead gull. She'd never been entirely at ease with the pranks, nor those who challenged his right to live alone, arguing by way of an excuse that it wasn't right to entrust the community's safety solely into one person's hands, but in fact uncomfortable with his choice to be apart.

Now, she began to understand his sadness and his contempt. Maybe she was even warming to him. Part of her wanted to ask more, but a larger part shied away from opening the floodgates.

'And I'm not the only outsider.' He leaned forward and lowered his voice, despite the fact that there was no one to hear. 'You look out for your taid, *fach*. Especially with her around.' There was no doubt who he meant. 'Can't for the life of me think why he offered for her to stay with you. Or why your mam agreed. Foolish. Too much at stake.'

'What do you mean?'

'You just watch what you tell her,' he said.

'What is there to tell? She knows that we exist now; surely it's in our interest that she knows about the good things we're doing, knows that we're harmless?'

'Can't argue with that.'

He refused to be drawn in further and deftly turned the conversation to Sandy's boat. Glesni enjoyed telling him about it, proud of her part in the repairs, and thought no more about his implied warning until after she'd drained her cup of water and left.

Idris's parting shot was to advise her not to disturb Taid if he was at the hermit's cave. So, having made the effort to climb the mountain, she decided to enjoy the views and took the undulating trail that led along the saddle of the ridge to the slightly higher peak at the island's north-east end. It looked like a haphazard heap of rocks, maybe a failed experiment by whatever mythical wizard gave Ynys Hudol its name. At times she liked to believe in magic.

As she walked, she glanced back from time to time at the squat tower, appearing and receding with the contours of the mountainside.

Whatever her feelings about Idris, she certainly felt safer knowing he was there, watching out for them, his faithful presence more effective than anything the Defenders might get up to. After all, hadn't he kept Ynys Hudol safe for the Seeders in the early days when the Clearance Crew came round? Glesni believed that meant he'd accepted the community's presence on the island wholeheartedly, contrary to what some believed at the time and a few still did.

From her seaward side she could hear the fractious bickering of colonies of kittiwakes, razorbills, terns and herring gulls that had whitewashed the cliff face to the appearance of chalk. It made it look taller than it was, somehow, especially from a boat out at sea. Even on land it was impressive enough, though the birds nested mainly out of sight of the safe path.

Accompanied by their glorious cacophony, she picked her way over dips and rises towards the rocky summit where the gorse and heather grew more sparsely. She didn't come here often, especially not on a hot day like this, but felt drawn to the top, anticipating the shimmering of the sun on the water. Another faint path led off to her right, and around to the cliff face; she ignored it. She'd been there of course, they all had, Haf and her friends daring each other on. The colonies were magnificent and once they'd conquered their fear – even her sister and the others had been scared, she could tell despite their taunts – they'd hung around for ages watching the birds come and go.

But not today. No one came here at this point in the breeding season.

She'd passed the dip and was beginning the climb, carefully choosing footholds and handholds as the path snaked its way upwards, when she became aware of a change in the piercing discords of the bird calls. It sounded almost human. She smiled to herself. There was definitely something enchanted about this place. A stone skittered from beneath her feet. A herring gull flew alarmingly close. Then another. As if they were seeking revenge for their dead companion. There it was again. Definitely a voice. There was only one person mad enough, or ignorant enough, to disturb the birds here.

She hurried back down the path and turned off the faint trail that led round towards the cliff, one cautious step at a time, until she could peer along the rock face.

'Over here!' Sandy was clinging to an outcrop, huddled against a persistent attack of swooping birds. A parched grassy slope stretched downwards below her, fairly broad but dangerous if she missed her footing. She shot a look of relief at Glesni, who raised her own arm in defence.

'They look worse than they are,' she shouted, trying to convince herself as much as Sandy.

Glesni inched along the path then, gripping a sturdy gorse trunk, reached out her hand. Sandy shook her head, petrified, trying to merge with the rock she was clinging to. She'd pulled her shirt up over her head, but the swooping continued. The fabric was streaked with guano.

'I can't come any further,' Glesni called. Unless Sandy made a move to help herself, they'd probably both end up on the rocks below in a flurry of squawking gulls. Staring at the white swell of the waves at a dizzying distance below, she kept the thought to herself. Sandy started flapping her arm at the birds. It was completely ineffective and probably even intensified the onslaught.

'I'm going to get help!'

Glesni made to turn.

'Don't go!'

'I can't... Just stay where you are. I'll be quick.'

She heard the familiar uneven footsteps and tapping of the walking pole before she reached the path. A wave of relief made her realise she'd been more scared than she first realised.

'What's going on?' Taid had a coil of rope and a climbing harness on his arm. 'I called by to see Idris. He'd seen the birds. I thought you knew better than to—'

'Not me. Sandy.'

He swore and made his way past her. After securing the rope he inched along the path then, ignoring the angry gulls, offered Sandy the harness. She shook her head, refusing to let go of her handhold. Glesni watched on as he managed to secure her; it took a while for the safety of the rope to thaw Sandy's grip. Taid patiently guided her back to the main path, where she collapsed, breathless as if she'd run up the main path to the summit and back.

'What on earth took you there?' he asked as she struggled free of the harness.

'Your bloody assistant...'

'Madog?' He frowned.

'Recommended this place for a walk... to see the birds close up...'

Taid waved a hand towards the well-trodden path. 'The summit not spectacular enough for you?'

'He definitely said...' She shrugged. 'I must have got it wrong.'

Taid raised an eyebrow but said nothing.

'He should have told you not to come alone,' Glesni said.

'If you haven't noticed,' Sandy said, 'I'm still not as fit as you lot. I thought I could make my own way, in my own time.' Putting the harness neatly on the grass beside her, she hugged her knees and glanced up. 'Wrong.'

Glesni looked helplessly at Taid. She felt sorry for Sandy, and they could hardly leave her after this. Taid shrugged; he seemed to agree. He gave her time to collect herself, then cajoled her up the comparatively safe path to the summit. Glesni followed.

At the top, a tumble of rocks provided seats that looked made for them. The smell of Sandy's white-streaked shirt wasn't too bad in the stiff breeze.

'You can make out the mainland of Cymru,' Taid said with a wave of his hand. He turned to face the west. 'And over there, you can even see Ireland on a clear day. Kid yourself it'd be an adventure to go there.'

'You don't think it would?' Sandy said.

'Not the kind I hanker after. Not any more.'

'You did once?'

He shrugged.

'You surprise me,' she said. 'I sometimes get the impression you'd like to get away. You don't seem entirely happy here.'

Glesni bristled; he belonged here.

'Listen, love,' he said. 'If you're looking for someone to ferry you across, I'm not your man, right?'

Glesni wondered if someone who didn't know him as well as she did would hear the tension in his voice.

'But don't you sometimes want to get away?'

Nothing but the distant murmuring of the waves far below.

Sandy would never succeed in getting Taid to help her. He wouldn't even go to the mainland on foraging trips these days, however much they begged him to accompany them with his practical and mechanical skills. He'd use the excuse that he was too old, he'd slow them down, maybe even put them in danger, but they all knew he simply didn't want to leave again.

'Are you troubled because of Helyg's mother?' Sandy continued. It was as if she was using outlandish questioning to make them forget her humiliating terror on the cliff face. 'What happened to her?'

'She died.'

'How?'

'One thing you'll learn, Sandy, about living in a small community is to respect other people's personal space.'

Steadying himself on a rock, he levered himself up.

'Work to do. You can guide her down safely, can't you, Pwt?'

He was on his way down without waiting for a reply.

Glesni wanted to applaud him. It wasn't very considerate of him to vanish, but Sandy's prying had earned it. Taid didn't need Idris to advise him when to keep things to himself.

But what things? As if unsettling nightmares and seagulls weren't enough, now she had Idris's cryptic allusions to contend with. *Too much at stake.* If Sandy hadn't been there, she'd have gone back and asked him what he meant. No matter; she'd rather ask Taid, or maybe Mam. She suddenly felt the weight of all the things she didn't know. Why on Earth would any of it matter to Sandy?

'Bloody hell, I obviously touched a nerve there. I didn't realise...' Sandy fell silent, as if by saying any more she'd lose her only remaining guide.

'He's just not in the mood to talk, obviously.' Glesni stood and held out a hand. With a smile, Sandy levered herself up, then followed her cautiously but without mishap down the steep, winding path.

PART IV

# NANT-Y-WERN

# BEAUTIFULLY APT

He thought of all those cut down in the fighting like the rainforest
they'd blundered in to try and save. The older ones who'd lived a
good life and deserved a better exit. The young ones with their
futures ahead of them. Even the bad ones, with their chance to turn
things around, to make amends, snatched from them. Would he
ever get a chance to make amends? Once he was healed, he could
start by helping this girl, this young woman. He laughed at himself.
What could he possibly have that she, Bela, would want, let alone
need? She'd finally told him her name, though most of the time she
communicated nonverbally. She'd shown him a picture in a book, a
pine marten. *Bele'r coed*. He doubted that was the name she'd been
given at birth, but it was beautifully apt.

He'd taken to getting up for breakfast, which consisted of coffee
and an assortment of nuts, grains and leaves. He still had no idea
where she got the coffee from; it tasted different – maybe it was
some kind of coffee substitute – but good. It had been so long that
it could be his taste memory at fault. He also wondered what she
did for food in winter when the harvest dried up. It was hard to tell
what time of year it was; it had been spring before he was ill but that
was hardly relevant. It was no different here than at home: the
weather veered wildly from intensely hot to surprisingly chilly.
Maybe it was the same for foraging these days, with things appearing
at unseasonal times. It would be a shame if winter never came, if he
never saw snow again, except for a freak squall at a time of year when
it shouldn't be there.

'*Iawn?*' she said as she appeared in the doorway.

He nodded and they exchanged a smile. He'd been relieved to
discover she could speak, though he should have known, since the
name, Bela, he'd found rattling around his head in his delirium had

turned out to be correct, so she must have told him. But though she'd found her voice, it was all in Welsh. She either couldn't, or more likely wouldn't, speak a word of English. He assumed it was Welsh; it sounded like the smattering he'd heard on a couple of childhood holidays. Like anyone else in what remained of Britain, he knew very little about the language; even in the fabled hills and valleys it had been effectively silenced since the unrest and the resettlement. Thinking about it for the first time, he wondered whether it was a policy born of pragmatism, to prevent covert communications, or punishment in the form of humiliation, a re-run of the conquering empire asserting itself by suppressing the vassal state's culture.

He was ashamed to realise that he'd never really given it much thought; the unrest over independence, or civil war as the Welsh called it, had begun in '36, only three years after he'd returned from fighting in the Amazon. By then he'd no longer been contracted for active service, which was a relief as Wales had seemed far too close to home to have felt like The Enemy. It had been a fairly short-lived conflict, though it had never really been won or lost: SarsCov-39, drought-induced food shortages and increasingly frequent power outages had ground down the resistance and the claims for independence had begun to fizzle, the final blow being dealt by the resettlement of rural populations. Although done for the more efficient – or fairer, according to government spin – management of scarce resources and medical care, the policy had nevertheless been called the Clearances by the Welsh and even he could understand the historical echoes. It therefore made sense that the remaining outlying communities, or individuals in her case, stubbornly stuck to their language as a form of resistance.

He'd never thought of himself as an oppressor. Even in the Amazon, hadn't he been fighting for a good cause? But didn't an invading force always claim the good-cause card? Laughable again. At least he was recovering well enough to laugh at himself. But surely no objective observer could deny that bringing down a government who seemed to have lost all reason, hell-bent on destroying what was left of the rainforest, 'the lungs of the earth', had to be for the greater good. Objective observers were hard to find in a polarised world where populist bullies had on ever-increasing occasions brought the international community to the brink of a third world war.

His thoughts circling around oppression, as he went into the kitchen for breakfast he noticed, not for the first time, that the bowl she took for herself had less in it than the one she passed him.

'You shouldn't,' he said, indicating each bowl in turn. 'You should share equally.' She shrugged. 'Or give yourself more,' he added apologetically.

'*Ti'n mendio.*' She gave him a look as if appraising a job well done. '*Angen bwyta.*'

He'd worked out that *bwyta* meant eat and *mendio* sounded comfortingly like getting better.

She wolfed her own breakfast then watched him, head tilted, eyes bright like the little birds who gathered on twigs, the wing mirror of the crumbling car, the rain barrels, waiting for the scraps she regularly gave them. Like the birds, she seemed to be getting warier the more he was able to move around.

A shaft of sunlight slanted through the open door, its warmth edged by the breeze it brought in with it. She glanced over as the door rattled on its hinges.

'*Fforio,*' she announced, waving towards outdoors. Then, as if an idea had occurred to her: '*Ti'n dŵad efo fi?*'

It was a question but that was all he understood. 'I'm sorry,' he said. 'I—'

'*Ti,*' she pointed at him, then walked her fingers in the direction of the door, '*yn dŵad efo fi.*' She made a beckoning motion and indicated herself at *fi*.

Leaning over, she grasped a basket from the far end of the table. '*Fforio,*' she repeated, '*Fforio am fwyd.*' Her free hand fluttered as she mimed picking and gathering in. He nodded, glad that he'd finally get to see beyond the garden fence and tangled hedge beyond.

'*Madarch*,' she announced with a smile as if they'd come to a decision together. '*Ti'n hoffi madarch?*'

He was saved from thinking of a reply by her getting up and vanishing from the room. Her birdlike timidity dispelled by a sense of purpose, she reappeared with a large waxed coat, stiff from disuse, which she took out into the yard and shook before kneading it into wearability.

He wrinkled his nose at the mildewy smell as she came back in and thrust it at him.

'*Rhaid*,' she insisted. '*Rhy oer i glaf. Oer. Brrr.*' She hugged herself in a pantomime of cold.

Though it was hardly freezing, he was still convalescing so he obeyed her and put it on, strangely relieved at not having to make decisions for himself.

Out in the woods, having negotiated a tangle of brambles and ivy like the barrier guarding a sleeping princess's castle, he learned that *madarch* meant mushrooms. He hadn't even known there were any about in spring, but she seemed to know instinctively where to find them and showed him examples of the ones they were looking for. She also made it clear with a dramatic display of retching and choking which to avoid.

It was something he'd occasionally thought about learning; he wished he had. He was humbled to realise how little he knew even about tree identification. Every mushroom he picked seemed subtly different from the examples she'd shown him and they sat roundly in his basket, taunting him and daring him to lick his fingers. He was struck by the individuality – hues, wrinkles, variations in size and shape – and thought of all he'd read about the underground community in the soil all around.

He sensed that she understood all that, maybe without consciously knowing it, while he felt privileged, as if he'd stumbled into a special world where he could only ever be a visitor. He breathed in the earthy smell, the rich leaf mould and the lighter must of the mushrooms. Suddenly he felt glad of the old coat, like a huntsman wearing the skin of his prey to conceal his alien scent.

The soughing of the branches and the irregular chatter of the birds were the soundtrack of childhood. No matter that he'd grown up in the city; he and his friends had gone out to play in the woods whenever they got chance. The serried plantations of struggling young trees that he'd known, with the low roar of traffic beyond, were a weak imitation of what he was experiencing now. Funny how his memory was more a childhood learned from books and stories.

A deep melancholy overcame him as he thought of childhoods, of whole lives, without this deep connection, of the mighty Amazon rainforest that was a shadow of what it should have been by the time they took action – too little too late – to save it.

He leaned on his walking stick, the thoughts of all that had gone and all that had never really been making the pain in his thigh and arm more insistent than it had been for a while. He urged himself on with the admonition that activity and a sense of purpose were an analgesic to rival Bela's potions.

If only he were stronger, this would be living the dream. He used to love getting out of the city. His opportunities grew less and less as they put him on call more often, until he ended up being continuously chained to the phone, unable to go more than five miles from home.

'Give me a nice, safe park any day,' Cass had said.

She'd seemed genuinely nervous when he took her out hiking, although the fells they climbed were too thronged to remotely resemble wilderness.

'If anything happened to us,' she'd declare, 'I like to think they'd know where to find us.'

That was the difference between them. What she found comforting was everything he hated.

That evening, Bela served him a rare feast. As he bit into his first mushroom and the light earthy taste answered something within him, he was surprised to realise how much he'd already come to trust her. His rational mind argued that if she'd wanted to harm him she'd had plenty of opportunity, but his heart insisted it was more visceral than that.

# A ROOM MUSTY WITH DISUSE

The house was silent. As she came and went, foraging and doing whatever else filled her days, Winter learned to differentiate the silence of her absence – the creaks and rustles of the house in the wind, the buzzing of a fly, the occasional unidentified rustling of creatures – from the quiet of her unspeaking, watchful presence.

Standing at the bottom of the stairs he looked up, wondering whether he was ready to brave it. Whether he should. She had never expressly forbidden him; she hadn't needed to, as they both knew it would require some effort – effort that until the last couple of days he simply hadn't had in him. He told himself he wasn't prying. He'd just try the stairs. Maybe there was a spare room up there and she could return the downstairs room to whatever purpose had been assigned to it before she took him in.

At the top he stood, leaning on the wall to get his breath back, suppressing the self-disgust at his weakness. The nearest door was ajar; he could see a bathroom, as airy and tidy as the kitchen and outside compost toilet. Three more doors, all shut. He opened the first and looked in. A bed with rumpled quilt, a chest-of-drawers and an old wardrobe with doors ajar indicated it was hers. He immediately stepped back and pulled the door to, respecting her privacy. He made his halting way to the end door, which was adorned with some kind of plaque. The spiky whirl of twigs, dried leaves and acorns indicated specialness, so much so that he was surprised the door opened to his push. A layer of dust and cobwebs shrouded a room musty with disuse. As well as the bed, the large room contained a wardrobe, a chest of drawers, shelving and a small table with a chair – a desk to judge from the notebook and pen lying on it, with only the dust indicating the owner was not going to return any minute and continue writing. He made his way across to it, then glanced over his shoulder to make sure he was still alone. His heart leapt at the sight of footprints – foot, shuffle, foot, shuffle, like some grotesque morse code spreading the news of his trespass. Like the rest of the house, the landing was swept clear, but here the dust was like a trap laid to let Bela know if anyone had been there. He doubted it was deliberate but still, he should never have been so careless.

Cursing his ongoing weakness of mind as well as body, he made to turn and leave before she returned. Maybe he could sweep the footprints away in the hope that by the next time she opened the door, enough dust would have resettled to conceal his wrongdoing. He shook his head at the hopeless notion.

As he dithered, his eye was drawn to a large brown envelope lying to the side of the well-thumbed books on the shelf above the desk. To be precise, it was the official insignia marking the envelope that drew his attention. It was so familiar that he almost hadn't registered it. With another glance out at the landing, he pulled the door to. He made his painful way back to perch on the chair, leg sticking out stiffly, and reached for the envelope. A cloud of dust billowed up and he paused for several uncomfortable moments, suppressing the urge to cough.

He drew out a bundle of documents. The form on top was as familiar as the insignia on the envelope. He'd processed enough of these forms before he defected. It would contain a dry, dispassionate report of sustained torture. He frowned. Yes, admit it, Winter: torture.

PRISONER ASSESSMENT DOSSIER
PROJECT ASCLEPIUS

He was unprepared for the tsunami of guilt that washed over him. He had only been following instructions, but what a thin excuse that was. The project was worthy research, they said, essential to provide protection from the ever-evolving virus – but what thin justification that was. When he found out what was going on, he'd stumbled from day to day finding ways to obtain more meds than the medical staff asked for, in the hope that he could alleviate the suffering of at least some of the prisoners. The impossibility of such a notion was why he had ultimately defected. Why he was in the predicament he was now.

He gazed at the impersonal cover of the form on his knee, unable to bring himself to open it and see the cold reckoning of suffering it contained. He knew by now what he was going to see, but his heart still jumped when he saw the distinctive initials in the bottom right-hand corner of the cover. *AS*.

Had Annabel Snow somehow made her way here? Of course not. Her signature was all over papers like these. Dust like this wouldn't have settled in the time it had taken him to reach here, and they'd left at the same time. They hadn't dared meet even to say goodbye, but he heard she'd managed to leave the country.

When she'd confided in him all those years ago, she'd said it was the first rescue she'd contemplated. Her fear confirmed it. Like him, she'd become disgusted with what they were being tasked with. She was a doctor, a researcher, but until then, her subjects for the vaccine research had always consented, always been meticulously selected for their health and suitability.

As a consequence of the increasingly insistent protests, which in many cities had erupted into rioting, side by side with waves of mutating viruses, it had seemed like an appropriate punishment to move those prisoners who were considered terrorists to a high-security medical research centre and deliberately infect them. Wasn't it essential to test the vaccines that were constantly being developed in a vain effort to keep pace with the emerging pandemics? Willing volunteers among the public had dwindled to almost none, and it was but a small step for the government to recruit volunteers from the prison communities. They'd all consented, hadn't they? But, as he'd asked himself from the start, who wouldn't if it meant a commuted sentence? The commutation never came, and the consent for subsequent medical trials grew ever more desperate. Eventually, consent was dispensed with altogether, until he wondered that participation in the Asclepius projects hadn't been handed down in the courts along with a jail sentence. But that would have meant the public knowing about it.

It became obvious that punishment – revenge even – was the aim, and he'd been increasingly sickened by the suffering in the name of 'beneficial research'. He'd tried to convince himself of the old argument: hadn't millions, including some of his own family and friends, suffered in the pandemics? But to repeat the process again and again, most of his colleagues revelling in it, was more than he could take.

When the trials were leaked and became public knowledge in the mid-40s, it seemed that the appetite for retribution was not as great as the government had calculated. *Death Penalty!* the headlines screamed. The issue caused yet another clash in the already painfully divided country. A select committee was appointed to come up with recommendations – presumably instructed to take their time about it, he thought cynically – and the Asclepius project was shelved.

Except it wasn't.

It merely went even deeper underground. Bound by an irreversible contract, he'd gone with it. As had Dr Annabel Snow. At first, he'd thought her a cold-hearted bitch, avoiding her like the plague she was ostensibly researching, until that evening when her rounds ended while he was on duty and she'd come to the guards' office for a coffee and a chat. What did he have to chat about with someone from a supposedly caring profession who would go along with this?

The second time, after she'd been talking about her husband's weeks in intensive care before he finally died, which drove home to him how lucky he was to still have Cass, his opinion of her began to soften. Everyone here had contracts, after all, and maybe the cold-hearted doctor was as much an exercise in self-preservation as the amiable but tough prison guard. Their chats became more relaxed, and following a crisis where several prisoners had become dangerously ill during trials of a particularly experimental vaccine, he'd gone to his senior officer and managed to wangle more staff and the proper ICU that Annabel kept pleading for. A tentative friendship was sealed by gratitude and a shared purpose. He could still hear her laugh. 'Adam Winter and Annabel Snow: with names like ours, we're destined to work together.'

There was one woman she was particularly concerned about. Implausibly strong given her small stature, she'd withstood several trials, but she was weakening. Annabel was amazed she'd come that far. She was also convinced that the woman, Elin Sherwell, had been scapegoated, not guilty of the more extreme crimes she'd been charged with. Winter knew her, too, from his rounds; he knew them all. Her gaunt features had a rare hint of warmth, compassion even, despite her contempt for a man who'd do a job like his. According to her notes, she insisted she'd never intentionally hurt anyone, though she'd caused plenty of public nuisance and material damage in an attempt to counteract lies and galvanise a disinterested world into taking action on the climate. He was surprised to find he pitied her.

Annabel had felt the same and had persuaded him to join her in a plan. He'd done the practical work of timing shifts and arranging transport to get Sherwell out while Annabel had faked convincing test results and a death certificate.

That rescue turned out to be the first of several, carried out over a number of years. How many did it take to atone for quietly getting on with your job, saving your own skin at the expense of others?

He still couldn't bring himself to open the file, but he wondered if it proved he'd come to the right place after all. When he went on the run, with nowhere to go, he remembered Elin Sherwell's promise, given in gratitude for his part in her rescue. If ever there was anything she could do to help him... Neither of them believed such a thing would ever be needed or possible. And if it were, he had no hope of finding her. Many prisoners, particularly those with a background in the Resettlement zones of rural Wales, Cornwall and the far north, had been taunted with photos of their ruined homes. But he'd heard a rumour that photos, films and documentary evidence of such destruction were as fake as his escapees' death certificates, shown to unfortunates whom the authorities knew would never be free to discover the reality.

He hoped the file he was now holding would prove the rumour to be true.

There was only one way to confirm it. Hand shaking, he gripped the cover, his whole body as tense as a man about to pull the pin on a hand grenade.

The door was flung open and the room exploded as if the grenade had gone off. Bela's screech deafened him. She was upon him before he could blink. Gripping his wounded bicep, she snatched the file from him, dragged him to his feet and kneed the wound on his thigh. His own bellow of pain filled the void left by her screech as he sank to the floor. He was too preoccupied to notice what she did with the papers as she dragged him up to stagger along the landing and stumble down the stairs to his own room, chattering her incomprehensible words with an anger he'd not heard before. Clutching his arm, she shoved him roughly onto his bed and slammed the door, reappearing moments later with a large cup of the sleeping draught.

Drained of the energy to fight it, he gave in and lay back, feeling the effects almost immediately. As nauseous oblivion came in waves, he heard something heavy being dragged across the door outside.

# HE CAN'T STEAL MY WORLD

He should wake up he's been asleep too long he's well he's not hot
not like when he came when I brought him to my house but he
won't wake up I gave him too much sleeping drink more than I
should it was Hers make you sleep make you mend but he's already
mending and I gave him too much wanted him away gave him too
much I was angry why did he go to Her room look at Her things it
hurts a stranger looking at Her things I don't want him knowing
She said no one must know only me and if he knows about Her that
makes him dangerous I had to stop him and I don't want him there
dirtying Her things Her memory I had to stop him I hate him why
did he go there didn't ask didn't wait till I tell him about Her maybe
I'll never tell him but he knows now and he didn't wait. I hate him
She said I was special I'm not special any more because he knows
too I hate him I want him to sleep forever so I don't have to talk to
him but if he doesn't wake up he'll die and when I saw him with
Her things I wished he'd die he's the only person been here since
She went to the owls the only man since those bad ones that stole
our food in the barn why we built the wall over the gate but I don't
need a wall for him didn't think I need a wall for him thought I
could trust him I want to trust him but it's only because he was ill
he was nice when he was ill when he needed looking after but now
I can't trust him I wish I could make him good keep him asleep just
wake him up to feed him then I have a friend I can trust but if he's
asleep it's not him and I liked going foraging with him liked showing
him my woods my trees my plants liked listening to him play the
guitar her guitar another thing he stole from Her I wish She'd taught
me how to play because now I need him to play if I could play myself
I wouldn't need him I could send him away stop him dirtying her
memory but then he'll be gone and I don't want that because I'm

not alone now he's here and I like being alone but just sometimes I like his company I didn't choose him but he's here and I haven't had a friend since She went to the owls.

I say his name Winter it means *gaeaf* but he's not cold he's warm and he's only sleeping I shake him shake shake shake *deffro'r dyn ffôl* he looks at me his eyes like he thinks I'm a dream I wonder if he's a dream a nightmare when he interferes with Her things but I'm glad he's here I shake him again hard he says stop he says *paid Bela* and the sound of his voice means I'm not shaking him any more I'm so glad he's awake I didn't want him to sleep forever but he shocked me he shouldn't go in that room he takes my hand and squeezes it weakly I want a friend She's not with me any more She was my friend and She was all I needed till he came and now he's here I don't want to lose Her.

I tell him he mustn't interfere and bring his man's world into Her room I ask him what he saw but he doesn't understand me I won't speak his language She told me to remember some words in case people came She said I might need the words from before but don't let them steal our world by taking our words he can't steal my world or Hers if I don't use his words he has to learn mine didn't he say *paid Bela* not stop it Bela. I know he can when he learns my words we can be friends it's true that we can be friends without that too but not the same like a bird comes to the house or *bele'r coed* the pine marten might come for food or a warm place for a nest but they see a human and they're nervous you think you've got their trust but not really that's how it is till I know who he is and what he wants and if he wants to stay. Until I know and he stops sneaking around I don't trust him like the pine marten doesn't trust people. But I want a friend and I ask him if he's hungry I say *t'isio bwyd* and he says *plis* he smiles and he says I'm sorry I didn't want to upset you and I just look at him I push his arms away and go to the kitchen I'm sorry I hurt him but I'm not going to tell him not until he says *dwi'n difaru do'n i ddim yn bwriadu niwed iti* maybe when he says that I'll be ready for him.

Now he's sleeping proper sleep without the medicine I leave him and go to hunt food gather mushrooms and herbs looking for little animals with my bow I always tell them sorry but we have to eat and then I hear a sound it's a long way off but I remember when Winter came and I forget foraging and go silent through the woods I know someone is there because a robin is shouting he always shouts but this is different I hear a bang it's not big but sends a flock of rooks rising black from their trees they're always noisy but I know this is more than squabbling I hear another bang a door of a car they didn't bring a car as far as the fallen tree last time but they're here now they won't find the men that came before I made sure of that I buried them they won't find Nant-y-Wern either because of that time that scare when we walled across the drive She took the sign and put it by the gate of an empty house the other side of the fallen tree Tyn Rhedyn was the empty house but She put the Nant-y-Wern sign there so no one comes to our house I watch this man and woman to make sure. Others have come too like that woman a few days before Winter arrived she looked around but she soon went away that house was empty when I came to Nant-y-Wern but maybe they're looking for the people who used to live there or maybe there are some things She never told me whatever I'm glad She was clever with the wall and the sign. I can see the strangers from above through the low branches the leaves the woman looks up she doesn't see me I can be still I can be quiet I stare back terrified unseen until she looks back at the paper in the man's hand they look over the fallen tree along my road that doesn't look like a road it's becoming wild with the grass the little plants claiming it they look at the paper again I can't see the writing but the symbol at the top of the page is the one on Her papers they've come to find Her but they won't have any luck She's gone with the owls there's only us now me and Winter the man says something they get in the car and reverse round the corner I hear them stop where the Tyn Rhedyn gate is with the Nant-y-Wern sign I stay where I am just listening they're there a long time I stay listening as they walk up to that empty house and walk back I wait and wait until the car moves and I wait again until its tyre noise disappears past the *Cofeb* the special memorial past the old village and over the hill and away I wait a long time after there's no more sound they won't find us and if they do I'm ready.

# ENGROSSED IN THE PATTERNS

After her vicious outburst, as he'd emerged fitfully from his drug-induced sleep, Bela had been warm, attentive, silently kind. Taking his hand in hers, she looked at him in a way that said: 'I wish you hadn't made me do that and I'm sorry'. She brushed his hair from his fevered forehead, felt his pulse then kept hold of his arm, as if drawn to touch him. Whenever he opened his eyes she fluttered back like a startled bird, jumped up and busied herself like a scurrying woodland creature. But most times when he woke he was simply aware of her caring presence. Her absences were usually filled with the comforting purr of a cat.

On a golden afternoon, early evening sun exploring his room on a scattering of dust motes, he became aware of an insistent headache and knew he was properly awake this time. When he heard sounds from somewhere in the house, he tensed. Whether it was Bela or Cass, reality or fever dream, he wasn't ready. He closed his eyes, knowing he couldn't feign sleep in front of either of them. How many times during the last few days had Cass come to taunt him? She'd come here to the woods, they'd chased through the streets, they'd lain in their bed in the cramped flat, rain streaming down the windows, wind shaking the building to its foundations. His heart had swelled to be back with her; she'd given him hope of forgiveness, the promise of togetherness, but always he found himself running, performing some impossible task, escaping from her clutches when she turned, teeth in a sneering grimace.

And Bela... if the tantalising distance that Cass's shadow created was predictable, Bela's closeness – there was no denying it – was more surprising than anything else she'd shown him since he'd been here. Maybe it was her vicious attack that was the fever dream, maybe he'd even conjured up the Asclepius file in the disused bedroom from the depths of his convalescent mind. Had even the series of rescues with Annabel Snow been a figment of his imagination, something he'd fabricated to bolster his self-image? If that was the case, what had he been running from, how had he ended up here in the woods with this strange young woman? She was certainly real, even if a living crash course in how concepts of reality could differ so widely.

He longed to know more about her, and confirm who was the guardian figure she kept referring to, but he'd have to go about it more carefully. In his first moment of wakefulness when she was at his bedside with her surprising tenderness, he'd been lulled into asking: 'Did you live here with your family?'

He'd been toying with the idea that Bela might be Elin Sherwell's daughter, though she looked nothing like the pictures he'd seen on his first escapee's file. But time and experience changed people. Or there could be a sister. He hoped it was a way in.

She tensed, drew away, looking at him in silent reproach.

'*Ti Mam? Tad?*' he added tentatively. His attempts to use her words, however pathetic, usually softened her. Not this time.

Bela stood, muttering in her impenetrable language, slammed the spoon she'd been about to hand him into the bowl of soup on the bedside table and stormed out of the room.

That reaction had taught him to curb his curiosity and wait for the right moment. What was the hurry? It looked like he was going to be here for some time.

He sat up and the headache pounded. Opening the window and taking in a deep draught of air helped. He saw her go out into the yard with the plate of scraps she regularly put out for the animals. She turned and betrayed no surprise as she saw him. Amazed by the way his curiosity had turned to fondness, amazed that fondness was possible after her outburst, he smiled. She returned it before putting the plate down, turning away and going off into the woods without a further sign. The setting sun's rays through the canopy made her path seem ethereal.

113

He hoped she'd gone searching for something to dampen his headache, then told himself not to be so self-centred. The fresh air seemed to be doing some good, so he dressed, pausing a moment to look at the shirt with the motley repairs she'd done for him, and went outside. On the way, he picked up a book from the shelf in the living room. Pausing to pet one of the cats that came, tail up, to meet him, he sat on a rough-hewn but comfortable seat carved from a weathered log and looked at the book he'd chosen, judging it entirely by its cover. It was a library book stamped in the old-fashioned way with a return date of 5 May 2035. He smiled to himself as he imagined playing the gallant and offering to pay the fine for her. It must amount to enough by now to buy a whole library, though they were extremely unlikely to come knocking at the door.

He opened it and looked at a woodcut illustration of a forest not unlike this one. There was something about a book that you just couldn't replicate on a PD. Though it couldn't auto translate like a PD: realising he'd picked up one in Welsh, he stared at the words, even more incomprehensible than Bela's spoken ones. He looked at a couple of random pages and saw from the layout that it was a collection of poetry. He never read poetry. Yet the allure of the words called to him, like holding an old CD or vinyl disc by a musician you love but with no means to play it. Drowsy in the dappled evening light, he leafed through, looking at the woodcuts, studying them in a way that he'd rarely, if ever, done before. As the evening air grew cooler, he moved indoors with the sitting room window open.

She found him there, engrossed in the patterns of the words and wondering if he'd ever learn to understand them. She said the name of the poet, a question in her voice. Reluctant to break the spell, he simply held up the book, pointing between it and her, eyebrows raised.

'Darllen?' she asked.

He nodded, eager to hear her read.

114

'*Bwyd yn gyntaf,*' she announced, turning to leave and head for the kitchen. She was right; he realised how hungry he was.

'*Heno,*' he said. She paused, turned back to him. '*Ti – darllen.*'

He must have made himself understood because she smiled. '*Ti – gitar,*' she said.

Far from the warm anticipation of an evening's togetherness of reading and playing to one another, the mood darkened when they sat down to eat. He could tell from her expression that something was worrying her before she pounced on him with the news. She began with her usual combination of incomprehensible words and expansive gestures.

'Stop.'

She stared at him.

'This sounds important. *Pwysig.* Please.' Whatever it was seemed too serious for lessons or language politics, though he held back from saying so out loud. 'Tell me.'

'They were here.' Her accent was strong, her voice hesitant in the unaccustomed language. 'A man and woman... from the same place that hurt Her like the men that hurt you?'

He put down his knife and fork.

'They can look but they won't find us.' She shrugged. 'They went.'

'Where were they? How do you know they won't be back?'

'By the dead tree on the road the one that keeps us safe.'

She told him about the encounter and the sign on the wrong house. For once pleased about the lack of power and PD signal, he nevertheless wondered if it was enough for them to believe that the house was wrecked and that he had moved on, seeking a different refuge.

'*Dan ni'n ddiogel,*' she said. 'Safe. *Paid â phoeni.* Don't worry but you must know you must be careful.'

He shook his head. 'I should leave. I don't want to mess things up for you.'

'*Na!*' She looked more scared by the thought of him going than any potential intruders. '*Ti ddim yn iach 'to.* You... you're not well.'

115

'But—'

'They won't come back.'

He recalled their first encounter, his heart sinking even further. 'You didn't...'

She shook her head. 'I didn't kill them I don't kill people only when... They went.'

She tucked into her food as if to prove a clear conscience, refusing to say another word on the matter. He had to agree with her that he was in no fit state to be setting out into the unknown.

# PART V

# YNYS HUDOL

The members of our Seeder community came with a wide range of belief systems, including no religion at all – even the two of us differ in this. One thing we all have in common, we believe, is a deep spiritual love of our island and respect for the wider world, as well as a sense of gratitude for the place in which we find ourselves.

We tolerate – if that's not too cold a word; let's say accept and embrace – all beliefs, even if we don't share them, and we have kept the old school and meeting room, itself a former chapel, as a public space for quiet prayer and contemplation when not in use as the schoolroom.

We believe, however, and this was agreed at an early Gathering, that a certain amount of ceremony gives cohesion to our society and a structure to the year. This is one reason we hold our Gatherings regularly, regardless of whether there are many, or any, pressing issues to discuss. We also have our own devised ceremonies – secular but with plenty of space and contemplative moments for people to import their own layers of meaning. This may seem artificial and contrived at first, but we hope they will become a natural part of our lives. We hold these at each solstice, not because we consider the pagan way to have precedence, but because it makes sense to mark the passing of the seasons – especially as our weather systems are getting ever more erratic. We mark the equinoxes with special games in spring and a cultural festival along the lines of the Welsh Eisteddfod tradition in the autumn.

'Frugality' is not the same as asceticism; just because we believe over-consumption is the root cause of humankind's problems doesn't mean we don't know how to enjoy ourselves.

*Extract from* Seeds of Change
*by Edith Turner and Bleddyn Price, 2047.*

# THE WEEKLY GATHERING

Since leaving home, Sandy had felt the rhythm of days slipping away. After the intense confusion of her illness and quarantine, she was now back to keeping track meticulously. Understandably, the islanders' weeks seemed to revolve around what needed doing rather than specified working days. They enjoyed leisure time, and possibly even had more of it than back home, but it wasn't defined by evenings and weekends.

Nevertheless, the weekly Gathering was held with strict regularity. Since she'd been on the island proper, she'd missed two and, despite tiring easily and generally being ready to retire to her room soon after they'd eaten, she decided it was time to see a Gathering for herself.

There would be drink – beer made from nettles to keep as much as possible of the grain they grew for food, and a selection of hedgerow wines and spirits – along with music, dance and storytelling: entertainment in a world without a TV in every house. She'd read in *Seeds of Change* that the business meeting was always followed by a social evening, which sometimes also extended to plays or films, since art and culture were essential to a flourishing life. She smiled to herself. It seemed like as good a way as any to do politics, if it worked. She gave some thought to her own story and how much she was prepared to tell. Despite Helyg's assurance that she didn't have to, she'd agreed to introduce herself publicly, and however brief she kept it, she was expecting to face a few questions. She couldn't blame them for wanting to know more about the stranger in their midst. And who knew, maybe she'd have the chance to find out more about some of them, too. For Liv's sake if not her own – she couldn't help wondering how much their Compassionate Silence was hiding.

She had no idea what to wear for the occasion. Helyg and the girls simply shrugged, saying it was up to her what she wore and no one would be judging, but she'd noticed that on evenings like this Helyg wore a colourful skirt she said had been her mother's, one of the few things she'd brought from her old life. Sandy took it as an opportunity to wear some of the clothes she'd been gifted. Someone had brought her a gorgeous linen skirt with flowers embroidered around the hem and it seemed that now was her chance; she'd never seen anything but practical trousers or shorts during the daytimes.

On her walks, she'd admired the roundhouse from the outside. Beautifully suited to its surroundings, from the outside it looked like a grassy mound, with an overhang around the base that, if you looked closely, was formed by eaves and a circle of windows. As they entered through a dusky passage, she realised the meeting area was slightly below ground and these windows poured down a gentle light from above. As she gazed up at the sturdy, spoke-like beams, Erik, who had shown no hard feelings since his abrupt departure from the clifftop a couple of days ago, explained that the smoke was simply allowed to drift out through the thatch. The accumulating smoke meant they only brought in the fire basket when the warmth or a ceremonial fire was essential. She didn't need him to tell her how ingenious the building's design was; nestling in a natural hollow in the ground, the circular space with its gently tiered circles of benches was insulated against extremes of temperature, and the solid, low-lying grassed roof shrugged off gales like a rock in the wildest riverflow.

He pointed out a passage leading through to the large store and kitchens where the weekly communal meals were prepared. She still hadn't been to one of these meals, since on communal days families sometimes chose to take food back to their homes if there were special circumstances – like having an invalid mainlander staying with you, she thought. Erik also told her that most of the community sheltered here during the worst storms, and the passage meant they had everything they needed without venturing outside.

A potent reminder of the increasing excesses of storms, here and back on the mainland.

The beams of the main hall were adorned with carvings and trinkets, and the circular walls hung with a mishmash of posters and artwork in varying degrees of home-made warmth and passion. Well-meaning slogans, such as Be The Change, The Waters Are Rising And So Are We, Conscientious Protector, made her shudder as she thought of the activism that had caused so much trouble and unhappiness for so many, and she concentrated instead on an intricate tapestry, clearly the work of several different but equally skilled hands, with scenes of nature and harmonious community surrounding the motto *Empathy-Humility-Frugality*. She also made out the Welsh words *Cyfoethog pob dyn a wêl ei ddigon*, which Glesni told her was the equivalent of 'enough is as good as a feast'. There were benches all around; for the first time she'd see the community come together and get a real impression of its size. Cai had quoted 'sixty-odd', but she imagined it would seem bigger with everyone together in this atmospheric space. Glesni arranged the blankets and cushions they'd brought and they sat down, Erik to one side of her and Glesni to the other, Tom beyond her. Haf had hurried over to a group of friends and Helyg, after staking a place next to her partner, went over to talk to a group near the entrance. As the Seeders drifted in, Sandy noticed that, although people were curious, some nodding a friendly greeting, they kept a distance as if she were still surrounded by an invisible miasma of disease.

She had the impression that the Joneses were respected members of the community, but that didn't necessarily insulate their guest from a tinge of wary suspicion. Only Glesni's friend Tahira, the one she'd heard speaking Arabic, came to sit by them, the two men with her taking seats on the row behind them. She recognised the doctor, Khaled, who smiled warmly and introduced his nephew Rashid, Tahira's brother, with a warm smile.

As the benches filled, Helyg returned with a jug from a table near the passage to the store, and Glesni produced some cups, filling one and passing it to Sandy with a flourish.

'Fruit punch,' she said. 'Special Seeder recipe.'

Glesni was starting to relax in her company and smiled as if mocking her own exaggerated praise of all things Ynys Hudol. It did taste good, and Sandy was relieved to learn that stronger drinks weren't served until after the business part of the Gathering; it had been a long time since she'd drunk alcohol, she had no idea of the strength of their beer and wine, and she was determined not to make a fool of herself or say too much.

Gwylan stood and a hush descended. To Sandy's surprise she didn't step forward to the central space. It seemed that at a Gathering people spoke from their place on the benches. She made out Cai sitting across from them; he saw her looking and gave her a friendly smile. His son, Madog, whom she'd seen working with Erik, gave her his usual scowl. Sandy still wasn't sure if his dislike was for her personally, incomers, or other people in general.

Gwylan spoke a few words of welcome, deftly switching between Welsh and English, and announced a moment of silent contemplation. Sandy's thoughts revolved around gratitude for the welcome she'd received. She was surprised to realise how comfortable she felt. Cai was asked to give a reading, which Glesni whispered was usual – often from *Seeds of Change*, but anything to suit the occasion, really.

Although Ynys Hudol is set apart from mainland Cymru, its identity is strongly Cymraeg. We feel it's important to maintain this – including the bilingual production of this book – just as we have in our own lives: Bleddyn is a Cymro, from generations of a Welsh family, while Edith learned the language and culture when we came together.

Our ultimate aim is for Cymraeg to be the language of the island; however we don't want this to be at the expense of inclusivity.

Anyone joining our community will be encouraged to learn the language as part of settling in; however, we realise this will be harder for some people than others. So for the time being, Gatherings and other public aspects of island life will be bilingual. We hope this will be a temporary concession and Cymraeg will eventually assume its true status as the language of the community.

However it's important, practically and culturally, not to lose English in future, particularly if we're to achieve our aim of taking our message to the mainland. Also, one of our primary principles is to avoid conflict, and this includes linguistic and cultural conflict. English and its musical, literary and artistic heritage will therefore also be taught to Seeder children and valued within the community, while ensuring that this is a matter of choice, not dominance.

May the two cultures live side by side, nurture one another and be fruitful!

After the reading, Gwylan formally introduced Sandy, which seemed a superfluous courtesy given the steady stream of people who'd passed through the Jones house during the last couple of weeks. A few people were still trickling in, glancing round and making their way to scattered empty places on the benches, avoiding their section. The only exception was Idris, who parked himself next to Erik. During one particularly irritable bout of shuffling Glesni caught her eye and smiled as if to say she'd tell her later what their usual penalty was for latecomers when they didn't have the convenient threat of a plague victim.

'Is everyone comfortable?' Gwylan threw sharp looks towards the fidgeters. 'The sooner we can get through the community business, the sooner we can hear Sandy's story and then move on to the music.'

Sandy hoped the business wouldn't include the so-called purists' attitude to her boat. She was intrigued to know how far back towards the Stone Age their opinions went, but would rather find out without being their focus. Gwylan began with the task rota. Sandy had seen this pinned to the wall of the store, but it seemed it was announced verbally every week at the Gathering, presumably to make sure everyone took note.

Helyg and Tom were among those allocated to kitchen duty for the next fortnight. Haf, Glesni and a couple of others were designated to look after the animals, including keeping an eye on the ponies. Sandy could feel Glesni's delight without the need for words.

They then moved on to more general plans. Idris was asked about the long-range weather forecast and it seemed the unseasonably hot weather would last a while yet – he emphasised *unseasonably* in a lugubrious tone. There was no need for emergency duties yet, though there was some discussion about irrigation in a certain part of the island. They also discussed the need to clear the coastline to protect the seals and seabirds as a raft of rubbish had drifted ashore. Glesni had said something about a seagull the other day, and Sandy recalled endless TV news items that used to wash over her, like the debris they featured, but assumed a new relevance here on the island.

Having assembled a crew of beachcombers, Gwylan went on to say they'd have to think about scheduling a mainland trip before too long, though the planning could wait for now. During her pause to allow for questions, Glesni whispered that, as well as obtaining provisions, they also took the rubbish they collected back to the mainland, in the forlorn hope that it might be reprocessed and recycled. Despite some muttering from the direction of Steffan and his small group, no one spoke, obviously keen to move on to the interesting part. Gwylan then introduced Sandy, who steeled herself, disconcerted by the nerves she felt.

*Over to you.*

With a smile, she surveyed the expectantly waiting faces, most of them encouraging and even Madog and his mates less hostile than some that she'd encountered on her travels. She cleared her throat, hoping they wouldn't see this most normal gesture as a sign of lingering disease, and launched into her brief introduction.

'You've probably all heard by now that I was searching for my partner, Adam, when my boat broke down and Erik here rescued me.' Glancing in his direction, she was surprised to receive an encouraging smile. She told them little more than she'd told Cai, concentrating on her journey across the unusually quiet landscape of northern Cymru. Despite the islanders' determined apartness there was a fascination for mainland life beyond the coastal stretches they visited on their occasional forays. Yes, the government was more or less the same (loud expressions of disapproval); no, she wasn't a particular supporter but she had to live.

'Did you work for them?'

Caught off guard by a voice she didn't recognise, and the hint of hostility it contained, she tried and failed to spot the questioner.

'The government may have been flooded out of London, but that doesn't mean that everyone in Manchester or Birmingham works for them,' she said, reluctant to lie outright but more reluctant to admit the truth. 'I was made redundant shortly before I left, so, since I was unlikely to find another job very easily, I took the opportunity to set off in search of my partner.' They didn't need to know that 'redundant' was a rather positive spin and her connection to him and his actions had been partly responsible for her losing the job. She also kept to herself the notion that finding him could be the key to getting her position back, or even a better one. After a final flourish about the possibility of tracking him down in Ireland, she finished on the flattering note that from what she had seen, her unexpected arrival on Ynys Hudol could mean breaking her journey for longer than it took her to fully recover, maybe even for good. She had no idea whether her listeners would believe that any more than she did.

As she sat down, she caught a look that passed between Helyg and Tom. Did they know her story wasn't the whole truth, some parts not even the truth? Did it matter? If she were called out at any stage, she could always rely on their Compassionate Silence, with the added proviso that story wasn't the same as a lie.

She must have missed Gwylan's closing remarks; she realised Helyg was offering her wine now her ordeal was over. She nodded; Glesni went to fetch it. Tom made his way down to the middle of the roundhouse to join a small group of others and, to Sandy's surprise, picked up a guitar and started tuning it. She'd never heard him play, or seen the instrument, in the house; he must come here to practise.

'You've really been through it,' Haf said, genuine admiration in her eyes. 'You must really love him to have come this far for him.'

As she thought of Adam, the sound of instruments being tuned adding an additional, poignant reminder, she hoped the guilt didn't show. 'Some things you just have to do,' she said, as if her journey were as inevitable as fighting the infection once she'd reached the Quarantine Rock.

'What's he like, your Adam?'

Helyg shot her daughter a look of disapproval, but Sandy said, 'He was loyal. He did what he had to.' The loyalty was true, however questionable its object.

'I meant, what does he look like?'

Helyg smiled indulgently at Haf's insistent questioning, in a way that suggested she was content to take Sandy's story at face value after all.

'I've got a photo among my things somewhere. I'll show you when we get back.'

Haf nodded with a smile before being swept away by a girl about her age; Sandy thought she recognised her friend Angharad. As the teenagers made their way down the gap between two sets of benches, Glesni appeared carrying a tray. Engrossed in gossip with her friend, Haf jostled her, causing the drinks to spill. It unleashed a flood of angry Welsh.

Helyg called over, her tone and the girls' sheepish expressions all the translation Sandy needed, then turned to her and rolled her eyes. 'I do wish they weren't at each other's throats most of the time.'

She took a handkerchief from her pocket and used it to wipe the base of a stoneware cup proffered by Glesni. She handed the wine to Sandy and took her own with a nod of thanks to her daughter.

'Do you have any brothers or sisters?' Helyg asked as Glesni put the tray down and went to join Tahira.

'I had a sister,' she said. 'Olivia. We were close. Oh, we had our ups and downs like those two. But you know how it is, deep down.'

'Not really,' Helyg said after a pause. 'I'm an only child.'

The music struck up and the people who had been gathering in the centre of the room formed a circle.

'You want to dance?' Helyg asked.

Sandy was glad of the excuse of fatigue; even if she'd been in the best of health she preferred to watch, though she looked forward to joining in once she'd got the hang of it. It was a circle dance, similar to the 'authentix' craze that had enjoyed a few months of being on trend back home, until the fashion moved on. The Seeders took it to new heights, with a level of feeling she'd never seen, maybe because the music was all acoustic, as she imagined it should be. The circle sometimes broke into pairs, apart for a while before effortlessly weaving back together. She watched, entranced, glad she'd sat it out until she'd seen more. After a climactic set, the lights dimmed, the dancers dispersed for a break and Tom sang, accompanied by a small group of others. Again, Sandy was amazed by the depth and intensity of the sound. Maybe it was the rich, sweet wine, maybe it was her growing drowsiness – maybe it really was as special as it seemed.

The set came to an end and the musicians moved aside. Above the chatter she could hear the occasional boom of an amplified system being set up and recalled what Glesni had said about the rationed powered entertainment. She saw her gathering on the dance floor with Tahira, Haf, Angharad and a few other teenagers – some older people too – and was impressed by the way they switched styles as effortlessly as they switched language. As the first beats filled the roundhouse, she was hit by another wave of nostalgia.

'Are you OK?'

Helyg looked concerned. Sandy felt guilty; everyone seemed to have dispersed, and Helyg must've been eager to join Tom and her friends. She smiled.

'I'm fine. You go and join them if you like. I was miles away.'

'Thinking of people at home? Your sister?'

Ambushed by the warmth of the evening, Sandy's guard was down. She nodded.

'You referred to her in the past. What happened to her?'

'You don't want to know.'

'I'll understand if you don't want to talk about it.'

'It's not that. I just...' Sandy felt closer to Helyg than at any time since she'd been there, and was reluctant to spoil it. She thought again of their Compassionate Silence. But no; they'd have to know sometime. 'She was one of the first "casualties" of the unrest – the civil war, as you call it. A victim of your resistance.'

Frowning, Helyg was looking across the room as if unable to meet her eye.

'Maybe that was a bit harsh. I doubt you had anything to do with it personally. But... Irlas?'

Helyg gave a slight nod, took a sip of her drink.

'My sister was a journalist.' Sandy kept her voice low. She was already regretting telling Helyg, and certainly didn't want anyone else to hear. 'Liv wanted to understand. She knew it wasn't as simple as a load of stubborn, narrow-minded nationalists proving a point, and she spent some time getting to know the people involved. There was a family at the heart of the protests. Liv got quite close to Elin Sherwell in particular. But as it developed into a siege – you remember hearing about it? – she couldn't gain access to the construction site where the protests were. However much she sympathised, and stayed around to report it, she wasn't going to go so far as to barricade herself in with them. She did her best to convey your people's concerns and point of view to her readers back home, right to the end. She wasn't actually killed in the bomb blast, though seventeen people were – seventeen, Helyg – but she might as well have been. She was paralysed and needed care for the rest of her life.'

'I'm sorry. I mean it.' Helyg twisted her cup in her hands. 'We—'

'My mum and dad both died in the SarsCov-39 pandemic,' Sandy said, determined to finish now she'd begun. 'Liv took her own life shortly after. She left me a note: *We're both free now.* She was free of her pain and her curtailed life, and I... I took it to mean she didn't want to be a burden.'

She took a drink from her cup. It was comforting.

'That's so sad,' Helyg said. 'It was a dreadful day. It should never have happened.'

'Really? I assumed... well, I got the impression that you – that most people here were nationalists.' She allowed her gaze to fix on the beams above them. Some of the symbols among the carvings were unmistakable.

'You're not wrong,' Helyg said. 'But most people – I'd say everyone here, even the Defenders – believe there are better ways of achieving our aims than violence.'

Sandy shook her head. 'But that's not what happened, was it? Keeping things peaceful?'

'It wasn't like you think.' Helyg's voice was almost inaudible.

'Think? I know. I saw my sister's fate with my own eyes. Liv totally respected what they were doing. Because she was convinced they were non-violent. Even afterwards, she wasn't upset so much by what they did to her, but because she thought they'd betrayed their own principles.'

'We – they – were determined not to hurt anyone. They were infiltrated.'

Sandy gave a snort of derision. 'You can't honestly believe that. I understand you want to make excuses, but—'

'The first time of many. The English government wanted to incite a war they knew our small nation could never win. They were safe because no one would believe they'd use such tactics. As your reaction shows.'

'You're right about *that*. I don't believe it.'

She put her cup down on the bench beside her and shook her head when Helyg offered her a refill. As she watched the kids on the dance floor, surprising herself with the closeness she felt for Haf and Glesni among them, she realised she wasn't the only one to have dropped her guard. Helyg had said 'we', and corrected herself. She'd been involved somehow. Sandy didn't have the energy to pursue it right now. A combination of the increasing volume and her own fatigue threatened to overwhelm her. She stood.

'I think I'd better be getting back. It's been lovely, but I'm tired now.'

Helyg made to stand but Sandy gestured for her to stay. 'I'll be fine.'

'Come on, I'll see you home; I've had enough sociability for one night,' Erik said, appearing at her side. Sandy wondered how long he'd been there. Whether he'd heard any of their conversation; whether he, too, had any involvement along with his daughter. This time, as they walked back, saying little beneath the friendly stars, she welcomed his lack of small talk.

# HIS BRIEF BOUT OF EXPANSIVENESS

Sandy straightened, taking a pause from weeding the raised beds, glad of her convalescence as an excuse for being totally unfit for this kind of work. She looked up the hill beyond the walls of the courtyard, wondering if her walk a couple of days ago had been frowned upon as prioritising pleasure over work. Though it had hardly been pleasurable. She'd heard raised voices from Erik's workshop the day after, and hoped it wasn't on her account. Thinking back, she'd managed to convince herself she'd got the lad's directions wrong. She hadn't spoken to Madog since – the workshop was empty now – and hoped he didn't blame her; he'd seemed hostile enough without a grudge to bear.

Through the open gates of the walled courtyard, she watched Erik making his way from the direction of the harbour. Not for the first time she wondered about his pronounced limp, surprised at how it rarely hindered him; he'd been agile enough when rescuing her from the birds' cliff. She asked herself if they were relaxed enough yet in each other's company for her to ask him.

He gave her a wave, then a friendly smile as he approached. 'You look as if you could do with a rest.'

Standing as she was, leaning a touch too heavily on the long-handled fork, she wondered if there was a hint of sarcasm in his voice.

'Fancy a cuppa?'

Sarcasm or no, she accepted gratefully and he went through the workshop into his cottage to put the kettle on the stove. She washed the dirt from her hands with water from the butt by the door and he called out that she was looking well.

It was all relative, she supposed. When she'd set out, the latest pandemic looked about to become the deadliest, percentage-wise, and she felt lucky to be alive despite the lingering debilitation. She wondered aloud to him whether her tiredness was actually post-infection fatigue, or maybe she simply needed to get used to the tough outdoorsiness of life on Aniseed.

He smiled again as he joined her on the outside bench with two mugs, steaming with the scent of his daughter's special blend of dried berries and flowers.

'I've always been into "tough outdoorsiness" – nice phrase, by the way – even before... before things began to change, so I couldn't say. Whatever, love, there's no shame in taking your time and letting your body toughen up at its own pace.'

Encouraged both by his words and his forthright manner, she found herself asking about the reason for his limp.

He frowned, gazing out over the garden and the fields to the sea. She'd pushed it too far; he was about to clam up again. 'I—'

'No need to apologise.'

She didn't know whether to feel relief or annoyance at his assumption.

'Sorry if I was snappy the other day. It's just... memories, you know?' he continued. 'I know we're not supposed to think about things as they used to be, but...'

He gazed at the sea through the archway as if putting the Seeders' Compassionate Silence into practice and she wondered how long to wait before nudging him. Eventually, he sighed.

'Every now and then it hits me.' He gave the slightest shrug. 'You've lost someone special, haven't you?'

She nodded.

'But you're hoping to find him. I wish you luck. Me, I know she's dead.'

It wasn't Adam she was thinking of. But this wasn't the time to bring up Liv. 'You were right; I shouldn't—'

'Not you. Memories,' he said again. 'Nothing to do with... Anyway.' He patted his leg. 'This. I guess you're expecting a good story?'

She gave him a *go on* nod.

'Sorry to disappoint. There are plenty of stories in this place, and plenty of people better at telling them than I am. Tom, for one. He's more of a singer, but between songs, on a good night... And our Helyg. Gets it from her mam, I guess. Certainly not me. Not that you can believe most of them.' He paused and took a sip of his tea. 'By the time people pick and choose what to tell, and those listening pick and choose what to believe – well, let's just say it's more interesting than real life. Depending on what you find interesting, of course.'

She smiled. 'If you don't want to tell me, Erik, just say.'

He laughed. 'There I was trying to give you a proper introduction. Ease you in gently to the king of all anti-climaxes.'

'Well?' She was relieved his momentary melancholy seemed to have lifted.

He drank his tea as if it were all part of the performance. 'I don't have a storyteller's imagination so I'll give it to you straight. I used to work a pub. Lovely riverside pub, it was. I daresay it won't be there anymore. Haven't been back since we moved away; years ago it was. Not long before Helyg was born; her mam wanted her to be born in Cymru, see – and she's, what, 34 now. Anyhow, that river was restless even then, the floods getting ever more frequent, which means the village, including the pub, has probably embarked on a Clearance of its own by now. Sorry, none of that has anything to do with my leg. I was cycling back from work one night – we lived just outside the village; maybe our place is still there if the river's been kind. And I got knocked off my bike by a hit-and-run driver.' He shrugged. 'Sorry there's none of the excitement you were looking for.'

'It sounds awful. Did they find the culprit?'

His expression darkened. 'Turned out it was someone we knew.'

'Really? That must have been upsetting.'

'Oh, it was. A long time ago now, though.' He stood stiffly and reached for her empty mug. 'A lot of water under the bridge. Now, I wonder if that bridge is still standing?'

He turned abruptly, as if Sandy wasn't the only one surprised by his brief bout of expansiveness. 'Stuff to do. Nice talking to you, love.'

He went inside and closed the door behind him.

Later, she was helping Helyg prepare the evening meal, the last one she'd make at home before their period of communal kitchen duty.

'I hope I didn't upset your dad earlier,' she said.

Helyg scoffed. 'Wouldn't be hard. Go on, what did you do?'

'I asked him about his limp.'

'Clam up on you, did he?'

'No, the opposite. I know men – older men in particular – don't like admitting signs of weakness and I regretted asking the minute I opened my mouth, but... He got to saying how he missed your mother, but then telling the story seemed to brighten him up. Maybe a bit too bright, to be honest, which is why I hope—'

'He *told* you?'

The chopping of Helyg's kitchen knife became louder and more staccato.

'In a roundabout sort of way,' Sandy ventured. It seemed she really had hit a sore spot. 'I'm sorry if I overstepped the mark.'

Helyg gave a brittle laugh. 'I suppose you can't stop men boasting about their war wounds.'

Sandy couldn't help thinking of Adam, who'd been physically unharmed but nevertheless changed.

'Less of the boasting.' Erik appeared in the doorway. 'She asked.'

Helyg put her knife down and turned to face him. If it had been a film, her movement would have been in slow motion. 'And you told her. I thought—'

'Hardly a war wound, though, was it, love? Not exactly heroic, to get knocked off your bike. Though you could say that cycling everywhere, in all weathers, was one way of fighting the good fight.'

Helyg tossed her head. 'Cycling everywhere in all weathers!' Her voice was as over-bright as Erik's telling of the story had been. 'What did I tell you? Boasting.'

'You remember it?' The question sounded stilted to Sandy's own ears, but better than asking outright how much of this she could believe. 'The pub, the village by the river?'

'Nah, Mam and Dad moved away before I was born. Didn't he tell you?' She turned to look at her father. 'Of course I heard plenty about it. I was named after the place – they grew willows there, my mam used to make baskets and stuff. That's what it means, *helyg* – willows. Though it's my middle name; my first name's Hope. They wanted to call me something more Cymraeg as I was growing up – and I guess there wasn't much hope left by then, was there?' She threw her father an accusing look. 'Mam once said she had real difficulty persuading him to have a child. Honestly, Dad, sometimes I don't know why you changed your mind.'

She turned away, hiding her expression.

'Listen, love, there's no need...' Erik moved awkwardly to put a hand on her arm.

She shook him off, turning to Sandy. 'I can never get him to talk about those days, about Mam.'

*But he talked to you*, she might as well have said.

'I'm sorry,' Sandy offered, 'I didn't mean to...'

'I know you didn't.' She sniffed. 'Look, if you want to help, can you pop out to the garden and get me a cabbage? They're down the far end, past the bean poles.'

Sandy hovered by the door as long as she dared but the pair of them had lapsed into their characteristic taciturnity. She was genuinely sorry to have raked up the past, but she was also fairly certain that Helyg's first *He told you?* was not referring to the same thing at all. She reckoned she had a pretty good sense of when people were hiding something – she couldn't help thinking of Adam – and wondered where Glesni was, whether next time they were on their own together she'd find a way of broaching the subject without upsetting her, too.

She got her chance a couple of days later. Glesni was laying a treasure hunt for the smaller children and invited her along. 'Taid said you'd appreciate the exercise.'

He did, did he? She decided to trust that he was thinking of her own good. And it sounded fun.

'It's the first time I've set it,' Glesni said as they set off. 'I was one of the little ones following the clues last time.'

Clearly proud to be allowed to lay the trail, she had a bag full of clues and as they went along explained to Sandy how it was a May tradition.

'We have a special Gathering to celebrate spring, and of course the kids' treasure hunt every year. We – they,' she corrected herself, 'they love it, but it's also a clever way of getting them to notice things around them.'

Sandy could see why Glesni had been chosen to set it – she certainly noticed things.

'So what's the treasure?'

Glesni patted the bag on her shoulder. She'd devised a series of clues, each one leading to the next via a trail of directions formed from arrangements of pebbles, sticks and leaves. At each point there was also an item, which represented the gifts they'd receive at the end. Cerys had been holding craft workshops during the previous couple of months as the days began to lengthen, and the adults came and went, making the gifts for the children. They were given out once everyone had successfully completed the treasure hunt.

'They used to be hidden in boxes with the clues, but some groups went faster than others, especially the older ones, and swiped them all – including special ones a mam or dad had made for a particular child. You can imagine the tears and the tantrums. This way it means everyone works together and they all get their reward. Though the winners still get an extra prize – we mix up the ages in the groups to make it fair.'

From the tangled roots of a sweet-smelling gorse bush to a dusty disused burrow at the base of a drystone wall, from familiar dandelions to less familiar pennywort, the course took them all over the island, to parts Sandy knew and hidden coves, hollows and coppices that she hadn't yet seen. They paused to rest after climbing a steep rise. As she got her breath back, Sandy broached the subject that had been nagging her, wondering if Glesni could give her any clue – even if she couldn't produce it out of her bag – about Helyg's strange reaction to Erik's story.

'Has your Taid told you the story of how he got his limp?'

Glesni smiled. 'The bike accident? Of course.'

So that much was true.

'He mentioned it to me the other day, but your mum didn't like him talking about it. How come?'

'I'm not surprised.' Glesni rolled her eyes. 'She never talks about the old days. Neither does he, really. I think he fell out with my nain – my grandmother. Don't ask me how or why, but if it's true I can see why Mam isn't happy about it. It's probably why he didn't come here till a couple of years after she did. I wish they'd tell me more. It's like our family's very own Compassionate Silence.'

Sandy was surprised at the note of disapproval in the girl's voice over the last two words. She never complained about their community's traditions. 'Don't you think that's a good thing? Leaving the past behind and concentrating on what you have now?'

'Of course,' Glesni said. 'I just hate not knowing about my own family. But if you have rules, and you agree they're there for a good reason, I guess you can't pick and choose when to obey them.'

She stood, brushing off her trousers. 'Come on, you've rested enough now. Time to get going.'

Sandy got to her feet. Although she was dying to know more about the revelation that Erik, seemingly estranged from his wife and family, had not come to the island with them, it was clear that now wasn't the time to pursue it. She told herself she was just being nosy, and she clearly wouldn't find out from Glesni.

The girl paused and pointed to a house standing on its own below them.

'Have you met Anti Martha?'

Someone was wheeling the old lady out in a wheelchair to look at the sea.

'Not yet, though I've heard about her.'

'The oldest person on the island,' Glesni said. 'Then Taid, then Idris. I love going to visit her.'

She shielded her eyes with her hand and watched the two small figures come to a stop not far from the house.

'Poor Martha,' she continued. 'She adores this time of year, but she can't go far now.'

'What's the matter with her?'

'Cancer. She had an operation, so they say.' She shrugged. 'Back in the days when we could still go to the mainland for that kind of thing, long before I was born. She was fine for years but it's crept back. Awen sees to it that she's not in too much pain, but Lucy, that's her carer, there, says she can't even be in the wheelchair for long before she needs to go back to bed. At least she's closer to the sea now.'

'Closer?'

'Have you seen the pictures in the roundhouse? There used to be a stretch of fields between Anti Martha's and the sea. This side of the island's getting smaller. I doubt Martha will be the last to live there, but it won't be long before the house will be in danger of flooding during a spring tide.'

Sandy thought it didn't seem close enough to the waterline to be a problem, and was struck by another hint of how bad the elements could be here. She was ambushed by respect for the tenacity of this small community.

# SHE STEERED THE BOAT IN SMOOTHLY

Glesni breathed in the special pre-dawn air, aware of birds waking up and boasting about it. Taid's house across the courtyard was silent and in darkness. It was hard to believe he'd left without her. Had he called her, quietly so as not to wake the others, and she'd missed it? Did he trust her to wake and rise without prompting? Something caught her eye by the courtyard gate. A flat stone with a smaller one on top. She noticed a leaf pinned to the ground by a twig, looking for all the world like a boat with a mast, and as she went closer to inspect it, saw an arrow sketched in the dirt, pointing down the track towards the harbour.

She smiled. His secret clue gave her a warm feeling. While she'd been out laying the trail the day before, they'd finished the work on the boat. He'd told them over dinner that Gwylan had suggested he took it for a test run. Which he'd inflated into a fishing trip.

'She wasn't too happy – said I should just go for a quick spin – but I know Gwylan; she wasn't going to argue too hard,' he'd said. 'Bloody purists. I should take it as a compliment, but even with my skills I'm hardly going to take every mackerel that ever swam the Irish Sea.' He'd grinned at Sandy. 'They don't have to eat it but the rest of us can enjoy a good, healthy bit of variety.'

Glesni was setting off down the track when she heard the door to the house open and close, followed by footsteps on the track.

'Glesni! Wait.'

Sandy came hurrying towards her.

'Are you going out on the boat? Where's Erik?'

'He's gone to get it ready.' She indicated the clues and Sandy smiled.

'There'll be room for another on board?'

Glesni shrugged; it was natural that Sandy should want to

come, but she was beginning to feel as if she followed them everywhere.

'It *is* technically my boat.'

She had a point. Glesni nodded, unable to think of an excuse. They set off down the track, the sky tinged by the sun as it rose unseen over the mainland. Hidden from view by the mountain, its pink hues lit up the clouds and the expanse of sea beyond the fields. A herring gull squawked and headed out over the waves, wings hardly flapping, gliding smoothly as if pulled on a string. She imagined it telling its friends of their intention and looked forward to them flocking around the boat. The sound of their sandals crunching on the gravel was whisked away by the stiff breeze. She savoured the coolness; it was going to be hot later.

As they neared the harbour she saw him, loading the boat with fishing tackle and a couple of crates. Glancing at Sandy, she put two fingers to her mouth and whistled. The Seeders' call, distinctively unlike any gull.

He looked round, his smile quickly fading. He might as well have said out loud, did you have to bring *her*? Glesni tried to convey without speaking that she'd had no choice and hoped that his expression hadn't been too obvious to Sandy before he turned back to his loading.

As Sandy clambered awkwardly on board, Glesni gave her a reassuring smile, hiding her disappointment that she'd invaded one of her special times on the boat with Taid. Once they were ready, she untied the mooring ropes and threw them on board, jumping on after them and coiling them neatly as Taid steered the boat beyond the jetty and out to sea.

Glancing at Sandy, who had taken a seat in the cabin, she took her place on one of the benches along the side of the boat. Like she always did. Not betraying a hint of resentment.

As they bounced gently away from the jetty she leaned over the side, rocked by the boat cutting through the undulating waves, mesmerised by the glinting spray. Looking back at the rocks she saw

142

a cormorant, wings spread out to dry. She often liked to mimic him, arms outstretched, building strength in her upper arms, stamina against the growing ache. Aware of Sandy's presence, she checked the childish impulse. Why childish? She wouldn't have felt self-conscious if it had been just her and Taid. Flexing her shoulders, she looked back to see the bird flapping away.

Once they were beyond the rocks that guarded the bay, she went over to the cabin. It felt strange not to be hoisting the sail – the *Otranto* had no mast, so as long as they were moving they'd rely on the motor, even beyond the stronger currents. She hoped that once he'd negotiated the rocks around the island and chosen a course, Taid would let her take control. Glesni paused in the cabin doorway, gripping the frame tightly despite the gentleness of the swell. She prayed he wasn't about to hand over to Sandy.

Taid gestured to the wheel.

'Can you take the helm, Pwt? I want to go check things over. You'll find she handles beautifully.'

Warmed by pride, Glesni went over to stand at the wheel, her relief tempered by embarrassment at his use of *she* for a boat, which irritated just about anyone who heard him. As ever she reminded herself it was stubborn old-fashionedness rather than disrespect, but she couldn't help glancing at Sandy. If she noticed, she didn't show it.

After briefly indicating the course and the area around a scattering of circling and diving gulls where they'd stop to try their luck, he started pottering about, leaning over the back to check the propeller, listening to the motor, taking out his battered glasses to peer at the charge gauges. Despite his activity she imagined him ready to step in at any moment, but he didn't stand over her. It felt good to be trusted. Heading out west on the open sea there were no hidden rocks lurking in wait, but even on a day like this the currents could be strong.

'You look at home there,' Sandy said after a long pause.

'I suppose so. I've been out quite a lot but it's only the last couple of times he's begun to let me take the controls, when we're alone together. Are you sure you're feeling well enough to be out at sea?'

'I won't get any better by sitting round on my arse. I've never had seasickness – not that I've been on boats much.' She sighed. 'Seriously, Glesni, I can't believe how weak I am. Knackered all the time. But Awen called by when I was sitting outside the house yesterday evening; said she thought the sea air might do me good. And... I wanted to see how my boat is after all the TLC.'

*My* boat. Fresh air or not, Glesni doubted she'd have been here if it had been *Berta*. Taid seemed to have the same idea. He straightened, tucked his glasses into his breast pocket and looked straight at Sandy.

'Like I said before, I'm too old to go off seeing the world in someone else's boat,' he said. 'Quite happy here, thank you.' He waved towards his granddaughter. 'And Glesni knows what she's doing. Your *Otranto's* quite safe on all counts.'

'I never meant—'

'No.' He laughed, an edge to his voice. 'I'm sure you didn't. Anyway, do you want to help me get the nets ready? Might as well have a go while you're here.'

'Make myself a few enemies?'

She caught Glesni's eye and smiled as she left the cabin, to lean against the newly painted metal wall and watch him.

'I'm sure you're more than a match for any purist,' Taid said.

Of course, Steffan had called round, rudely interrupting the family meal, and had made a fuss about seeing Taid readying his fishing gear. The same old arguments. As if the *Otranto* was equipped with vast lengths of mechanical trawling gear.

By the time they stopped to drift among the diving gulls, the sun was well above the horizon. The hint of sea mist had dissipated and the sky was clear. Before settling in to fish, Glesni took off the thick shirt she'd had on to protect against the onshore wind. She'd have to put it back on before too long to avoid sunburn, but for now she had her sun hat and enjoyed the freedom and fresh air of short sleeves. Sandy followed suit; Taid passed her a peaked cap they'd found in one of the cupboards that lined the cabin.

Before readying the rods, Taid set up the awning he'd brought from *Berta*. It wasn't perfect – *Otranto* was longer and wider so its coverage was limited – but the shade it gave was welcome. Glesni showed Sandy how to fix the bait and cast. Despite the shade from the awning, there was only a slight stirring of a breeze from the sea and it was getting hotter by the minute. Taid's activity, though hardly exertion, had brought him out in a sweat.

'You must be sweltering, wrapped up like that,' Sandy said.

He shrugged, fingering the oak-leaf pendant at his neck, which drew attention to Bleddyn's paisley scarf he'd been given and always wore since his friend had died.

'I'm not wearing anything under this shirt.' He glanced at her before gazing out over the sparkling waves. 'I could tell what the weather's going to be like so I didn't see the point in layering up.'

'But aren't—'

'We can't just pop to the shop and buy a new garment when things wear out, you know. No click-and-collect here. You get used to wearing what's necessary, nothing more.'

'You could take it off. I wouldn't mind.'

'I'm fine.'

'Don't want you getting heat stroke.'

He laughed. 'I'm not used to being fussed over. Carry on, I'm loving the attention.'

'Don't flatter yourself.' She rolled her eyes. 'It was the same when you were working on the boat the other day. I don't want you being uncomfortable on my account.'

'You can rest easy. I'm just trying to protect myself.'

'Bullet-proof fabric?'

His laugh sounded forced. Glesni thought of the magnificent tattoos covering his arms and upper body like a garland. Even though she rarely saw them, it had never occurred to her before that

145

his scarf and long-sleeved shirts might be deliberately hiding them. Why would he?

'Over-exposure to the sun,' he said. 'Skin cancer.'

He looked relieved when Sandy gave a little shriek as her fishing rod bobbed and he showed her how to reel it in. No sooner had she got over her squeamishness about dealing with the flapping fish than she got another bite. The gulls had shown them the right place. After a while they reeled in the net, and even after selecting the fish carefully the box was almost full, the iridescent scales reflecting the sparkling sea. Enough to share with those who wanted it for a treat that night and some left over to hang and dry for leaner times ahead. Looking at the topsy-turvy plight of them drowning in air, Glesni wondered about the predator in people.

Satisfied that they'd caught enough, they paused for a while to enjoy the snack they'd brought.

'Don't eat too much,' Taid said. 'Fish supper tonight.'

They sat, admiring the easy grace of the gulls. A couple of dolphins approached – a rare sight even for Taid and Glesni. Sandy was ecstatic. After a while, they swam off; time to leave. Glesni was proud to be at the helm, Sandy sitting in the cabin beside her, and Taid outside tidying up the equipment. The island grew larger and she got that wonderful feeling of home. She loved being out at sea, but she loved more the sight of Ynys Hudol's magical rocks spreading towards them like welcoming arms. She wondered what it felt like for Sandy, still new here.

'Who owns the island now?'

Clearly she wasn't entirely overwhelmed by the magic of the place.

'I've never thought about it,' Glesni replied.

'Your founders, Edith and Bleddyn. Did they have family?'

She sounded serious.

'Not on the island,' Glesni said. 'As far as I know they never had kids.'

'All of us.' Taid appeared in the doorway, arms braced on the frame, swaying slightly with the movement of the boat. At first it sounded like he was making a philosophical statement about community, metaphorical brothers and sisters. 'It belongs to all of us.'

'Did you resurrect the trust?'

He shrugged. 'Nothing so complicated.'

'What if they have relatives on the mainland?' Sandy peered at the dark smudge on the horizon as if summoning a tribe of sons and daughters.

'They'd be welcome to join us. We'd sort out an empty house, or get a work party together to convert or build a new one. Like we would for you if you decide to stay. That's the way we do things.'

'You know that's not what I mean. So... they died intestate?' Taid shrugged again. 'And you don't—'

'Nope, we don't. We pool our resources. Share it all. Between ourselves and with the birds and the animals and the crawling insects and the grass and the flowers and the ancient lichens... You get the idea? We're happy with it.'

She said no more. As they neared the harbour – everyone's harbour – Glesni saw a small group waiting.

'Looks like we've got a welcoming party,' she called out.

Taid finished what he was doing and came to join them. 'Can't say as I'm surprised.'

It made no difference to the purists how infrequently the boat went out. Even if Taid and whoever was with him found anything worth catching, they only took what they needed, yet Steffan and maybe one or two others were there without fail like a self-appointed conscience. This time, however, Madog was there too, standing slightly apart.

Glesni offered to step aside for Taid to take the helm, but he shook his head. 'Go on, show them what you're made of.'

She felt more nervous than usual in front of an audience, but steered the boat in smoothly.

'Nice one,' Taid said as he jumped out onto the quay with a rope.

Madog stepped forward.

'Where is she?'

'Glesni? Who do you think steered us in?' Taid finished tying up at the bow, then reached on board for the aft rope.

'Don't try it on, Erik. What are you playing at?'

'Ask Gwylan. I agreed with her to take the boat out today.' He busied himself with the rope, without so much as a glance at Madog. 'I know our friends there don't approve,' he nodded towards Steffan, 'but we were lucky with the catch. A rare and wonderful shoal of mackerel. Even surprised me. We'll all be a bit better fed for a while.'

'Stop pissing me about. You were out of sight for a couple of hours. Where—'

'I appreciate your concern.' Sandy's voice was calm as she emerged from the cabin. She looked beyond him to the others. 'As you can see, Erik didn't chuck me overboard. I've no idea why you might think he should.'

Madog looked uncomfortable for a moment, then tried to hide it by jutting his chin aggressively. 'You were gone for ages. Long enough to get to the mainland and back.'

'And what would we want there?' Taid said. Glesni watched through the wheelhouse window as he walked up the ramp without waiting for an answer, leaving Madog looking slightly pathetic as he hovered for a moment, then strode after him. She wanted to run after them, to be the one to harness Ffred to the cart as usual, but she saw Steffan approach, and came out of the cabin to guard the crate of fish. The boat gave a mighty wobble and her childish satisfaction at his ungainly clambering quickly gave way to trepidation.

'Don't,' she said as he moved to push past her. Glesni stood firm, testing whether his nonviolent principles were as strong as the rest of his worldview. He glared at her but held back from shoving her aside.

'Rather a lot there,' he said.

'You should have seen how many were still swimming around when we left.'

Glesni turned, smiling at Sandy's unexpected intervention.

'She's right,' Glesni said. 'And you've got to admit—'

'I've got nothing to admit,' Steffan said, the flush on his face deepening. 'Even you can see there are far more than necessary here.'

*Even* her? 'Nothing will go to waste. We'll dry what we don't eat now, and my sister and Cerys are going to make leather from the skins.'

Steffan huffed dismissively and glanced up towards the store, where Taid was returning with the pony and cart. Madog was still talking at him. Hoping he didn't scare Ffred into a stubborn standstill, Glesni willed them to come quickly so they could offload the catch and get it up to the kitchen.

'If you'll excuse me, Glesni,' Steffan insisted.

She stood her ground. She'd seen him tip fish back before now. He claimed it was to put food back in the chain for the seals and other sea creatures, but it was nothing but temper and waste as far as she could see. When Taid finally started down the ramp with the pony and cart, Steffan took a step forward, as close as he could get without actually touching her. He was beginning to scare her.

'Don't be a dick.' Sandy put a hand on his arm; he shook her off roughly.

'And what would *you* know, mainlander?' His voice was suffused with blame for all the world's ills.

'I know that this trip was agreed,' she said coolly.

The boat rocked as Marc, a fellow purist, scrambled aboard in Steffan's support.

'Get your arses off the boat!'

Glesni was relieved to hear Taid's commanding voice and see Mam and Cai behind him. She noticed Madog walking away and wondered what he and Taid had said, and if she'd ever find out.

'Can't you see how wrong this is?' Steffan said.

Cai stepped forward. 'What's wrong, mate, is using force to express your opinions. Like it or not, we decided it. You don't have to eat any. Leave it.'

'I'm sure no one decided a whole fucking crate.'

'*I said leave it!*'

It wasn't like Cai to raise his voice and Steffan flinched.

'Hey,' Taid said before he could start up again. 'Let's all calm down. Steffan, you're the first to point out when the weather affects the harvests and it looks like we might go short of food. Think on it for a while. If you still feel you have to complain, that's what Gatherings are for.' He spread his hands in a gesture as calm as his voice. 'I wonder what they'd think about you threatening my granddaughter.'

Steffan glared at him. After a moment's silent face-off the two purists left the boat, their attitude once they were safely back on land indicating they were trying to do them all a favour, saving them from decadent decline. Mam and Cai followed them after Taid waved away their offer to help lift the crate. Mam rolled her eyes at his insistence, but allowed him to prove he was still up to it.

'Fuck's sake, does that happen often?' Sandy said as, cart loaded, they led Ffred up the slope towards the houses.

'Fishing trips don't happen often; that's the point,' Glesni said. 'But when they do, they're usually waiting.'

'Like our own little marine enforcement officers,' Taid said cheerfully. 'Inspecting and checking the quotas.'

She smiled. 'What was all that with Madog?'

'Just some daft notion; nothing important.'

He was breathing heavily from the exertion but Glesni knew he wouldn't have said any more if they'd still been sitting on deck surrounded by the sun-jewelled sea.

# HOW PRECARIOUS SHE STILL FELT

Sandy was late and Martha's funeral ceremony had already begun. She saw Helyg and hurried to stand with her in one of two rows lining an avenue of young trees that led to the *Llannerch*, the clearing in the island's only woodland in a small, sheltered valley, where they gathered for ceremonies. As Glesni and the procession of robed children approached, Helyg leaned forward and said in a whisper loud enough for both her daughter and Sandy to hear: 'See? Everything's just fine.'

Sandy noticed she spoke in English, and felt included. She'd played her part in getting Glesni to cooperate. Haf had now outgrown the children's procession and this was the first ceremony in which Glesni was the oldest and therefore in charge of the little ones. She'd protested loudly that she, too, was too old to 'dress up and parade around with a bunch of flowers', though Sandy could tell she was hiding a touch of nervousness about shepherding the younger children. Her main objection, however, was in Sandy's view totally justified. This was Anti Martha's funeral, Glesni had been close to the old woman, and she'd probably be unable to immerse herself in the emotion as her eyes would be on the little ones with their even littler attention spans.

Sandy had done her best to help, meeting Glesni after school a couple of days previously, where together they'd helped the children choose the ribbons and other trimmings with which they personalised their brown, green and blue robes. Glesni had gone for shades of brown, orange, red and yellow liberally sprinkled with feathers, saying they represented the robins and goldfinches who came to Anti Martha's window for the gossip.

As they'd gone out early that morning picking flowers for the posies, she'd enjoyed hearing Glesni talk about Anti Martha with her wicked sense of humour and conspiratorial laugh. She and Tahira would visit her regularly and she'd tell them tales of growing up in a city then moving to the country when she was in her teens, before she came to Ynys Hudol as an adult. Sandy suppressed a smile as Glesni said that the mainlanders in her stories sounded like the people here on the island, no better, no worse, with caring communities punctuated with petty squabbles and personality clashes.

She never lost her spark even when she was ill, and Glesni was going to miss her. At the last minute she realised she'd forgotten the necklace Martha had given her, made from shells gathered from coves and rockpools. Sandy had dashed back to get it for her. As she searched the girls' room, she felt like a trespasser; not a good feeling to have immediately before a close community ceremony.

Still slightly breathless, she watched Awen bringing up the rear of the little procession. She'd seen her role in the Gatherings, but still found it hard to imagine her leading a ceremony. On the few occasions they'd met, she'd found her shy to the point of aloofness, most of the time immersed in her walled garden fragrant with flowers and herbs, or closeted away in her studio, drying plants or preparing powders and tinctures; Sandy sometimes imagined her casting spells by moonlight.

The healer's demeanour when Sandy consulted her during her debilitating post-infection fatigue had initially led her to question the woman's abilities. At first annoyed at being given little more than advice to rest and take it easy, as she recovered she became grudgingly appreciative of the tonics and tinctures Awen proffered at apparently random moments, and came to realise that maybe it was a question of perspective. Awen wanted to take things at their natural pace. It took time for the effects of a remedy to become apparent. Not for her the inexorable haste of the mainland, the insistence on instant knowledge when answers were not immediately knowable.

Having helped Glesni with the children's procession, robed and adorned as they were, she had expected similar of Awen. White, diaphanous robes, hair flowing, maybe bare feet. Yet there she was in her usual brown tunic and green skirt, the same earth-hued homespun she wore every day, tattered sandals providing all-too-human protection from the stones and weeds in her path.

Once the procession had passed, the two lines of Seeders followed them into the grove. As Sandy looked around the gathered mourners, she had to admit that Awen had presence. Despite the more pragmatic members of the community's claims to the contrary, despite Sandy's own resolute rejection of gods and monsters, when Awen surveyed the congregation purposefully, she felt something.

A small group, including Tom, began to sing, and everyone joined in. It was beautiful – not the earthy, characterful sounds she knew from the roundhouse, but more like an ethereal cathedral choir. Her mind drifted and she tried to remember when she'd last heard one of those. How were cathedrals faring these days? She'd seen plenty of crumbling churches, for sure. The *Llannerch*'s high vaulted roof was formed by the trees and ultimately the sky. Not quite the same acoustic perfection, maybe, but it sounded glorious.

They watched the shrouded figure being lowered into the freshly dug grave among the trees to the side of the clearing, and the children stepped forward in turn to lay down their bouquets as Awen and her choir sang. Anti Martha had been the oldest member of the community; that distinction would now pass to Erik. She realised he wasn't with his family and glanced round but couldn't see him. Strange; he'd looked devastated when Helyg broke the news of Anti Martha's death. Maybe he was waiting in the wings for some special role in the community's funeral rites.

Awen led a second chant, which carried them away as if they could follow Anti Martha's departing soul to wherever it had gone – the earth, the sky, the sea. It was clear that, whatever the individual beliefs people had brought with them, this shared ritual made them feel as one.

Then they shared their memories in whatever way they chose –

music, poems, just a few simple words. It was a long, moving ceremony; almost everyone had something they wanted to say about Anti Martha. Having lived on the island for years before Bleddyn and Edith bought it – she'd been one of the trust members responsible for finding sympathetic buyers – she'd stayed on and contributed enthusiastically to the community as it was established. Committing to this way of life for longer than a holiday was admirable in Sandy's book, whoever you were.

There were not only memories, but more music, too. Helyg sang a song that her mam had written, which Martha loved. Once again Sandy was reminded that Erik was absent, and again when Glesni read a poem. Her friend Tahira sang a song in Arabic. Clearly nervous at first, as her confidence grew her voice soared, weaving effortlessly through the island's traditions. At the back of the gathering Sandy saw that Khaled had tears in his eyes. He gave Rashid a manly pat on the shoulder and Sandy noticed Erik next to them, looking slightly breathless and dishevelled.

The final communal song, more celebratory and joyous, took her by surprise. As the little band of flower children led everyone to the roundhouse where they'd continue to tell their favourite Anti Martha stories over food and drink, Sandy glanced back and noticed Erik step aside to stand by her grave. Surely he hadn't missed the funeral? His sadness was almost tangible. Helyg caught her eye briefly, a slight frown creasing her brow, and as she looked back at the Grove, the trees hid him from view.

The festivities in the roundhouse were a gossipy celebration of Anti Martha's life, in contrast to the reverence of the outdoor ceremony. Sandy sat on the edge, insisting that Helyg didn't have to stay with her, and a succession of people came over with anecdotes about the old lady, or the early days of the community.

Her fatigue was beginning to return and it looked like things could go on until well into the evening, so after finishing her second cup of mead – another favourite of Anti Martha's, since until her illness she'd been primarily responsible for the beehives – Sandy decided to call it a day. Her way over to the door took her close to where Madog was drinking with a group of friends. He glowered at her and moved a step away from his group. Not now, she thought.

'I hope you're pleased with yourself,' he said, his voice quiet, menacing.

'I haven't a clue what you mean,' she said, deliberately refusing to lower her voice. A couple of the lads looked round.

'Don't give me that. You know perfectly well.'

Shaking her head, she walked on. He stepped closer, almost barring her way. This time almost inaudibly, he said, 'Don't know how you've got the nerve to show your face here today after—'

'All right, Sandy?'

She felt relieved to see Cai appear. Then silently berated herself for it: she could handle a drunken young lad. Throwing his son a look of displeasure, he accompanied her to the door.

'I'm glad I caught you.'

Sandy was disconcerted by the warmth his announcement sent through her. 'I – I'm just leaving, I'm afraid. I wish I could stay longer, but I don't know when I'll stop feeling knackered all the time.'

'I could do with a bit of fresh air. You mind if I walk with you some of the way?'

'Of course not. Though it's hardly far or dangerous enough to "see me home".'

Cai laughed. Once they were away from the building, he said, 'I'm sorry about my son's behaviour. Don't know what's got into him. And the other day – you know, when you came in on the boat? I haven't seen you since. Totally uncalled for; I'm sorry.'

She smiled. 'No need to apologise on his behalf. Steffan was far worse. And in any case, Madog's an adult; he can mend his own fences, though judging from that,' she tossed her head towards the roundhouse, 'he's got no intention of mending anything.'

Cai walked with his hands in his pockets, eyes fixed on the lane ahead, apparently relieved she wasn't angry with him. She was almost tempted to mention Madog's false directions to a dangerous section of cliff-top path.

'Maybe you can tell me what was going through his mind, though,' she said instead.

'No idea. Erik hasn't said anything?'

'Unsurprisingly, no,' she said. Ever since the boat trip, he'd been more absent than usual, and now he'd even missed his friend's funeral. The few times she'd passed the workshop he and Madog had either been arguing over trivialities or working in silence – she could feel the atmosphere drifting out like a fog. 'Look, forget it. I'm not taking it personally. I'm sure people are suspicious of any newcomer. You were probably on the receiving end of it yourselves when you came over. A few years ago, did you say?'

'More than a few: fourteen years now. I didn't really sense any hostility – I was just glad to be here – but Madog's always been edgy.' He looked across at her, as if gauging whether to confide. 'I suppose it's not unexpected; he was only eleven when we arrived. Funny age, and he's got his mother's temper. He chose to come with me – thought it was an adventure – but then a few months later changed his mind. Resented me like hell. Typical teenager, you could say, though I suppose he had more of an excuse than most his age, having been wrenched from his home and brought to "the arse end of nowhere".' He sighed. 'Once we were here... well, there was no going back.'

'Really? I've been wondering what will happen if and when I decide to leave.'

He laughed. 'It's not that. It's unlikely that anyone will actually try to stop you, you know. It was me. I just couldn't face going back, to more endless explanations and recriminations, let alone trying to find a new job. And I could hardly pop across and dump an eleven-year-old on the first stretch of beach we came to.'

If she'd had Madog to deal with, that was exactly what she'd have done. 'I guess not,' she said diplomatically.

'He was trouble for a few years. Bullying the other kids, even stealing stuff.' He nodded towards the workshop. 'Until he started working with Erik.'

She laughed. 'I'd hardly call Erik the social worker type.'

'But he was prepared to take him on. Told me once that things had been difficult for him when he was young. He'd been bullied himself; lost his mum, never knew his dad – I believe he was taken in by his uncle, so he knew the importance of having an adult to turn to. Madog seemed to trust him from the start – the way he just quietly gets on with things.'

'He hasn't been back to see his mum?'

She immediately regretted getting too personal.

'I've got no idea where Lowri is now. You know what communications are like round here. We... we parted on pretty final terms.'

'Because of the reason you came?'

'Partly. All connected. We'd been going downhill for a while, but when I resigned it was the last straw. She was annoyed about me giving up the chance of a decent career, but probably more concerned about how it affected her own prospects.'

'A decent career doing what?'

'We were both in the police force.'

She raised an eyebrow. 'That explains the interrogation when we first met.'

He frowned, feigning hurt. 'I thought I'd been the master of tact and subtlety.'

She smiled. 'So what *did* make you leave?'

This time his frown was serious. 'It just got on top of me. Society becoming ever more fractured, seeing humanity at its worst, day after day.' He paused again. She said nothing. He gave a slight shake of his head as if recognising that this wasn't a good enough explanation for her. 'But what really got to me was policing the riots. Protests, in normal language – that's the point. Laws became increasingly draconian, and more and more pressure

157

groups got labelled as terrorists. Everything got twisted, punishments got worse, enforcements more violent, until I felt I couldn't be part of it any more.' He sighed, gazing down at his feet on the stony track. 'You might say I took the coward's way out. Believe me, I tried changing things from the inside, in my own small way. I was only a sergeant, though – not enough influence. It didn't work, so I left.'

The resemblance to Adam wasn't only physical, it seemed. 'But some of these supposedly peaceful protesters *did* carry out terrorist attacks,' she said. 'The Irlas Dam, for one.'

He shook his head. 'They weren't—'

'My sister was at Irlas, and took her own life – later, but as a direct result. They killed her.'

'I'm sorry for your loss.'

He sounded genuine but she pushed on. 'Though it was all in a good cause?'

'I didn't say that,' he countered. 'I will say that no eco group planted that bomb. Like the others that came after, it was a disruptive but peaceful protest till it was infiltrated.'

'Infiltrated? By whom? The Welsh separatists?'

'Not them, either.'

'By whom, then?' Not Cai, too. She realised she was shaking her head. How many times had she had this conversation with Adam?

'I'm sure you know as well as I do, Sandy. It was just what the establishment needed: an excuse to brand them all as terrorists.'

'Oh, come on,' she scoffed. 'You seem too grounded to be a conspiracy theorist.'

'I base my opinions on what I saw.'

They walked without speaking for a while. No doubt he was wondering, as she was, how the conversation had become so heated. A sharp breeze was rising, drawing her attention to the darkening of the sky over the sea, spears of rain clearly visible above a clouded horizon. She pulled her collar tight against the breeze; such a contrast from the warm sun of the ceremony earlier. She was still unused to being so closely aware of the world around her. Maybe the approaching weather had affected their mood.

Cai was the first to speak. 'You know... I'm no apologist for criminals – of any kind. But sometimes you have to let go, for your own sanity.'

Some things were too deep to let go of. She said nothing.

'It... Living here has made me see the world differently.'

'I'm not sure I'll stay around long enough to test that one out.' She doubted that any amount of time here would blunt her desire to find Adam, to make him pay for his betrayal. An outlier drop of rain on her face made her flinch.

'I hope you're not planning on leaving just yet.'

She turned to him in surprise. 'I... haven't really thought about it.'

They came to a stop as they reached the house, and two figures appeared round a bend in the evening light. She recognised Erik and Glesni.

'Cai!' he called. 'Just the man I want to see.'

'Oh yes?' He seemed wary. Maybe they'd had an argument after the boat trip. Sandy hoped they weren't going to resume it right then.

'A little mystery to test your leadership skills.'

Cai relaxed slightly. 'Tell me.'

'In case you were wondering why I was late to the funeral – I was down on the shore this morning. You know how Martha loved beachcombing? I wanted to find something to lay on her grave.' He'd found what he was looking for – told them to go to the grave later if they wanted to see it – and was just making his way back when an unfamiliar movement caught his eye at the harbour. 'The boats. Come loose. *Otranto* was caught on the rocks. I haven't checked the damage but I managed to wade out, push her off and take her after our *Berta,* which was drifting out... We're lucky it's not any rougher. Could've lost both of them.' He shook his head. 'I thought I'd miss the funeral altogether. Two rocking boats, one of them taking water... leaning out and trying to tie one to the other. Not easy.'

'Why didn't you get help?' Cai asked.

'Didn't want to spoil Martha's send-off for everyone else.' He shook his head as if fighting his own thoughts. 'Still don't. I've just been back down to check and they're both secure. We can break the news when the time's right.'

'You think it was deliberate? When were you last down there?'

'They were both firmly tied yesterday.' Erik glanced behind him towards the harbour. 'What kind of fucking idiot would pull a stunt like that?'

They exchanged looks. 'I think we've got a pretty good idea,' Cai said.

'I bloody hope not, for their sakes. All that stupid posturing over a few fish – that was bad enough. If it *is* Steffan and co., they've gone too far this time.'

'Couldn't the boats just have come loose?' Cai said.

'Both of them?'

'One could've bumped the other free.'

'Hardly.' He glanced at Glesni who held up a length of rope. 'Evidence. Cut. Deliberately. I'll leave the detective work to you. Now, if you'll excuse me.'

He strode past them into the courtyard, then paused and turned. 'I'll need help to get them up on dry land tomorrow. You heard about the storm?'

He disappeared into his cottage, leaving Cai and Glesni to tell Sandy: Idris had brought news that morning of an approaching weather front. As they spoke Sandy felt the growing evening wind more keenly, although they said that it wasn't likely to hit with full force for at least another twenty-four hours. It had been deemed safe to pause for the funeral, but the following day would be spent in a frenzy of battening down the hatches.

Sandy recalled being told how they all sat out a storm together in the roundhouse; she was clearly going to witness its ferocity for herself. Watching Cai leave, she thought the sea beyond him looked quite innocent, though a growing swell indicated more to come. It felt as unnerving as the thought of being cooped up in a hall full of inquisitive Seeders.

That night, despite her fatigue, Sandy was unable to sleep. An almost full moon was hidden by cloud cover, but its benevolent glow meant the night was not fully dark. She stood, gazing out of the window and hoping they were right that the full force of the storm was at least a day away. She'd been surprised at their trust in the international radio weather reports that Idris plucked from the air like the moths he studied in his traps.

The occasional gust battered the corner of the house as if tapping her on the shoulder and reminding her how precarious she still felt – physically, but also in terms of acceptance. She'd slipped into family life with a disarming ease, and although she wondered how much longer she'd be welcomed, for now her presence wasn't questioned. And many others had made her feel the same way. But where there was hostility, it was unnerving. She thought of Madog earlier in the evening. Maybe he'd already known about the boats somehow, and blamed her for it. Surely if that was the case, he'd have raised the alarm?

Without taking her eyes from the ghostly scene outside, she reached for the crumbly biscuit Glesni had left her for supper, spares from the batch she'd made for the funeral wake. At home she'd have popped a slice of bread in the toaster or unwrapped a bar of chocolate. She wondered if any of the older ones – the girls and their generation wouldn't know any different – ever missed these simple pleasures, without having to grow, thresh, mill, make. She recalled Glesni saying how the work was an essential part of life and if people became too distanced from all that went into the things they had, they could hardly be blamed for consuming indiscriminately. So far, Sandy's convalescence had kept her from too much of the soul-nourishing grind of work, but she could see that those who lived it, and not only the purists, tended to share Glesni's view. No one seemed to miss easy toast. Not out loud. She stopped her yearnings with a delicious mouthful. Honeyed for a special occasion. Yes, there must be plenty they missed; why wouldn't they? But they knew how to appreciate what they had.

Adam would have fitted right in here. Maybe she was affected by the funeral, but the buffeting wind, like a child tugging at a parent's sleeve for attention, seemed wistful. Despite what he'd done, and the deep differences that made their parting inevitable, she was still ambushed by moments of longing for what they'd had. She imagined his arms around her, warm, comforting, and tried not to think of his uncanny resemblance to Cai. She brushed thoughts of both of them away; she hadn't been able to afford that weakness for a long time. Not since Adam had gone off to war.

Why had he ignored her pleas and gone on that fool's errand? Why hadn't she listened to Liv and forgotten about him in his absence?

He'd returned, changed both by the destruction they'd sought to stop and by the bloody, cruel reality of war, but her sister was immersed in her work and later incapacitated, and Sandy welcomed him back. Soothed him as he saw out the remainder of his duty participating in that project they knew was wrong but didn't feel in a position to question. Waited for the man she loved to resurface, resigned to the notion that it was as unlikely as him ever being able to afford leaving that job. Cursed him as he defected, not sure if she hated him for his betrayal, for vanishing without a word, or for not taking her with him. Set out to track him down, in the hellish fury of a woman scorned. Sitting here now, immersed in the silvery moonlit panorama that he would have loved, the idea crept up on her that she needn't report him if ever she found him.

She felt for the crumpled paper in her pocket. It was a tenacious thing, refusing to disintegrate, impossible to lose. It was barely legible in the moonlight, but she knew it by heart.

*I still love you*
*But it's better if I go*
*Better you don't know*
*Please don't try to follow*

She ought to write it out again; the paper was getting tatty. Something always held her back. No matter that the writing was hers, not his – she'd copied it from a quickly deleted message – no matter that the words were seared on her brain, she held onto it as if it were infused with his DNA.

Of course she'd had his PD traced. Of course it had been found, destroyed, in the bins of the adjacent building to theirs.

Looking at the words now, she couldn't help smiling. Maybe Cai had a point when he said she should try to put past hurts behind her. Regardless of what Adam had done, and his ultimate abandonment of her – though admittedly, she'd played her own part, telling him she never wanted to see him again as long as she lived – she couldn't help the fond memories. His musical ambitions. Maybe if he'd succeeded it wouldn't have come to this. He wouldn't have joined up, wouldn't have come back changed. The words looked clunky on the page, but when she imagined them sung, in the way he'd sing and play them, she was overcome by a long-dormant nostalgia. With the ever-present anger snapping at its heels. She untensed her hand, which had been about to screw the message into a ball or tear it up. The gesture was almost as familiar as the words.

Not for the first time, she wondered if the chance acquisition of a decrepit boat had accidentally brought her closer to succeeding in her task of finding Adam, whether through being a step closer to Ireland – maybe it really was worth going – or through unearthing some helpful information. It was obvious that several of the Seeders knew more than they were willing to tell her.

But right now she felt ready to have a go at forgetting.

There it was again, that insistent notion that had begun to creep up on her. Maybe she could stay. Maybe she didn't need to spend the next months or years of her life on a futile hunt for Adam so that she could redeem herself by uncovering his crime and betraying him. She might find she had all she needed here.

After all, who was left to miss her? Her close family, small enough to begin with, were gone. She'd lost her job. If anyone had been monitoring her nevertheless, well, her PD had given out shortly after she entered Wales. That meant a lot of territory to search and they had plenty of other preoccupations to ensure they didn't look too hard. Missing, presumed dead. That would do. Maybe, in due course, she could come up with a plan to confirm the assumption. She wouldn't be the first.

Perhaps she could find peace here. Begin to hear people's stories because she genuinely wanted to know them; not to mine them for information, that all-important commodity that people pursued mindlessly as if it had taken the place of the wild animals they'd originally evolved to hunt.

A door banged in the walled courtyard below. The wind, or Erik going out for one of his solitary nocturnal wanders. She realised she hadn't thanked him for rescuing her boat earlier. He'd hardly given her the opportunity. She resolved to catch him soon, recover a friendship that she hoped hadn't been too badly eroded by her nagging suspicions, which were beginning to feel totally unfounded.

# THEIR STOIC ACCEPTANCE

The storms got worse each year. Everyone said it and Glesni had seen plenty of evidence herself. They kept their houses in good repair with thick roof slates that even the strongest gales couldn't shift. As more people arrived and usable stone became too scarce, some delved into the sloping ground and hillocks to build underground homes. Those who preferred to remain in the light fitted thick shutters and barred them in place at the first sign of bad weather. Glass was fragile and replacements hard to get when it broke. They got the harvests in the minute they were ready, all pulling together so as not to waste a day. They sowed early. The storms came early. In good years they sowed second crops between stormy seasons, practising careful rotation, and stored what they could. Good years didn't happen often and the seasons were increasingly unpredictable. They'd huddle in the roundhouse in warm clothes and blankets – the fire was rarely lit – and say at least the storms brought rain to replenish the springs and cisterns so they wouldn't have drought.

On this occasion, the timing was completely wrong. Late spring, just before the barley harvest. They'd taken a gamble and sown ridiculously early. It paid off as there was no serious frost. But the crops hadn't fully ripened and now it seemed they never would.

Three days it had lasted so far. Glesni missed Taid. Like some others, he hated the forced communality of the roundhouse, preferring to sit it out at home, compensating for a minimal existence with the relief of not having to indulge in small talk. Idris would come down from the watchtower but hunker down in one of the squat stone hides, watching for birds blown adrift, and Awen, equally solitary but in a different way, remained apart. Some said she danced in the rain, warding off the worst of the damage. Tahira would be there or not, depending on whether she was in one of her alone-time periods when the storm hit. This time she was absent and Glesni missed her. She smiled as she thought maybe her friend would join Awen in her rain dances – she imagined there were rituals her people had developed in desperation when the refugee ship was hurled about on the sea.

Arguments broke out, as they always did when they were confined together, the wind battering and the rain lashing relentlessly. Glesni would look up from the book she was reading and wonder what was the point in blaming one another. Someone would voice concern about the ponies and goats, and wonder about venturing out to them; others would say they were hardy and sensible enough to use the shelters, and what more could anyone do? Then the purists would chip in with their arguments against keeping animals. Whatever the debate, the lads, especially Madog, always thought they knew best. Or maybe they just wanted trouble to pass the time. A sharp word or two from Gwylan, with the threat of being thrown out to fend for themselves in the storm, was enough to dampen the scuffles that broke out.

On the whole, they used their enforced time indoors to good effect. Glesni had helped to bring skeins of flax fibres in from the drying shed to make room for the sharp-smelling bundles they'd hastily rescued from the retting field, and her mam was teaching her to spin. She was beginning to enjoy it; the hours passed like the smooth fibres through her fingers, frustrating and laborious at first, slowly settling into a rhythm as she learned – and it kept her safely out of the kitchen.

Sandy had been set to mending work-clothes. She didn't seem to be enjoying it, nor was she very good at it, probably because she spent most of her time pausing and watching the ritchety-clunk of Glesni's spinning wheel. She fingered the shirt she'd been given.

'Has this really come from what you're spinning?'

'Mm-hmm.'

'Your fabrics are gorgeous.' Sandy had been similarly enthusiastic and even asked to join them in their craft sessions with Cerys when they were learning about different plants for dyeing. 'Do you sell them when you go to the mainland?'

Glesni shook her head, still concentrating.

'You should. You'd get a fortune.'

She came to the end of the skein she was spinning. It was slightly uneven but that would all be part of the effect when it was woven. 'You've seen for yourself what a long-drawn-out process it is. It's all we can do to make enough for ourselves. Anyway, it's not like what you're used to, is it?'

'People pay a fortune for handmade stuff – if they can get it these days. There's hardly anyone around who has the skills or the time. What we do see is imported, but even that's in short supply these days.'

'Bring it up at the next Gathering,' Glesni said, thinking it would be interesting to see Sandy debate with the purists about keeping what they produced. For once she agreed with them; she liked knowing who'd made her clothes and was looking forward to the next time she needed something – it would feel all the more special knowing she'd had a hand in spinning the flax into linen.

Her fingers grew stiff and her back began to ache. Mam said it wouldn't be as bad once she was more experienced – she wasn't sure if that meant it wouldn't affect her so much, or whether she'd simply stop noticing. Once Sandy had finished the small pile of mending she'd been given, Glesni challenged her to a game of World's End. Sandy took to that somewhat better than sewing – so much so that her serious consideration of every move slowed the game down almost to the point of tediousness. Every so often she'd ask something completely unconnected, and Glesni suspected she was probably thinking more about the tactics of talking to her than those of the game. She was getting better herself at parrying the questions.

'Why hasn't your Taid come to the hall?'

'He never does.' She shrugged. 'Too much sociability for one thing. And he hates being confined indoors.'

'Even in this weather?' Sandy gave her one of those 'tell me more' looks.

'You've seen what he's like,' Glesni said.

She nodded. 'He's said more than once that he's always been an outdoors kind of person. What did he do – you know, before they came here?'

'They lived at Nain's family place; they'd moved there before Mam was born. Mam says it's partly because Nain's mam and dad were getting old and needed help, and partly because they wanted her to be born in Cymru. The civil war hadn't happened then, of course, and neither had the Clearances.' Glesni shrugged. 'They helped to run the farm at first, but then got together with some neighbours and started a rewilding project under the stewardship schemes.'

Sandy leaned across the game board and picked up a card from the pile. Again, she raised her eyebrows in silent encouragement for Glesni to continue. What could she say? She knew that the commitment to regenerative farming and rewilding, including the introduction of certain species, had been unpopular with some, but a beautiful thing to those involved. It was ironic to think that those most against the project were likely to have supported the same government that introduced the Clearances policy – which had probably done its own rewilding rather well. As far as her family's contribution was concerned, she realised how patchy her knowledge was, and was relieved to see Sandy's expression as she looked at the card she'd picked up, and her triumph at winning the game for the second time.

It was one of those storms that ended suddenly. Sometimes the weather would grumble on for days, gusting and squalling, reluctant to leave as if it had mistaken their stoic acceptance for a welcome. Sometimes the storm simply stopped, in an oasis of relief. After days of violent struggle as the elements staked their claim on the roundhouse and the community around it, suddenly from one moment to the next it was silent. Clean, hopeful and sun-filled. They knew there'd be destruction, but when the air was like this they could face it in a spirit of renewal.

As they emerged, people scattered, hurrying to check roofs, gardens and fields. Glesni was the first back to their house, intending to hurry past it and check Taid's cottage and workshop. She stopped short by their own door. Two new planks stood out, bare wood against faded green paint, and part of the frame pieced in. She continued across the courtyard, leaving Mam and Haf to puzzle over the door, but sensed as soon as she crossed the threshold that Taid's place was empty. She assumed he was the one who'd repaired the door and that probably meant he was fine, but wanted to find him nevertheless. The boats. He'd dragged them out of the water with Cai, Madog and Tom the day before the storm hit, but the two they'd lost in the previous gales had also been well secured. Taid had thought they were safe that time and never stopped beating himself up about it. She ran like the recently departed wind down to the harbour. *Berta* and *Otranto*, apparently untouched. No Taid.

She stood for a moment watching the sea on the rocks, still hurling itself at the land as if escaping kidnap by the departing storm. Shutting out the activity back at the houses, she lost herself in the everchanging heartbeat of the sea. The metallic sheen of the water, mirror images of the clouds drifting in shape-changing clumps, the wheeling of the gulls, the crunch of gravel and hiss of spray. The overwhelming freshness, sea air mingling with wet grass.

Looking up the lower slopes of the mountain, she became aware that the turbine, normally just visible from the cove by the jetty, was not there. She walked briskly up the slope, her breath rising in her ears, and as she crested the rise felt the tug of a mischievous breeze as though the storm was on its way back. The shoulder of land was not the highest but seemed to be a hang-out point for every breeze, gust and gale. A perfect place for the turbine. Almost. One of the guys that held the mast in place had worked loose and it was lying across the scrub. Watched by Ffred, Taid was crouched by the fallen turbine, cradling the housing like Idris would hold an injured bird, inspecting it for damage. The blades, which he'd already detached, lay like forlorn wings.

'Is it OK?'

'I think so. It must have taken a knock when it fell. I need to check it over.' He gestured to the cart, which he'd brought as far up the rough slope as he could get it, and she helped him secure the turbine in place. 'Then we'll need to get a team together to anchor this...' He glanced at the guy rope.

'What happened?'

He shrugged. 'It was sound enough. There are burrows round here so it could have been undermined, but it was probably just the strength of that gale. Though it's survived plenty of others. Who knows?'

He started off down the hill, leaving her to lead the pony down the track.

'The main thing is to get it back in action as soon as possible, Pwt. The tidal array's fine as a baseline but we always use extra when everyone's cooped up in the roundhouse, and the batteries are almost drained. People are going to need power for all the repair work.'

The questions Glesni was dying to ask him were still there like the errant gusts of wind from the retreating storm, but she struggled to keep pace with him, despite his limp. They reached the workshop and she hitched the lead rein to the bar outside the door, pausing to give Ffred a pat and a whispered thanks.

'Come in,' Taid said. 'Watch and learn. Let's turn adversity into an opportunity.'

It wasn't hard to put away the guilt she'd felt as they passed neighbours' houses; people retrieving wind-blown debris, beginning to patch up damage, tending to uprooted plants. This work was important, too.

At first, she was absorbed as she watched, passing tools and parts to his soothingly calm commands. He stripped the casing from the turbine and had her clean and inspect the parts as he examined the mechanism. Her own task completed, she watched him work in rapt fascination.

Once the turbine was inspected and reassembled, Taid rummaged in boxes at the back of the workshop for a replacement ground anchor. Glesni picked up her discarded jacket, noticing the chill now this part of the work was done. Taid always worked with the door open, as if the cold never touched him. Glancing at her with a smile, he went over to shut the door. A moment for themselves.

'Cuppa?' He looked round, hand on the latch of the connecting door to his cottage.

'I'm fine, thanks. Brewing tea's all there is to do in there. Shouldn't we be getting it back in place?' She hated her conscience for ending their time too soon. 'We can talk on the way.'

'It can wait a few moments. You don't have to justify yourself to me.'

Relieved, she perched on the little three-legged stool she'd made under his guidance.

'So,' he said, 'how were things in the chicken coop? No one driven to murder?'

It was as if he sensed she had things to say.

'Close. You know, the older lads arguing.' She took a deep breath. 'But there are some things I want to ask you. Stuff Sandy was asking me.'

She paused.

'What things?'

She appreciated the prompt. Like a mother gull nudging a fledgling off the edge of a cliff into flight.

'She asked me what you did before. I kind of mentioned the nature reserve, the rewilding, but realised there wasn't much to say, because I don't know. I don't know how the Clearances affected our family or how Mam came to be here. Or why you didn't come till later.'

He raised his hand to his cap, pushed it aside and rubbed his temple.

'Did you say any of that to her?'

'Not about Mam or you.' She felt an unexpected sob welling in her throat. 'Because there was nothing I could say, was there? No one's told me anything. I could hardly ask Mam, could I, in the crowded roundhouse? So I'm asking you.'

He fingered the oak leaves at his neck and turned to the window. It prompted her to recall their patched-up door, but this was more important.

'What *did* happen? Where were you?' Silence hung between them. She tried to sound casual. 'You know, so I don't accidentally say the wrong thing.' The cobwebbed window seemed to hold a fascination for him. 'To Sandy or anyone else,' she finished lamely.

He got stiffly to his feet. 'Long story, Pwt. Too long for now.' He gestured to the workbench. 'You were right. It's time to brave the elements and finish the job. Want to come?'

'Not until you...'

They heard footsteps and Haf burst in. Glesni suppressed a sigh. She might get a chance to push him further while they were working.

'There you are. Glesni. Taid.' Haf glared at her sister. 'Mam's been looking for you. Both of you.'

Taid raised his eyebrows.

'We've been doing important work,' Glesni said. 'The turbine came down in the storm. We've been checking it for damage.' She circled her finger in the air. Haf stared it down just as the wind had toppled the real thing. 'So what does Mam want?'

'She's worried. There's all sorts of stuff to be done.' Haf glanced over her shoulder at the scattered debris littering the courtyard. 'She says you can fiddle around in here later. You know – since we've not been too badly affected ourselves, we ought to go and help others who haven't been as lucky.'

'Which is exactly what I'm doing,' Taid said. 'You'll have noticed I fixed our door?'

Haf blushed. 'Thanks,' she mumbled.

'Well, now I'm making sure we get full power back on.' Glancing at the turbine, he reached for his coat, then gestured to Glesni to untie Ffred and ready the cart. 'We'd best get going.'

'We?' Haf looked daggers at Glesni.

'Extra power, to help with the repairs and stuff,' she replied.

'I know why, *twpsyn*. I mean why you?'

'Glesni's got to go and drum up a work party,' Taid said with world-weary patience. 'And then come and help get it back in place. I may be pretty useful round here but even I can't raise a turbine on a mast by myself. In the tail-end of a gale.'

'But she—'

'You can come too, if you like, Haf.' He made Glesni smile – there was no surer way to silence her. 'Come on, Pwt.'

'I'll tell Mam you're safe,' Haf said as she turned her back on them.

As if there had been any doubt about that.

# PART VI

# NANT-Y-WERN

# NOT JUST LEAVING IT TO CHANCE

I go west away from the sunrise though the sun is swallowed up by clouds I can feel where it is in the sky and that's how I'll know my way back too I'm going further than I've been before further than the landslide where the mountain swallowed our road keeps us safe like the fallen tree keeps us safe from the other direction. She said not to leave our home and I don't want to I'm scared not at first but the trees don't go on forever and now I'm facing the other country the moors with wind whistling in the scrubby grass the crumbling walls the open mountains the rocks the giant metal towers striding some of them with trailing wires like cobwebs for spiders to catch their prey. She told me they were like our turbine tower but carrying power for lots of people that's weird to me they look harsh and menacing like they're there to hurt people hurt the animals hurt the world but our turbine was a good thing when it worked She didn't have an answer for me not one I understood She only said it was good for us that the giants didn't work any more because it meant people had no power and went away so we're on our own safe funny how such menacing structures meant people could live here so often things aren't what they seem. I try not to look at them still claiming the land the land itself windblown unfriendly the only friendly thing a stream but a band of mist hovering along its length makes me think it's not friendly is it hiding something more than water but it's only mist on a stream but this is all new country I don't know if it looks after me but I've never been this far west and the men coming makes me think I need to see what's there.

The wind in the grass the open ground away from the road makes me nervous should I wait till Winter can come with me I think of him at home he doesn't question me going I like that I like the freedom just to be me after She went with the owls I like to be just me I like him in my house too now I know he won't steal Her space he knows respect he didn't mean harm and it's good to have him there I help him he helps me but I like some time for me I don't want to need him he might go I have to hold on to the alone of me.

The first farm looks a bit like ours at first but as I come near I can see it's been empty for a long time like Tyn Rhedyn the one near the fallen tree with our name on the gate no things in the rooms or the falling down buildings no rubbish except some rusting bits of machinery no useful things except a large flat trolley close up I see it's got one wheel missing I could repair it and use it for something so I pull it down the stony lane not easy because it keeps wanting to roll in the deep rut carved by rainwater but I drag it on three wheels to the gate and leave it just inside so no one else can see it can steal it. If there's someone nearby I'll have bigger problems than losing an old trolley but if trouble comes let it come in its own way I won't tell trouble how to find me by leaving a trolley where someone can see it.

I look back and see the gateway the stone pillars and the broken gate only I know the trolley is behind the gatepost it makes me glad we changed our wall it was only a few years ago after the people came and looked round and stole some food from our store but went away again She said they might have done worse and we should be more careful. I sometimes hear people on the road footsteps not vehicles not tyres crunching since the tree came down and sometimes voices but I don't feel scared because there is no track now and why would they climb the wall and come to my house if they don't know anyone's there anything worth stealing She was wise and all I know I know from Her. All this thinking of gates and walls and old trolleys and safety makes me check I'm walking on the tussocks of grass in the road not leaving footprints in the mud but of course I'm already taking care of that my mind makes me do these things even when I'm not thinking them.

That's how the world works and how it takes care of me guides my mind my instincts even when I'm not looking I know it does even though She taught me how to make sure it happens not just leaving it to chance I miss Her I miss Her every day then I hate the world I hate that it didn't take care of me when it made Her die took Her away from me. I wonder if Winter will take Her place he doesn't know the things She knew but he knows other things and when he's mended he can tell me but when he's mended I think he'll leave so I don't think too much about what the house will be like with him living in it all the time he makes me think I should look for things to replace my old ones things like fabric my things are all holes the old clothes in my house nearly all gone so even now he's helping by making me come here and look for new things.

The next place appears suddenly I see it as I reach the top of a rise it sits in a hollow guarded by trees huddling round then straggling up the mountain the trees probably meet my woods somewhere over there beyond where I normally go. I'm glad to see the trees at this new house because I can get near unseen the roof is whole and it looks like they've been using the yard and the track not long ago maybe people are still there now I have to be careful. A window is broken the door hanging open it looks silent and lifeless but I know if anyone comes to my house they'd think no one lives there but they don't have my instincts I can feel there's no one here but still I creep up through the trees and peer out from the cover of the leaves for a long time twice I see two blue tits fly in and out I feel safe because blue tits wouldn't go in and out if people were there.

I watch for a long time the birds coming and going a high sad cry of a buzzard behind me maybe warning maybe not it could go somewhere else to hunt if anyone was here so probably it means the place is safe. I slowly creep out and ever-so-quietly across the yard keeping by the wall I wish I had something my bow my knife but I'm not hunting today and I didn't think of being scared and needing them why would I a robin hops on the wall scolding me telling me something probably that it's his place which means there's no one there I move from the wall and walk in the first room is a kitchen I have to be careful I look around the place is bare not like anyone living there cold and dusty and a smell like our old store but different. All the furniture still there I look in cupboards nothing there just some old bottles under the sink no food nothing that smells good in the bottles a few odd knives and forks in a drawer I put them in my backpack and a knife and some string in my pocket another drawer has some towels I gather them up they need washing but I need fabric I can wash them I find two pans in another cupboard and put them on the worktop to take on my way out.

Into the living room furniture is still there and pictures on the walls but nothing useful no food but no damage looks like the people left on purpose but fast all the good things gone only important things they could carry leaving not-useful things still here on shelves like ornaments and books maybe I can read again can't concentrate but maybe new books will take me in I glance over the spines pick a couple at random and stuff them in my bag one fallen on the floor behind a chair I pick it up open it see it's handwriting not print someone's writing with photos I turn the pages the land the trees the sky look familiar I see a photo it's Her looking at me watching me guarding me I feel safer than I did a moment ago glad I turned the page but I don't relax She's with a group of people all look friendly guarding all watching me watching over me but I must be alert I stuff it in my bag and look round the room making sure it wasn't a trick I go to the door and peer up the stairs maybe I have enough new things now but her picture makes me feel safer it means She knew the people who lived here I go upstairs same story empty rooms furniture but only a few clothes left in the cupboards some trousers and shirts much too big but I can sew I take a couple of each and there's a blanket it won't fit in my bag I think about leaving the books behind the printed ones not hers but I want them I hang the blanket over the rail on the landing look in the bathroom get some soap not much but nicer than the soap I make not nicer but different a hairbrush with more bristles than mine everything else mouldy I have enough I fasten my bag and I wrap the blanket round

180

my bag and fasten it with the string I found in the kitchen and move silently She always said how silently I can move to the top of the stairs then creep down the stairs a movement I jump but it's the bird dashing in storm on its way I look at the door and I know no one's here but now there's a storm coming should I go home or stay here I don't want to stay even if this house belonged to people She knew they're not here now but someone else might come back and Winter is waiting for me at home.

I'm not scared of the wind and rain I grab the pans I left ready and say goodbye to the blue tits and the robin and hurry outside until I'm in the trees then I stop to tidy up the backpack and put the books inside the pans inside the clothes and tie the blanket round the lot and put it on my back start moving I don't know these trees and the sun's gone now just grey sky getting darker part storm sky part dusk on its way I go back down to the grassy road I know there will be no one there but then I think he came Winter didn't he and the men who followed him and the men from a few days ago they might come back and the wind might hide the sound the smell of them they could creep up I stay alert I'm partway home over the landslip when the rain comes maybe if I hadn't gone upstairs in the house I could have been home and dry by now but I don't mind getting wet I can make a fire and dry the things the books won't spoil deep in my bag anything else will dry I just hope the rain doesn't hide the sound of someone or something coming for me but I know these woods better than anyone She said I'm part of them and move like a blown leaf or a scurrysmall animal so if there's anyone's sound being hidden it's mine and I'll see them first.

I settle by the fire after a nice meal a stew Winter made he's tired he's asleep in his room the wet smell of the things from the empty house out to dry I'm happy with the things I got I didn't get any food but we won't go hungry I know the plants the mushrooms their secrets and sometimes I hunt the animals no food from that house but I have everything else I need pans fabric. When I set off

181

this morning I didn't think I'd get books Winter says he'd like to read them too they smell a bit musty but I arrange them neatly with the others on the shelf in the alcove by the fireplace they'll dry I feel good inside thinking about them. Sewing first I have to do the useful things first but when it's done when I miss Her miss talking to Her singing with Her playing games when I'm lonely I'll enjoy reading She taught me that. I have Winter now but sometimes I just want my world Her world and I have to protect my alone for when he goes.

No sewing tonight I'm tired after my journey and the washing and putting away but before I go to bed just one thing I sit in my chair with the handwritten book on my lap I didn't show it to Winter it feels too personal if he decides to stay I'll show him I open it I scrabble through the pages till I find that photo there She is I look for a long time I relax then I fold the corner of the page down and turn to the beginning there are photos lots of photos of a family I don't know babies children doing different things dressed in different clothes playing by the sea I want to go to the sea one day I'll make a longer journey today I wanted things fabric useful things but it was practice for the longer journey I want to make just once and I'll come back if I can journey safely and come back I want to see things towns the sea films music paintings maybe even other people all the things I hardly remember but She told me about. Apart from the sea I'm not interested in this family I flick through till I come back to it that picture I saw of Her it's a newspaper cutting like the ones in the box in Her room I look and She's happy in a group of people there are names beneath the picture the tall man next to Her is Her husband She told me about he's smiling too I know She loved him like I love Her I look at him for a long time I look at a girl between them I wish she'd been here with us like she was with them then she could have been my friend but families lose each other I lost mine I was lucky She found me and let me share Her home and now I'm safe I keep looking at the picture don't know the other people but I'm lost in the faces of my family I think of

Her as my family so the man and the girl are too after a while I read the story from the newspaper it was a long time ago before I was born before the *Digartrefu* when people lived in the farms and worked together I look again at the picture and I thank the neighbour people for leaving this book for me I'm sad we didn't have it when She was alive sometimes She was upset because She didn't have any pictures of the man and the girl I have them now and I think of Her I hope that's enough.

# SAFE AS HOUSES

As the days grew longer, they grew closer. No one else had come near the house; at least, not that she'd told him. He believed her and the fear, the constant looking over his shoulder, faded as his scars healed.

He was changing in other ways; he noticed more than he ever had before the approach of the longest day. The air seemed to hover around the extra hours of sunlight and he was glad to be surrounded by it, away from crowds and buildings designed to shut it out. Occasionally, he'd feel a pang for the bustle and cheerful activity of urban life, but the feeling didn't come often. His fleeting thoughts of Cassie were less frequent, too.

They were driven indoors for several days by a storm that shook the house and made the trees dance manically. He sometimes heard a creak above the howling wind, which made him wonder how safe they were from falling branches. It reminded him of a phrase from his childhood, *safe as houses*, which didn't seem too apt in these times of storms, floods and rising sea levels.

They had enough supplies to last them a few days, and so with no real reason to venture out, they used the time to read, play music and teach each other songs. And for language lessons. He persuaded her that, although he might pick up rags of her language through going about their business together, learning songs or listening to her read, it would be better if they made a positive attempt at teaching and learning. She bristled, both at having to explain and at the fact he liked to write things down to help his memory. An impatient teacher, her system of reward and punishment was simple: if he spoke English she'd pretend not to listen, though he now knew she understood him – an unorthodox but effective method that bore results. In the absence of anything to measure it by, he had no idea whether the results were better or worse than any other way. He soon found he understood her well, though it took longer for him to be able to speak himself.

One evening when she made one of her regular references to Her, the guardian woman who had lived with her here, he ventured to ask, *Pwy ydi hi?* He'd guessed who she was from the documents he found, but wanted to be sure. After a while, once she'd considered what was obviously a huge step, Bela took down a book from the shelf. A photo album. He felt closer to her when she sat down beside him, cradling it reverently. It fell open at a particular page and she showed him a newspaper article featuring a picture of a group of people involved in a community regenerative farming project. She didn't need to point out Her. Elin Sherwell-Jones looked happier and healthier than he'd ever seen her and he was terrified to speak, dreading Bela's reaction if she knew his part in her life. If he stayed she'd have to know, but for now he nodded in a coward's silence. His smile upon seeing the image was genuine, but he was glad when she unfolded the article and passed it to him, saving him from having to speak.

## WATER IS THE NEW OIL
*Olivia Wellesby*
*The Guardian Long Read, 11 August 2036.*

It has been a privilege to spend time with an unprecedented alliance of Welsh independence campaigners and environmental activists, who have come together to take over the site of a proposed reservoir and dam in the Irlas valley in Wales.
One aim of the reservoir project is to help control the flow of the Irlas, which eventually joins the Severn, thereby alleviating the ever-increasing flooding problem downstream, along the Wales-England border.

However, the main purpose is to regularise the water supply to regions of England. Construction work has already begun on a massive pipeline that will carry water from the Irlas reservoir to an undisclosed point in the Thames Valley catchment, and from there to London and the Home Counties. Counter-intuitively, another branch will divert water when needed to the drought-affected agricultural areas in Herefordshire and other Marches counties.

The project has been a subject of controversy for many years with the devolved government in Wales. They claim that decades of underfunding from Westminster have been little more than an attempt by the UK government to blacken the reputation of the Senedd, giving them an excuse to refuse the Welsh bid for independence, and maybe even take away some devolved powers. In retaliation, the Senedd have implemented a series of emergency laws requiring the English water board to acquire expensive licences to develop the reservoir and its associated infrastructure.

'These are our natural resources,' said First Minister Lewis in her speech following the success of the Independence referendum. 'We have to remember that the water shortages over the border have been caused by decades of mismanagement. As a nation on the verge of independence we will no longer be taken for granted.'

The UK government, still dealing with the after-effects of Scottish secession, is dragging its feet over the Welsh independence issue. The Irlas Dam controversy is seen as a key bargaining tool in the Welsh fight to leave.

I'r Gad!, the hardcore independence movement, want to take it further. Payments, however large, are not enough. They refuse to accept construction work on Welsh soil for a project that will benefit English communities almost exclusively. 'Why should they drown our valleys yet again?' says group representative Alun ap Ifan. 'There's plenty of scope for catchment and storage on or under English soil. Do they not remember Tryweryn?'

Back in the 1960s, the damming of the Tryweryn river that flooded the village of Capel Celyn, creating the reservoir that still feeds the city of Liverpool, became the focus of Welsh language and national identity as the destruction of a traditional Welsh village symbolised the continuing domination of the English over Wales. The rallying cry, *Cofiwch Dryweryn*, in its distinctive red cloud, was resurrected in the early 2020s as the YesCymru independence movement gained ground, and the fight for Cwm Irlas is now seen as the successor of Tryweryn.

'It's not only a matter of language and culture. Here in the Irlas Valley, our Welsh communities are practising sustainable stewardship of the land,' says ap Ifan. 'The dam project will wreck swathes of what we've achieved so far.'

This is where the independence and environmental movements have joined forces. Environmental groups say that too much established woodland and regenerative farming land will be lost beneath the extensive reservoir, and the changes to the drainage will affect upland bogs which have re-established themselves since the local rewilding project began. Modelling has shown that side effects such as these may in fact exacerbate the very flooding that the dam is intended to mitigate.

Catrin Hywel, spokesperson for the Gwyddonwyr Gwyllt/Wild Scientists (GGWS) campaign group says that downstream flows are better regulated naturally by encouraging wetland habitats and their ecosystems to slow the flow along the river's upper reaches. 'We're already seeing the huge benefits from the rewilding scheme by local farmers and landowners,' she says. 'Woodlands and other important habitats have been allowed to re-establish themselves, and the controlled introduction of alpha predators will ensure that balance is restored. This oversized reservoir would undo so much, drowning the valley and destroying woodlands that cannot simply be replaced by new planting.'

'We're not going anywhere,' says Elin Sherwell-Jones, whose family farm is one of the collective of landowners at the heart of the rewilding project. 'The reservoir would drown land that my family has owned for generations, land where we're now practising permaculture. It would decimate a large chunk of the area we've given over to rewilding, not to mention the vast swathes of habitat elsewhere – in England, too – that would be disturbed by the pipeline.'

She typifies the movement. Appearances are deceptive. Although you could imagine her, along with her rugged husband Bede, tattooed like a Pict, and their 14-year-old daughter, charging down the mountainside at the head of a pack of wolves, she is in fact well-educated and articulate. In the past, the local farming community would have baulked at the project, but her family are not untypical of the new generation. 'We've had to diversify in recent years to make a living, but it's more than that. We know the land, respect it and understand how best to regenerate.'

This is not merely blind optimism. Before he died, her father was supportive of their ideas, though he had his reservations, and her mother has been instrumental in uniting the local community, many of them initially sceptical, behind the rewilding. Most of the farms and smallholdings in the project have been in their respective families for generations, with only a couple of what the hostile press like to call 'well-meaning but misguided incomers'.

What concerns scientists, environmentalists and nationalists alike is the speed with which the government is determined to press ahead with construction.

'Both our countries' backs were turned,' says Alun ap Ifan. 'Here in Cymru we were focused on the Independence vote, while across the border they were once again succumbing to election fever.' The sweeping victory for the government was of course helped substantially by the substantial numbers of Welsh voters who boycotted the election, claiming the Westminster government no longer represented them. 'So while people were preoccupied elsewhere, they swept in and began felling our ancient trees when they haven't even finalised the scheme. Just like they did with HS2 during the Covid-19 pandemic, they're hoping most people won't notice the scale of the destruction and once they do, they can say it's so far down the line there's no going back. That's not going to happen here.'

A sizeable camp has been established with a community of tree houses in the valley and protesters, many of them local residents, occupying the houses by the river that are ultimately scheduled for demolition. Supporters are holding rallies in Cardiff, London and Manchester. The new government has threatened to tighten up security and bring in the full force of the policing reforms begun in the early 20s.

'We're ready for them,' says Sherwell-Jones, with a friendly smile as she leans out of the ground-floor window of one of the houses. 'We've taken to the streets before, many times. As well as our ecosystems, we're protecting my Anti Gwen's house, and my daughter's set up camp in the trees where she made dens as a little girl.'

Her 76-year-old aunt appears by her side. 'This is nostalgic, in a way. I was at Greenham Common and I'm as scared and angry now as I was then.'

She looks at her niece, who nods.

'We're not afraid and we're ready to put up a fight.'

# SEVERAL LAYERS OF SADNESS

The lights and the heating were becoming more erratic. On colder days he'd wondered why she didn't light fires – the fireplace in the living room looked as if it would work with a good sweep – but her regular trips to inspect the downed tree at one end of the lane and the landslide two miles beyond their house at the other made him realise she didn't want the smoke to be seen.

One day she took him to inspect the shed full of ageing batteries, along with the solar arrays on the house and in the clearing. He'd made a show of examining them, peering at gauges and checking connections, but what did he know? He was a townie, with these things done for him. The best he could do was apply the knowledge of army equipment he'd gained during service. Having your life depend on it was the best incentive to learn. But however laterally he applied the knowledge, there was no denying they needed replacing. Or overhauling. He had no idea. He asked her if there was somewhere – a town with a functioning builder's merchant, or even an abandoned place they could scavenge, but because he was still unable to ask in her language, she made a show of ignoring him.

Only a show. One morning, she beckoned him as soon as they'd had breakfast. Announcing they were going to fetch *batris* – he understood that all right – she took him outside to where a large wheelbarrow was waiting. It contained the well-equipped toolbox he'd been impressed with from the start, and a wheel. He knew her well enough to suspect she had a purpose for it. He'd find out soon enough; there was no time to ask as she set off, no doubt keen to make the most of the day.

He helped her heave the wheelbarrow over the wall that disguised the bottom of their track. It had been done a while ago; moss and lichen combined with the brambles to give an appearance of age.

Together with the log fall and landslide blocking the road, it reminded him of the winding ramparts of prehistoric hillforts, almost precluding the need for violent defence.

Almost. He remembered the day he'd arrived, without knowing the precise location of the house. Of course, he hadn't actually found it; she'd dragged him there, probably using this very wheelbarrow, though he'd been unconscious for most of it.

The road was potholed and fast succumbing to the predation of roots and weeds, but despite having to step on tussocks – her understandable safety precaution to avoid leaving footprints – it was easier going for boots and wheelbarrow than tangled undergrowth would have been. After negotiating the landslide, they reached a gateless entrance and she stopped. He could see the farmhouse it guarded and thought it unlikely that any of the huddle of derelict buildings could possibly produce useful batteries. Bela vanished behind one of the crumbling concrete gateposts and tugged out a trolley. With a missing wheel. He smiled to himself. She was hard to fathom sometimes but she never did anything without good reason; the trolley had been either stashed or observed there by her, in waiting until it was ready to serve a useful purpose.

They fitted the wheel, with the help of rusting wire from a fence that hadn't seen livestock for a long time, and a tangle of binder twine. The wheel was the wrong size, of course, but no worse than the supermarket trolleys that decades of design refinement had never managed to perfect.

It was slow going with the limping cart; they paused twice to patch up the makeshift repair. It must have been half an hour before they reached another house, closer to the road. This one, too, was abandoned, but it seemed more recently. She chattered away as they approached and he understood that this was where the people in the photo album had lived.

The occupants had taken most of their belongings when they left but it seemed that the house hadn't been ransacked. He found the remoteness oppressive, despite the safety it offered. He hadn't been aware of anyone coming this way since the day he'd barged in with his pursuers; there were several layers of sadness to this house. These neighbours had clearly known Elin Sherwell-Jones, yet must have been unaware of her return. Sensibly, she had chosen to stay hidden.

The solar roof was intact – its dull surface could soon be cleaned – and in an outbuilding they found a stack of batteries. Bela flicked a switch and he was relieved to see the beginnings of it coming to life. Having ascertained its usefulness, they set about disconnecting the system and harvesting the components, loading what they could onto the trolley and wheelbarrow. He was once again amazed at her agility and resourcefulness, especially as she clambered about on the roof, but was satisfied he'd made himself useful. By the time they'd finished, the sun was beginning to sink towards the horizon. Stepping back from securing the last few parts, she announced *Yfory*. Tomorrow – they'd come back tomorrow; time was running out since the journey over the pitted road would be much more slow-going with heavy loads. She carefully hid everything from view in an outbuilding, though if thieves came – *other* thieves, he thought with a pang of conscience – they wouldn't be hard to find.

As she started towards the lane, he asked why didn't they camp out for the night in the house and was startled by the intensity of her reaction. Her pine marten would have raised its hackles, and did pine martens hiss? She strode off down the lane as if his suggestion had put a curse on the place, and he hurried to catch up.

They were nearly home when she turned off the potholed road, pushing aside some brambles to reveal a faint path downhill through the trees towards where, on windless nights, he'd heard a river. The recipient of their tributary stream.

As the gradient began to level out towards the valley floor, he heard the rushing river above the soughing of the wind in the branches. The trees seemed different; even his unaccustomed eye realised that although there were as many if not more crowding each other as the ones higher up the slopes, they were younger, competing with denser undergrowth.

They paused as they came to a wider road; she spread her arm to hold him back as she stood listening. Like their lane, it was potholed, the verges merging messily with the crumbling asphalt, but he could tell it was used occasionally. He supposed this must be the road he'd been travelling when he paused to eat on the fateful day of his ambush. He turned to ask Bela, but her attention was entirely on the road, head cocked as she sensed the air.

She darted across, beckoning him to follow. He was surprised how wary he felt. As they made their way down to the river and turned to follow its bank, parallel with the road above, he thought about fate and the way his attack had brought him to Nant-y-Wern. He doubted he'd have found the parallel lane, let alone the walled-off farm track, left to his own devices.

They hadn't gone far when, through the young trees, he saw the road veer away from the river, following the contours of the land. They came to a clearing around the remains of a building. Again, she indicated for him to pause while she listened. At first it looked like the shell of a barn; then he realised it was a house with a sagging roof, stumps of walls running away on the far side indicating it had once been joined to a row of others, their absence amplifying its loneliness. Satisfied there was no threat, Bela led him round to the side, where the neighbouring house should have stood. All signs of habitation had gone, but both storeys of the wall were covered in a colourful but fading mural. Richly painted scenes of land, defiant people, dragons and daffodils surrounded the words *Yma O Hyd*. Even across the border they'd seen it everywhere as the slogan of the civil war. We're Still Here. Now it was doubly ironic, adorning the walls where a family had lived years ago, and representing the hopes of a downtrodden nation. Yet it stood out defiantly against the faded glory of the mural. Someone was still here to touch it up in a mix of desperation, vain hope and love, though it was clear even they hadn't visited for a while. It occurred to him: Elin? Bela herself?

She was standing reverentially, contemplating the dead house. Not the time to ask.

Standing in respectful silence, he looked around him. The river chattered in the background, a quiet roar with the occasional gloop as it leapt round a stone. The houses were gone, but crumbling walls drew the lines of gardens down to the road, stones of further derelict buildings visible through the trees. The sound of the river grew as they stood and he became aware of voices, distant singing. He tensed, but Bela was calm. The peaceful river noise grew to a roar, drowned the singing, drowned the wind in the trees, drowned the birdsong. He stood, spellbound, transported.

A bird darted from the socket of an upstairs window. His eyes followed the movement and caught hers.

'*Llatai*,' she said, eyes wide with delight.

As he breathed, shaking off the tension, as the sounds of river, trees and breeze returned to normal, he recalled a line from a song that had become a favourite of theirs, about a blackbird messenger, *llatai*, between two ill-fated lovers. The spell broken, she led him around the front of the house, relatively free of undergrowth as if whoever touched up the paintwork also gave similar gruff care to the garden, to the other gable. In contrast to the artwork of the first mural, this was a scribble of graffiti in messy layers, even the most recent less than new. Among the scribbles he recognised that other rallying cry, *Cofiwch Dryweryn*, recalling the drowning of a different Welsh valley by the English back in the 1960s, and knew where he was.

Sure enough, after a brief pause, she led him downstream along the river, all the while alert, keeping to the shelter of the trees, until they came to another clearing where a huge mass of concrete debris, spiked with the curled tentacles of broken metal bars, confirmed that this was the site of one of the first confrontations of the civil war. The tumbled blocks and rusting remains of abandoned machinery were similarly daubed, their predominant red and green fading but defiant in the setting sun.

They were standing close and, without thinking, he took her

hand. She let him as if it were the most natural thing in the world.

It wasn't long before they turned back. Clearly the remaining house was more important to her than the site of the dam, since she paused again as they passed. She seemed to love it as a shrine, revelling in all it represented. Maybe he still hadn't quite shaken off the oppressive rising of the river and unquiet ghosts, but the whole place seemed ineffably sad to him.

They struck off uphill through the trees. It was growing dark by now and he felt safe from the world he'd left behind, the 'real world' that had begun to feel increasingly unreal long before he went on the run, now enmeshed in a ghostly aura of lament and regret. He thought of Cassie. What was she doing now? She'd coloured the edges of his thoughts often enough since he'd been here, but this was the first time he'd truly wondered about her in the real, present world. Would she try to find him before he was ready to make contact with her? Did he want her to? The crepuscular light dimmed further and he wondered if it was the ghost world talking. Suddenly, he feared for her.

He gave himself a mental shake and concentrated on following Bela, who clearly knew her way, confident yet slowing her pace enough for him to follow her without stumbling too badly.

That evening, they ate a meal she'd prepared in advance and toasted each other with a bottle of elderflower wine, in the glow of a single lamp. An air of contemplation settled over them as they sat, blanket-wrapped, on their old sofa. Emboldened by the wine, he asked her if the house in the valley had once been her home. She laughed, genuinely surprised and amused. This had been her – Elin's – house; the house in the valley had also been in the family, but no one had lived there since they killed the village twenty years ago. Even with his limited grasp of the language he was sure she said *killed*.

Bela had come here eight years ago and She had taken her in, given her a home, taught her how to live again. Eight years ago. She'd have been in her early teens, little more than a child. Feeling like he was stepping out onto thin ice, he asked where she'd come from. There was a long pause. He couldn't see her expression properly in the faint light.

After a moment, she said, '*Rhyfel. Pla.*' Her matter-of-fact tone implied that everyone's lives had been changed by war and plague so what was there to say?

He was about to prompt her when she stood and moved across the room towards the shelves. He waited in anticipation, thinking she was going for a book, a diary, another photo album, but she returned with the guitar, which she passed to him. He played some rippling arpeggios, anticipating her story and silently agreeing that the music was a good way of cushioning the starkness, but she gestured impatiently and asked for the *llatai* song.

He played the opening chords then paused, hoping as vainly as the ones who kept the graffiti alive that she might give him her story. She told him that she'd been to the memorial house, talking to the ghosts, the day before he arrived.

He paused, taking this in, wondering whether she believed she'd somehow summoned him, a companion, into the loneliness of her life. Did *he* believe it?

She gestured impatiently. '*Canu.*'

He sang the *llatai* song for her.

It began to rain, light but persistent, as they returned to the neighbours' house. The old coat she'd given him was waterproof, though drips inevitably found their way in, and his boots were leaky. On their return, with wheelbarrow and trolley both heavily laden beneath protective tarps, the wonky wheel proved even more of a hindrance with a full load, but they were making reasonable progress, more than halfway home, when he became aware of an unfamiliar sound over the pattering of the rain.

He felt it before he heard it.

By the time he'd processed the sound – the crunching tyres and hum of an approaching vehicle – she was rushing with the wheelbarrow to the gateway where they'd picked up the trolley the day before. She hurried back to help him drag the trolley into concealment. He felt panic rising, expecting the car to appear at any moment until he recalled the landslide and the fallen tree, and the direction of the sound assured him that it was on the road below. He thought ruefully that not so long ago he'd have been delighted and flagged them down to ask for help transporting their load. Now he shared Bela's instinctive caution.

They crossed the lane, scrambled down a short way and peered through the trees. The vehicle drew level, then passed. He couldn't make it out, but caught a flash of metal as the car went on its way. He started to relax; then it stopped. So did his breathing. A muted beat intensified as a door was opened: a strangely sinister reminder of his old world. The music stopped, car doors slammed and he heard footsteps on gravel. Two pairs; indistinct voices.

They waited.

He was damp, cold and aching beneath the scant shelter of dripping branches; she looked unconcerned by the worsening weather, but totally alert to what was happening down the valley. With a flap of her hand, she signalled to him to wait. He pointed to the gateway where their things lay hidden, but she shook her head vigorously. She vanished swiftly, gone before he could suggest going with her. Resigned, he huddled into a hollow beneath a bush, wrapping his coat tightly around him.

The wait was a reality check and he wondered how paranoid he'd become. But she knew how frequently vehicles travelled this road. He only had to remember what happened the day she found him to respect her caution. Time slowed and he wished the waiting would end. He thought he caught snatches of voices, the occasional footstep through the rain, but even his fear-heightened senses couldn't be sure. Occasional gusts of rain-spiked wind startled him and he told himself to get a grip. The absence of activity began to nag, and he decided he should go and see what was happening.

Fighting stiffness, he emerged from his hiding place. He'd gone a few paces when he heard the car doors, the muffled thump of the music resuming like a distant approaching horde. Wheels crunched and the sound of the car vanished oh-so-slowly into the distance. He paused, listening to the sound fade. She'd be back soon; maybe he wouldn't need to scramble down the slope.

The wind was rising, roaring in the trees overhead. It made him increasingly uneasy, not only about the possibility of falling branches, but by the conviction that they'd seen her, overpowered her and taken her with them. Rooks cawed in the branches above and it spurred him into movement. He ran down the faint path. His foot caught a moss-covered root and he tripped, his healing leg giving way and arms flailing uselessly. The landing winded him and he lay muddy, wretched and useless. The sound of something approaching through the trees gave him the energy to roll to the side but they were there before he could burrow into the brambles. The terror of that day paralysed him; she wasn't here to help him this time. No one—

He looked up in time to see her annoyance dissolving into hysterical laughter.

Face glowing, infuriated beyond words, he got to his feet and stormed up the hill. Resolutely refusing to turn back and look at her, he crossed to the gateway and dragged the trolley back out onto the lane. He'd recovered enough to regain some of his strength and if ever there was a time he needed to prove his physical fitness, it was now.

He'd reached the stretch of wall closest to the house and started unloading the cargo to dump it over, ready to transport up the other side, when she caught him up.

She was smiling, affection rather than mockery in her eyes. Too bloody late for that. He turned and continued unloading.

She grabbed his arm with surprising force. It was his injured arm; despite himself, he allowed her to stop him.

'*Sori.*' She drew him towards her, stood on tiptoe and kissed him. 'You looked so funny.'

He broke into a smile, amazed at hearing the English words. He was even more amazed to find himself kissing her back.

# PART VII

# YNYS HUDOL

One of our main aims is to be self-sufficient, yet we're realistic enough to realise that, for the foreseeable future at least, there are some things we'll need from the mainland. Technology is one: although a certain amount of physical work is good for body, mind and soul, it's not our intention to go without certain benefits, such as light and power. It is, of course, up to the Gatherings to decide on the extent of this and the frequency of our mainland trips.

After we'd bought the island's freedom (as we like to think of it), we converted what we had left to cash and have it in safekeeping on Ynys Hudol. Others who came did likewise – voluntarily – and to date our reserves have served us well for our mainland trips. This is not some cult whose members donate their worldly goods to enrich the leader, as we have no permanent leader. Every penny is accounted for, and its use approved, at Gatherings.

We have no need for money within the community, both as a deliberate policy and practically. Mundane jobs are shared in a fortnightly rota and specialist work is accounted for by bartering, or the offsetting of rota tasks, such as the ever-necessary work in the fields and gardens.

It seems to be working, on the basis of honesty and people's genuine desire to do their share.

*Extract from* Seeds of Change
*by Edith Turner and Bleddyn Price, 2047.*

# THE ONSHORE BREEZE WAS INNOCENT

Her morning stint in the garden complete, Sandy went upstairs to her room. Fairly sure that the family were all occupied elsewhere, she locked her door. They'd thought her eccentric enough when she'd asked about a lock; having fitted it, who knew what their response would be if they caught her actually using it. She had to admit that the atmosphere of community and trust had made her quite forgetful and she rarely did lock up. The broken house door had unnerved her. It was unlikely that anyone would have braved the storm simply to snoop around her room but she wanted to be sure. After a pause to listen for footsteps on the stairs, she lay down and lifted the loose floorboard beneath the bed.

She felt a wave of relief to find that the file, the PD and the small, waxed fabric bag were there. A quick flick through the official papers and her notebook reassured her. She listened again for anyone approaching, then drew the small pistol from the bag. One thing she had to thank Adam for, at least. She recalled her fears as the rioting got worse, made tangible when he'd presented her with the gun. The few firing-range sessions he'd arranged for her were hardly reassuring, nor his insistence that she carried it. More than once since arriving on Ynys Hudol, she'd wondered about approaching the Defenders. One afternoon, a volley of shots peppering the air, Glesni had told her that, despite the community's main defence of invisibility, there was a small group prepared to defend them if needed, practising with the few weapons brought by new arrivals and confiscated for the common good. The Defenders were allowed to train when they weren't needed for practical tasks, though some said if it came to violence they'd have betrayed the Seeders' principles and there'd be nothing left to defend. The community kept a watchful eye on the Defenders to make sure no one started acting aggressively, and they in turn accepted the strict limits on their activities, satisfied that the community would be grateful if their services were needed. Despite the islanders' suspicion, Sandy thought it was eminently sensible; though when she thought of the likes of Madog, who she knew was involved, having access to a store of weapons, she could begin to understand, if not share, the islanders' doubts.

Satisfied that nothing was missing from her cache, she tucked her notebook beneath her mattress to update later before secreting the other things away again. It seemed the broken house door really had been carelessness. Madog, come too late to help Erik patch it up, had immediately asked her if she'd been the last to leave the house for the roundhouse when the storm hit, as if she were the only person incapable of shutting a door properly, but she'd assured him they had gales and storms in Manchester, too.

Looking out of the window over the sun-warmed fields, she was reminded of summers back home when Adam had insisted on trips out to the country. Even the onshore breeze was innocent, as if keen to deny that a storm had struck them only a few days ago. Everyone had pulled together to repair buildings and replant uprooted crops, hoping the next storm and its inevitable destruction wouldn't arrive too soon.

Setting out for a walk, she made her way across the fields, past one of the marshy stands of whispering willows that she'd been told had originally been planted so previous generations could make baskets and lobster pots, followed by a period of preservation as cover for migratory birds, and were now fulfilling both purposes. Reaching the shore, she turned towards the south, the harbour and the boats, where she hoped Erik had made a start on patching up *Otranto* again.

It was surprising how well she'd come to know this rugged terrain, each little cove with its unique character. Each one home to one or more seal pups in the autumn, which she was looking forward to seeing. Glesni had told her how worried she was about their wildly fluctuating numbers. They'd moved north, most of the colony abandoning the island as the sea rose inexorably to shrink their beaches. But a few had begun to return, finding new favourite haunts as the sea nibbled away at the coast. It coincided with a series of much colder winters. Sandy was well aware of that in the city; she shuddered to think what a stormy, freezing winter would be like here. All down to the weakening of the AMOC, the currents that gave them the Gulf Stream, so Idris had told her. She'd been surprised at the detail of his account of the effects of the various oceanic flows, but reminded herself that because they chose a life apart, it didn't make them ignorant.

She reached the harbour to find Erik and Glesni loading the rudder from her boat onto the cart. It was in two pieces and looked a sorry sight.

'Timing,' Erik said as she approached. 'You can help young Glesni with the pony and cart while I make a start on fixing the hole in the hull.'

'Hole? That sounds serious.'

He shrugged. 'Easy enough to patch up.'

She and Glesni set off up the track, leaving him to clamber up and disappear into the boat. Not for the first time, she wondered if she detected a coolness in his attitude towards her. From what others said, maybe it was his early warmth that had been uncharacteristic. She even wondered if Glesni was being unusually quiet.

'I can't believe how quickly time's passed,' she said. 'Hard to believe this happened during Martha's funeral.'

'Tell me about it.' Glesni rolled her eyes. 'Earth Day's coming up soon – another one I've got to get dressed up for.'

She gave Sandy a confiding look that banished her fears of a rift. 'Earth Day?'

'Do you have that on the mainland?'

Sandy shrugged. 'Heard of it. It's not a big thing.'

She tended to shy away from major celebrations – Christmas,

Easter, Halloween. Most people did, or partied to feverish excess with little concern for meaning. There were always bad memories and guilt: the ghost at the feast to be appeased or banished by drunken oblivion.

'It's a shame, really,' Glesni was saying. Sandy frowned. 'We don't have many special occasions and these two have come so close together.'

Relieved that the girl hadn't read her mind, she made a light-hearted comment about Martha not doing it on purpose, immediately feeling crass then relieved when Glesni smiled. She asked about details of the Earth Day festival. Glesni told her that the Seeders celebrated their Earth Day on the solstice, as the obvious date to mark the turning of the seasons and celebrate the resilience of nature in the face of humans' excesses. The summer ceremony included vows to walk lightly upon the earth from now on, and also honoured those who had tried in whatever way to stem the inexorable tide of so-called progress.

Sandy was not surprised when Glesni told her that the purists had called more than once for the honouring aspect of the ceremony to be reworded, because they believed there was little to celebrate and some of the declarations could make people feel dangerously self-righteous or, worse, lull them into complacency. Apparently Awen scoffed at their concerns. The basic shape of the ceremony had been agreed at a special series of Gatherings and could be given whatever meaning or emphasis people liked in their own hearts and minds. It was considered by most to be a beautiful day when the community came together. Whatever their views, everyone attended.

A slight hesitancy in Glesni's tone made Sandy wonder if she'd agree with the purists, but she nevertheless looked forward to seeing it for herself.

Once again, Sandy couldn't help but be impressed by Awen's presence as she led the procession into the *Llannerch*. Gwylan was by her side this time; it was unclear whether this was in her capacity as co-leader or the healer's partner. She thought Awen and Gwylan a most unlikely couple. This woman with her head so wispily in the clouds seemed the least compatible partner she could imagine for Gwylan, with her down-to-earth, practical efficiency and leadership qualities. It was a shame that the leader was only a temporary position. Sandy could understand their mistrust of power and its consequences to an extent, but it seemed a waste when you had someone as capable as Gwylan at the helm. What would happen if it fell to Idris, keeping himself apart in his tower, immersed in his nature-watching? Or Erik, only slightly less apart and hardly a natural-born leader. *Seeds of Change* stated that no one would judge a candidate who felt compelled to refuse, but no criteria for refusal were specified. She felt thankful that she'd arrived on Gwylan's watch. It was hard to imagine what her time here would have been like if the role had fallen to Steffan, the arch-purist, or Madog, who had taken a dislike to her for some reason she had yet to fathom. She felt a momentary panic that the changeover might be about to happen at this ceremony, but remembered with relief that they considered midwinter to mark the turning of the year, just like in the real world. The mainland world, she corrected herself.

Although she knew that the decisions essential to the running of the community were made at Gatherings and the co-leader's role was primarily as a kind of facilitator, she could see the benefit of keeping the spiritual side of things separate, and whatever her personal view of the woman, Awen was probably the ideal spiritual leader. Having spent her life back home steering clear of most aspects of religion, Sandy could understand how the islanders' ceremonies, and even the weekly ritual of holding a Gathering, provided a grounding, a moral reference, continuity in the face of shifting change.

Indeed, as the final notes of the children's choir echoed through the whispering leaves of the grove before they dispersed to stand with their families, she felt something. A shared experience of togetherness. Enough of this and she might start to believe in something more. There it was again, that sense that maybe she should think about staying.

Glesni had given her a translation of the Welsh lines. She'd read through them a few times, until she could almost feel she understood the language. She let herself drift, only glancing occasionally at her crib sheet.

*We love the earth and all the life it sustains.*

After each line Awen paused, an infinite moment in which the breeze-rustled leaves, the noisy wrens and robins, the harmonious blackbirds, the distant soughing of the sea, were a choir singing an ethereal response.

*In sincere apology we do our utmost to live in ways that cause no further destruction.*

*We give back, to our Mother and to one another, that which those who went before us, and those who continue elsewhere, have taken in their greed and their refusal to learn.*

*We give thanks for our lives when others are suffering.*

*We give thanks to those who devoted their lives and those who gave their lives. For the martyrs and their sacrifice.*

*Whether they failed or succeeded, they gave what they could.*

*We will do the same.*

*We honour them.*

Awen the priestess fell silent. Awen the woman said, 'Edith Turner, *ti ydi'r pridd sy'n maethu'n gwreiddiau.*'

You are the soil that nourishes our roots.

She'd practised it with Glesni and was now sufficiently able to get her tongue round it to join in with the group as they intoned the refrain that grew with each iteration.

Cai, co-leader, took up the sequence: 'Bleddyn ap Hywel, *ti ydi'r pridd...*'

And round the group it went. It seemed they'd each chosen, or been given, a name. The refrain took on a special quality, a warmth. Sandy looked at the family to her side. Helyg and Tom, Haf and Glesni. The girl caught her eye and they shared a smile. Erik beyond her seemed elsewhere, his attention somewhere in the tree canopy beyond the far side of the group, his lips shaping the refrain but no voice.

Thanks were given to individuals and groups from around the world, close to home, past to present. As the first drops of drizzle fell like tears for the martyrs, her unasked question about the roofless Grove was answered. They got on with it. They got wet. They embraced all weathers. Why should sun and a rustling breeze be a more appropriate backdrop to their ritual than the pattering of life-giving rain?

As the litany continued, moving at random from past to recent present, far to near, she heard names she knew – Thoreau, Attenborough and, more surprisingly, Winstanley, some that were new to her such as Brazilian activist Chico Mendes, and some, such as Berta Cáceres after whom their boat was named, or Polly Higgins who had pioneered the concept of ecocide, that she'd picked up since she'd been living among them.

She allowed the naming and honouring to pass over her. It was only now that she realised she'd have liked to play a part greater than simply being there. It came to Glesni. Greta Thunberg. Of course. Glesni must have fought her sister for that one, to judge from Haf's glare. She didn't recognise Haf's own contribution. Helyg had a faint smile as she named Gareth Llywelyn, her partner, the girls' father, who'd died only a couple of years after arriving on the island.

Erik was next. 'Elin Sherwell,' he said, quietly but steadfastly.

How could he? He knew that Sandy's sister had been fatally injured at a protest that woman was responsible for! Sandy's fingernails dug into her palms and she kept her eyes to the ground, refusing to intone the refrain. They'd invited her to name her own martyr, but she'd declined, feeling unready for that. Now, though, she felt an urge to shout up out of turn and name Liv, yet something made her suppress her emotion and she merely glared at him. Deep in his own thoughts, he was oblivious to the world. The remaining names that she recognised seemed more harmless, at least.

209

'And who will be the Earth's guardians of the future?'

Sandy glanced down at Glesni's crib sheet as Awen called the children back to form the procession and talked about the importance of future generations – the adults' responsibility to nurture them, to listen to the children's voices, to give them courage to make the best of the world that had been left to them. And to take the Seeders' message out to the mainland world one day, when they were ready.

Finally, the rain offering an apt if uncomfortable drumbeat – they were getting quite wet by now – Awen announced that the Flame of Ages, representing the ancients who lived in harmony with the Earth and gathered around campfires to share stories and wisdom, would be lit in the firepit in the roundhouse, their only concession to the elements. Before moving indoors, the children came together again for the final song. It was as beautiful and uplifting as the first had been, but Sandy's unease was too great for her to immerse herself this time.


'I couldn't help noticing some, er, controversial names among your "martyrs", she said as they sat drinking punch around the dancing flames of the fire.

'One person's terrorist is another's freedom fighter,' Helyg said. Sandy fought the urge to roll her eyes at the cliché.

'Helyg told me about your sister,' Erik said quietly. 'I was sorry to hear it. If it means anything, I respected her work. It was a terrible… mistake. Most people there had no intention of using violence, and were as shocked as anyone by—'

A bitter laugh escaped her. 'Shocked? That the use of explosives kills and injures people?'

'That a bomb was planted in the first place.'

'You know, do you? What their intentions were?'

He remained impervious to her attempts to provoke a reaction.

'Our movement – environmental and pro-independence – was non-violent,' he said, the low light of the room making it hard for her to read his expression, though she noticed he said *our*. 'Anything counter to that was a reaction to what *they* did to *us*. Maybe some people gave in to provocation, did things they shouldn't—'

'Out of desperation!' Helyg cut in, eyes blazing. 'Government inaction was – still is – killing millions of innocent people around the world.'

'Two wrongs don't make a right,' Sandy insisted. 'In a democratic—'

'Can you look me in the eye,' Erik said, 'and tell me you've never done anything you regret?'

# THE MOVABLE FEAST OF MORALITY

The midsummer ceremony always made Glesni think. She'd never really understood why some societies revered ancestors just because they'd gone before. Ancestors made mistakes like anyone else, didn't they?

After all, their immediate ancestors were the people of the nineteenth and twentieth centuries. The ones who engineered an explosion of greed and consumption. The Industrial Revolution – they were taught that mainlanders considered it a force for good. Not the beginning of the end, a way of making things easier for the few while perpetuating poverty and division for the rest. Distancing people from the reality of what they consumed, seeking endless growth from finite resources. As more and more bought into it, they could see it was costing the Earth. Well, her generation could – with hindsight. Those who saw it then, who refused to go along with it, were the ancestors they honoured.

But they made mistakes too. As she changed from her robes, Glesni acknowledged to herself that this Earth Day honouring didn't leave her with the usual warm feeling. Maybe she simply felt apart from the chattering children, old enough to think rather than merely feel. The Seeders' ceremonies were simply an attempt to tap into some greater good, and to bring the community together – she understood that. There couldn't be false gods, as people like Idris claimed, if they didn't believe in gods at all. He still came to the Earth Day ceremony, stating in no uncertain terms that it was for the good of the community, *Empathy-Humility-Frugality,* not because of any change in his beliefs. After naming Jesus of Nazareth as his martyr, he went straight to the altar in the schoolroom, as if to atone for his sin.

It was Sandy's reaction to the honouring of the martyrs that worried her more than anything. Glesni had so wanted Sandy to be a part of things but could sense she didn't feel right about it all, despite her keeping a neutral expression as they went round the circle. She worried about the painful memories of her sister, Liv, even though it would surely be cathartic for her to feel and allay them, and wished now that she'd broached the subject of honouring Elin Sherwell with Taid, not only because of her association with Sandy's sister, but to use it as an excuse to ask him what his connection with her was. Several other people, Mam included, always named the same martyrs, but there was a reason for it, even if the Compassionate Silence sometimes obscured it. When she entered the roundhouse after changing from her processional costume – she hoped for the last time – she could see them having a discussion that looked less than friendly.

Tom was playing the guitar; not one of the rebel songs, Glesni noticed. Glancing over at the family, she made her way round the back of the roundhouse to the group of older kids in the far corner. She'd have preferred to sit with Mam and Taid, listening to the music, but her desire to distance herself from the little ones after her final children's procession would be more pointedly served with Haf and her crowd.

'I don't know what he was trying to prove, naming Elin Sherwell,' Haf hissed in her ear, moving away from Angharad and the others as she approached. 'He knows about Sandy's sister and Irlas. She looked upset.'

Glesni shrugged, suddenly feeling defensive. 'If he hadn't named her, someone else would have.'

'Sure. Someone who isn't playing host to the woman. Not that Taid knows much about manners.'

Before Glesni could reply, Haf turned back to her friends. She watched Tom call the band to take their places on the stage as people started to form a circle for the dance. As if she'd heard Haf's snarky comment about manners and was trying to prove her wrong, Mam was urging Taid to partner Sandy and teach her some of the steps. Cai approached and Sandy accepted his offer, saving Taid the embarrassment of refusing. Tom came across, took Mam's arm, and they all stepped up to join the others on the floor. They were smiling, laughing, and it warmed Glesni's heart to see any hint of coldness, real or imagined, gone. She looked round at Haf and her friends; they were making a good show of being aloof from such idiocies. The traditional *twmpath* dances were for little children or adults; teenagers knew better. They were making it clear that Glesni wasn't old enough to be admitted to their clique yet; she headed for the door to get some fresh air, not wanting to give Haf the satisfaction of seeing her sit at the family's table with Taid. In any case, it would have been impossible to talk above the music and sounds of merriment.

The sky was still quite light, but the moon moved in and out of fast-moving clouds like a shuttle weaving a silvery fabric. She stood watching it for a while, enjoying the sounds of music drifting out towards her, without the awkwardness of watching from the edge, feeling like she ought to be joining in when in fact she was quite happy not to.

'Where's your friend?'

Glesni spun round at the sound of Madog's voice. 'Which friend?'

'The mainlander.'

'In there, dancing, last I saw.'

He shook his head. 'It's one thing that the woman's been snooping around old Erik, though God knows what for.' She tried to interject but he carried on regardless. 'Don't say you didn't notice. Hanging round him ever since she's been here, asking a million and one questions, sneaking off on that boat – got to give you credit, there, getting on board to make sure they didn't get up to whatever it was they were planning.'

'What on Earth—?'

'But now she's after Dad.'

'What do you mean?'

'They're all over each other.'

'Dancing, Madog. What's your problem?'

'Think about it! He's been on his own since he and Mam split up. Since we came here. Now she's getting her claws into him.'

'And? Two lonely people—'

He gave an ugly laugh. 'Oh, grow up. You were sharp enough to find out who she works for. Don't play the innocent now.'

'I haven't a clue who she works for.'

He rolled his eyes. 'That logo on her phone, the one you showed the old man.'

'How do you—'

'A government department, Glesni. You didn't believe all that crap about getting lost while chasing after her partner, did you? She's here for a reason.'

'What's your dad got to do with it?'

'How should I know? Something from back when he was in the force.'

'What about Taid?'

'Secretive old bugger. Nothing would surprise me. But she's got no right coming here and causing trouble. What's in the past should stay in the past.'

'And what's in your imagination should stay in your bloody head.'

Glesni turned away and headed back inside, for once pleased with herself for thinking of the right reply at the right time. Most of his questions she'd already asked herself, but Madog was the last person she'd want to discuss it with.

Taid was sitting it out at the edge of the room. The circumstances weren't ideal, but she went over to talk to him. He smiled as she made her way across to sit with him. She tried to smile back.

'What did you have to tell Madog for?'

'Tell him what?'

'About the logo on Sandy's PD.' He frowned. 'You know, the one I showed you—'

'Good grief, Pwt, I'd never talk to him about that kind of thing. Not Madog, not anyone.'

215

'So how come he knew? He said "the one you showed your taid".'

He shrugged. 'I remember now. When you showed me. Didn't I say I thought I'd heard someone? Sneaky little bastard with his ridiculous suspicions. I'm getting seriously fed up with him.'

Glesni suppressed the thought that she might be able to take Madog's place in the workshop if Taid dismissed him. She was still too annoyed. 'He said it's who she works for.'

'If he knows it's because he's asked her himself. And that's hardly likely, is it?' He wasn't looking at her, but gazing across the room. 'He's just guessing, trying to provoke you into giving something away.'

'But I don't know anything!'

'Exactly. Because there's nothing to know.'

'Really?' She took a deep breath. 'I think there is. Like why, if you believe in non-violence and all that, why do you always honour someone who planted bombs?'

'She didn't. They—'

'Were infiltrated, deceived, whatever. *If* that's true, what is she to you anyway? Can't you share it around and choose someone else to honour, for once? People are talking.'

'What people, Pwt?'

Glesni frowned. Haf had mentioned it, but who else? 'I don't know,' she said sullenly. 'No one talks to me. But *why* do you always honour Elin Sherwell?'

He looked past her and held up his empty cup. 'I'll tell you, but now isn't the time. Take this over and get me a refill, will you, Pwt?'

Wishing he'd talk straight with her, Glesni made her way over to the bar table. Mam was dancing with Tom, looking happy and carefree like she rarely saw her. Gwylan and Awen were there, too; beyond them, she spotted Cai and Sandy. Why shouldn't they enjoy themselves? Madog didn't seem to have come back in.

She refilled Taid's cup and managed to persuade Lucy to give her another punch, though she was already feeling the glow from the one she'd had. By the time she returned to the family table, Mam

216

and Tom had come to sit down, flushed and smiling. Which saved her from the futile task of pushing Taid further; she was certainly no match for the three of them. When she looked back at the dance floor, Sandy and Cai were nowhere to be seen.

The next day Glesni was out in the garden, digging over the ground and removing the worst of the weeds to create a new patch. On her own. Haf had got distracted some time ago by Angharad and hadn't yet come back. Her back was beginning to ache, even though the plants didn't fight back. Well, some did – nettles fought back. And others clung on, refusing to budge, leaving traces of roots behind as if to say they'd as much right to be there as the community's poxy veg, and who were they to decide which were to go and which to leave or plant in their place? She said a silent apology as she coaxed or yanked each plant from the ground, remembering how when she was a little younger she'd asked, if people didn't eat animals, and she understood the reasons for that, why was it OK for them to eat plants? After all, they were living things, too, sharing the same world. What had they done wrong to be torn from their homes just because people chose to 'garden' there? And what about the ones they cultivated – planted in a place of humans' choosing and forced to grow? They seemed healthy and happy enough but it wasn't their choice, was it, in the natural scheme of things. And to add insult to injury, they were reared for the sole purpose of being eaten. Why, she'd insisted with a child's logic, was that more right than doing the same to animals?

When she raised it again in a recent discussion at school about the interconnectedness of all things, Tom suggested it could be her introduction to philosophy. While it was up to individuals and societies to decide on what they would and wouldn't eat, provided it wasn't destroying the planet like factory farming, they should remember that predator and prey were natural, and living beings had to eat. All things in proportion, the movable feast of morality.

Glesni was brought back to the reality of weeding when she

scratched herself on a thorn. Green in tooth and claw. However much she'd thought about it over the years, she still wasn't totally sure why animals had it over plants and why people thought they had it over the lot of them. Not to mention some people having it over the rest.

'Need a hand?'

She looked up, not sure that Sandy's hands would be much help. She handed her Haf's fork nevertheless and showed her the outline of the new garden plot. She showed willing, if not great skill, and Glesni appreciated the company. Sandy said how much she'd enjoyed the ceremony, complimenting her on the procession and the singing and surprising her by admitting how she'd felt a spirituality she hadn't expected.

'I can see why... It really makes you feel part of something.'

'I'm glad,' Glesni said.

She went on to ask her about the honouring, her voice casual enough to suggest that in fact it was the only reason she'd begun the conversation. Glesni explained how the names were divided out and agreed in advance, usually at random, to make sure no one got honoured twice. She deliberately didn't mention that some people always named the same person, especially if they had a connection to them. Sandy asked about some of the names she hadn't heard of. Surprised by her ignorance, Glesni told her as much as she knew about what their contributions had been. It wasn't until she asked, even more casually than when she started, about the Sherwells, that she wondered if it was some kind of test. Whether there might be some truth in Madog's crazy notions.

'They weren't just at Irlas, you know. They were campaigners in both the environmental movement and the Wales Freedom Alliance,' she said, the nonchalance of her voice probably sounding even more forced than Sandy's. 'Which makes them important to us on two counts.'

Sandy tugged at a stubborn weed. 'Funny that your taid named Elin Sherwell but no one mentioned Bede.'

'Martyrs are usually dead. He disappeared but it's only assumed that he died.'

'Don't you think some of the choices are a bit extreme? People who've been involved in terrorist acts?'

'They've all been decided on at Gatherings. Someone proposes, we have a vote. Not everyone likes every choice. But not everything someone does is all good or all bad.'

'But from what I've heard, you're totally committed to peaceful action.' She glanced up the hill. 'Apart from the Defenders. Even then, I suppose they'd only react, with reasonable force.'

Glesni nodded. 'And not everyone totally approves, remember.'

Sandy had given up on any pretence of gardening. 'Hm. But what about those who were at Irlas Dam, though? I mean, even with your Seeder ethos of forgiveness and understanding...'

'The authorities needed scapegoats.'

Sandy was looking at her with something like pity.

'I don't blame you, Glesni. You only know what you've been told.' She shook her head. 'But I'm getting fed up of the constant references to scapegoats and conspiracy theories.'

'That's probably because they're true.'

Glesni made sure she sounded determined, but in truth she wished she knew more. The whole conversation was disturbing her; she had a feeling there were things being deliberately kept from her, too. She hated to think the adults still believed her too immature not to say the wrong thing. Then she felt paranoid for even thinking it. Surely there were other people Sandy could pester. She wished she could think of a way to turn the story to Cai that was a bit more subtle than *Why don't you ask your new friend; he knows far more about these things than I do*. She and Madog couldn't have been the only ones to have noticed them leaving together the night before and she was dying to ask her about him. Glesni sympathised with her, being here all on her own, but knew she'd never confide in a young girl like her.

'You're not the only one being evasive,' Sandy said. 'All this stuff about forgiveness and not traumatising people by raking up the past.'

However excluded Glesni might be feeling, Sandy's words triggered a sudden wave of loyalty towards her community. 'We'll probably never know who planted that bomb. Why can't you just let it go?'

Sandy laughed, ruffling her even further. Then she turned serious. 'You know what happened to my sister. I'm beginning to think there may be people here who had a hand in it and are on the island to hide away from the consequences.'

Glesni could only shake her head; this was taking it too far now.

'Believe me, it wasn't why I came,' Sandy said. 'But I'm going to find out.'

# TO CHANGE WAS NOT A WEAKNESS

Sandy woke up with a mild but nagging backache. Beautiful though it was, sleeping on a mountainside under the stars would need some getting used to before she could truly enjoy it. Light was beginning to tinge the edges of the sky. She looked across at Cai, still blissfully asleep. They should be getting back.

She lay for a moment, gazing up at the fading constellations. She'd found the darkness on the island – and before that, across post-Resettlement Wales – oppressive at first, but soon grew to love the display. Last night they'd gazed up at the stars massing to infinity in a density she could never have imagined, the Milky Way floating through them like the silky scarf of a sky goddess.

'It makes you wonder if anything matters but the here and now,' he'd said.

When they weren't absorbed in each other, they'd lain back and he'd pointed out some of the constellations, telling her their stories. It was the kind of knowledge, like the names and habits of plants and animals, that the islanders talked about like people back home talked about politicians or that day's bad news. Things she'd hardly thought about for quite some time now.

'Rise and shine,' she said, shaking him gently.

He woke, sat up and gave her a lingering kiss. They were both tempted to stay, to rekindle the previous night's passion, make the most of these opportunities before the weather turned again, but by instinctive understanding they drew apart and dressed as the horizon grew lighter and pinker. The previous morning, after the night of the honouring, they'd both made it home unnoticed. Sandy doubted whether Helyg, Tom or the girls would have batted an eyelid, but Madog was another kettle of fish.

As they made their way down, she felt she'd left some of the night's magic behind in the hollow of the hillside. She could hardly believe it had happened. Outside the roundhouse two nights ago, so different from the night club where she'd met Adam, the music poles apart but the same rhythm of life drifting towards them on the air, something had crystallised between them. As the revellers drifted away, so had they. But not to their homes.

This had been their second night. After a brief hug and a kiss, they went their separate ways, agreeing they would try to meet that night if they could slip away unnoticed after the Gathering – it seemed that, although the community had come together for the ceremony, the weekly Gathering would be held come what may. She tiptoed into the house and crept to her room, turning the key. She had a new reason to be glad of the lock.

She walked over to the open window to watch the dawn enrich the landscape's colours, moment by moment. Breathing in the island breeze that whispered up through the grass in a beeline for her room, she smiled to herself, wondering why she felt the need to act like a naughty teenager. In truth, she didn't want the attention. She knew Cai was worried about Madog's reaction. Either way, no point causing trouble when the affair would probably be short-lived.

Or would it? Did she have to give it up, this new life? Aside from Madog's accusations after the fishing trip, which had been brushed off as one of his crazy outbursts, no one seemed to believe that she was anything other than an ordinary office worker whose life partner had been cruelly driven from her by a vicious regime. Only Madog, and maybe Cai, seemed to suspect she had a different story. But he hadn't pushed her to tell. She'd felt nothing but welcomed and had no doubt that if she wanted to stay, they'd form a work party – after agreeing it at a Gathering, of course – and help her make a home for herself, as Erik had said.

Erik.

To stay would mean turning a blind eye to atrocities. Yet hadn't she turned a blind eye often enough at home? She'd worked for a government department for fuck's sake. Hadn't her skin crawled more than once at things she'd been tasked with? Even if she wanted to, going back was hardly a realistic option. Liv's voice nagged her. Was she really going to allow lust to derail her from her search for Adam? She had to see it through, bring him to justice. It was her chance to make amends, for herself and her sister. She was beginning to accept she might never find Adam, but it seemed she'd found a more than adequate substitute.

When it had dawned on her who Erik really was, that the woman he'd named at the honouring had meant more to him than simply a respected martyr to the cause, it had felt like a physical blow. She'd tried not to think about it, wanted not to believe. He came across as such a likeable person behind that gruff exterior. Troubled by experience, but one of the few genuine souls in this world. Proof in itself of the insidious effects of this place and its people: she never waxed lyrical like that.

She was dismayed not only by who he was, but the fact that he'd taken her in so completely, playing the genial, harmless old man when his past actions had been anything but harmless. As if her clumsiness in attempting even the simplest practicalities of this life wasn't enough, the ability of such a man – not to mention his thirteen-year-old granddaughter, for fuck's sake – to pull the wool over her eyes caused a huge loss of self-esteem that Cai's attentions had gone only some way to restoring. Her conscience beginning to nag that she'd allowed her growing emotions to hold her back from saying anything to him, she justified not speaking up as fairness to Erik, telling herself she should prove her suspicions before voicing them to anyone else. In any case, she realised that she'd be only mildly surprised to discover that Cai knew Erik's background, that they all did.

And what about Glesni? She was no innocent, Sandy was beginning to realise, though she suspected there was plenty that the girl hadn't been told. If she didn't know, she deserved to, and decide for herself. If Sandy had turned a blind eye more than once in her life, it was to faceless government departments, distant colleagues, anonymous news items. Here, they were face to face with at least one terrorist. Yet she hesitated to break the spell. The notion of an idyllic, innocent childhood might be a fiction, but the children here were at least able to enjoy a rare respite from the consumerist world. Maybe even that was wrong; maybe it was delayed cruelty, since surely this community wouldn't last forever. Not for the first time, she worried about how attached she was becoming to the girl.

She kept revisiting the scene at the – what was that word? *Llannerch*. The Grove. Their leafy cathedral. The togetherness, the desire to connect with the Earth, to live in a way that was right. Neither Erik nor anyone else had given her the impression of being anything other than ordinary – with the exception of Madog, maybe; who the hell had he been in a former life, if he wasn't too young to have had one? He'd been following her around as if she presented a threat to someone, or indeed the whole community. Well, if her suspicions about Erik were right, the lad might just have a point. Yet if someone truly had moved on, had atoned for their actions in some way, shouldn't they be given a chance? Was she showing precisely the lack of empathy they might expect of a mainlander, a city-dweller, a civil-servant cog in the wheel of the system that they had rejected?

One thing she'd learned since she'd been here was to slow down. Maybe she shouldn't judge too hastily. Give him another chance. If she was mistaken, or if he showed the slightest hint of remorse...

The island wind swelled the curtains in an attempt to remind her that to change was not a weakness.

She tracked Erik down in the workshop, the *Otranto's* battered rudder on the bench with a wooden replica in a vice before him. As ever, she couldn't help noticing the tidiness of the place. Only the window was untouched, covered by what she'd come to think of as the world wide web as she passed a succession of blind, empty windows on her journey through Wales. The skin of cobwebs contrasted with the rest of the room, as if to emphasise his desire to keep the outside world at bay.

Watching him finishing off the replacement for the rudder, she commented on his skills.

'I've always had a fascination for how things work,' he said. 'Taking things back to basics, finding solutions.'

She held herself back from wondering aloud whether his knowledge extended to explosives.

'Mighty useful experience,' he continued, 'now things aren't done for us.'

She nodded and he continued working in silence. It almost felt companionable. After a while, he paused.

'Penny for them.'

She'd been wondering how to say it; his prompting caused the words to spill out. 'I know who you are.'

Was that a momentary fear in his eyes? Only for a split second, before he drew down that steady indifference like a window blind. He turned his attention back to the rudder gripped in the vice on the well-worn workbench. This is who I am.

She envied him his calm. Despised him for it.

'Don't mess with me,' she said. 'You're one of the Sherwells, aren't you? Bede Sherwell.'

The rhythmic whirring of the lathe, the rasp of a file, took the place of words. It was impossible to tell whether he was confirming or denying it. She decided to play him at his own game, sitting there watching him work; after all, it was her boat he was repairing, so it was in her interest to let him get on with it.

At long last he unclamped the rudder from the vice, gave it a polish and showed it to her with pride. It looked good, though really she had no idea.

'Do you know who it was?' she asked. 'Who untied the boats?'

Talk about something else; lull him into a false sense of security. She had time.

'I dare say it'll be the centrepiece of tonight's Gathering,' he said. 'Proves my point, doesn't it? We need a spare boat in case something happens to the other. We had three till the autumn storms last year.

I shouldn't have let that happen; should've hauled the other two out of reach of the highest tide.' He sighed. 'I was just damn careless.'

He tugged his sleeve down. Glanced at her, his hand moving to the scarf at his neck. He went back to his sanding. Stopped and tugged at his sleeve again as if to make sure.

'Maybe you were. Careless.'

She remembered what he'd said on the fishing trip. Lots of people wore long sleeves all the time in these days of sunburn and skin cancer. There was no sun in this shadowy workshop. Lots of people had distinctive tattoos. But they didn't keep trying to hide them.

'The fault wasn't mine alone. I'm not the only person in this place capable of winching a boat up the slipway.'

'Maybe I wasn't talking about boats.'

He stopped what he was doing and looked up. 'What *were* you talking about, then? I'm crap at riddles; you should know that by now.'

He sounded weary: Just say what you've got to say and let me get on.

'You're also crap at dissembling. If someone suggests you're one of the monsters of the twenty-first century, most people would react in some way.'

'I've been called plenty of things in my time.' He removed his cap, scratched his head, and put it back on. 'OK, Sandy. You've had a chance to get to know me. If you still think I'm one of the "monsters of the twenty-first century", that wounds me to the core. But I'm long past letting things like that get to me. Satisfied?'

'Who else knows?'

'Knows what? That I keep my emotions to myself?'

'Who you are. What you did.'

'I don't know what you've heard.' She was glad it was hard to see his expression in the dim light. 'One thing I do know – it's who you are in here that matters.' He patted his heart, then stood and strode round the workbench towards her. There were times she found it hard to believe he was in his seventies. This was one of them. She forced herself to stand her ground.

'You don't deny it?'

'I don't deny a name.'

'Irlas Dam? The bomb, the violence?'

'I paid the price. A price that wasn't mine to pay.'

She wished she didn't have to look up to meet his gaze. 'Really? No price is enough to bring my sister back.'

'I've told you, I'm sorry about that. Believe it or not, I mean it. I understand you. They murdered my wife.' His voice was menacingly quiet. 'I refuse to believe she harmed anyone. Property, maybe. Things, Sandy. But people, no. She was murdered just the same.'

The woman he loved. Helyg's mother. Glesni and Haf's grandmother. Murdered? Sandy held on to the bloody images of the Irlas Dam bomb. Elin Sherwell-Jones had got away from that one, but had eventually been jailed, and subjected to the lethal drug trials as part of her punishment for other acts of terrorism. Regardless of her ultimate fate, it was justice.

'Whereas you got off early, on some dubious pretext. There was no such reprieve for my sister.'

'I'll say it again: I'm sorry it happened. You probably won't believe me, but I liked Olivia Wellesby and respected her work.'

'I don't give a flying fuck about your opinion! The fact is—'

'The *fact*, Sandy, is that there was a plant. Government agent. There were things I did, but not the bomb. Come now, if I'd been involved, do you think it'd have gone off at the wrong time?' He actually smiled, though there was no mirth in it. 'Seriously, those of us who were there from the start fully intended to be non-violent, like we always had. It's not hard, even for the likes of you, to believe they wanted a civil war. Fewer homes to power; someone to blame for their failings. Fewer mouths to feed as they fucked up the food supply.'

She scoffed. 'You're claiming you're innocent?'

'No one who lived through the last few decades is innocent.'

'You can't—'

'Sandy. Whoever you are. I'm guessing you've got blood on your hands, too.'

'How dare you?'

'Tell me, who's this Adam? What's he done? Why are you chasing round the country after him? Rescue or... the opposite?'

'I told you—'

'And I believed you. *We* believed. Why wouldn't we?' He twisted the oak-leaf pendant at his neck. 'Tell me, Sandy, have you ever fought for something you believe in?' He gave a bitter laugh. 'Have you ever actually believed in anything?'

'Justice.'

'Oh? I think the word you're looking for is revenge.'

She failed to see why that couldn't be part of the mix.

'So where do we go from here?' he said after a loaded pause. 'What do you want from me?'

He glanced round as the door latch clicked.

'Hey, Pwt,' he said, relaxing as the door opened and Glesni came in.

'Hiya.' Her face fell as she saw the rudder on the bench. 'You've done it. I wanted to help you make it but I couldn't get away and—'

'Not to worry; you can come and learn how to fix it in place.' He smiled. 'You coming, Sandy?'

'I'll leave you to it.'

She watched them walk down towards the harbour, wishing she felt differently. But she was seething. Whether he was baiting her, had truly brainwashed himself into believing his own innocence, or was protecting someone else, he'd had his chance. His indifference, along with the whole community, incensed her.

Back in her room, the breeze through the open window for once unable to soothe her, she did her regular check on the treasures beneath the floorboard. She'd locked her room during her night-time absences, but maybe there was a spare key. Her heart performed a hollow lurch and she looked accusingly at the open window. The papers were there but the PD, which she was sure had nestled beneath the file, had gone. She lay down and shoved her arm deep into the gap. The waxed cotton pouch was still there, in it the pistol. Partial relief. She felt again: no PD. She looked everywhere – pockets, drawers – even though she knew she hadn't moved it. Her first thought was to find Cai. He'd told her she should let go more – did that make him a sympathiser? Maybe she could talk to him before the Gathering. About that, and about Erik Jones's true identity. Hoping fervently that he'd be as surprised as she was, she went in search of Cai. He wasn't at home, or in the office he shared with Gwylan, in the fields or gardens or any of the workshops. Then she remembered he was on food-prep duty; she had to remind herself that being co-leader didn't put him above such menial tasks. In the kitchen they told her he was late. Had Erik said something? Or was Cai avoiding her because of their budding relationship? She'd passed Madog after she left Erik's workshop and his look was deadly, but that was nothing new.

She resigned herself to seeing him at the Gathering, after all. In the roundhouse, she took her usual place with Glesni, who'd settled into her role as unofficial translator of anything people said in Welsh. Maintaining a pretence that nothing had changed, Sandy nevertheless made sure she put the rest of the family between her and Erik.

The business included an interminable back-and-forth about the mainland foraging trip that had been postponed because of Martha's death and funeral, the storm and the Earth-and-hero-worship ceremony. Steffan ventured to suggest that the two former events were fate, an omen, clearly telling them that now was the time to stop polluting themselves with relics from the decaying mainland world and become truly self-sufficient, whatever the sacrifices. What amazed Sandy even more than the proposition itself was that the Gathering actually discussed it as if they were taking it seriously. The purist ideal was crazy enough, but they were actually debating omens? Even more preposterously, some kept glancing her way as if she somehow added a whole new layer of danger to the mainland trip.

She couldn't help smiling to herself. Maybe that part wasn't so preposterous.

Once the discussion had come to an end and the trip planned for two days' time, those interested in going were told to meet after the Gathering. Gwylan then announced they had another important matter to discuss. The possibility of sabotage: the downed turbine and the liberated boats. Sandy thought it best not to add that her PD had gone missing, despite the lock on her bedroom door. Since she'd failed to tell anyone about it, that was something she'd have to sort out herself. And she'd called Erik careless.

Gwylan outlined the circumstances – the funeral, the storm, both times when most people were preoccupied. Glesni had told her on the way to the roundhouse about their customary two minutes' silence during which the culprit, if known, could explain their actions, and if not known, had the chance to come forward and confess and apologise before explaining. Then be forgiven. Sandy smiled to herself at the naïveté. There was a haphazard system of punishments to suit the crime, usually centred around making good in some way, and counselling. She looked round the roundhouse and found herself wishing they didn't always have to sit right opposite Madog. He stared at her the whole time.

'No one?' Gwylan finally spoke out, an edge of exasperation to her voice. It seemed people usually confessed. She turned to Cai.

He asked Erik, without specifically mentioning the coincidence that he'd discovered both instances of damage, to describe what he'd seen. He swore blind that he'd inspected the turbine's ground anchor recently, but the storm had been a bad one and these things happened. They were lucky; the damage could have been much worse. As for the boats, he'd regretted being late for his friend's funeral. He produced the length of rope from the scene of the crime and held up the severed end. There was no doubt that this was deliberate.

'Thank you,' Cai said. 'The incidents weren't necessarily connected, but they both happened when the community was gathered elsewhere. So, let's start by asking ourselves, who wasn't here during the storm, and who didn't go to the funeral?'

Idris was already on his feet. 'I was in the watchtower during the storm,' he said in a voice that pre-empted any mistrust: he was always in the watchtower.

'Did you see anything?'

'I noticed the lads going out to check stuff during a lull in the storm. The young lass, Tahira, went out of her house one time. Like she was drawn to the sea.' All eyes turned to the Husseins. 'I was worried for her. But her uncle went out to get her before I felt moved to come down the mountain.'

'The lads? Did any of them go beyond the houses?'

He laughed. 'I was watching migratory birds driven off course by the winds, not young lads I see every day! Most of the time I was inside with my books in any case.'

'But you didn't see them.'

'Wouldn't I have said if I did?'

'What about the funeral?'

'Martha and I went back a long way. I paid my own respects, in my own time.'

'And did you see anything then?'

Idris shook his head. Cai turned to Steffan. He shrugged.

'I was in the roundhouse throughout the storm,' he said. 'Plenty of witnesses.'

'Your feelings about the overuse of electricity are well-known. You could have loosened the turbine's ground anchor beforehand.'

'My feelings about unnecessary waste are equally well-known. I'd argue against replacing it, but to damage a perfectly well-functioning item is a different matter.'

Sandy thought he looked shifty, refusing to meet Cai's gaze – but didn't he always look shifty?

'You came to the funeral at the very last minute.'

Steffan gave an exaggerated eye-roll. 'As you're fully aware, we've been saying for a while that the ceremonies are getting ever more extravagant. We liked and respected Martha as much as anyone, but just wanted to avoid the fuss. Did I look out of breath? As if I'd nipped down to the jetty and back? And like I said about the turbine, I may not like the use made of the boats, but deliberate damage is waste.'

Cai paused, then moved through a couple more absentees before the focus settled on Madog. A murmur suggested many suspected the lad; to Sandy that was hardly surprising, though his attitude was all hurt and personal affront.

'Yes, I did my bit during the storm – went out a couple of times when it abated to check for damage we could secure when it was safe to do so. But I was with Aled,' he looked to his left and his friend nodded, 'and we were never out long.'

'The boats? The funeral?'

He gave an irritated sigh. 'Yeah, I was late. I was fixing the axle on the trailer – Erik'll confirm it...'

'He was in the workshop when I left.' Erik shrugged. 'Told him to leave it, finish up later.'

'When was that?'

'About an hour before I found the boats.'

Cai exchanged a glance with Gwylan. 'So, time enough for him to have got to the harbour,' she said, clearly stepping in to save him from having to confront his own son.

'Are you accusing me?' Madog jumped to his feet, though it seemed to Sandy they'd been accusing him all along. He could have any number of muddle-headed motives to stop them from leaving the island. Or from reaching the mainland. His own father had suggested he'd been a troublemaker when he was younger. 'I got distracted by the job, didn't I? You know how it is.' He looked at Erik, who gave a hint of a shrug. 'Then I had to go and get changed. Didn't want to be all disrespectful in my work clothes.'

'Can anyone confirm it?'

They'd all been too immersed in the preparations for the funeral. 'I don't believe this! Why's everyone always looking at me?'

Hardly surprising, Sandy thought. She recalled her mishap with the breeding gulls on the cliff; now time had gone by, she was certain she'd followed the directions he'd given her.

'Enough!' Gwylan stepped in again. It wasn't just the personal connection; Cai was simply too mild-mannered sometimes, as if to prove he'd never been connected, however distantly, with police brutality. 'You know how it works. Keep to the facts and the Gathering will decide.'

'What about her?' Madog glared at Sandy. 'I saw her arriving at the funeral after me. A bit weird that there are two suspicious incidents after a mainlander arrives, isn't it?'

Keep to the facts, hey? Sandy thought.

Cai turned to her, his expression apologetic.

'There are plenty of people who can confirm I didn't leave the roundhouse during the storm.' She tried to keep the indignation from her voice. 'I wouldn't know where to begin tampering with a turbine. As for the funeral, Glesni will vouch for the fact that I went back to the house to fetch a necklace she'd forgotten.' She glanced at the girl by her side, who nodded.

'Took your time,' Madog muttered audibly.

Ignoring Gwylan's glare, she couldn't help replying: 'It can take a while to find something in someone else's room.'

If it made him think of her PD, he didn't show it.

Helyg spoke up. 'It's true. She was helping Glesni.'

Cai looked relieved, as if he really didn't want to find Sandy guilty of anything. A low buzz of opinions was growing around the room.

'Am I allowed to say something in my defence?' she said, looking between him and Gwylan.

'I can assure you no one's accusing you,' he said. The muttering suggested otherwise. 'But of course.'

'Thank you. Tell me this...' Sandy glared at Madog then looked around the room, speaking slowly and deliberately. 'If I'm up to no good, why would I sabotage my only means of escape from this place?'

She'd intended the question to be rhetorical, but the little speech she'd been about to give was interrupted by Madog.

'Maybe you like it here,' he said, glancing at Cai, 'and you're worried we might send you away. Which we couldn't do if the boats were gone.'

'Why on earth would I think that?'

He turned to face her.

'Or maybe you only intended to lose one boat. So you couldn't be followed.'

'Followed?'

He let the accusation hang for a moment.

Sandy cautioned herself against trying too hard to justify herself. Don't feel you have to fill every pause.

'It just doesn't make sense,' she said, despite herself. 'I'd have no credible reason to damage my own boat.'

'Maybe you were trying to leave, you fumbled and the boats got away from you,' Madog said.

'Oh, for fuck's sake!' Erik surprised her by speaking up. 'I thought I'd taught you better than that. Gwylan made it perfectly clear, as if you didn't already know: stick to the facts.'

He sat down and examined his folded hands in his lap, clearly intending to take no further part in the proceedings. Madog glared at him but said nothing.

After a little more discussion, around the room and between Gwylan and Cai, the Gathering was brought to an inconclusive close. If it had been a court, it would have adjourned, Sandy thought, though she doubted the case would be revisited. They simply gave a warning for people to be more vigilant.

Oh great, she was being watched now, and with much more intent than being peered at as an exotic mainlander.

Incredibly, the courtroom atmosphere dissolved and there was the usual entertainment. Someone struck up a guitar. She helped Helyg and a few others move the benches back to clear the dance area, as a small group left to discuss the mainland trip. No one beckoned Sandy to join them – why should they? It wasn't as if she knew that corner of the mainland any better than they did. She was surprised, however, to see Erik at the side of the room, chatting to Idris – she'd assumed he'd automatically be going on the trip. Then she recalled his strength of feeling when he'd thought she was asking him to take her to Ireland.

She looked around for Cai, trying to be subtle about it. Deep in conversation with Gwylan and a couple of others, he glanced in her direction and smiled, but gave her no sign of special recognition. Frustrated, she slipped outside before she could get drawn into any irritating conversations, keen to talk to him first, though she asked herself why she should trust him more than anyone else. What did physical closeness matter? She thought of Adam. What indeed?

Outside, she took a deep breath. She paused to admire the waning moon and showers of stars, thickening to the Milky Way that arced across the sky above the fields and sea. Standing on the track below the roundhouse, she wondered whether to wait or abandon hope of seeing him. A night apart would probably do them both good – and it would do no harm to leave him guessing. The sea beckoned. A chance to clear her mind. Try to make sense of it all. She walked a short way then stopped to admire the moonlit waves, wondering if the dark specks she could see were birds, dolphins, seals – or rubbish. She wouldn't see any more clearly for being by the shore, but the sound of the waves might lull her.

Or drown out the sound of someone approaching. She shuddered as a nameless fear crept over her. She recalled Glesni mentioning something about mainlanders choosing to flood the skies with artificial light because they were irrationally scared of the dark. She might have been scared back home, but not here. Not till now. Maybe she should forget the sea and head for the house. But what if someone was waiting for her there?

She took the first few steps down the track as if wading through treacle, every nerve tensed. She wished she had something to defend herself with, then told herself not to overreact. Voices from the direction of the roundhouse suggested someone with small children was heading for home. Her body relaxed a little.

'My dad stood you up, then?'

Sandy hoped the darkness was enough to conceal her jumpiness and jangling nerves.

'Madog.' Good, her voice was coming out steady. 'No idea what you mean. I'm going back to the house for an early night.'

The lad was standing on the edge of the track, hands in pockets. She wished she could see what, if anything, he was hiding.

'Fed up of everyone looking at you as if you're guilty?' he said.

'They're not.'

Walk on, go home. There's the young family over there. He wouldn't...

'Not satisfied with my dad, hey? Got old Erik twisted round your little finger, too.' He cocked his head, eyes reflecting the moonlight in a stare that made her tense with fear. 'I'm watching you.'

He turned and strode back towards the roundhouse. How wrong he was. But why had Erik cut him off in the meeting? Maybe he was simply as fed up with his assistant as most of the others seemed to be. Or was it something else? If she didn't leave – and by sticking up for her, he was helping her to stay – she couldn't cause him trouble. Perhaps.

The sea felt distant, the black dots merged into the moonlit ripples, the land lying before her like a vast, menacing predator. She looked away, caught a shadowy glimpse of Idris climbing the path to the watchtower. She saw the young mother shepherding her two little ones towards their house, then watched Madog enter the roundhouse, before making her way home.

# QUESTIONS BETTER OFF NOT ASKED

Glesni walked and walked, as if she could allow the playful wave-goading, seagull-buffeting, flower-nudging wind to blow away the atmosphere of the previous night's Gathering. They'd had their problems in the past – wrongdoings, accusations – but she couldn't remember an investigation that had remained inconclusive. It left her with even more doubts, piled on top of the nagging questions about Sandy, her mam and her taid. And underlying it all was the huge disappointment that she wouldn't be allowed to go on the foraging trip.

It was at times like these that she felt small, unable to engage with the island's wonders – trapped, even.

A part of her never wanted to leave, and she shuddered at the thought of what went on beyond the grey smudge that rimmed the eastern horizon, which she knew to be the mountains of mainland Cymru and, in the other direction, on a clear day, Ireland. On the other hand, she feared never having the chance to experience that grey smudge becoming real grass, stones and concrete beneath her feet, to turn and see the grass, stones and sand of the island as nothing but a tiny smudge on the horizon.

Sometimes as she stood on the harbour wall, with the peeping oystercatchers and scampering sandpipers below her, the choughs standing guard then suddenly taking to the air as one, the seals' singing would turn to bickering mockery all around her – experts in relaxation on land, they could suddenly vanish into the sea, transformed, escaping, leaving her stranded, longing, her curiosity reaching out to somewhere beyond fear.

When that wanderlust struck, she couldn't settle; she'd walk the coast, dreaming of seeing a new place, fighting down anger and resentment that they thought her too young and irresponsible to go with them.

Someone came into view, heading in her direction. The path didn't branch and it was too late to turn without seeming rude. The way she felt about talking to Sandy echoed her conflicting feelings about the mainland. The last person she wanted to talk to, or someone she felt would understand? Glesni paused and looked out over the rocks to the gently white-capped waves to avoid those awkward moments of closing in while being too far away to talk.

'How was the meeting last night?' Sandy asked as she came to stand beside her, slightly out of breath.

'You were there.'

'Afterwards. About the mainland trip.'

'Haven't they been to see you yet? They'd like to take your boat as well.'

'They? I thought you were going.'

'I'd hoped...' Glesni stared at the sea and sky, trying to keep her voice light; to complain would be to betray her community.

'But I know how much you want to go! You're perfectly capable.'

'Pity you weren't there.' Glesni brushed a lock of wind-teased hair from her face.

'I'm surprised your taid isn't going.'

'He hasn't been the last couple of times. You heard him when we were up the mountain. Whether he's going or not, he's the worst when it comes to mithering about me. Makes you wonder why he's bothering teaching me about the boats.'

'Doesn't that mean they need you more? If he's trained you...'

Glesni smiled involuntarily: someone was taking her seriously.

'Listen,' Sandy continued, 'if he won't help you, I can. They can't refuse me; it's my boat.'

'I thought you weren't going.'

'I didn't see what use I'd be – the mainland I know is rather different from the remote corners of north Wales. But I've been thinking... I'm not sure I'm ready to continue my journey yet. You know, to Ireland, to find Adam. If I do choose to stay here, well, something like this might help me feel part of things. Show willing, with the boat and everything.'

'You're probably right. But there's no way you could persuade them to let me come.'

'So how's this for an idea? Come to the boat with me, I don't know, to help carry my stuff, and get on board, lie low in the cabin or something. Once you're there – I'll stick up for you – they won't be able to say no. Stand your ground. What do you say?'

'But it was agreed that I can't. I'd be in trouble.'

'After what I saw last night, there won't be much of a penalty. Surely it'll be worth a few extra chores for a while afterwards. What's the problem?'

'I'd be letting everyone down.'

'They're letting *you* down, Glesni. I'd have thought they knew and respected you better than this. Especially Erik.'

Glesni's first instinct was to refuse Sandy's offer, but she swallowed her scruples and smiled. 'Thank you.'

'Deal?'

She nodded, the warmth of conspiracy adding to the glow of anticipation. They began to walk in the direction of the harbour.

'Can I ask you a small favour in return?' Sandy said.

'Depends what it is.'

Sandy's turn to smile. 'I need your help. You remember my PD?'

Of course she did.

'It's gone. I don't suppose you know anything about it?'

Glesni stopped. 'Gone from where?'

Sandy turned back to face her, raised eyebrows chilling the warmth.

'Honestly,' Glesni insisted. 'I haven't thought about it since you showed it to me.'

'I'm sorry.' Sandy's voice softened. 'I didn't mean any offence.'

'It's OK.'

'But you're better placed than me to find out—'

'Did anyone else know about it?'

'Not from me.' Sandy's voice was neutral.

Glesni regretted telling Taid, especially after what he'd said about Madog overhearing them. She had no idea how to tackle either of them.

'I'll do my best.'

The conversation echoed in Glesni's mind as she continued along the shore path. Sandy had gone to find Gwylan, to tell her she'd decided to go on the foraging trip. It was strange; she'd only been there a matter of weeks but it was hard to imagine everyday life without her. And she'd seen the way Sandy and Cai looked at each other.

As the harbour came into view, she saw *Otranto* out of the water at the top of the ramp, Taid on his back underneath. Seeing him didn't cheer her like it should.

'Everything seems OK,' he said, without looking up. He always seemed to know she was there, acknowledging her without fuss. He shuffled his way stiffly from under the boat and got to his feet with a muttered curse, bracing himself on the side of the boat. 'Of course, we won't know for certain till we get her on the water.'

He grinned conspiratorially. She knew he didn't really need to take it out for a spin; a simple inspection would be enough. But the shared mischief was irresistible and she helped him winch the trailer with *Otranto* down the ramp. He let her do everything, from starting up to navigating past the Quarantine Rock, out into the open water. Once at a safe distance, he indicated for her to cut the motor and let the boat drift.

'Nice one. You're learning well.'

'But not well enough to go to the mainland.' She swung the pilot's chair round to look at him.

'That wasn't my decision.'

'But you agree with them, don't you?'

He gave the slightest shrug, then turned and beckoned her to come and see the emergency repairs he'd done. She enjoyed talking about it, despite herself. They drifted in the sun, rocked by gentle waves. He took out a flask of cordial and they shared it, in no hurry to go back. Glesni felt as though he was trying to make up to her.

'It won't work.' She hated herself, but the words came out all the same.

'What won't?'

'This is lovely. But I still want to go. Can't you say something? Please?'

'I've probably pissed everyone off by not going myself. Nothing I say would make any difference. Leave it, Pwt. Your time'll come soon enough.'

He looked sad; that melancholy he sometimes failed to hide. She thought of Sandy's offer. How it meant that she'd be disappointing him – Mam, Gwylan, everyone. He looked away. The hurt welled up inside her. If only he'd help her, she wouldn't have to let anyone down. But he was right. No point in pursuing it with him. It would have to be Sandy. Passing him the flask back, she took a deep breath. 'Can I ask you something?'

'As long as it doesn't concern the mainland trip.'

'There's something I need you to ask Madog about.'

'Madog?'

'You're the only person he'd listen to.'

He grinned. 'In that case there's no chance.'

They exchanged a look and she almost let it drop. A glance across the water to the hazy mainland renewed her purpose, and she told him about the PD.

His face clouded and he shook his head. 'No point asking Madog,' he said.

'But we've got to try and help her. She can't continue her journey without it.'

'I'm sorry, Pwt.'

He stood abruptly, then leaned over the side. She heard a splash. Too late, she grabbed his arm.

241

'That was it? Sandy's PD?'

She scrambled to open the equipment chest for a net. He put out a hand to restrain her.

'Too late for that.'

He gently shut the lid of the chest and sat down on it, indicating her to join him. 'I'd have thought she'd find a less obvious hiding place,' he said. 'In her own room! But I guess I can't blame her for not knowing anywhere better.'

Glesni shook her head. 'But you should have—'

'Told everyone? Been more open about it?' He sighed, looked overboard as if making sure the gadget had gone. 'There are things... it would have led to questions better off not asked.'

She remained silent, waiting for him to continue. The fact that he'd dropped the device so obviously, in her presence, suggested he wanted to talk.

'Stupid, really,' he said as if he'd read her thoughts. 'It won't make any difference. Might buy some time. Whether it does or it doesn't, it makes me feel better.'

'Buy some time?'

She willed him to look at her but his gaze was fixed on the horizon. 'She'd have used it sooner or later,' he said.

'But what's that to you?'

'She says she's not going but I don't believe her.' Glesni felt strangely guilty for her pact with Sandy, though her anger at what he'd just done was stronger. 'Whether it's this mainland trip or the next, without her PD it'll be harder for her to turn me in.'

'What?'

'To the authorities.'

'What for?'

'She believes I played a part in her sister's fate.'

'But you—'

'I didn't, no.' He turned away again, a wall of unspoken story rocking with the boat between them.

'So why?'

'Why not me? She's highly unlikely to find her Adam so... why not a different trophy?'

Glesni glanced at the water lapping insolently at the side of the boat, having digested the device and now hungry for more.

'But if you're not going, she can't do anything to you.'

He shrugged. 'Even without her PD, she'll find a way to get back to where she came from. Send someone out here. Put others, the whole Seeder community, at risk.'

'But she was talking to me just now about settling here. If she did go on this trip, it would be as part of the community.'

He laughed. 'And you believed her?'

She looked at him. 'It was you, wasn't it? Tried to sabotage the boats.'

'Wish I'd thought of it. But no. Do you think I'd endanger us like that? I'm no purist – we can't cut ourselves off from the mainland forever.'

'I wish you'd tell me what's going on! Why are you so important to her? Turn you in for what?'

He remained silent. She felt anger and frustration rising. '*Did* you have something to do with her sister?'

'Liv Wellesby was a journalist, sympathetic to our cause. There weren't many of those.'

He stood and made his way over to the wheelhouse. On impulse she grabbed his arm to tug him back. 'I'm sick of all these hints! You obviously want to talk – you chucked Sandy's PD overboard in front of me. So just talk! Tell me what the fuck happened!'

He frowned. No stranger to others swearing, she was surprised to find the word passing her own lips.

'I didn't hurt Liv Wellesby.'

'You did something. Why didn't you come to Ynys Hudol at the same time as Mam?'

He said nothing.

'You're supposed to love me,' she insisted. 'Show me some respect.'

'There are some things you're better off not knowing.'

'*You're* better off not confessing, you mean?'

He stood in the wheelhouse door, silent.

'If you don't tell me, I'll think the worst anyway.'

He sighed and made his way back to the bench. She sat beside him. He looked out over the waves, scanning the horizon for words. He turned back to her, reluctantly, as if he found it hard to meet her gaze. She found it hard to meet his, as tears were beginning to sting her eyes.

'It's not because I wanted to deceive you, or keep you in the dark,' he said. 'God, that's the last thing... I just... after all these years I find it hard to talk about it. It was the last time I saw your grandmother, your nain. Elin. The last time she spoke to me.'

'Just a minute.' Glesni realised she'd never known her nain's name. Just Nain, someone they rarely mentioned. Now it dawned on her. 'Elin? Sherwell?'

He nodded.

'Who was at Irlas Dam.' He nodded. 'So you're...?'

He nodded again. 'Was. Bede Sherwell.'

She was beginning to see why Sandy had it in for him.

'I don't believe what you're saying!'

'Please. Let me finish before you judge.'

Momentarily lost for words, she had no choice.

'Where to begin? You know about our rewilding project, yes?'

She nodded.

'Did you know that part of the ecosystem – not to mention some of our land – was set to be decimated by the Irlas Dam scheme?'

Of course she didn't. 'You...?'

He nodded. He clearly found it difficult to tell. She found it just as hard to take in.

'I hated the notion of that reservoir. I wanted to stop them as much as anyone. But how? We'd protested, made our opinions known since the bloody scheme was first dreamed up. We were achieving so much, so many people were behind us, the land was starting to recover, the animals and birds we'd reintroduced were flourishing. The red squirrels, the beavers. Pine martens. Birds of prey, songbirds. Butterflies, insects. There was a huge way to go and we were only a tiny part of the country, the world. But it was happening; it and other similar projects showed people what was possible.

'And they wanted to come along and drown it under a vast expanse of water to make up for other people's incompetence. Our home, Pwt. Imagine Ynys Hudol being under threat. I know you're itching to leave, but only on a trip, yes? You'd want to come back.'

She nodded.

'And even if you didn't, you'd want to know the island was still here, wouldn't you? And our community. For us, but for everyone else as well. That's how we felt at Irlas. We felt so privileged to live there, but we'd worked hard to foster it all. And it was more than that. I'd moved there as an adult, but Elin, your nain, grew up there. As did your mam. She was born there, and fourteen when it happened. Our farm, Nant-y-Wern – Elin's family home – was up on the hill above it all, but her aunt, Gwen, lived down in the valley by the river and we occupied her house – built up stores, barricaded ourselves in as they threatened to demolish the village. There were people in three of the houses. Your mam was camped out with another crowd, protecting an ancient woodland in the valley.

'We'd been there for weeks. We knew they were going to come for the trees soon. At other protests they'd gone in heavy-handed, even cutting them down with protesters still in them. You can imagine how worried we were about our Helyg, but we were unable to leave the house without immediately getting arrested. We got messages but we couldn't go anywhere as they'd be straight in to demolish the lot, and it would all have been in vain. No one, including young Helyg, wanted that.

'I found out that one of the security guys was one Sam Markham, my stepbrother. He and his brother had it in for me when we were teenagers. I hadn't seen him since I left home. Turned out it was no coincidence he was there – gave me some shit about how his chance had come to make amends for the past. He had this plan – to arrange for the coast to be clear under cover of darkness so I could get to Helyg and persuade her down to safety without her having to waste months or even years of her young life in jail. Then get back to the house we were occupying.

'I still don't know to this day if his intentions were good, or if this was one more opportunity for him to make trouble for me. Of course, the Seeder me shouldn't care; I should just forgive...'

He paused again. She said nothing, sensing worse things to come than not forgiving.

'The first bit went as planned. Helyg and her buddy, who'd come down with a stomach bug, were actually relieved, so I didn't have to do much coaxing to get them down and on their way up to the farm unscathed.

'The next day was when they came for the trees. As we'd feared, they injured several protesters and even killed one poor lass – you don't hear Sandy banging on about that, do you? As the news reached us, as if it wasn't terrible enough, there was this almighty rumbling, enough to make the house shake. We thought they'd decided to deal with us at the same time, demolish the houses with us in them and have done.'

He paused with a sigh.

'But no. It was the dam. Bomb went off at the wrong time, didn't it? Rumour was that it was supposed to have happened at night, with plenty of warning to allow people to get out of the way. Something went wrong.' He looked out over the waves, then back at her. 'Though I have no idea to this day whether that was true, or how anyone knew what was supposed to have happened. I certainly didn't.'

He paused as if waiting for her to comment, but she said nothing, still taking it all in.

'That's when I realised Sam Markham hadn't kept his word – or maybe he'd planned it all along. They did come, battering the place down by force, and it was me they were after – the guy who'd been spotted the previous night by the woods. Spotted by whom, hey?

'Sam was there among the police. "Sorry," he muttered as he moved to grab me so they could make their arrest. *Sorry?* If he really was sorry, why was he first in? Maybe he thought he could make it easier for me. I ought to be a good Seeder and give him the benefit of the doubt.

'He didn't get his chance to do anything. All the interminable days cooped up in that house, worrying ourselves to death about our daughter, on top of years of shit in the past from him and his brother, not to mention the disaster of the bomb.

'I knocked the taser or the gun... whatever it was, I knocked it out of his hand and went for him. No excuses, Pwt.'

He shook his head. She hated him using her special name at that moment.

'I can still... The blood and the crunch of my fist. Again and again. Until they shot at me. My leg's never been right since, but that's nothing compared with the guilt. That I allowed anger to get the better of me.'

'So the bike accident was yet another lie.' She sounded trivial to her own ears.

'No, it happened. That injury was properly treated and healed straight; a "terrorist" didn't merit the same care. I'll leave the interrogation to Compassionate Silence. I couldn't tell them anything because I didn't know anything, but they must've had a handwriting expert busy for weeks creating the documents to show I'd helped to plan the bombing.

'Seven years for GBH and a concurrent life sentence for conspiracy to terrorism. Those seven years can be left to Compassionate Silence too. I'll just say Tamsin Henderson, my solicitor with a legal charity, Justice for Protectors, was an angel. I was beyond caring, but she worked tirelessly to appeal the terrorist charge on the grounds that, although they'd found no one else – and they still haven't to this day – there was no evidence that I was actually involved. So I was out by the trees, not far from the dam – that meant nothing. She got me off shortly after the seven-year term expired. That's what Sandy, with her personal stake in it all, can't accept.

'The absence of an actual, proven bomber is why most of us believe it was infiltration. It was one incident of many, but it was the spark that ignited the independence war. The civil war they still refuse to call a war.'

Finally, he looked at her. She turned away. Even if she believed he'd had no part in the bombing, he'd confessed himself that he'd lost it and attacked his own stepbrother. She got up and went into the wheelhouse. Stood there, unable to move. It would have been dangerous to start the boat with her vision blurred by tears. She sensed him hovering behind her.

'Glesni.'

She gripped the wheel without moving or saying a word as the waves slapped indifferently against the side of the boat. She wasn't about to make it easy for him.

'I'm sorry,' he said quietly, his voice almost drowned by the sound of the waves.

He'd just said himself how meaningless that little word could be. She stared through the salt-frosted window as intently as if she were steering the boat between rocks.

He put a hand on her shoulder. She didn't have the heart to shrug it off like she wanted to. 'I realise—'

'I didn't even know your *name!*'

He murmured another useless apology.

'What's that all about anyway?'

'When I was released, I... They suggested... It didn't make sense to go round using the name of a "terrorist". I didn't care. Hated myself anyway. But I took the vowels of your nain's name and her family name, as if that could bridge the eternal gap between us. As if. You can't imagine the despair I felt when I was told she'd died, angry and disillusioned with me, before I ever got the chance to talk to her.'

'Does Haf know?' Glesni felt petty and childish, but unable to voice the things that really mattered.

'No one but your mam – who uses your nain's surname, not mine, for the same reason – and Gwylan.'

'Gwylan?'

'She was there.'

'Oh.'

'She wasn't called Gwylan then. I still have to stop myself calling her by her old name. Just like she must find it hard not to let Bede slip out sometimes.' If that was meant to make her feel better, it didn't. 'No one else. Haf knows no more than you. Did. Till now.'

'Lucky Haf,' she said, standing aside. 'Can we go back now?'

He moved to the wheel and sat on the stool, but didn't switch the motor on. 'And Sandy – she guessed. Then insisted. I couldn't deny it.'

'God forbid you should lie to Sandy.'

'I'm sorry, Pwt. I... I didn't mean to keep it from you. The time was never right. It didn't seem like there was any need.' He shook his head. 'I'm still the same man I was half an hour ago.'

'You attacked him. Your own stepbrother.'

'It was a single moment. With personal history. Have I ever done anything you found threatening?'

Glesni shrugged. All the Seeders' talk of compassion and forgiveness crumbled to nothing in the face of reality. She realised she knew even less about her nain. Elin Sherwell. They said she'd been wrongly accused of the terrorist crimes she'd committed. Was that true? Glesni also knew next to nothing about what her mam had done. Maybe he was right; maybe she was better off not knowing.

# ONE THING WE AGREE ON

Glesni spent the morning after Taid's revelations trying not to think about all that he'd told her. She hardly said a word over breakfast, shrugging off Mam's and Haf's concern with a story about a bad dream she'd had. They seemed to accept it. By the time Sandy appeared, they were ready to leave for school. She was relieved that she could put off telling Sandy about Taid and the PD. As she and Haf passed the courtyard on their way out, she could hear sounds from the open door of the workshop but didn't call in as she usually would. If her sister noticed, she kept it to herself.

She felt an emptiness inside. Everything seemed wrong. There was a bit of an uneasy feeling in the classroom, too; a couple of days after the Gathering about the acts of sabotage, the older ones were still speculating about who could have done it, blaming each other and various family members half in jest. It seemed trivial to Glesni in the face of what Taid had told her, though she didn't like to be reminded of yet another thing wrong. During class, Tom assured them that inconclusive Gatherings had happened before and the community moved on, but it felt strange not to be able to trust each other. There was something in the air, a hostility or suspicion without focus.

Back home at lunchtime, she mentioned it to Mam – she had to say something to stop herself asking about Irlas when Sandy could appear at any moment – and she said it had been the same down on the beach where a group of them were collecting dulse. Nothing tangible, but the conversation had been a little too halting, the banter a little too sharp.

Taid hadn't joined them for lunch, and afterwards Mam asked her to take his plate of salad to the workshop. He was on his own. She put the plate down on the workbench and turned to leave before he had a chance to look up. He called and she paused in the doorway without looking round.

'Madog's not well.' He sounded the same as he always did, as if the previous day's revelations hadn't happened. 'Or so he says. Probably sulking under the weight of accusation, who knows? So, I'm a bit short-handed to be honest. I'm finishing off a permanent replacement ground anchor for that turbine now there's a break in the weather, and I could do with your help?'

'Sorry, I can't. I've got to help Mam and the others with the seaweed.'

She pushed herself off the door frame as if that would propel her away quicker. Her heart wanted to talk to him so much that her head hurt.

'Listen, Pwt.'

She glanced back and finally caught his eye; immediately she turned away from the sadness there. She was saved from having to disentangle her feelings by Mam coming into the courtyard.

'It seems we're all needed in the roundhouse,' she said as she approached.

Glesni looked back again and Taid nodded. 'You'd better go,' he said. 'We can talk later.'

She wasn't so sure. Mam moved past her.

'Dad,' she said, in that exasperated voice she saved exclusively for him. 'All of us. Emergency Gathering.'

She told them that Gwylan had gone to get the money they saved for the mainland trips, and found it gone.

'Believe it or not, I don't know anything about it,' Taid said. 'You don't need me.'

'You've got to come!' Mam's exasperation faded to weariness – the inevitability that he would do what he wanted and nothing else. 'If you don't, you'll be suspect number one.'

Taid shrugged, glancing down at the work bench. 'I'll be in bigger trouble if this doesn't get done before the next storm.'

They didn't think about money very often. Someone had ironically coined the term 'shopping trips' for their mainland forays, but they tried to buy as little as possible, preferring to forage for materials from abandoned items – things like tools that they couldn't make as their own wore out, metals to melt down, and materials such as timber that were scarce on the island. Bulky items like scrap metal and wood were limited by space on the boat, of course, though at least they'd have two boats this time.

It wasn't all scavenging, though. They stocked up where they could on food and clothes to boost their home-made and home-grown stocks, though that opportunity was limited, too. Sometimes they'd find the shops had empty shelves, and many were closed and boarded up. Their savings dwindled with each trip as they had little surplus to sell or barter. It was true what Glesni had told Sandy: anything they had of value was worth more to them than the money they could get in exchange.

And it wasn't just a case of finite reserves. Every time they went, the money itself dwindled in value with inflation, and there was even a nagging fear that one day the currency might change.

Despite all that, and despite the purists saying they shouldn't dirty their hands with money from the old system, what they did have nevertheless proved useful on every mainland trip. Although no one had ever said outright, some suspected it had even been used more than once to buy information or silence.

Of course, no one at the Gathering owned up to taking the money. Expressions ranged from quiet shock and horror that anyone among them would do such a thing – their chief suspect was obviously Sandy – to I-told-you-so satisfaction from the purists: what good could possibly come from the double sin of hoarding money and consorting with the devil of consumerism on the mainland? The Gathering seemed to go on forever and people got restless. The perfect day for outdoor work beckoned, while some people were eager to get their things together for the foraging trip. Eventually Gwylan and Cai sent people off to their various tasks while they and a small group of volunteers went round to question those who weren't present.

As she was leaving, Glesni saw Sandy in a heated discussion with Steffan. There was no doubt she could hold her own, and it delayed the moment when she'd have to tell her about the PD. It felt like a confession even though she'd had no part in it, and if Taid was right that Sandy wanted to betray him, which there was no reason to doubt, his theft of her precious PD would harden her resolve. Inaction was a choice, she'd always been taught, but right now it was a choice she was happy to make.

She saw Mam and Gwylan heading towards their house and slipped away to tag along with them. She knew they were going to find and question people who weren't at the Gathering, but even so, she hoped she'd get a chance to talk to one or the other of them – to persuade Gwylan that she'd make a competent member of a mainland team, so she didn't have to rely on Sandy's scheme, or to find out more from Mam about the family's dubious past so she could try to get her thoughts in order.

Taid's workshop was empty. Gwylan headed off up the mountain to Idris's tower. Glesni and Helyg were to go to the harbour, but her mam paused. 'We can wait a while to see if he comes back. Help me spread out the dulse to dry, and you can tell me what's bothering you.'

'Bothering me?'

Her mam nodded. 'You've been moody all morning. And yesterday evening.' She led the way to the store across the track from their courtyard and climbed the ladder to the loft above, where the air was warm. Glesni passed up the basket of shiny, sea-smelling red fronds before joining her. Helyg tipped the dulse from the basket then paused, giving Glesni a meaningful look. With all the questions churning in her mind, she had no idea where to begin.

'Is it because you weren't chosen for the trip?' Mam said.

She shrugged. It was partly that, but she had no idea how to broach the rest.

'What did Dad say to you? When you were out on the boat yesterday?'

She'd thought no one had seen them.

'Don't worry; he didn't give the game away. I started to worry when Haf came home alone, didn't know where you'd got to. I went down to the harbour and saw you both, still out at sea. He's not offering a way to sneak you in on the shopping trip, is he?'

'He thinks I shouldn't go, like everyone else.'

Her mam smiled. 'That's one thing we agree on.'

Glesni started to spread the fronds, trying to think of how to ask her about the rest. Her mam continued before she could find the words.

'Isn't it enough, what we've got here? What do you think you're going to find?'

Her mam busied herself, giving Glesni space to answer. The expectant silence was punctuated by a warm breeze raising a pungent, briny smell from the red sea of dulse.

'No need to answer that one.'

Glesni smiled, letting her believe she'd þeen thinking about what the mainland meant to her.

'I know how I felt when I was your age. I wanted to take on the world! Spent several weeks living up a tree once, thinking it would make a difference.'

'But you did make a difference! They... the reservoir never got built.'

Her mam raised her eyebrows. Realising what she'd said, Glesni nodded wordlessly. Yes, she knew, but she wanted to hear her mam's version, uncoloured by anyone else's.

'That wasn't a difference I made. It was the bomb – not something any of *us* would have dreamed of.' She shook her head. 'None of us had anything to do with it – you do believe that, don't you?'

'But Taid was violent all the same,' Glesni said, despite herself. Her mam looked at her in surprise. 'He told me. On the boat, the other day.'

'Did he now?'

'He told me about his stepbrother. About rescuing you. And how they came for him, accusing him of plotting it all. And how he lost it...' She felt the tears pricking her eyes. 'I can't believe he'd do that.'

Mam reached for her hand. 'I know how you feel. I felt it too. And Mam – your nain, Elin – was so angry with him, though she didn't need to be – he hated himself for losing control, allowing a darker side of himself to come to the surface.'

'I wish I'd never asked! I'll never be able to trust him again. How can I believe he wasn't behind the bomb?'

'Don't say that, love.' Her mam came over and hugged her and Glesni sniffed as the tears overflowed. 'It was a really stressful time. And he never told me much, but I know his stepbrothers bullied him in his teenage years, especially after his mam died – and his stepdad wasn't much help. I guess he carried it all with him, and then with the enormous stress of Irlas, it all spilled over.'

Glesni nodded, drying her eyes on her sleeve.

'But that's easy for me to say with hindsight,' Helyg continued. 'At the time I felt as disillusioned as you do. Just as Mam did. Because of that fight, the intensity of it, we couldn't entirely believe Dad had nothing to do with the bomb. I do now, of course. But still... Under the terrorist laws we weren't allowed to visit him in jail and I'm ashamed to say we never fought very hard to challenge it. Then, when we heard he'd been released, he made no attempt to find me or visit her – she was locked up herself by then, after her part in sabotaging an oil refinery. Even when he came here, I wanted nothing to do with him. Couldn't believe Gwylan had tracked him down. Turned up with him after a shopping trip – some acquisition that was!'

'Gwylan tracked him down?' Glesni was only just coming to terms with her as someone he and Mam had known before.

'You didn't think he just happened on a boat, took to the water and turned up here by chance, did you?'

If she'd thought about it, that was exactly what she'd have

assumed. 'He told me Gwylan had been there, at Irlas,' she said, to hide her embarrassment.

'She was a good friend of theirs. She managed to visit your nain in jail once or twice – that was why she stayed on the mainland for so long – but eventually her visiting passes were stopped. When all their appeals failed, that was when Gwylan came to Ynys Hudol. Finding me and your dad along the way. As... as you know?'

Her voice trailed up in a guilty question. Glesni shook her head. Something else.

'You know your great-grandmother Delyth left our home in the end, in the Clearances?' No again. Her mam's words tumbled out as if Glesni was about to sail off to the mainland, never to return. 'Your dad and I stayed. Gareth was a researcher on the nature reserve; that's how we met. When the Clearance Crew came to turf us out, we hid; we knew the land, the bird hides, the secret places. We were young, believed we could live like that forever – or at least until it was safe to go back to the house. Then I got pregnant and both of us got scared. That was when Gwylan came to find us and brought us here. Haf was born on the way.' She smiled. 'Lucky that Gwylan's group had Jo among them.' A silence lingered. 'I thought you knew all that.'

'I should have asked.'

Mam shook her head and Glesni gave her a tear-stained half smile. 'We should have told you. There never seemed to be a right time.'

She went on to tell her that Nain Elin had asked Gwylan on her last jail visit to find Taid and try to reconcile things between them. Gwylan also believed he'd let them down – them and all they were fighting for. But when they heard that Elin had died, it seemed her friend couldn't ignore her request. He deserved to know that, at least. Gwylan was on Ynys Hudol by then and maybe it was the spirit of forgiveness of this place, who knew? Eventually she went to find him, persuaded him that life was worth living and brought him here to be reunited with his family.

'We did up the cottage and workshop for him, but I hated the idea of that man coming here to live with us. Gwylan practically had to drag me to see him. I wanted to accept him – however much he'd changed, still I could see my daddy in there, all the lovely times we'd had, the love, before Irlas. But I couldn't see past the betrayal – like you're feeling now. Then, during a row, I let it slip that I'd thought he was dead, since he'd vanished without trace after his release, and wished it were true. I immediately regretted being so harsh. But that was what did it. "You thought I'd died." He looked at me in that way he has. "They told me that *she'd* died. And you. Our home in ruins. Showed me pictures. Actual pictures!" That was why he'd never come back to us. Don't let anyone tell you a camera doesn't lie, Glesni.

'He's a difficult old bugger, not all Daddy and his little girl in the sunshine of summers past, but we've done our best to make up for lost years. You in particular mean the world to him. You're a lot like your nain, *fach*.'

Glesni tried to believe she wouldn't always feel disillusioned. Her mam squeezed her hand, then drew away.

'I wish that bitch would leave him alone,' she said suddenly.

'What does she want? It's true he had nothing to do with the bomb?'

'I firmly believe that.'

'And if he's been in jail he's more than atoned for what he actually did.' Glesni could imagine what being trapped indoors for years would be like for him. 'He wasn't anywhere near her sister Liv.'

'He was there. I guess she thinks he was let off on some technicality. I suppose I get that.'

'But can't she accept that—'

'It's not so simple. Protests were increasingly portrayed as acts of terrorism, so in her eyes he's a terrorist, and it was terrorism that killed her sister. He was cleared of the bombing for lack of proof. People like Sandy argue that wasn't enough – that there should have been proof he *wasn't* involved. There were many who thought so-called terrorists should never see the light of day again.'

257

No wonder he'd changed his name.

'And part of the deal of his release was to report in regularly. Behave himself.' She smiled. 'Refrain from disappearing off to remote islands to live out his life in peace.'

'You think that's why she's here? She's been after him all along?'

Her mam ran a hand through her short-cropped hair. 'I don't think so. She began to realise who your taid is and saw her opportunity.' Glesni was surprised to see tears in her eyes. 'I'm so glad he's not going. Or you. I lost him once. I lost my mam and then I lost Gareth. I couldn't bear to lose him again. Now you know why I'm so afraid of you going.'

Afraid.

Glesni hugged her and her own tears spilled over again. She'd never seen this side of her. She was always Mam – capable, there: caring but distant. All that she'd lost like a wall between them. There were times when Glesni had hated the way her mam held her back, had called her unfair because she'd had the chance to be out there in the world, to act, to be involved – what right did she have to deny it to her own daughter? She understood now.

Understanding was not the same as being happy about it.


As they left the drying loft, the outside air smelled fresh and clear. Glesni wished her thoughts were the same.

'He'll be up on the south hillside,' she said, remembering they were supposed to be looking for Taid.

'What makes you—'

'Said he was doing the turbine anchor.'

'Of course. Come on, then.'

Helyg set off purposefully.

'I'll walk with you as far as home,' Glesni said.

Her mam slowed. 'You can't avoid him forever.'

Glesni said nothing, wishing she could unknow what she knew, start the day again. Start the last few months again; go back to before Sandy arrived, let someone else find her, someone else have their family irrevocably changed by her presence. As they neared the house, she slowed her pace.

'I understand,' Mam said. 'Take the time you need.'

'Thanks.'

She turned into the yard, thinking that time wasn't all she needed. It seemed she wasn't even going to get a minute, as Sandy appeared in the doorway with a large basket of washing.

'Your mam was just finishing this when the Gathering was called. Can you help me hang it out?'

She could hardly refuse. Sandy was all smiles.

'They're happy for me to go,' she said as she delved into the peg bag. 'Especially since I offered to help with the money. Though I confess that was putting the cart before the horse, as I'll need the PD to get through to my bank.' She glanced around. 'Any joy with that yet?'

Glesni concentrated hard on Tom's clean, damp shirt, as if the PD were hidden in its folds.

'Did you manage to speak to Madog?'

'It wasn't him.' She could have kicked herself.

'So... you know who's got it?'

Glesni secured the shirt, shaking her head. It wasn't entirely a lie. No one *had* something that was lying on the seabed.

'But you know who took it?' Trust Sandy to see through her. There was a harshness to her voice. 'It was one of your family, wasn't it? Who else would have access to my room?'

'But— '

'I don't believe it! I thought we were friends.'

'You think I took it? No!'

'Well, it wouldn't be Haf, would it? I can't see her being at all interested.' She bent down to the laundry basket. 'Which leaves your mam, your dad or your taid.'

Glesni shrugged. She could feel her cheeks reddening. She willed the breeze to cool her face.

'I doubt your dad would do something like that. He's too sensible. And he's kept his distance from me. What reason would he have?'

259

'Same with Mam and Taid. Why would they?'

'If you don't know, I'm not the one to tell you,' Sandy said, her expression softening unexpectedly. 'I'm not going to push you. It's hard, I know. But, listen – you were worried before about betraying your values by stowing away on a boat. One of them has *stolen* from me. Isn't that worse?'

The same thought had crossed Glesni's mind. Not just stolen, but destroyed. She tugged at a sheet from the laundry basket. It felt endless.

'Help me with this, will you?'

How many times had she tamed a wind-flapping sheet? She wanted the billows to drown Sandy's piercing gaze.

'I'm sorry,' she said, her eyes determinedly on the pegs and the line. 'There was nothing I could do.'

By refusing to name anyone, she was doing her best to compromise. She was surprised when Sandy kept to her word and didn't push it.

The washing hung out to dry, Glesni walked down to the shore. She needed time to think, and their room could be invaded by Haf at any moment. She glanced back up the hill towards the place where Mam and Taid would be deep in conversation. Probably arguing. The thought grated on her. By chucking the device into the sea in front of her, did he think he was bringing her closer by sharing the misdeed? He'd only compounded the betrayal of the years of silence. Stealing, wrecking – it was so out of character when he was usually obsessed with repairing, recovering, reusing. But now she realised how little she really knew him. He'd even forced her to lie for him. So much for their closeness. Mam she felt differently about. But she'd only be away for a day – even if Sandy was lying to her, and actually had plans to abandon them and leave altogether, that didn't mean Glesni had to go with her. She sighed, annoyed with the community, too. If they'd simply let her go on the trip, she wouldn't be driven to scheming to get on board the boat. Sandy's reasons for going needn't have concerned her at all. But now she'd been drawn in, her mind had effectively been made up for her.

# PART VIII

# THE MAINLAND

# FASCINATING IN A HORROR STORY KIND OF WAY

It seemed to take forever until Haf fell asleep. When Glesni was satisfied her sister's breathing was heavy she got up, dressed quickly, and drew out the bag from under the bed. She'd packed it earlier after saying she wanted an early night, letting people think she was sulking for not being able to go. She'd tiptoed round, packing a change of clothes and some bits and pieces including a first-aid kit with some of Mam's special salve. She was no nurse, but it might come in useful.

She paused to look at Haf sleeping in the faint light of the crescent moon, silently saying goodbye before creeping out of the room. She paused in front of Mam's door to do the same. Goodbye and sorry. There was no sound from Sandy's room, either. She hesitated, hand tensed ready to tap. Turning away, she told herself she didn't want to wake the others, be discovered and lose her chance to go, but really she preferred to head down to the harbour alone. She hoped she wasn't too late. The plan was for the party to leave shortly after sunrise when the tide was at its highest, but plans were one thing and reality another. That much she had learned. Crossing the courtyard, she threw a silent farewell towards Taid's cottage, trying not to wish he was coming, reminding herself of the way he'd kept her in the dark for so long. Plagued by conflicting thoughts, she was relieved when she came in sight of the jetty, the water glimmering in the moonlight, and saw both boats moored there, dark and silent.

She stood on the jetty, looking down at Sandy's boat, *Otranto*, creaking with the gentle nudging of the waves. The tide was coming in, just high enough to pick it up and float it, before reaching its peak around dawn. Clutching her backpack, she climbed on board and made her way towards the deckhouse at the front. She felt beneath the flap that had covered the fuel cap, when it still used fuel, and found the key. Letting herself into the cabin, she realised she wouldn't be able to return it *and* lock the door back up. Hoping Sandy would arrive before anyone else, she stowed the key in its place and shut the door, firm but unlocked. No one used keys anyway; it was a mere courtesy to Sandy, so it wasn't out of the question to have left it open. She hoped the trip wouldn't be jeopardised yet again by an inquisition into who had forgotten to lock up.

She checked the store compartment just inside. Her heart sank; it was tinier than she'd remembered. She did a trial run and after rearranging some of the stuff that was in there, moving some to the other compartments, she just managed to curl up inside with her backpack. The slap of a wave against the hull made her jump. Heart pounding, she froze until she was certain it had only been a wave.

She'd planned to snatch some sleep in her hiding place until Sandy arrived, then they'd agreed she'd stay out of sight until they were underway and it wasn't worth them turning back. Given the discomfort, however, she decided to wait in the cabin. The moon was a sliver, but there was still enough light to see the track clearly. As she waited, she wished she'd brought something to eat.

The seals were singing their eerie accompaniment to a solitary herring gull gliding over the silvery water, its course occasionally buckling in the wind. She watched it wheel round and make its way back, wondering if it had a purpose. The moon vanished but the water retained an ethereal glow. Annoyed with herself for getting distracted, she looked back at the land, which was now a dark mass.

Another wave slapped the side and the boat bumped gently against the harbour wall. She heard the footsteps before she made out the shadow. The harsh white dots of a torch flashed on and she caught a momentary glimpse of Sandy before ducking down out of sight in case she wasn't alone.

The boat rocked as Sandy stepped on board and Glesni tensed, holding her breath. She heard the key rattle a couple of times in the cabin door, then it opened.

'Oh,' Sandy said. 'You're here already.'

Why so surprised?

'Yes,' Glesni replied, getting back onto the captain's seat.

Switching her torch off, Sandy breezed in on a waft of cool night air and dumped her large bag on the cabin floor. The one she'd arrived with all those months ago. Glesni's first thought was to wonder why no one had lent her a day bag. Then she realised it was full.

'Listen,' Sandy said as she sank down on the side bench. The moon had returned and Glesni could see she looked worried. 'I've been thinking... Are you sure about this?'

'Of course! I thought—'

'I understand how much you want to come. But when we were talking about it... what you said about being secretive. Going against your principles. Letting people down. I don't want to be the one—'

'Is this because of the PD? I really tried...' She stopped herself, still reluctant to betray him despite everything.

'Oh, don't beat yourself up about that.' Sandy reached out with her foot and drew the bag towards her. 'It's just... plans have changed. I really don't think this is the time for you to come.'

She propped the bag neatly in the corner between wall and bench. As if giving herself an excuse not to look Glesni in the eye.

'Not you as well.' In a wave of disillusionment, Glesni swung the seat back round to face the front. 'I might have known I shouldn't trust you.'

'Believe me—'

'It's for my own good.' She gazed unseeing at the control panel. 'Thank you for your concern. But I'm coming. As we agreed.'

Sandy sighed. 'Please, Glesni. If you go back now, no one will know you even considered it...'

She fell silent as they heard footsteps approaching at a run.

'Shit,' Sandy whispered. 'Get down.'

Glesni hopped off the captain's seat and moved to crouch below the window. The footsteps outside drew level with the boat and stopped.

'Stay there,' Sandy hissed. 'Keep out of sight. Let me deal with this.'

'But—'

'Just lock the door and be ready to start the boat if I tell you. Don't do anything stupid.'

She went out on deck, shutting the door silently but firmly behind her. The sound of her voice had been chilling. Surely it was just one of the foraging party – what was there to 'deal with'? Glesni turned the key, glanced down at her hiding place – hadn't that been the plan? – but instead peered out through the salt-opaque window.

'Where is she?' His voice was breathless. No way would Idris be part of any foraging party. What was he doing here?

'Where's who?'

'Don't mess with me, *hogan*.' The boat dipped as he climbed aboard. 'Glesni.'

As Sandy protested, he strode across to the cabin and rattled the door.

'Why's it locked? Let me in.'

'I haven't got the key,' Sandy said. 'It wasn't in its usual place when I got here.'

'I know she's in there.' He rattled the door again. 'Glesni?'

Bewilderment held her still and silent.

'What makes you think she's here?' Sandy's voice was all calm and reason.

'I saw her come down to the boat. Knew something was wrong.'

'Wrong?' She laughed. 'Too much time alone up there's obviously given you a vivid imagination. I couldn't sleep. Arrived early to wait for the others.'

'One lie after another.'

Glesni gasped as he moved surprisingly swiftly, and after a brief struggle had Sandy down against the side bench in a headlock, a knife to her throat. She'd only ever seen him wield it to free sea creatures from human rubbish.

266

'I know why you're here,' he said. 'Erik came to see me last night.' She struggled; he held on. 'To ask my opinion. I gave it to him, but he decided to go with you anyway. I'm surprised at him, trusting you to keep to your word. But what amazes me more, and saddens me, is that he's allowing you to put young Glesni in danger.'

'I keep telling you, she isn't—'

'I'm not stupid,' he snarled, pressing the tip of the blade harder against her skin, causing a red trickle to ooze from it.

Sandy struggled again and Glesni suppressed an urge to leave the cabin and help her. Fear held her back – Idris might flinch with the surprise and cut her. Or worse. She wondered what he could mean. Taid had been adamant he wasn't going. Sandy's plan had been made with *her*. Had she told him about it? She was about to let herself out of the wheelhouse when, as if summoned, she became aware of Taid's distinctive gait. Turning from the view of Idris and Sandy's deadlock, she turned to look through the front window, and as she saw him, heard the crack of a gunshot from just the other side of the door. Taid stopped abruptly and a cry escaped her. Her heart stood still as she stared at him, motionless on the track, dreading the moment when he collapsed to the ground.

After an extended moment he gathered himself and sprinted towards the boat; she started to breathe.

Before daring to unlock the door, she peered again through the cabin window. Sandy had a small pistol aimed at Idris, who stood facing her, clearly as shocked by the gunshot as Glesni. In her other hand, Sandy had the knife, which she hurled behind her into the water.

'That was a warning,' she said, glancing down at the handgun. 'Next time it'll be for real. Now get off the boat.'

He shook his head.

'Go!'

Taid had reached them and Sandy glanced across at him. 'You took your time. Untie the fucking boat and let's be going. Once your friend's left us.'

He started to untie one of the lines, looking up at Idris. 'Do as she says, mate. I appreciate the concern, but it's my decision.'

'Not entirely,' Idris said. 'It affects us all. I still say you should have put it to a Gathering, let the community decide.'

Sandy cut across with a laugh. 'The community of saints!'

'But whatever you do,' Idris continued as if she hadn't spoken, 'you really shouldn't have dragged Glesni into it.'

'What?'

Taid shook his head as Glesni stepped out on deck.

'What the hell do you think you're doing here?' he snapped.

'I... Sandy said... We're just waiting for the others. She's going to make sure I'm OK.'

'Oh, is she?' Taid held out a hand to her. It was shaking. Glesni made no move to take it. 'Sandy's leaving and not coming back.' He nodded towards her bag. 'So come on. Off the boat.'

'But... if you're coming... You said you weren't.'

'Sandy – explain.'

He turned to where she was standing, the gun still pointing at Idris.

'I tried to warn you, Glesni,' she said, her voice familiar again despite the weapon. 'I really think you should go back with Idris. But if you insist on coming, I'm not going to stop you. I'll see you back safely.'

'Oh for fuck's sake! You expect us to believe that?' Taid reached for Glesni's hand again. She held back, scared by the anger he was radiating. 'Please, Pwt. Off the boat – now!'

'But what about you?'

'I'm going, yes. Change of plan.'

'I mean why won't you be seeing me back safely?'

He turned. 'Sandy?'

She shook her head. 'Don't blame me for your inability to talk to your own family.'

They froze at the sound of a shout. It came again, from the rocks above the jetty. 'Stop right there!'

'Christ on a fucking bike,' Taid muttered. 'Sounds like Madog. Let's leave before this turns into a bloody Gathering.' He turned to Idris. 'I'm sorry, but I'm going through with it. Please go before you get hurt. Glesni, go and untie the lines.'

'No. You just want to get me off the boat.'

'I just want to get us moving before anything happens.'

'I'm obviously not going to change your mind,' Idris said. 'I'll cast you off. Glesni?'

She shook her head. As he jumped down to the jetty, a shot rang out, immediately followed by a whining ricochet off the hull of the boat. Glesni threw herself to the floor; Sandy ducked beneath the side. Taid emerged from the cabin at a crouch, keeping the solid metal wall between himself and the rock where the voice had come from.

'That you, Madog?' he called up.

'Get off the bloody boat.'

'I know what I'm doing.'

'Well, come and tell us all! You're welcome to put yourself in danger, but not the whole community.'

Taid looked up towards where Madog was lurking. 'I'm going with her for the *good* of the community. Idris will explain.' He sighed. 'Though it seems like he has already,' he muttered under his breath.

Two more shots sliced through the grey air. After a moment another rang out, shockingly closer. Glesni turned to see Sandy's small pistol aimed above the side of the boat. She fired again. A cry of pain from the rocks froze them to the spot.

'Shit,' Sandy muttered into the silence that followed. She looked at the handgun as if someone else had fired it. Taid rushed to the side of the boat as if to jump ashore.

'Don't move.' Sandy had recovered herself and turned, pointing the gun at him.

'What have you done?'

'Brought it on himself, didn't he?' Her voice was brittle.

'We've got to go and see—'

'What we've *got to* do is leave.'

'We don't know how badly you've hurt him.'

'Shut it, Sherwell. It seems violence has a way of following you around. Idris can see to him.' She waved the pistol. 'We need to move.'

'Or what?' He laughed. 'Go on. Fire. I might even thank you for it.'

'You might. I doubt Glesni feels the same.'

Sandy turned, slow as a nightmare, and Glesni saw the gun pointing directly at her.

'All right, all right, put it away!' Taid said irritably. He nodded at Idris, who busied himself with the ropes, then disappeared into the wheelhouse. Idris threw the first rope onto the boat then, as he unwound the second, beckoned to Glesni, who leaned over the side.

'*Cymer ofal,*' he said, using their language as a veil of privacy. 'You know the woman. Do your best to stop her harming your taid or the Seeders.'

'What...?'

'He'll tell you.'

Sandy moved a step closer. 'What are you on about?' she snapped.

'He's just wishing me luck,' Glesni said.

Sandy huffed. 'You won't need it if you get off and go with him now.'

Glesni shook her head and grabbed the aft rope from Idris. As Taid manoeuvred the boat away from the jetty, she went into the wheelhouse to join him. Slowly and carefully: throughout it all Sandy kept her pistol trained on her.

Taid glanced back at Sandy. 'You can put your fucking toy down now,' he said.

'Once I'm sure you're going to cooperate.'

'I can't concentrate on anything while I'm scared for Glesni. You'll have us all on the rocks.'

She backed away and lowered herself to sit on the crew bench

270

across from where Glesni was now crouched. She lowered the pistol but kept it firmly gripped in her lap.

'Well, Pwt,' Taid said without taking his eyes from the water. 'It looks like you've got your way this time. Sorry it's not quite how you would've wanted.'

Once they were on the open water with less need to concentrate, less paranoia from Sandy that they'd scarper at the first opportunity, Taid turned to her, eyes blazing.

'Nice one, Pwt,' he said, knuckles white on the boat's wheel. 'You always have to get your own way, don't you? I hope this'll teach you that sometimes others *do* know best.'

She'd never heard him so angry with her. 'But—'

'But no, you had to have your adventure. Well, ask Madog about adventure! Stupid, stupid girl. Let's just hope he isn't badly hurt – or dead.'

'Why was he there?'

He took a deep breath. 'Half the time I have no idea what's going through his head.' His voice was low and he glanced out of the wheelhouse door to make sure Sandy was out of earshot. 'But although we argue, believe it or not, he cares about me. He's been making that clear ever since Sandy came. And no... he doesn't know about me and Irlas. I've tackled him about the sabotage. The turbine, I think, was the weather, but I'm pretty sure the boats, and the money, were Madog. However stupid, he was acting for my benefit, so who am I to push it? As for tonight, well, I'll just say Idris didn't seem at all surprised he was there. So he must have seen me last night when I went up to the watchtower, and then paid his own visit. I don't know what he thought he'd achieve, but I do believe he meant well.'

'So why did you go to see Idris? What's this decision of yours that's going to put everyone in danger?' What she wanted to say was, why didn't you talk to *me* about it?

He killed the motor and beckoned her to his side at the helm. He told her he was going to let Sandy turn him in. She'd persuaded him that if he didn't, she'd send people out to look for him, among an island community that harboured terrorists, as she saw it. The consequences could threaten the very existence of the Seeders.

They stood there, the boat drifting and swaying beneath them as she cried into his shirt and felt his breath deep and shaky but silent, until Sandy put her head round the door and said 'Enough,' surprisingly gently. They drew apart and continued on their way.

By late morning they had arrived at a gloomy harbour that both Sandy and Taid called small but looked huge to Glesni. Desolate-looking buildings hulked in a line set back from the harbour wall and there was a scattering of boats in various states of disrepair. It was hard to believe how many there were, and the numbers of people they represented. Tattered curtains flicked as someone peered at them from one and she was glad that Taid had moored them to a broken section of jetty that was a scramble to reach from the land. Not land as she knew it. She'd seen expanses of weed-blown concrete in pictures but it was fascinating in a horror-story kind of way to see it there in front of her.

She and Taid sat together on one side of the deck, Sandy at the other. No one said a word as they ate their picnic lunch. None of the three seemed to feel like eating – Glesni certainly didn't – but they went through the mechanical process of refuelling.

Despite the sun coming and going from behind a series of scudding clouds, the place felt dismal and abandoned. It suited their mood. How badly hurt was Madog? Two shots, then nothing. She felt for him more than she would have expected. Taid's words had made her see him differently, driven to act in an attempt to drive Sandy away before she could do any harm. All in vain.

A gull gave a mournful cry and she cwtched up to Taid. He hugged her.

'I never meant it to happen like that,' Sandy said, her voice raised in the offshore breeze.

'Sure you didn't,' he replied.

The boat rocked gently against the broken jetty, buffeted by a sharp wind.

'I'm sorry,' Glesni whispered, not for the first time, hoping only he could hear her.

'Not your fault.'

It was good to hear it at last.

The gull flapped away over the derelict harbour sheds and alighted on the gable of a house beyond. A house that was bigger but not so different from one of the older homes on the island. Yet the surroundings were immeasurably different.

Taid stood abruptly. He paused for a moment, looking up at the sky, then shrugged. 'Looks like any serious weather's going to hold off for a good while. We're safe enough here.'

It didn't feel safe. Part of her was desperate to go with him, to see what this mainland town was really like. A larger part of her simply wanted to untie the boat and head straight home to Ynys Hudol.

# IT HAD BEEN ABANDONED

Sandy envied their closeness. Despite all Glesni had learned over recent days, everything she'd had to face up to, she still stuck by him. Still looked to this man for comfort. Maybe she was just clinging on to the life she thought she'd known.

Sandy recognised that feeling. She'd been through it all on that rough crossing. Wondering what had happened to Madog. That ominous silence. Regretting it all. Even though she'd had no time for the lad... And he'd fired the first shot. She'd only been protecting herself. Try telling that to Cai. Her heart plummeted. But she'd never intended going back. Or had she? If she was honest with herself, she'd wondered more than once if she really had the resolve to continue with her search for Adam once they'd completed the first part of her plan, with Sherwell. Would she even see that through now?

She was relieved when he stood abruptly.

'I'm off to see how the land lies.'

He seemed suddenly eager to move, as if delaying the moment for talking.

'Give me a moment,' she said.

'I said *I*.'

Glesni moved to his side. He hesitated, clearly weighing up the pros and cons of taking his precious granddaughter into the decaying town or leaving her on board with the enemy. Sandy had got used to the way their minds worked with little need for words. It used to make her feel excluded, but now she preferred it to the arguing – and by this stage she was excluded in any case.

'Can't stop either of you following me,' he said finally. 'But let me do the talking.'

'You think there'll be talking?' Sandy said, surprised.

He shook his head in exasperation. 'It may be the Wild West, literally, but even here people tend to prefer verbal communication.' Holding up two fingers in imitation of a gun, he glared at her. 'No point me telling you to leave it behind, but don't even fucking think of using it.'

He turned and climbed out of the boat.

Judging from the seaweed and barnacles, the tide was relatively low, but they were all wet by the time they'd clambered across the collapsed section of jetty onto land. If there was ever a next time, she'd make sure to get herself a boat with a tender.

The dockside buildings seemed to hover over them as they headed for an alley between two warehouses. No signs of life, but threatening all the same. It was the place she'd departed from, but her memory was vague. They followed a bleak street that led onto another, more welcoming. Some of the empty buildings were boarded up, some simply hollow, but several shops and houses showed signs of life, with cheerful paintwork and even some plants in window boxes.

They came out onto an open square, with no people in sight but signs of life. Again, there was a patchwork of lived colour and monochrome abandonment, but the colour seemed to be winning. Sandy was struck by a proliferation of wooden planters on the side of the square most likely to be sheltered from storms, containing a variety of food plants.

Sherwell paused in his purposeful stride. 'This has changed.'

His expression implied *for the better*. Glesni was staring wide-eyed and Sandy reminded herself that the girl had never seen so many buildings in one place, such an expanse of paved street. She was glad for her sake that they weren't in a city with crowds of people to add to the bombardment of experience, though she herself would have preferred that to the eerie calm and the feeling of being watched.

'Where is everyone?' Sandy asked.

'They'll have clocked us the minute we came into view on the sea,' he said. 'They don't fully trust us, and who can blame them?'

After studying the square for a few moments more, he made for a place with a neatly painted sign proclaiming Siop Seren. A mishmash of household goods and food was stacked behind a small-paned frontage. Even in the cities they were gradually abandoning the plate-glass displays that were so vulnerable to storms. And riots, Sandy thought drily.

He put on a face mask and handed one to Glesni, indicating to Sandy she should do the same. It had been a while. At first she'd felt strange without it on the island, but probably not as strange as it felt to them to be using them. He went over to the shop and opened the door. An old-fashioned bell rang out, a sound she knew from films but couldn't recall actually hearing.

'Erik?' A slight woman, younger than him but older than Sandy, came out from the back of the shop, her eyes wary above the face covering she was fiddling with.

'Seren.' He smiled. 'Good to see you're still here.'

'Where else would I be?' Her eyes returned the smile in his, but looked anxiously past him. He turned to them.

'This is my granddaughter, Glesni.'

'*P'nawn da*,' the girl said shyly, and added a few more words in Welsh. The woman replied, visibly relaxing at the sound of her own language.

'And this is Sandy. Got marooned with us and we helped her out for a while. I'm just seeing her safely on her way home.'

The two women nodded at one another. He produced two jars of honey from his bag.

'I've missed this. Thank you! *Diolch*.' The woman winked at Glesni.

'*Croeso*,' he said, intercepting their look. 'I don't have anything else. The others are on their way.' He glanced at the window as if they might appear at any moment. 'We came in Sandy's boat, see. There was a bit of a delay back on the island.'

Sandy tensed, but Seren didn't ask and Sherwell didn't elaborate.

'Things seem to be looking up since last time I came.'

Seren shrugged. 'Took matters into our own hands, didn't we? Couple of families who'd left in the *Digartrefu* returned and it galvanised the rest of us into action. Well, a good number of us. No point sitting around watching the place go to ruin. Or leaving.'

Sandy detected a hint of bitterness on the last word.

Seren talked with pride about some of the projects they'd been putting into action. 'We'll be welcoming tourists back next.'

He laughed. 'You're joking.'

'Too bloody right I am. And yet... You won't have heard. About the election? There were massive protests, and they had to re-run it. Even brought in UN observers to make sure it was all above board. Total change, it is.' She turned, searched a shelf behind the counter and handed him a well-thumbed newspaper. 'It won't be easy, but it's a start. Not that anything they do down there will affect us.'

Sherwell scanned the front page, his expression brightening. 'You never know. The Clearances affected us, didn't they? Positivity might trickle through, too. Just think...'

He handed the precious copy of the paper back to her without offering it to Sandy. She'd seen the headline – Surprise Win For Left-Green Alliance – and she could guess the rest.

'Whatever happens, I still think we're better off relying on ourselves.' Seren smiled, looked in the direction of the sea beyond the buildings. 'I'm sure you'll agree. Talking of which, we've got some scrap metal for you. It's been so long, we weren't sure if you'd be coming again. I'll get someone to fetch it.'

'Owain?' He turned to Glesni. 'Seren's son. I first saw him when he was your age. How is he?'

'Gone.' The word plunged between them like a stone dropped into a lake. She looked away. 'Left some time last year. I... I wish he hadn't but he was determined to get away.'

Sherwell shifted uncomfortably. 'What can I say? I'm sorry. I dare say he'll be back when he's had enough.'

'I doubt it. Him and Jac and Mabli. They waited long enough and none of you showed.'

'None of *us*? Someone promised…?'

'I'll go and find someone to fetch your stuff.'

'No hurry. Like I say, I'm going inland with Sandy some of the way. Gwylan and the rest of them will pick it up. I hope they'll be here soon.' Too late for the kids, his pause seemed to say, and I'm sorry about that.

Seren nodded. 'Are you stocked up for the journey?'

He shrugged. 'We've got enough.'

'Wait here, I'll get you some bits.'

Sandy reminded him in a whisper that she'd still got a little cash, but he dismissed her with a wave of his hand.

They left the shop with a good selection of things Sandy would once have considered staples but now thought of as luxuries, and a few treats that were special under any circumstances. They crossed the square in the direction of the harbour. The afternoon sun was now hidden by clouds and the wind was rising, bringing drops of rain with it; they'd tacitly agreed to head straight back to *Otranto*.

'Hey!' A small gang, two teenage boys and three girls, stepped towards them as they walked out from a side street onto the harbour front.

'Evening,' Sherwell said, moving imperceptibly to put himself between them and Glesni but barely altering his pace.

'Haven't we seen you before?'

The two lads sidestepped to block their way.

'Maybe,' Sherwell said irritably. 'Don't recognise you, though.'

'Not you, old man.' The one that was obviously their leader stood menacingly close. He was not as tall as Sherwell, but thickset and, of course, had youth on his side. 'Her.'

Sandy's heart started thumping. Glad of her mask, she shook her head and shrugged.

'That your boat?' The second lad waved towards the harbour, moving uncomfortably close to her as he did so.

'Yep, and if you don't mind—' Sherwell shoved past them and

hustled Glesni in front of him down the quayside. The girls moved closer.

'We do mind,' the leader said. 'Ask your friend here.'

Sandy gasped as the two lads grabbed her. Sherwell stopped and turned, motioning Glesni to get out of harm's way. Sandy was surprised he didn't scarper himself.

'So? What you got to say for yourself? That's my dad's boat, that is.'

'I was told it had been abandoned.'

'Who told you?'

'No idea. It was months ago. Didn't get his name. Paid him good money for rowing me across to it, though.'

'Not our problem.'

'Not mine either.'

The leader nodded to one of the girls, who stepped up. 'Get the key, and anything else we can use.'

Sandy struggled to free herself, but she was no match for the two lads who had her arms pinned. As the two others yelled encouragement from the sidelines, the girl unzipped one of her pockets.

She was suddenly gone. Sandy heard a screamed curse then a splash. She felt a release of the grip on one side as Sherwell punched the smaller lad on the jaw. As surprised as they were by the old man's strength and readiness to fight, but sharp enough to take her chance, she managed to turn and knee the leader in the groin. She tore loose and ran to Glesni, who was watching, motionless. Sandy shoved her hand into her pocket and got the boat keys, handed them to the girl.

'Go!'

'But—'

'Just go. Get the boat ready to leave as soon as we get back to you.'

She turned back and saw both lads had recovered from the shock of the unexpected attack. The leader was a couple of paces away from Sherwell, a knife glinting in the evening light. The girl who wasn't helping her friend from the water had also closed in with a blade that looked too big for her.

Sherwell took a swipe at the unarmed lad, who staggered back. Sandy pulled out her pistol, but a moment too late. She gasped as she saw the gang leader grab Sherwell. The girl closed in with a stabbing motion and he staggered a little.

'Stop!' She fired a shot into the air.

One of the girls screamed and the small gang froze momentarily, then ran. Only the leader kept his grip on the old man, looking insolently into Sandy's eyes. She fired again, this time at the concrete ground by his feet. With a final blow that floored Sherwell, he scarpered after his mates.

Her breath roaring in her ears, Sandy kept the gun aimed at the alleyway they'd disappeared into. After a moment that seemed to last forever, she heard steps behind her.

'Get back!' Sherwell yelled.

She glanced and saw Glesni, paused mid-step.

'Both of you – go,' he said.

'But—'

'Get on the fucking boat...' With gritted teeth he hauled himself up. 'Just winded. I'm right behind you.'

Relieved that he was on his feet, though certain that *just winded* was more than an understatement, she waited for him to catch up.

'Thank you,' she said quietly.

That was all anyone said as the three of them clambered onto the boat, no longer caring about the soaking as they scrambled across the breach in the jetty. Glesni finished untying the last mooring rope and hurried into the cabin.

She steered the boat away smoothly as the gang began to emerge from their alley. Her grandfather, slumped on a side bench, gave no word of protest as they rounded the harbour wall and headed out along the coast, away from the town.

'Let's have a look at what's wrong with you.'

The left side of his face was beginning to swell. Sandy went into the cabin to fetch the first-aid kit.

'Don't worry,' she said in an attempt to reassure Glesni. 'He'll live.'

'I'll be with you as soon as I get us out to open water.' The girl's voice was calm. Or numb with shock.

Out on deck, Sherwell reached for the first-aid kit. His open coat fell aside and Sandy saw a blood stain seeping across his shirt. She stifled a gasp.

'How bad is it?'

He waved her away. 'Didn't think you were the kind to fuss.'

Before she could protest, she felt the boat slow and, letting it drift, Glesni appeared from the cabin.

'Oh, Taid.' She hurried over.

'Thick coat,' he said. 'Only a scratch.'

It was more than a scratch, painful but not too serious, provided he could avoid infection. He allowed Glesni to tend to his injuries, pushing Sandy away. She turned her attention to making tea. Proper tea, from the shop.

'Didn't you tell us you paid a good price for this bloody tub?' the old man said as they sat cradling hot mugs.

'You're accusing me of stealing it?'

'*I was told it had been abandoned,*' he said in a mocking falsetto.

'You prefer to believe a gang of thugs rather than me?'

'I wonder why, Sandy. Why I'm not inclined to believe a word you say.'

'You weren't exactly straight with me yourself, were you?'

He shrugged, rose stiffly and headed for the cabin. Starting up the motor, he set the boat back in motion.

Glesni followed him into the wheelhouse and sat beside him. Sandy moved to stand in the doorway.

'Listen, you didn't have to help me there,' she said. 'Thank you.'

He stared straight in front of him, unmoving except for the slight adjustments of his hands on the wheel.

'You had half our supplies in your backpack.'

# FEWER PEOPLE LEFT TO DREAM

As they moved down the coast Glesni saw scattered houses and, once, a row of storm-battered caravans standing out above the cliff like a mouth of mouldering teeth. One or two were less rotten than the others – families still clinging to beloved holiday haunts maybe, or opportunists finding a home in places they could never have dreamed of, now there were fewer people left to dream.

They went just far enough to put a safe distance between themselves and the town before mooring up in shallow water just off a beach that seemed deserted but somehow welcoming to Glesni's island eyes. The few cottages they could see looked just as vacant as the harbour buildings they'd left behind, but nowhere near as eerie and threatening. They decided to rest there until the following morning, keeping an eye open for any signs of life from the houses or the road that ran past them, before venturing back onto land and continuing on their way.

She hated to see Taid's face swollen from the blows he'd received, and the way he moved carefully to protect the knife wound in his side, but she was relieved his injuries weren't any worse. He produced a stove from one of the equipment boxes and they heated up two tins of the soup they'd got from the shop. Thick and tomatoey, with noodles and other bits of vegetables, it was like nothing she'd tasted before, though she also found herself thinking about the cans and what they could do with them when they got back home – if they got back home.

Taid finished first, opened a compartment in the bench beside him and produced a flask. He unscrewed it and took a swig.

'That's better. Nature's painkiller,' he said, easing himself back on the bench seat. 'So tell me, Sandy, why?'

Sandy looked up from the bowl she'd been scraping clean. It had taken her longer than either of them to eat; her mind must have been as preoccupied as Glesni's. 'Why what?'

'Why you wanted to get away so badly. Was it worth injuring, maybe killing, young Madog? Whatever his faults, he didn't deserve *that*. Or have your experiences made you immune to violence?'

The hollow look in her eyes suggested she wasn't.

'All for what? What do you really want from me?'

'Justice.'

'You don't think imprisoning a man for seven years, one hundred and thirty-five days is justice enough.' It wasn't a question.

'And you clearly don't think that taking the lives of eighteen undeserving people is a crime worthy of greater justice.'

'I've told you—'

'Yeah, yeah.'

He got to his feet, towering over her. 'Don't talk to me like that.'

'You've told me what you claim and I've told you I don't believe you.'

'So why not just kill me and have done?'

'Justice has to be seen to be done. Ask the families of those you killed.' She held her hands up in mock apology. 'Sorry, those who *were killed* – by your people – at Irlas.'

He sat back down. Took another mouthful of spirit. Looked at her quizzically. 'Why do I matter so much to you?'

'Don't flatter yourself. I was amazed how easily you came.'

'You threatened our community. One of the few bloody decent things left in this world. You shot a friend of mine and threatened my granddaughter. I must mean something.'

She shook her head. 'Not really. I didn't choose to pursue you, *or* your nest of terrorists.'

'You decided I'd do when you couldn't find Adam.'

'More than that. I realised you're in a unique position to help me track down the treacherous bastard.'

His laugh had an edge to it. 'I knew some people. Moved in certain circles.' He raised the flask to his lips. 'Then lived on a remote island for years.'

'Can you guess what Adam's line of work was when he was discharged from the army?'

'Security guard, you said.'

'Well, I wasn't quite telling the truth.' She ignored Taid's ironic laugh. 'He became a prison officer.'

Taid shook his head. 'You showed us his photo. Never saw him in all my seven-and-a-half years inside.'

'He was a warder at the Harbridge facility,' she said, as if explaining algebra to a particularly unwilling pupil. 'The secure hospital where they carried out the Asclepius Project. The drug trials?'

Her sarky tone wasn't warranted but she had their attention.

'You know what his crime was?' She paused for longer this time as if they actually wanted to play the guessing game.

'Oh, come on,' Taid said. 'I've told you before I can't be doing with riddles. Just spit it out.'

She told them about a doctor, Annabel Snow, who was involved in the drug trials but came to regret her work, despite all official claims that the prisoners had consented and the work was essential given the ever-present threat of new virus variants. 'It seems the good doctor had a crisis of conscience and clearly worked her charms on a gullible prison warder to help her, shall we say, liberate some guinea pigs. Human guinea pigs with the free will to consent, I hasten to emphasise.'

'And the "gullible prison warder" was your Adam?' Taid said. 'If so, I congratulate him and he can rest assured that if I knew his whereabouts the knowledge would be safe with me.'

Sandy rolled her eyes. 'So quick to judge. The project has saved thousands, maybe millions, of lives in immunisation research, and very few of the prisoners were harmed.'

'Which is why your good doctor was prepared to break the law and risk her life's work?'

'It went on for years,' Sandy continued as if he hadn't spoken. 'One here, one there. She'd fake their deaths with convincing test results and documentation, and he'd arrange their escapes.'

'If you think Ynys Hudol's part of some underground fugitive network, I'll have to disappoint you.'

'They were finally found out last year, by which time Annabel Snow was on the other side of the world – the government's still fighting a futile battle for extradition with New Zealand. Meanwhile, Adam...'

She gave an expansive shrug. Her gesture and the catch in her voice suggested she thought Dr Annabel Snow and her Adam were more than associates, another cause of her determination to track him down. Even Glesni could tell that. Did Sandy really think she could convince Taid to help her in a personal vendetta? Glesni looked at him. His eyes were focused on the middle distance, fingers fiddling with his oak-leaf pendant, and she willed him to come to the same conclusion and overpower Sandy, shove her overboard and take them home. The mainland had lost its allure.

She felt him tense beside her. He shook his head. 'No.'

Sandy looked at him with raised eyebrows.

'I can guess where this is leading and I refuse to believe you!'

He locked eyes with her. She seemed to be enjoying the moment.

'What?' Glesni asked, helpless in the weight of silence.

'The first prisoner they "rescued" was Elin Sherwell-Jones,' Sandy said. 'They made sure her death was all over the news, but—'

'Tell your fucking lies to the wind!'

He stormed into the cabin and slammed the door shut.

'You get it, don't you, Glesni?' Sandy asked.

She wasn't getting anything.

'I'm asking him to lead us to their old home, Nant-y-Wern. It's a win-win situation. He gets to be reunited with her, and I have the chance to find out if she has any information that leads me to Adam.'

Glesni stared at her. 'Why didn't you tell us all that before we left?'

'You'd never have believed me.'

When Glesni knocked on the cabin door a moment or two later,

Taid let her in and lowered himself gingerly to a makeshift bed on the floor, fully clothed, wrapped in his coat and the big warm blanket.

'Bitch took the key,' he said, waving at the control panel. 'Otherwise we'd be halfway back to the island by now. You don't know where she's put it?'

She shook her head.

He shrugged and waved half of the blanket at her. She lay down beside him. 'Looks like we're going with her tomorrow, after all.'

The next morning Glesni went out on deck to find Sandy fiddling with the small stove to make the coffee she and Taid had made so much fuss about. Glesni failed to understand what the big deal was – it tasted foul to her. Sandy was wrapped in her blanket and she almost felt sorry for her having to spend the night huddled beneath one of the outside benches, a tarp draped across to make a tent. The rain had held off, but the wind was increasingly strong, cold and blustery. She checked her sympathy; Sandy deserved everything she got, and she and Taid had hardly been wallowing in luxury.

Taid emerged. 'Coffee. I could almost like you.'

Glesni wondered if he'd slept. There hadn't been a moment when she was awake and he wasn't.

'If it's any consolation, I didn't sleep a wink last night.' Sandy looked up from the stove.

'Glad to hear it,' he said conversationally. 'Though it's more or less what I'd have expected of the undead.'

'Grow up. I'm serious.' She sat back on her heels. 'I can't stop thinking about Madog. I'm sorry.'

'I doubt you're so concerned about the lad. More what his father will think of you.'

'Oh, please.' A flush to her cheeks suggested he wasn't far wrong. 'So if you're really sorry, you can prove it by ditching the weapon.' He held out his hand, waited.

'No way!'

'I wouldn't expect you to trust me.' He gestured overboard.

'It's going nowhere. To you *or* the sea. What happened with Madog, that was self-defence. For God's sake, he actually shot at us. In any case, we may need to defend ourselves on our travels. Not amongst ourselves – you have my word—'

'For what that's worth.'

She glared at him. 'And not against the ones we're going to find. But who knows what we'll come across on the way – remember the gang yesterday?'

He shrugged. During breakfast, he scanned the horizon at regular intervals. Sandy seemed to notice.

'You know them better than I do,' she said, 'but I doubt—'

'This is one of our landing places. They'll come and find us here once they realise we're not in town.'

'All the more reason to get on our way.'

'We're not going anywhere.'

'But—'

'Not until I've got Glesni on board our *Berta* or taken her home myself.'

'But I'm coming with you!' Glesni said.

'Listen, lass.' He turned to her, his expression stern. 'It's not safe. Especially not in the company we're keeping. Yesterday proves it and I'm sorry I let you come this far. Besides, have you given the slightest thought to your mam? Haf? Idris will have told them you're with me, but small consolation that is. Can you imagine what they're feeling?'

'Mam told me she was glad you weren't going because she couldn't bear to lose you again. And *you're* not intending to go back!'

His head dropped and he stared at the floor of the boat, hands clasped tightly on his lap, his face hidden by the peak of his cap. 'She actually said that?'

Glesni nodded, though he wasn't looking at her. She hugged her coat around her against the wind. He straightened slowly and turned to Sandy. 'I don't exactly have a choice, do I?'

'You wouldn't anyway, not yet,' Glesni insisted. 'Don't you want to see your old home?'

'Ynys Hudol's my home.'

'See if Nain's still alive?'

'You believe her lies?' He gestured at Sandy.

'All the more reason to see for yourself,' Glesni said.

'She's got a point.' The boat rocked gently as Sandy stood, the pistol in her hand gleaming incongruously in the morning light. 'And I promised, didn't I? I'll see Glesni safely back.'

Taid snorted. 'Glesni, who you threatened yesterday.'

'I'm sorry. I needed... You know I wouldn't really hurt her.'

'I don't know a thing about you.'

She stood, unflinching. 'Enough of the emotional blackmail,' she said briskly. 'Get the stuff together. We're going.'

In a daze, Glesni gathered the coffee mugs and rinsed them out, then busied herself in the cabin packing the big bag. She paused as she heard Taid come in behind her. The salty sea wind on deck had made his eyes water.

'You're right,' he said quietly. 'Maybe I do want to see for myself. And I'm glad you'll be with me, Pwt.'

# TO JUDGE HERSELF

Four days. Four whole days holed up in an abandoned house at the edge of a deserted village. The sea, which would once have been on the far side of the road, was now lapping up the garden as if the house were venturing to dabble its toes in the water. Every now and then the gale whisked items of debris past, adding to the pollution of the seas item by item, and the occasional freak wave lashed the ground floor. It was one of those upside-down houses, designed not to withstand rising sea levels but to make the most of views that Sandy would have killed for once upon a time.

Killed for. She turned away from the view of the grey sea with its spray-capped waves and looked at the others as if checking whether they'd read her thoughts. Glesni was hunched over the notebook she'd been writing in while they'd been holed up here, saying she wanted to create a record of the recent events as a companion piece to *Seeds of Change*. The old man – she felt safer thinking of him as that, rather than either the pragmatic, multiskilled Erik or the notorious, nothing-to-lose Sherwell – was sitting with his beaky nose in one of the mouldy books they'd found on the shelves, sprawled in a chair by the wall furthest from the windows. It was as if he had a point to prove: after years of life on a windy, storm-lashed island, either he was unimpressed by views of the majestic sea – which she doubted – or he was well aware of the fragility of picture windows in gales such as this.

A squall hammered the glass with skittering drops and she forced herself not to flinch, though her fortitude was wasted since neither of them so much as acknowledged her presence. Never had she felt so lonely, not even since her PD had lost signal, leaving her stranded halfway across Cymru. Better to be alone than despised.

The old man rose and stretched, then winced from his injury.

'I'm off to find us some food. Can't be doing with all this inactivity.'

'You seemed engrossed enough in that to me.'

He looked at the book he'd put aside and shrugged as if to say it was crap but preferable to having anything to do with her. They'd found a selection of games on the house's shelves, and taken it in turns to play with Glesni, but when the girl had said she wanted to get back to her writing, he hadn't offered to play Sandy and she'd be damned if she was going to ask him.

'It's still too dangerous out there.' Sandy wondered at her social conditioning – showing concern when in fact she couldn't care less if he got hit by a flying road sign or dashed onto the rocks by a rogue wave.

His only reply was to pick up his coat and start searching through the pockets.

'She's right, Taid.' Glesni looked up from her notebook; it felt like the first time that day she'd acknowledged Sandy's existence.

'I'd rather die trying than fade away from starvation.'

The girl shook her head and returned to her writing.

'Won't you need some money?' Sandy asked.

She'd hardly finished speaking before he was pulling the door to ungently behind him. Clearly he was less sniffy about stealing if the alternative was accepting anything she had to offer. When they'd taken shelter here after almost a day's walking, the storm gathering around them, they'd found an ancient car in the garage on higher ground behind the house. When she suggested he checked it over, he'd looked at her in exasperation: hadn't she learned anything from her escapade with the boat? It still peeved her that he believed some small-town lowlife over her – no matter that he was actually right to. Later, they'd found the car keys in a kitchen drawer and even Glesni had suggested it was meant to be, but he'd made some snide remark about not being the criminal some people insisted he was. Sleeping in someone's house in a hurricane was borrowing; taking someone's car, abandoned or not, was another matter entirely. And playing with bombs is different again, Sandy thought. When things were back to something like normal, she'd come on holiday here, paying over the odds to let it, by way of a thank you for this respite. She sighed. Face it, that wasn't going to happen.

As far as taking her cash was concerned, he probably had a point; the shop and café they'd seen in the village seemed long shut, with no one around to take payment. He might be lucky and find something. Maybe he'd surprise them again with a shopkeeper friend they'd known nothing about. The supplies Seren had given them were running low; they'd searched the house but the cupboards were bare.

Eventually she heard him return. Glesni snatched up her journal – another snub, though Sandy had to admit that yes, she would have taken a sly look if she had the chance – and dashed downstairs.

They were gone a long while. Eventually she heard feet on the stairs. Glesni appeared cradling a basket with an assortment of sorry-looking but fresh produce, closely followed by the old man.

'I found a couple of cans of diesel as well,' he said. 'In someone's shed. It just might still be viable. Couldn't tell. The car wouldn't start. Old bloody heap. I'll have a look at it – I can remember enough about the old engines; used to work with them. It'll give me something to do. Could even have it going by the time the weather's fit to travel.'

He stopped as if realising he was talking to her like a human being.

'Fix the car,' she said. 'The car you're not going to steal.'

'You can steal it. Me and Gles'll hitch a ride.'

Completely deadpan. She had no idea whether or not it was an attempt at humour.

'And that? A load of veg? You found someone to take pity on you?'

He looked hard at her, weighing up whether to condescend to reply. 'I knocked on the door, though it was hanging off the hinges. Same place I got the fuel. The garden was more weeds than veg. Can't stand waste.'

He disappeared into the kitchen. 'OK, Pwt, what feast are we going to concoct from this little lot?'

They were stuck in the house for a couple more days. Every time it seemed the gales were dying down, a new storm threatened from the horizon. They were rationing the coffee; she'd welcomed it at first but now it was making her edgy. Or maybe that was the company. She could feel the two of them watching her, despite each being buried in a book – one writing, one reading. Judging her. Or simply challenging her to judge herself. How different it could have been on the island – but it had been her own decision to leave; her own actions that led to the inevitability of leaving.

She just wanted to get going. To find Adam. She reminded herself he no longer represented comfort – was that her fault, too? No, it was not. He was the one who'd decided to help criminals. He was the one who'd decided to enlist in the first place, setting in motion a train of events that ultimately put him in a position where helping criminals was his best option. None of this, none of the betrayal she was going to be forced into, was her fault.

# TUNED IN

I go up the hill behind the house I want to think. The rain keeps coming but I like the rain it cools me not just on the outside but my thoughts keep me calm the rooks the jackdaws the little birds tell me it's all right I just have to think I'm a different person now this morning still no blood it's been storms for days I haven't seen the moon but I know the blood is late and there's new life inside it scares me it's right it's a good thing like the plants and the little animals in spring but they can all do it they all know how to look after their little ones the little ones know how to grow I have to care for this one like She cared for me and I don't know how to do it he can help me but he'll want to leave I know he'll want to leave soon before the winter before the gales are here all the time maybe bring more trees down stop him going even town people know storms he'll see it's going to be worse and he'll leave while he can no one to help me I can do it I don't need him I think of Her in the photo with the girl if She had a girl I can have this life but She had her man the tall man but I don't need Winter I want him to stay but if he goes I don't need him it was months after She went to the owls before he came and I didn't need anyone I looked after him mended him so I can look after this new one it's what we do what we're made for I don't know now but I'll know when it happens.

All morning I waited for him to say he knows. We don't use any language much now he knows he learns the woods the birds and the animals know him so he should know what's happening that's why I think he does know and he's scared and he's leaving he hasn't talked about family about a child where he came from so he doesn't know how to look after it maybe he's scared like me but I'm not scared it's just a new feeling maybe he doesn't know yet because it's not inside him it's inside me but I know and surely he can feel my knowing? I have to think think think he's not going to leave me he knows the woods now the weather he goes out in the rain without thinking it's going to kill him. He's still learning because I teach him maybe I have to teach him there's a new life growing I have to tell him he can't just know and if I tell him then he won't go I don't want him to go I have to tell him I don't want him not to know such a good thing.

I told him he's outside the rain's slowed to drizzle he's outside weeding not really weeding looking at the garden where we grow food for us and this child funny to think when next season's food grows the child will be here he was worried I told him it's nothing to worry about it's a good thing he still doesn't believe we know for sure but I'm certain and he's worried about help how will we get help when we need it I say we won't need it I'm strong he says we'll have to leave I say I'm not going anywhere but we have time we have months to agree. Not to agree for me to persuade him I'm not going anywhere and no one else is coming here we don't need help the animals don't need help the birds don't need help and he says yes but lots of their little ones die I say that's animals not people he says suit yourself you always do you know a lot but you don't listen you only listened to Her if only I was Her you might listen to me. I don't like it when he talks like that I wonder if he wants to leave he said he never wanted to go back never wanted to see the woman he used to love who loved him but wants to hurt him I don't know how you can love someone and want to hurt them at the same time maybe the time he interfered with Her things before I was ready but that's not like planning to hurt someone and that was before I knew I loved him I think I loved him then but I didn't know it.

Outside he watches me approach leans on his fork a weed in his hand chucks it into the barrow it's a nettle we can use that but there are lots of them and it's more important that he's smiling this preparing for new life in the soil makes him calm and happy about the new life in me I'm about to go to him when I hear a noise a low hum I know it's a car it stops it was so far away I hear nothing else I wait he asks what I heard he knows when I'm listening even if he hasn't heard it I put my hand on his arm he stays still too then we hear the noise again he says nothing but I know he's heard it this time now I'm tuned in She used to say tuned in I thought it was the hum of noises making a tune but She told me it meant radios but this hum now I'm ready for it I know it's going to the *Cofeb* the memorial the house the dam the ghosts people go to remember to respect then they go away again like the people that came the day we fetched the batteries that was the last time anyone came to the *Cofeb* that was the day we came together I wonder what this one will bring but people have been to the *Cofeb* before and nothing happened or maybe I just didn't know. It's a special place but it can be special for itself and for people coming without making things happen to us.

I grab his arm and lead him away these people will go away after visiting and remembering but I want to be sure I lean the fork against the wall of the house and shut the door and we go into the woods down towards the road stop our side of the wall to listen to make sure they're gone.

After a while they come the car stops it doesn't fade away it stops like they've come to the fallen tree they'll turn round but they don't I think I hear a car door bang and soon we hear voices from a long way away the little animals scurry they always scurry but it's different when people are coming it's not long before we hear footsteps people never come here the tree the landslide there's nothing here they only come when they're looking the last time anyone came it was the two men looking for Winter the ones that went back to Tyn Rhedyn then went away again we wait for these people to go away they don't I grab Winter's arm I'm scared.

We're hidden in the trees the bushes the wall that hides our track the footsteps go past he looks at me like he says I told you so but then the footsteps stop and voices just too far to hear them then the footsteps come back. He wants to talk to them but I say no we stay hidden until we know who they are what they want it's safer to let them come and go away even if they steal things they're only things that's what She said the time the men came before we changed the wall they're only things and if we stay hidden the strangers can't hurt us. I scurry to the house like *bele'r coed* I get my gun I climb the tree next to the house I can watch from there he doesn't like me climbing the tree now he knows about the child but I say *bele'r coed* climbs trees when she's pregnant squirrels do it's fine I'm not hurting it or myself but these people might and he promises to stay hidden.

# CUT OFF FROM ITS HEARTBEAT

Glesni wanted to see their family home really badly. Maybe she even harboured a tiny hope that Nain would be there, and after a happy reunion they could take her back to Ynys Hudol. If that unlikely series of events came to pass, she was sure even Sandy would relent and let Taid live out the rest of his life in peace while she continued with hers. Glesni tried hard not to think of any of it, because to expect the worst felt safer than having hopes dashed. She could tell Taid was doing the same, probably just as unsuccessfully.

The rain was like a waterfall on the windscreen and she was glad Taid had got the old car going, had even relented and decided to use it. Not steal, or even borrow. *Use.* That way they could all kid themselves they'd simply return it on the way home. She was mesmerised by the beat of the wipers, and by the surface of the road converging into fuzzy lines as it passed under the car. Sandy was happy to let her sit in the front. Glesni liked to think she was aware of what a new experience this all was for her, and wanted her to enjoy it to the full, but maybe she simply felt she could keep an eye on them both better from the back. Both Sandy and Taid complained of slow progress but it was faster than Glesni had ever been, even when racing the ponies with Haf and the others or piloting the boat, and although she'd grown up believing that the speed of cars was an unnatural, unnecessary luxury, now she was experiencing it she couldn't help enjoying it. She told herself she didn't feel guilty. The perspective of land extending so incomprehensibly further than the horizons of Ynys Hudol felt completely different in reality from her imagination and the pictures and films she'd seen.

She'd never been away from the sea. She was enjoying the trees and the mountains and the wide vistas that opened up at certain turns of the road, before plunging into lanes where the trees arched overhead to form tunnels. She loved it all, but it felt uncomfortable to think she was moving so far from the sea, cut off from its heartbeat. She was glad of the car that would take them to their destination, then back to the coast, without days of longing as they walked. Again, she felt a tinge of guilt.

They passed through a couple of towns and villages, with a mixture of ancient and fairly new houses – not unlike the settlement on Ynys Hudol. Unlike there, though, where they were pushed for space and there'd even been talk of building new homes during the next season of repair, so the Bowens and the Lewises could have their own space, many – probably most – of these houses were empty.

'Where is everyone?' she asked.

'This is it,' Taid muttered darkly. 'The *Digartrefu*.' He went on to expound about the severe rationing of power supplies, the way people had left, or been forced to leave, for the new towns in England, and how it was all so run-down because the few who stayed were too worn out to care beyond their own little circles.

They left a village behind with its patchwork of scrubby fields. The land became more mountainous beyond the trees that crowded in and arched over the road. The rain had cleared a little as they crossed a plateau of bleak moorland. Going downhill again, they turned off onto a smaller lane. It must mean nearing their destination and she felt a quiver of excitement. The road headed towards a shoulder of the mountain that came down to meet them, skirting it closely to their left. The wooded slope fell away to their right and she caught a glimpse of a river far below. They slowed as the lane became a garden, with grass, bright yellow dandelions and cheeky daisies claiming the cracks in the asphalt. It was beginning to peter out altogether when they rounded a bend and Taid swore and stopped the car suddenly, jolting them in their seats.

They were confronted by a wall of rocks and stones, with grass and moss already colonising them. They peered out of the windows up the steep slope, hardly stirring as if the landslide had merely paused for breath and was about to rouse itself again and bury them.

Once the surprise had faded, she saw that there was a visible track around the lower edge where people had walked over the landslip. It had been there a while.

They got out and in the damp air, rain dripping loudly from the trees, went to inspect it. They clambered over the path. The obstruction was far too big and dense to consider digging out a path for the car. The road continued beyond the impassable obstacle.

'You sure it's the right road?' Sandy said.

Taid gave her a killer look. 'We can walk the rest of the way but it's a couple of miles at least. Maybe more. It's a long time since I've been here.' He looked up as a gust of wind shook the trees, releasing a tattoo of raindrops. 'There's another way. Let's try that first.'

They got back into the car and Taid reversed it, turning as soon as the road widened enough to allow it. Glesni held her breath, scared they were going to end up rolling down the slope through the trees. The wonder she'd felt only a short while ago as they speeded through new landscapes turned to an awareness of the danger of entrusting themselves to a mechanical box. Once they'd negotiated the weed-strewn lane and turned back onto the original road they'd been following, Taid turned to her and smiled. Trust me.

The road gradually dropped towards the valley floor. The trees seemed different here. Younger, and the undergrowth patchier. They rounded a bend and saw a clearing to their right. The road widened to a potholed area on that side, tyre tracks indicating that others had been there before them. Taid pulled the car over and stopped.

'Where are we?' Sandy asked from the back.

'Use your eyes.' He gave a dismissive shake of his head, then stared out of the windscreen. A row of derelict buildings had been kept clear of weeds. Little was left of them but low walls, except for one house at the end of the row. This stood desolate but almost complete, like a proud castle keep, although the door and window sockets told her it was only a house.

'Anti Gwen's,' he said, his voice almost a whisper.

She glimpsed Sandy in the rear-view mirror, sitting in stony-faced silence. Glesni thought of her sister and almost felt sorry for her.

Glesni and Taid got out of the car, careful to shut the doors quietly. After a moment, Sandy followed and banged hers shut, raising a chorus of cawing from a rookery somewhere nearby. As they waited for the echo to fade, she heard the rushing of the river nearby, its voice the closest she'd heard to the sea. Flashes of graffiti daubed the front wall, people marking their visit and recording the events of a place special to them. The side wall was a riot of colour, tangles of leaves, flowers, water and words. It had clearly been touched up over the years. *Yma o Hyd*. We're still here and we won't forget.

Something was drawing Glesni to the house. She looked at Taid; he didn't look her way but with a tiny movement of his hand gestured for her to go ahead. She pushed the tired front door open and stepped inside, taking in the atmosphere of a room that was nothing but cold emptiness, dust and cobwebs. Outside, Sandy turned away and walked towards the river in search of her own ghost.

Glesni moved to the back wall where the faint light from the window caught a patch of wall where someone had painted a tangle of leaves, insects, birds and creatures. Vines entangled a script so beautiful it almost obscured the words. It made her look closely, demanding that she concentrated to read.

*They said we were selfish.*
*They said the people of Cymru brought it on themselves.*
*They didn't realise that we were willing to share.*
*We wanted to help, it hurt us to see their suffering –*
*The suffering they'd brought on themselves with their ways.*
*Sharing wasn't enough for them, they wanted give and take –*
*We were to give and they would take.*
*They wanted more than we could spare.*
*We were willing to share, but we weren't prepared to die for them.*
*They laughed. We were prepared to die for our cause, weren't we?*
*That wasn't the same and they knew it.*

As she wondered who this person was who'd chosen to shelter their words indoors, away from the other memorials outside, she looked around and saw signs of life all over the abandoned room. Not only the spiders, but the green of ferns in a crack where the light from the broken window seeped. The ragged ball of twigs where wall met ceiling and a bird had made its home. Droppings from some animal on the floor. It was sad, but not entirely so: she was sure that Anti Gwen would have preferred her home to shelter creatures than to die like the others in the row.

Through the wind and the distant river she liked to think she could hear children playing in the gardens enclosed by the old walls, singing, the bustle of life. Looking out of the window she saw Taid standing unmoving in the rain, his back to the house. As she wondered what it felt like to be at the place whose defence had stolen years of your life, she realised she really had forgiven him. Which in turn meant she must believe he was innocent.

She went outside, hood up, waiting for him to indicate he'd had his moment and it was OK for her to approach. Sandy was waiting by the car, hands in pockets.

He pressed a button attached to the key in his hand. They heard a click from the car and the lights flashed as it unlocked. The novelty of it, which had given her a childish pleasure when he'd shown her how the car worked, now seemed an empty gimmick.

The lane branched before a rickety makeshift bridge that had taken the place of the ancient stone remains beneath. Taid stopped the car again beside a huge, broken concrete mass with only a tentative covering of the ubiquitous brambles and moss. He looked back at Sandy. She shook her head.

'I don't know what you're trying to prove.'

They drove on without speaking, taking the road that followed the contours of the hill upwards. Before the trees closed in, Glesni looked back towards that forsaken place.

The gradient levelled as they wound back on themselves, parallel to the valley floor. This must be the road that had been blocked by the landslide at its far end, but the warm feeling of nearing their destination didn't last long.

A fallen tree made the road impassable. This time they got out and left the car carelessly in the middle of the road. No one would be coming this way. As they scrambled over the huge trunk, she felt warm inside to think that nature was protecting their family home. A small voice whispered that they might find the house had been similarly crushed by some natural disaster. Somehow she knew they wouldn't.

As they followed the road between an ivy-hung fence on the lower side and a dry-stone wall on the other, Taid strode ahead. Being so close to home made his limp almost imperceptible. Intermittent fat drops from the earlier downpour dripped from leaf to ground in an irregular rhythm.

She stopped as a little creature rippled across the road in front of them. Its smooth motion flowed from its furry body to its magnificent tail. It paused and looked at her, bright-eyed, before scurrying under the fence and up a tree without pause, the vertical climb as natural as running across the ground. She'd seen pictures of squirrels; this one seemed smaller than she'd anticipated, because pictures were always in close-up, but its reality was more beautiful than she could have imagined. The animal, an ambassador for the sounds she could hear all around her, was like a fairy story come true. They had lots of birds on Ynys Hudol, but few land mammals. Knowledge of wild animals was passed down from the adults, their memories embellished by the previous generation's stories of better times, theirs in turn reaching back to Eden. She thought of the broken-tooth houses they'd seen on their way and the ruined village in the valley below, and what happened when people in fairy stories failed to fulfil the conditions of their destinies.

She glanced ahead; Taid and Sandy had stopped and were following her gaze up into the tree. The squirrel had vanished round the back of the trunk. She saw it briefly, high above, before it merged with the wind-rustled leaves. Taid smiled.

'Come on. You'll see more before we're done.'

They walked on. When Sandy asked how much further, he looked at her irritably, but Glesni was feeling similarly weary by now. At a bend in the road which she found hard to tell apart from any others they'd rounded, he paused, frowning, and looked back down the road.

'We've come too far. I must be losing it. Did you see a gateway, Pwt?'

She shook her head. She'd been admiring the undulating length of wall, her mind forming patterns in the stone, and marvelling at the multicoloured splodges of lichen to distract herself. She'd have noticed an opening.

He smiled to himself. 'Clever.'

They retraced their steps and he stopped at a certain point. The stones were as moss-grown and lichen-patched as their neighbours, the ivy claiming its customary hold, but the trees on the other side seemed to part ever so slightly despite the brambles filling the space between them.

They climbed the wall and picked their way through the tangle of undergrowth until, some distance from the road, a way became clear. They hadn't gone far before a house became visible in a hollow of land. Glesni sensed that someone lived there.

She reached for Taid's hand and he squeezed hers.

# LOOKED LIKE TENDERNESS

Sandy felt like a trespasser. Her irritation had been chipping away at her for days, fuelled by their deliberate refusal to include her. Now they were on the mainland she simply wanted to get this over with, get home and safe, and try to pick up the threads of the life she'd once had. Without Adam. If they found him, she had no idea whether she'd relent or pursue her intention to its bitter end. But they weren't going to find him; they weren't even going to find Sherwell's terrorist wife.

She was annoyed at herself for missing the house last time she was here. If she hadn't allowed herself to be fooled by this deceit of concealed entrances and house names – though she couldn't help feeling a grudging admiration – she could have saved herself the whole Aniseed episode.

After they climbed the wall she hung back. Let them have their nostalgic visit. It was futile. Clearly no one used that road and Sherwell had said the farm had been demolished. He'd been shown photos as proof. But he'd also been told his wife and daughter were dead. His wife had been rescued by Adam in 2046 and his daughter was alive and well on Ynys Hudol. She saw Glesni take her grandfather's hand and the simple gesture of hope told her the house had not been destroyed either.

As it came into view she thought it looked quite a homely place – far from derelict. A cat came towards them, tail held high in greeting, and Glesni gave a little cry of delight. She crouched down, hand out, and silently coaxed it to her. Sandy realised she hadn't seen a cat during her whole time on the island. Something to do with it having been a nature reserve in the past. She couldn't see Sherwell's expression but he waited remarkably patiently. She kept a respectful distance. He said something to Glesni, who stood, and together they went to the house. The door was ajar. He knocked and waited. The moments stretched endlessly. He knocked again, called hello. Glesni called hello.

He pushed the door open; the action looked like tenderness. They went in and Sandy sat on a low drystone wall to wait. The wind was loud in the trees above. She pulled her coat more tightly around her, thoughts wandering.

# TAKE AWAY THE YEARS

Winter hated Bela being up the tree. It reminded him of the day they met. The day she'd rescued him. It wasn't the memory that concerned him: today the wind was gusting and he was scared for her. Bela's news that morning had shaken him. He'd been happy here, their growing closeness warming him and giving him purpose. He was still happy, but he hadn't expected to become a father and he hadn't expected to commit himself so soon. The shock of her news mingled with protectiveness, heightening his unease at the approaching newcomers.

From his hiding place behind a holly bush, he watched the little group walking towards the house. A man, a girl and, slightly apart from them, a woman. He lost them from view in a dip of the land. When they emerged, the woman was no longer with them. He'd hastily agreed with Bela that they'd stay out of sight until they knew whether or not the party spelled danger. He couldn't move to check on the woman; he just had to hope she'd stopped and wasn't creeping round to come up on them from behind. His attention was held by the man and the girl. As they neared he thought the man seemed familiar. Tall, too old to be out here roaming the remote moors and woods for no reason. The girl was too young to be his daughter. But she seemed comfortable, here of her own volition. He clearly didn't mean her harm; as if to confirm it, the girl took his hand as they approached.

Something about them, especially the man, suggested this place was familiar to them. Surely they weren't old neighbours, returned to reclaim one of the nearby abandoned farms? He froze. *Neighbours*. The photo Bela had by now framed and hung on the wall above the fireplace. The cat came out to greet them and they paused. The man gazed fondly at the girl, then looked round, so directly that Winter feared he'd been seen. Tense with nerves, senses heightened, he appraised the old man's face. That photo had been taken a long time ago. Imagine him with longer hair beneath that cap, take away the years and the wrinkles.

As the two of them continued towards the house, he peered up at Bela, perched above him in the tree. Their eyes met and he wondered if she'd recognised the newcomer too. Gesturing to him to stay where he was, she flitted effortlessly down from her lookout. Under cover of the couple's hollering at the back door, Bela quietly told him that the other stranger, the woman, had hung back. She left him to keep watch and moved silently towards the house, following the old man and the girl inside.

# NOT HOSTILE BUT WARY

The house with its well-tended garden felt so right. It was the first time Glesni had stroked a cat. She'd imagined that moment so many times, but never thought it would be when they came to her family's home. Whether or not Nain was there she felt they were welcome. *Whether or not Nain was there.* They'd both got used to the idea she wasn't; she'd never see her and Taid would never see her again. She could feel him holding back as if he'd never really believed she might be. After they'd called and no one answered, she and Taid looked at each other and slowly went in. The room, a kitchen, was clean and tidy. It renewed her hope.

He called again into the house. His voice was swallowed by the still air. There was no answer and she took his hand again. She'd never seen him look so old, so vulnerable. Hand in hand they went through into a hallway. The house looked dull, reflecting the weather outside. Faint light reached the hall from an open door and they entered a living room. An armchair. A well-worn sofa. A shelf with a few books. A guitar leaning against the wall. Above it a sculpture of twigs framing a photo.

'It's so different,' he said. 'The same but different.'

She gripped his hand. People changed. Places changed. Hope still hung in the air, stirred by the rain-damp curtains swelling in the breeze.

He remained motionless, said nothing. Despite his negativity dragging the air out of her, Glesni clung to the hope. 'She might still—'

'No,' he said. 'I can feel it.'

She thought she heard a sound from the kitchen. They both tensed. Everything was still.

'How can you know?' she said once she was satisfied no one was coming.

His brief half-smile lit up the gathering gloom. 'It's probably for the best.'

She was overwhelmed by an intense sadness. Sandy shouldn't have used him to come here. Glesni herself shouldn't have insisted. Didn't she have a perfectly good home on the island?

She heard a rustling again and turned to the door. A young woman had appeared there, not hostile, but wary like an animal. She seemed more curious than anything.

Glesni felt herself gaping; she'd been expecting someone Taid's age.

'*Croeso*,' the woman said, looking past her at Taid. '*Do'n i ddim wedi dy ddisgwyl di.*'

'She wasn't expecting you,' Glesni half-whispered, though she knew Taid had understood.

They looked across the room at one another in an extended moment. She was Glesni's height, though a good few years older, her earthy features sharpened by experience, confident yet tensed. In her open shirt collar Glesni noticed a chain with an acorn that matched the oak leaves Taid never took off.

In a sudden movement she was by his side and led him to the picture on the wall. Glesni was surprised to recognise him, and Nain, who she knew from the photo he treasured but kept tucked away so it didn't fade, with her mam as a little girl between them.

'You?' The young woman's voice was more a statement than a question.

A momentary aura of sunshine seemed to light up the air around him. 'I remember that day.'

The young woman looked from him to the photo to Glesni, a small frown creasing her brow. 'Her?'

'No, that's our daughter, Helyg. Glesni here's her daughter. My granddaughter.'

The young woman's eyes flicked to her then down to the floor, uneasy. 'She died. Elin.'

He nodded. 'I know.'

He hadn't known; he'd hoped just as Glesni had hoped.

The young woman looked up defiantly. 'Last year. She was ill I looked after her like she looked after me. Like my mam she was.'

She told them to sit. Speaking Welsh as if her English had been out of momentary sympathy for Taid, she told Glesni how much she looked like her nain, then said she had things to show them. Glesni heard her footsteps on the stairs. In her absence, Taid attempted a smile that looked like hollow desolation, then stood and walked from the room. His tread heavy with the weight of Nain's absence on his shoulders, she heard him cross the kitchen.

She knew instinctively to allow him a moment of alone time, but when he opened the door they'd so recently come through, deceiving themselves with hope, she heard voices. One was Sandy's.

# ACROSS A CHASM OF DIFFERENCE

Sandy hadn't been waiting long when it began to rain again. A crowd of rooks bickered noisily somewhere in the branches above. She tugged her hood up and as she did so, noticed a glimpse of movement near the house. Had someone gone in through the door? She stood and set off to investigate. This may have been Sherwell's house once, but not any more. She no longer cared what happened to him but she worried for Glesni despite herself. Her hand tightened around the pistol in her pocket.

She was about halfway to the house when she heard a movement to her left. She steeled herself as a man stepped out in front of her. She gaped at him. He looked as shocked as she was.

'Adam?'

'Cassie?'

She felt a rush of adrenaline. Surprise, yes, but also triumph. At last. The hurt and anger at what he'd done, the way he left her, surfaced, with a tangle of emotion that held her unmoving. They stared at one another across a chasm of difference. The growth of his hair and beard, his patched clothes, his weather-beaten skin, rooted him here. There was something else, something indefinable, too. She wondered what she looked like to him. The smell of damp ground rose fresh around them beneath the gentle brush of the rain.

He broke the spell by glancing over his shoulder to the house. That simple, loaded movement brought her hurt and anger, his betrayal, to the fore.

'So you're here,' she said.

He nodded, impenetrable.

'There was the tiniest chance I'd find someone here who knew where to find you. But here you are. How come?'

'Same,' he said. 'Slim chance of finding someone.'

His voice was the same. She took a breath in the deep silence. Thought of what that *someone*, Elin Sherwell, meant to him. To her.

'So, Cassandra.' He only used her full name when they argued. 'You wanted to find me. What now?'

Despite herself, she dared to hope. 'That depends on you.'

The rooks resumed their noisy bickering. She almost wished that she and Adam would bicker – anything to bridge the heavy gap between them.

'Why have you come here?'

His voice made her heart leap again. A moment ago, waiting in the wind and rain, she would have answered immediately. Now, with him here in front of her, maybe... She pushed the feeling aside.

'Is anyone else here?' She indicated the house.

'Your friends have just gone in.'

She swallowed her irritation. 'You're living here alone?'

He shook his head.

'Who?' she insisted.

Tensing visibly, he took a small sideways step as if to block her way.

'Just leave her alone, Cass.'

Enough. She tried to push past him, towards the house that seemed to stand in judgement. She had to know. Had to see the woman for herself. An ageing terrorist who'd played a part in her sister's murder. Adam took hold of her arm to stop her.

'What?' he said out of the blue.

She realised she was smiling as she saw Sherwell, come to rediscover some idyll that had never been, standing in the doorway. She imagined him facing Adam, claiming back his wife and his home, doing her fighting for her.

'I'll introduce you to my "friends",' she said. 'You can introduce me to yours.'

'It's not what you think.'

'We'll see.' She tried to shake him off, move towards the house. His new life had strengthened him. Her dashed hopes had weakened her. She almost slipped on the rain-slick ground. He held on to her sleeve. Impatient, she used her free hand to whisk the handgun from her pocket.

He froze momentarily; enough for her to break free.

'Cass, please—'

A shot rang out from an upstairs window. She felt a jolt and stumbled. She heard Adam's voice shouting no, no, thudding footsteps as a searing pain spread from her shoulder. The world looked sharp, leafy branches, the black shadows of birds, swirling as she hit the ground.

'It's all right.'

His voice was kind, soothing. Strong arms lifted her. In the fog of pain and disorientation, she wanted to turn and bury herself in the comfort of his embrace. Give in at last.

'We'll get you into the house,' he murmured. 'Take a proper look at you. Then you can get some rest. You're going to be OK.'

The flow of words continued, half-whispered, to distract her from the agony of movement. Words for words' sake, but the meaning... he cared. Nothing else mattered. She had no strength for anything else to matter.

Out of a dreamlike whirl of sensations, she became aware of being lowered gently onto a surface. A bed. Indoors. As he drew away she reached out. He took her hand.

'Thank you,' she said, her voice horribly weak.

He gave it a brief squeeze, made as if to let go.

She clung on weakly. 'Adam...'

'No.'

Wide awake now, she opened her eyes. Sherwell shook his head, his expression one of concern. Glesni appeared from the dream, offering her a drink to help her rest and take the edge off the pain while they tended to her.

'I'm sorry,' he said quietly. 'For not being who you wanted me to be.'

# NO LONGER SCARED HER

A gull came to the windowsill of Glesni's room the following morning, bringing a touch of salt to the fresh green of the woods and fields. Like her, it must love the house despite missing the sea. After a good night's sleep, she was beginning to feel safe.

As she and Taid were enjoying a morning cup of tea, Bela appeared, an envelope in her hand.

'*Well iti adael am shelan fach,*' she said to Glesni, then turned to Taid. 'I think she should go. This is for you. She...'

'There's nowt you can tell me that I don't want Glesni to hear.'

His words enfolded Glesni like the warmest of hugs.

Bela showed him a letter that Nain had left in case he ever came home. That was how she said it. *Adra*. Home.

*Dearest Bede,*

*If you're reading this it means that I'm no longer here, but that you're alive and free.*

*I just wanted to apologise. To say how much I regret how I rejected you for so long. Selfishly, I hope you didn't feel the same about me, despite everything.*

*If you ever meet Winter, please don't blame him for leading you to believe I died. I can only apologise that it hasn't yet been safe for me to try and find you and our lovely Helyg. I often wonder where you both are, whether you're together and whether you have family around you.*

*For my part, I'm happy here with Bela and have had plenty of time to reconsider my feelings.*

*I can't deny you weren't always easy to live with, but I still love you and hope that we'll meet again, that there'll be no need for this note.*

*Yours forever,*
*Elin*

There was a drawing of an acorn surrounded by oak leaves, like Taid's pendant and the acorn that Bela wore.

It was the first time she'd ever seen him weep. If only they'd come sooner. If only he hadn't believed she was dead, that the house was in ruins.

Bela took them out and showed them where she'd buried Nain, in a special clearing in the woods. Taid took the oak leaves from round his neck and left the pendant on her grave. Bela did the same with the acorn that Nain had given her, so they would always be together whatever else happened.

Bela flitted back to the house. It felt like the first time they'd been alone together since leaving Ynys Hudol. They went for a walk so he could show Glesni some special places and tell her about the rewilding project. He laughed and said that nature was dealing with that very nicely on its own, thank you, though he hoped their work had given it a helping hand towards recovery. Age had settled heavy on his shoulders when they'd arrived at the house that was no longer his home, but he seemed more youthful now.

Sandy was recovering; although the bullet didn't cause any critical damage it left a nasty wound in her shoulder. She lost a lot of blood and the shock made it worse, but Winter's first-aid skills saw her right, once they'd persuaded him to help her, and Bela knew some effective remedies that she learned from Nain Elin. Some were similar to Awen's, but there were several plants they didn't have on Ynys Hudol. Glesni was glad of Bela, since Taid and Winter kept their distance. She also made sure that Taid's knife wound continued to heal.

Winter asked them to call him by his surname, which he'd adopted with everyone except Sandy from military service onwards, because he said that was how he felt back then, cold and wintry, and now it was the name Bela knew him by. Sandy didn't like it, which was probably why he insisted on it. Bela refused to tell them her name from 'before' or anything about herself up to when Elin took her in, but Glesni was OK with that. Her Compassionate Silence.

After a few days, Sandy began to spend increasing amounts of time helping in the garden, like she did on the island. As if to prove she learned from her time there. Aside from a bare minimum of care, Bela avoided her, as did Taid and Winter, even if they were more subtle about it, but Glesni liked to join her, guide her. Didn't she deserve a chance? She said little, but sometimes looked wistfully at Winter, though it was clear to anyone with eyes to see where his heart was now. Or maybe Sandy was simply wondering what was happening back on Ynys Hudol, how badly she hurt Madog, and whether Cai – who Glesni couldn't help thinking looked a bit like Winter – could ever forgive her.

Glesni wondered whether the changes they'd read about would make a difference to the Seeders' contact with the mainland, and whether people would return to the farms and villages of areas like Cwm Irlas that had been hollowed out by the Clearances. She couldn't help hoping that people might stay away from there and from Ynys Hudol forever, but knew deep down that it was selfish. Their founders had always intended them to take the knowledge of all they'd learned in their Seeder society out into the world. Mam had even said Glesni would be a good person to do it. Certainly not yet, although the mainland no longer scared her – not only because of its trees, birds, squirrels and confused inland gulls, but also because of places like Nant-y-Wern and Siop Seren.

As the days passed and thoughts of Helyg and the others became more frequent, she and Taid began to prepare to leave, eager to get back although keen to enjoy their remaining time at Nant-y-Wern.

The elements made the decision for them. About a week after they arrived, they agreed that the weather was on the change again and they needed to get going in case it became a full-blown storm. But Taid might have wanted to stay in his old home for a little longer – with the excuse of waiting out the storm there – if it hadn't been for Sandy.

316

Glesni was awoken that morning by their voices. Taid yelled 'Stop!' and Glesni jumped as if his voice was in her dream. By the time she got to the window, Sandy, carrying her bag awkwardly because of her injured shoulder, had turned to face him.

'Where do you think you're going?' he was saying.

'Home. To Manchester.'

'Oh no, you don't.'

'Fuck off, Sherwell. What is it to you anyway?'

'Everything. I—'

'I've no intention of turning you in. I'd have thought that was clear enough by now.'

'Maybe, if I could trust you. But you may recall that you threatened to send the Clearance Crew, or whatever worthy body has taken their place, out to Ynys Hudol. The government might have changed by now, but attitudes probably haven't.'

She shook her head. 'I've given up on you, and bloody Adam. So I've got no reason whatsoever for saying anything about the island or the Seeders to anyone.'

'That's not a decision for me to make. Since I've got no other way of ensuring you don't endanger my community, you'll have to come back with us until everyone gets a chance—'

'Oh, for fuck's sake!'

'If they decide it's worth the risk of letting you go back, I'll come across and help you on your way. If you still want to leave. If it wasn't for Winter... Adam... I'd got the impression you were coming round to the idea of life on the island.'

'You're joking! They all hate me. Like him and his weird woman. Like you do.'

'I don't hate you, Sandy.' He reached out and touched her elbow, took her bag, which she seemed to yield with relief. 'I'm less than impressed with what you did, obviously, but I haven't the energy for hate. So if you've truly dropped all that...? People will understand, eventually.'

Glesni was pretty sure he meant Cai as much as 'people'. With his hand still on Sandy's arm, he guided her kindly but firmly back into the house and she couldn't hear any more of what they said.

Sandy spoke to her a bit later, though, after breakfast when the others went out to secure things in readiness for the bad weather – which made Glesni hope that Bela and Winter would be coming with them, at least for a short while. Sandy asked her opinion about whether she should go back to Ynys Hudol. Glesni didn't reply immediately, and she continued, saying she could have ignored Taid and just left, but really, she didn't have much to go back to. Her family were all dead, her relationship with Adam was clearly over and most of her friends back home had turned against her when it came out about what he'd done.

'I'm surprised your taid's as friendly as he is with him – he was part of the system that imprisoned your grandmother and, who knows, probably shortened her life.'

'But he was also the one who rescued her. That's how it is. That's how it could be if you came back. Apologise, prove you've changed, that you don't mean the community any harm. It won't be easy – I guess it depends on how badly Madog was hurt, or... whether he's alive... but after all, he did fire the first shot.'

She didn't say that if Sandy stayed on Ynys Hudol it would save them having to decide how to make sure she didn't betray them if she returned to Manchester.

'I don't have any choice, really, do I?' Sandy sighed. 'But you've made me feel better about it. You've been a friend, Glesni, and I'm sorry I messed that up.'

Glesni nodded, unsure what to say, or how she felt. She was more sure of her feelings about heading back to the boat and home. They'd decided they were all going, though even at the last minute she could imagine Bela changing her mind. She couldn't wait to see Mam, Haf and Tom. And Tahira, and the ponies. She wanted to be back on Ynys Hudol, where she belonged.

## The journal of Glesni Jones,
## Saturday 29th August 2056

Well, we're about to leave. Looking back at what I first wrote in this notebook, and how I was feeling, I wonder why I keep writing. To remind myself, I suppose, of how it feels to leave home for the first time and, though I haven't experienced it yet, the joy of going back. A moment ago, Bela was flapping at the gulls in the garden to stop them from stealing her seeds, but soon stopped, as if to say that humans have always taken their fish, so why shouldn't they have a few? Give and take. One of them – I'm sure it's the same one as before – has taken refuge on my windowsill, peering in at me like the spirit of the one I had to kill, that hot day when Idris first voiced his suspicions. Who knows, maybe this gull and its friends here at Nant-y-Wern are migratory. Maybe I've seen these very birds on Ynys Hudol.

Someone's just knocked at my door. The gull flew off, but I'm sure it'll be back. Just like I will, one day.

# ACKNOWLEDGEMENTS

No woman is an island, and the island of Ynys Hudol would not have come into being without my own community of support.

I'm indebted to Rebecca Parfitt, Gemma June Howell, Lynzie Fitzpatrick and Janet Thomas at Honno for their enthusiastic and comprehensive championing of my novel at all stages of the publishing process. Also to the wonderful family of Honno authors, past and present, of whom I'm honoured to be a part.

My friends Martine Bailey and Elaine Walker have given me invaluable friendship, writing feedback and encouragement for many years. Thank you also to the wider writing community for ongoing warmth and support.

I'm grateful to my early readers: Ed Layland, Trina Layland, Ann Stonehouse, John Stonestreet, John Maskall, Abi Woods and Jen Skade, whose reactions and comments helped me to shape the novel in its early stages.

Ynys Hudol is fictional, but largely inspired by Ynys Enlli/Bardsey Island. Substantial parts of this novel were written during stays on the island and I'm grateful to the Bardsey Island Trust, the Bardsey Bird Observatory, the wardens and staff for making me so welcome, and for safeguarding this wonderful place as a haven for both wildlife and people.

Thank you to XR Oswestry & Borders and Oswestry Climate Action Hub for being such an inspiring part of my activist journey, and to all similar movements everywhere who are pushing for urgent action on climate change and helping to build resilience in their communities.

And huge gratitude to David for everything.

# Riverflow

by Alison Layland

Would you like to know more about Bede and Elin Sherwell's earlier life?

Alison Layland's previous novel, *Riverflow*, explores the genesis of their activism, living off-grid in our present times of increased flooding and gathering protest.

*A novel of family secrets, environmental action and dangerous deception*

After a beloved family member is drowned in a devastating flood, Bede and Elin Sherwell want nothing more than to be left in peace to pursue their off-grid life. But when the very real prospect of fracking hits their village, they are drawn in to frontline protests. Mysterious threats and suspicious accidents put friendships on the line, and Elin and Bede's marriage under unbearable pressure. Is there a connection with their uncle's death? Who is trying to stop them saving not just their home and village but the wider world, and how far will they go? But far from a global threat, it seems the enemy could be closer to home.

*"I was completely drawn in by her characters and their environment... The sense of unease that pervades throughout was heart-stopping at moments. A terrific read."* Emma Curtis

*"A haunting and elegantly written novel about family secrets and their shocking consequences. It builds to a twist that nearly made me miss my tube stop."* Louisa Treger

# ABOUT HONNO

Honno Welsh Women's Press was set up in 1986 by a group of women who felt strongly that women in Wales needed wider opportunities to see their writing in print and to become involved in the publishing process. Our aim is to develop the writing talents of women in Wales, give them new and exciting opportunities to see their work published and often to give them their first 'break' as a writer.

Honno is registered as a community co-operative. Any profit that Honno makes is invested in the publishing programme. Women from Wales and around the world have expressed their support for Honno. Each supporter has a vote at the Annual General Meeting. For more information and to buy our publications, please visit our website www.honno.co.uk or email us on post@honno.co.uk.

Honno
D41, Hugh Owen Building,
Aberystwyth University,
Aberystwyth,
Ceredigion,
SY23 3DY.

We are very grateful for the support of all our Honno Friends.